THE EVIL THAT WOULD NOT DIE

Martin lifted his eyes from his plate. He fought to keep from screaming.

Joyce's face had changed. Liquid ran in greenish-yellow streams from her pig-snout nose, dripping over rotting and hairy and protruding lips. She snorted and oinked and curved back her lips. Her fangs were long and discolored. Her hair was all tangled and ropy and filthy. Fleas jumped about in the mess.

"Kiss me, Martin," she grunted.

The horror had begun . . .

D1559237

CARNIVAL

William W. Johnstone

ZEBRA BOOKS
KENSINGTON PUBLISHING CORP.

ZEBRA BOOKS

are published by

Kensington Publishing Corp.
475 Park Avenue South
New York, NY 10016

First printing: February, 1989

Printed in the United States of America

To: Ronne Johnstone-Dowling

BOOK ONE

And the wild regrets, and the bloody sweats,
None knew so well as I:
For he who lives more lives than one
More deaths than one must die.

—Oscar Wilde

Nowhere to go but out,
Nowhere to come but back.

—Benjamin King, Jr.

ONE

He experienced a very odd sensation in the pit of his stomach as the trucks of the carnival began rolling through town. They looked old, but they were all gaily painted and appeared to be in good shape. The drivers all waved and smiled at the people who stopped on the sidewalks and watched them roll past.

But that feeling? . . .

Very odd. Martin couldn't remember ever having a feeling quite like it. And he couldn't put a name to the sensation. It was all a jumble: fear, excitement, revulsion, anticipation—a mishmash of odd emotions that he could not understand.

Why would the sight of carnival trucks produce such a myriad of emotions.

And add one more sensation, Martin thought.

Dread.

"But dread of . . . what?" he muttered.

"Getting senile when you stand on the street and mutter to yourself, dad."

That jarred him out of his . . . whatever the hell it had been. He looked at his daughter. He had not heard her come up beside him. The sixteen year old smiled up at him. Beautiful. And Martin knew he was not being parent-prejudiced in thinking that. She was beautiful. Honey-colored hair, heart-shaped face, blue eyes. Just like her mother. And about that . . .

"Where is your mother, Linda? I called home and got no answer. And why aren't you in school?"

11

The girl rolled her eyes and made a face. "Questions, questions." Her father laughed at her. "Mom went down to the fairgrounds with Joyce and Janet. I saw them pass just as I was leaving the school. I came into town to get some stuff for Miss Houston."

"The fairgrounds?" Odd. "What would possess her to do that?"

The teenager shrugged her shoulders.

"Your mother doesn't like carnivals. She's told me so." A lot of things your mother hasn't liked lately, Martin silently added. "Why would she go to the fairgrounds?"

Again, the girl shrugged. "Beats me, dad. Maybe it's because we've never had one here before. They've been working on the old fairgrounds since spring, trying to get ready for this thing."

Her remark triggered another odd emotion, surging from deep within him. And as with those other strange sensations, Martin did not understand the emotions or what was causing them.

"No, honey," he corrected. "We used to have carnivals here—back when I was just a little boy. Had a big fair every year. I just faintly remember them." He started to tell her why they had stopped having fairs, then checked himself.

Then, as violently as if he'd been punched, a strong sudden surge of memory staggered him. Martin grabbed hold of a lamp post for support. The memory came bursting forth, ugly and savage and totally unexpected.

And then it was gone; gone so swiftly he couldn't grab any of it, only the absolute horror of it.

His daughter's voice came through the fog circling around his brain. "Are you all right, daddy?"

He blinked, shifting his eyes. The town was all wrong. Where the hell was he? Those cars—they were all old. All of them models from back in the early 1950's. And that boy over there, that looked like . . . No! That was impossible. He died years ago. Martin heard music from a juke box. Jesus God! He hadn't heard that song in thirty years.

Then he looked at his daughter and thought he was losing his mind.

12

It wasn't his daughter. This was some horrible-looking creature standing before him. The old hag was ragged and filthy and grotesquely ugly. A savage-looking old witch of a woman. The creature opened its mouth, exposing blackened stumps of teeth. The breath from the rotting mouth smelled of death.

Martin blinked his eyes. The hag was gone. Linda stood before him, worry furrowing her brow. Martin looked around him. All the old cars were gone. That 1950's music no longer played.

Linda touched his arm. "Daddy?"

Martin sighed and leaned up against the lamp post. He looked around to see if anyone else had witnessed his strange behavior. Apparently, no one had. He tried a laugh that almost made it. "Tell you what, kiddo: you go on back to school. I'm going to see Dr. Tressalt. I think I'm coming down with a bug."

"You want me to go with you?"

"No. I'm all right. It's just a short walk. And don't tell your mother about this, either. I'll tell her myself."

"OK." She grinned at him and walked on.

Martin did not tell the doctor about his hallucinations. Not just yet. Nor anything about the strange music or his odd play of emotions at the sight of the carnival. Just that he hadn't felt well all day and wanted a quick checkup.

After fifteen minutes of poking and prodding and temperature taking and checking blood pressure, Dr. Gary Tressalt leaned back in his chair and lit his pipe. Through a plume of smoke, he grinned and said, "Well, you smoke too much. And don't give me any crap about physician, heal thyself. Martin, as close as I can tell, you're as healthy as a race horse. You went over to Scottsbluff for a complete physical just last month. I read the reports, remember? Your CAT-scan was fine. You haven't been experiencing any headaches, have you?"

"No."

"Well, it's awfully warm for this time of fall, Martin.

People are coming in complaining of flu-like symptoms. There's a virus going around. Hell, maybe you just got a touch of the sun. Wear a hat, damnit! Now get out of here, I've got sick people to see."

Holland, Nebraska, located in the northwest corner of the state. The largest county in the state. Miles and miles of nothing to see but miles and miles. Three towns in the whole county. Holland was the largest town, but not the county seat. That was Harrisville, some fifty-odd miles to the south of Holland. Five thousand one hundred and twenty-two souls resided in Holland. Three doctors, one of them so old he only treated old friends one day a week. One small, ten bed clinic, that, surprisingly enough, was well equipped and staffed. A number of churches scattered about the town. One bank. Half a dozen juke joints and honky-tonks and one fairly decent lounge. One movie house that had been closed for years. One funeral home: Miller's. Three very small factories that at the most employed about three hundred people. Farms and ranches dotted the area around Holland. Two rivers flowed through the county. A dozen or so small creeks.

Nothing much ever happened in Holland. The P.D. was made up of four men and one woman and the chief. Not counting the office crew. One sheriff's deputy manned a substation.

A carnival used to play the Holland fair every year, in the fall. Last one was back in '54. That was the year of the big fire at the fairgrounds. Everything burned up, all the buildings, the pavilions, the rides, the trailers, the tents, everything and damn near everybody connected with the carnival. 'Bout a hundred people got all burned up, all of them carnival people. Terrible sight it was. Folks around Holland don't talk none about the fire back in '54. Not none at all. Mention the incident to anyone who was old enough to remember it, and they'll just turn right around and walk off.

The fire was a lot of things, but what it was mostly, was disgraceful.

14

By the time the state police got to Holland, sometime around one in the morning, all the gruesome stuff had been done and was over, and boy, was there ever some stuff done that night. Holland, Nebraska made the national news for that night. Only year it had ever made the national news, before or since.

That was the night that Western vigilante justice popped back up and took care of things. Showed them goddamn carnival people a thing or two.

Ended it, right then and there.

Martin walked back up the street and paused for a moment at his hardware store, leaning up against the door jam. Most of the carnival trucks had rolled through; only a few of the concessionaires were still pulling in.

Madame Rodenska's fortune telling truck and trailer rolled slowly up the block. Damn trucks all looked practically ancient. The truck rolled past the block of stores that the Holland family owned. The entire block; on all sides. Holland square, some folks called it. And it was a long block. The Holland family was the richest family in the county. They owned the lumber shed and the hardware store and a real estate office and this and that and the other. Martin's greatfather had built the first store, a trading post, on the banks of the Niobrara River. Then he moved the store north about twenty miles, and founded the town of Holland.

Several more carnival trucks rumbled past, one big one with the sign NABO'S TEN IN ONE painted on the side. Damn truck was old. Martin wondered what in the hell a ten in one might be?

An elderly man came walking up the sidewalk and stopped in front of the store. "Mayor," he greeted Martin. Martin had been the mayor since his return from Vietnam. Nobody ever ran against him and it was doubtful that anybody ever would. Job only paid fifty dollars a month and Martin never took that. Nobody except a Holland had ever been the mayor of Holland.

"Mr. Noble," Martin greeted the man.

The elderly man waved a blue-veined hand at the carnival trucks. "Don't like this, Mayor. Don't like this at all. It's a bad idea of yours, Mayor. Bad, I tell you."

But it wasn't my idea, Martin thought. As a matter of fact, he didn't know whose idea it had been. "Oh, come on, Mr. Noble," he kidded the man and smiled to back it up. "It'll give the kids—of all ages—something to do. It's all in fun. It'll give the people a chance to get together and socialize."

Noble snorted in that old man's way. "Oh, yeah? Well, you just remember that's what they said back in '54, too." He walked on up the sidewalk without another word.

Martin sighed and began the walk toward his car, parked in the lot of Holland Enterprises, about a block away and behind the main part of town. A peaceful little town. Stuck 'way to hell and gone out in the middle of nowhere. And because it was a small town, isolated, it was a fairly close-knit community. Everybody knew who was screwing whom—most of the time; who was in financial trouble; what marriages were going bad and usually why. The weekly newspaper—Martin had sold that some years back—still carried news of the local box suppers, homespun and homegrown poetry, who busted who in the mouth at the Dew Drop Inn, and in general would utterly bore anybody not from Holland.

Martin walked on. A tall man, with dark brown hair, just graying at the temples. Big hands and thick wrists. A powerful man, but very slow to anger—usually. But when he got angry, look out, for despite his wealth and education and position, Martin could and would duke it out with anybody just as fast as a cowboy with a snoot full of beer at a juke joint. And Martin would hurt you, too. Had him one of those white-hot tempers when he got the red-ass. And knew how to fight.

His shoulders were wide and his waist was still trim. Not a handsome man. His face was more interesting-looking than handsome. Rugged, was the word. Square-jawed. Dark eyes. Forty-one years old July past. 'Nam veteran. Won a bunch of medals for bravery and had absolutely no idea where they were. In the attic, probably, stored up there in cedar-lined boxes with his daddy's army clothes and his grandfather's World War One uniforms and a bunch of other stuff.

He wondered why Alicia had gone to the fairgrounds. She sure had been acting oddly the past months.

"Because I think it is an important event, Martin. Not that I particularly care for carnivals, I don't—they attract the same type of people as wrestling matches. But this town is dead. Lord knows I've tried to bring it some culture." That was a direct dig at him but he ignored it. Damned if he was going to get started in another argument about the little theater group. "Something is needed here, if only for a few days."

Martin stared at her. She was lying. She always pitty-patted her hands silently together when she was fibbing, and she was fibbing to him now. Alicia had pitty-patted a lot lately. Martin didn't know what the trouble was between them. As far as he knew, they were still very much in love, and up until about six months ago, they had enjoyed a much more than satisfactory sex life for a couple married as long as they had been.

"All right," he grinned at her. "I'll go along with that."

"Fine," she replied, a coolness in her eyes that touched her voice.

Martin fixed them drinks at the wet bar and handed one of the martinis to Alicia. "I'm getting more and more feedback from some of the older citizens. They don't like this carnival idea at all."

"Oh? I haven't heard that. Is it about that stupid fire years ago?"

There were times that Martin had difficulty understanding his wife's lack of sensitivity. "I was seven," memory prompted the words. "I remember now. Strange how the sight of that carnival rolling through brought it back. It happened thirty-four years ago."

Martin knew, or felt, there was something else he should

17

recall. But he could not drag it to the light of recollection.

"And I was four," Alicia said primly. "I recall that you acted forty when you were seven."

Martin ignored that cut, too. He had always been a serious type of person, for the most part, even though he had a good sense of humor, when he turned it loose. "You're fast approaching the big four-oh, kid," he said with a smile.

"Thirty-nine forever," she replied, but did not return the smile. "I shall never turn into some old poot."

"Like me?"

She looked at him for a moment and then dropped her eyes.

Martin wondered, again, if nearly nineteen years of marriage was going down the toilet.

"You don't really believe all those rumors about the fire and the cover-up, do you?" she asked.

"I sure do. Two town girls were raped and the townspeople reacted rather badly, to put it mildly. They blamed some carnival people and the carnies fought back. The fairgrounds was destroyed. Fire everywhere. All the rides and concessions and trailers and trucks of the carnival people destroyed. Some carnival people were shot, and rumor has it that some were horsewhipped just before the fire. Almost a hundred people were killed. All carnival people. By the time the state police got in here, it was all over and the townspeople stood together with their stories. Nobody ever went to jail for anything."

Alicia shook her head. "All rumors, Martin. And I don't believe any of them. And I do not believe it was really some townspeople who raped those girls."

They didn't agree on anything, anymore. But then, Alicia would never think harshly about the town. Most of the residents might not be as uppity-uppity as she thought she was, but they were still residents of Holland— although slightly beneath her.

"Well, I'll take Dad's word for it," Martin countered. "He was there and we were not. Besides, he as much as admitted to me that it was a cover-up. Then he never said another word about it."

"Was he drinking at the time?"

The question had just enough grease on it to irritate Martin. He ignored it. Martin's father had been known to tip the jug a time or two.

"If it had been the town's fault, there would have been lawsuits. I never heard of any."

"Who was left to sue? Besides, dad told me the insurance company paid off the wives and kids of those killed and that was that. As far as I know. I read about it once, over at the newspaper offices, but all those accounts are gone. Destroyed by someone."

"Now why would anybody do that?"

He shrugged his muscular shoulders. "I don't know. To cover guilt, to bury the past, to kill the memory." He had not told his wife about his hallucination that afternoon, or of his visit to Dr. Tressalt. He sipped his martini and asked, "Where are the kids?"

"Linda's over at Jeanne's, with Susan Tressalt. Spending the night. Mark has a date."

"I thought he and what's-her-name had broken up?"

"Betty. Yes, they did. He's out with Amy."

"Ah! Who's Amy? Never mind. He flits around so much I can't keep up with him."

Friday evening. Most other kids and many of their parents would be all hyped up for The Big Game that night. But Holland didn't have a football team or basketball team; hadn't had either in years. The distances the teams would have had to travel were just too great and the school board wisely felt that money would better be served on education. But Holland did have a place for the young to congregate on weekend nights: a huge old warehouse that had been converted to a teen center. They could dance, play pool or ping-pong, have parties, or just sit and talk. And it was only loosely supervised by adults. The kids themselves kept order, and since its inception, the young people had done, for the most part, a damn good job of it.

Martin glanced at his watch. "What's for dinner?"

Alicia smiled sweetly and smugly.

"Oh, no! I forgot."

"That time again," she reminded him.

Martin drained his glass and headed to the bar for a refill. He took note of his wife's disapproving look and set the glass on the bar, returning empty-handed to his chair.

Been a lot of disapproving looks lately, he thought.

On the third Friday of each month, a half dozen couples, all approximately the same age, gathered at a home for dinner and gossip. The women enjoyed it, the men professed to hate it. But they really didn't.

"Where are we suffering tonight?" Martin asked.

"Eddie and Joyce's. But cheer up: next month it's here."

"What's goin' down tonight?" Jeanne tossed out the question.

Susan shrugged and Linda said, "I don't want to go to the center, that's for sure."

The three girls all had that sun-tanned and wind-fresh healthy look of typical country girls. Susan grinned and Jeanne said, "What's the matter? You afraid that Robie might be there?"

"Not afraid." And she wasn't. Like her father, Linda was self-assured and resourceful, and had a lot of raw nerve. "But I sure don't want to see him. He makes me sick. He wants Suzanne, he can damn sure have her."

"I always thought you and Robie had an agreement?" Susan said.

"Yeah, so did I. You should have seen the expression on his face when I punched open the console and found those panties in there. And they sure weren't mine. My butt is not that big."

The girls laughed, Jeanne asking, "Did you really hang them over his head?"

"I sure did. Then I got out of the car and walked home."

"You tell your folks?"

"Mother. She thought it was disgusting. But she's been weird lately." No one commented on that. They all knew what was going on. The grapevine of the young. "I didn't tell daddy 'cause he never was thrilled about me seeing Robie. Thought he was a wise ass. I guess he was right."

Neither Susan nor Jeanne said: I told you so. But they both wanted to.

Jeanne rolled off the bed and dangled keys in front of her friends. "I got daddy's truck. Come on. Let's ride."

Robie Grant stood in front of the teen center with several of his friends, including the unspoken leader of Holland's answer to a gang, Karl Steele. All had agreed that it was boring as shit inside. Ping-pong. Who wants to play ping-pong?

The boys were dressed very nearly alike: jeans, boots, cowboy hats, dark shirts. And they all had one thing on the brain.

Karl Steel vocalized it. "Let's ride. See if we can chase up some pussy."

"Suzanne and Missy said they'd be around tonight," Hal informed the group, "lookin' for us. Suzanne's got her mother's car."

"Let's roll," Karl ordered. "Get us a case of long-necks."

And the others followed.

Martin looked at the glob of eggplant casserole the hostess had plopped on his plate. Never a picky eater, there were, nevertheless, a few things he disliked to the point of barfing.

Eggplant casserole was one of them.

To Martin's mind, the damn stuff looked like it had unwanted visitors wandering around in it. It was almost as bad as boiled okra—and that looked like snot.

"I'm telling you, Martin, that is the absolute best food you have ever put in your mouth," Joyce was assuring him with a smile.

Martin lifted his eyes from the crawly goop on his plate. He fought to keep from screaming.

Joyce's face had changed: mucus ran in greenish-yellow streams from her pig-snout nose, dripping over rotting and hairy and protruding lips. She snorted and oinked and curved back her lips. Her fangs were long and discolored. Her hair was all tangled and ropy and filthy. Fleas jumped about in the mess.

"Kiss me, Martin," she grunted.

Martin recoiled, almost dropping his plate. He blinked his eyes and the apparition was gone. The Joyce he had gone to school with stood before him, frowning, worry-lines creasing her forehead.

"What's the matter, Martin? You suddenly went white as a sheet. Alicia!" she called as the room went silent. "Hey, girl, you'd better get over here."

But Dr. Tressalt was there first. He sat Martin down in a chair and took his pulse. "Racing like a trip-hammer." He looked up at Alicia. "You better take him home. I'll get my bag and be right behind you." He patted Martin's arm. "You got a bad bug, my man. You're probably coming down with the flu. The symptoms are right. I'll see you in a few minutes."

"I damn sure have something," Martin agreed, standing up and moving toward the door. But for some reason, as yet unknown to him, he did not think it was the flu.

As the front door closed behind Martin and Alicia and the doctor, Milt Gilmer said, "Ol' Martin better lay off the sauce." He knocked back the rest of his bourbon and water. "End up like his daddy."

TWO

Martin Holland the third got in his truck one day, drove off to the north, and never came back. That was in 1969, while Martin the fourth was doing his thing over in 'Nam. A massive search went on for days, but neither the truck nor the man was ever found. Some theorized that he was kidnapped, with the kidnappers losing their nerve and just killing him. Others felt he was drunk and drove up into the badlands and got lost. Others didn't really give a damn what happened to him, those types of people being what they are: envious of anyone with more money and material things than they happen to possess.

Martin number four had been adamant that with the birth of his son, the numbers behind the name would cease. So the boy was named Mark. A year later, Linda came along. Alicia said there would be no more.

Good kids, most would agree. Never in any trouble, respectful to elders, and both worked for their money—unlike a lot of kids with monied parents—and made A's in school. And both kids preferred the company of their father over the company of their mother. Which suited both parents just fine.

Back at the Holland house, with Janet coming over with Gary, Martin leveled with them all about the hallucinations he'd been experiencing. Alicia looked scornful, Janet seemed worried, and Gary did not respond at all.

The doctor took Martin's blood pressure, his pulse—which had settled down to normal—looked into his eyes and down his throat. "Everything is normal, Martin. Like

23

I said, I think you've got a bug roaming around in your innards, just winding up for the big punch that'll put you down for a few days. You get some rest tonight and take it easy tomorrow."

Martin shook his head. "Gary, I feel just fine! Maybe somebody slipped some acid into my drink this evening?"

The doctor sat on the ottoman, facing his friend since boyhood. "OK, buddy. Let's pursue that line. Hey, we're all out of the sixties, that time of great unrest and social change and experimentation. Did you ever take any LSD at good ol' U of N? Or anywhere else for that matter—like in Vietnam, to name one real good place where nobody would blame you for wanting to get zonked out? I mean, acid, or so I've read, can come back on a person."

Martin shook his head. "No, I never dabbled in acid. I smoked some pot in college." He waved his hand. "Hell, we all did—remember? Took some speed. But I never got into psychedelics. By the time I got to 'Nam, I'd been clean for over two years. I never liked grass anyway; all it ever did for me was make me hungry, horny, and sleepy—at the same time."

Gary and Janet laughed at that. Alicia did not. That was too crude for her tastes.

"Gary, I don't have a fever. I don't have the sniffles. I don't have a headache, or sore throat, or any aching in my muscles or joints. It isn't the flu. And it didn't start until I saw those carnival trucks begin to roll through town."

At that, Janet walked to the wet bar and fixed a pretty good bump of bourbon.

"What's with you, love?" her husband asked.

"Ah, well, here goes—even though you're probably going to think I'm crazy."

He grinned at her. "What else is new?"

Janet turned, facing the men. "Gary, I'm serious about this."

"About what?"

"Some . . . damnit! Something pulled me to the fairgrounds today!" she blurted.

Gary stared at her. "Say—what?"

24

"Gary, now I told you I'm serious. Don't make fun of me." She looked at Alicia for support.

"Oh . . ." Alicia waved her hand. "All right. It was more something pulling me than it was Janet and Joyce. It was probably just my imagination and when I told them, it became infectious, that's all." She seemed anxious to dismiss the whole matter.

"Could the carnival have brought some sort of virus in here, Gary?" Martin asked.

"Oh . . . maybe. But it would have to be a fast-moving sucker and everybody in that show would have to be infected with it."

Martin stared at his wife. "You felt a pull? Would you explain it?"

"It was like, well, someone had planted subliminal suggestions in my brain. Then all of a sudden, something triggered them. I just could . . . not help myself. I had to go to the fairgrounds."

"Weird!" Martin shook his head.

"It's bullshit!" Gary muttered, careful that the ladies didn't hear him say it.

The phone rang and Alicia stilled it. "Yes? Oh! Yes, he's here. I'll tell him. Is the boy all right? Very well, doctor. Surely." She hung up and looked at Gary. "That was Dr. Rhodes. He was called over to the teen center. Some boy named Harold went into convulsions and then began screaming about monsters coming out of a fire. The doctor would like for you to join him."

"That's odd," Gary said. "Don made it clear some time back that he doesn't care for me at all."

Martin stood up.

Gary looked at him. "Where in the hell do you think you're going?"

"With you." He lifted a hand, cutting off the doctor's protests. "Gary, I feel fine. Look, something very odd is happening in this town. And I'm going to find out what it is. Let's go."

*   *   *

25

The fairgrounds lay quiet. The carnies would start putting up the equipment in the morning; but for now, they stayed in their trailers and campers—a very few in tents. The mess tent was up and open. But nobody was using it.

The road manager of the show, Jake Broadmore, and his front man, Slim Rush, stepped out of Jake's old trailer to stand in the quiet darkness.

"Our last play-date," Slim spoke softly and with a slight smile on his lips. He was called Slim because he was five feet, six inches tall and weighed two hundred and fifty pounds.

Jake smiled his reply.

"They got the place all fixed up real nice, don't they, Jake?"

"Real nice," Jake agreed.

"But it don't look much like I remember it."

"They changed it around some. Some rebuilding. Tell the boys there ain't no big rush in settin' up. Things don't crank up for six more days. Next Thursday at noon. Mayor's supposed to make a speech, then some lady's gonna sing the national anthem. Same old stuff. But I've missed it."

"Yeah, me too. We got time, lots of it. We wanna do this right."

"Amen, brother."

"Almost thirty-four years to the date. I rememer it all well."

"Will be exactly thirty-four years come next Thursday night."

Both men's eyes seemed to burn at the memory.

An extremely tall man walked past them in the night. He was almost eight feet tall. He glanced at the men, nodded his head, and walked on.

"You lookin' after Dolly?" Jake called.

"Don't I always," the carnival's giant man replied, without pausing.

"Still surly," Slim muttered.

"Have you ever knowed him when he wasn't? Looks

26

after Dolly though. Even though he don't have to no more."

Dolly Darling was the fat lady. Six hundred and fifty pounds of blob. Five feet, five inches tall. Her special-made truck was her home. Tiny the Giant drove the truck. Backed it right up to a special-made stall in Nabo's Ten-in-One, wheeled Dolly to the tommy-lift, and lowered her. That's where she sat, from noon to nine at night. Except when she had to go take a crap—which was an event in itself. The potty was also special-made, and was placed right behind a flap just to Dolly's right and a couple of steps back. Dolly Darling's place was between Tiny the Giant and the Dog Man.

The others in Nabo's Ten-in-One included: Carlson, the world's most tattooed man, who lay on a bed of spikes. Nuru, the Indian fakir, who stuck needles and pins through his lips and cheeks and arms, and chewed up light bulbs and soft drink bottles. Samson, the strong man, who bent horseshoes and crowbars and who had an I.Q. of about fifty. At the peaks. At the valleys he was a slobbering idiot who was very capable of tearing a normal human being into bloody chunks with nothing but his bare hands. There was Balo, the beautiful young woman who handled snakes, including rattlesnakes and pythons. Lulu, the half man, half woman, with both male and female organs. For a slight extra charge, one could see the Geek, watch him tear the head off living chickens and drink the blood. At the end of the big tent housing the Ten-in-One, was JoJo, the ape man, billed as having been found as a child in the deepest, darkest jungles of Africa— half ape, half man. JoJo was known, in carny lingo, as the main blow-off. Meaning that he could, if he had to, carry the whole show. The blow-off is the most important part of a Ten-in-One. Before the carnival got JoJo, they had only the Dog Man as a human freak.

Nabo himself ate fire and swallowed swords and neon tubing.

"I can't hardly wait," Slim broke the silence.

Monroe, the Ten-in-One's talker, joined them in the

night. A circus uses a barker, a carnival uses a talker. It was Monroe's duty to gather the crowd, usually with a half naked Balo on the platform with him, a fifteen foot snake wrapped around her, the tip, or crowd, gathering, and then Monroe would turn them; in other words, coax the tip into the tent with his line of patter—a talker.

"It's begun in town," Monroe informed them.

"How wonderful!" Jake replied, excitement in his voice. "We've waited so long!"

The Harold boy had settled down by the time Gary and Martin had arrived at the teen center and pushed their way through the kids. Dr. Rhodes knelt by the boy. The boy's lips and tongue were bloody where he had chewed on them during his convulsions.

There was a peculiar odor lingering around the boy.

"Smells like charred wood," Martin noted.

"Yes, I noticed." Dr. Rhodes looked up, "but he has no burns on him that I can find." He smiled oddly.

Gary thought it was a hell of a time to be smiling. He knelt down beside the boy. "What did you give him, Don?"

"Nothing. He was already quiet when I got here."

"He was talking crazy," a teenage girl said. "Some mumbo jumbo language."

"But it was a language," another girl spoke up. "I mean, it had definite word-sounds and obvious meaning."

Don Rhodes looked irritated that the kids had brought that up.

Strange behavior on his part, Gary thought. "It had meaning . . . to whom?" he asked the girl.

"I don't know, Doctor. But it was a language. I've studied languages for the past four years and intend to become a linguist. It was a language."

"Nonsense," Dr. Rhodes said.

The Harold boy was taken to the town's clinic and

nurses called in. Members of his family agreed to sit with him during the night, and the nurses would call if his condition changed.

He would be transported to Scottsbluff first thing in the morning.

Dr. Don Rhodes had walked off without another word.

"Odd fellow," Martin commented.

"More like a horse's ass would sum it up better," Gary replied. "But he's a good doctor," he grudgingly added.

"Gary, the boy doesn't belong to one of those religions that go off the deep end every now and then and start speaking in tongues, does he?"

"I thought of that and asked his friends. No. Not according to the kids."

Gary dropped Martin off at his house. He told Martin to get some rest and if he felt like it, he'd meet him at the club for their regular Saturday morning golf game.

"The kids aren't back yet, Alicia?"

"It's still early, Martin. It's not even nine o'clock."

"Damn! So much has happened it feels like it should be around midnight."

"How is the boy?"

"His vital signs are perfectly normal. The boy says he doesn't know what happened. He doesn't remember anything except the horrible visions of fire and the monsters coming out at him. He'll be checked for epilepsy down at Scottsbluff."

"Strange."

"Yes. But there was definitely a smell of charred wood on and around the boy."

"Was anybody cooking on the outdoor grill at the center?"

"No. I looked." He yawned hugely. "I hate to go to bed so early, but I'm just plain beat."

He waited for their ritual goodnight kisses. They did not come.

Alicia sat and looked at him. "Then you go on to bed. I'm going to read for awhile."

Both Martin and Alicia were avid readers, preferring

29

books over the tube, and they had encouraged their kids in that direction.

Martin liked adventure books. Alicia preferred horror stories.

For some reason, or reasons, that none could explain—although no one had asked, many of the townspeople, young and old, had gathered at the fence surrounding the fairgrounds. They stood, mostly in silence, and stared at the darkened trucks and vans and trailers of the carnival people.

There were still a few of the locals working in the long sheds and pavilions that would house the cattle and sheep and goats and pigs. Others worked in the small booths that would display the cakes and pies and other local culinary endeavors. One by one, those booths began to go dark as the shadows thickened and the hour grew later. They shut it down and went home.

Outside the fence, the people remained. Standing and staring in silence.

The girls drove by in the pickup truck. "Wonder what the fascination is over there?" Jeanne asked, her eyes taking in the knots of people standing by the fence.

"Turn around and come back," Susan said. "There's Binkie."

Jeanne found a place to turn around and came back, stopping at a knot of young people.

"Hey, Binkie!" Linda called from the truck. "What's up?"

A boy left the crowd and walked over, to stand by the pickup and stare at the girls. Jeanne, behind the wheel, and the farthest away from him, could not see his eyes.

But Susan and Linda could. His eyes were odd-looking. Something seemed to dance behind them. If it wasn't such a stupid thought, both girls felt it looked like tiny flames.

Linda asked, "What's everybody doing, Binkie?"

"Nothin' much. Standin' around is all."

Something was the matter with his voice, too. It was

very flat-sounding. Totally without inflection. Weird.

"Why are you standing around, Binkie?" Susan asked.

Binkie shrugged and stuck his hand inside the cab, trying to fondle Linda.

"Goddamnit, Binkie!" she yelled at him. "Keep your hands to yourself!"

"OK," the boy said, very matter-of-factly.

The girls noticed a giant of a man walking among the shadows, behind the fence. "God! would you look at that!" Jeanne breathed. "It's a giant!"

"Probably got a dick a foot long," Binkie said with a grin.

The girls groaned in unanimous disbelief. It just wasn't like Binkie to try to grab a feel or say something like that. Binkie was everybody's favorite. Binkie buddied with the boys and palled around with the girls. Everybody liked Binkie.

"He'd probably show his dick to you if you'd ask him," Binkie added.

"Binkie!" There was exasperation in Linda's voice. "Knock that off. Who are you out here with?" Then her eyes found Karl and Robie and the others. "Oh, not them, Binkie. Not that bunch."

"They're my buddies. You wanna see my dick, Linda?"

"Let's get out of here," Linda said wearily, not understanding what had gone wrong with Binkie.

Jeanne put the truck in gear. "Goodnight, Binkie. You'd better go home and sleep it off."

Driving away, Susan said, "What's got into Binkie? I never heard him talk that way before."

"I don't know," Linda replied. "But I don't think it was the beer. Place is getting weird. All those people just standing around the fence."

They stopped at an intersection and Jeanne spotted Linda's brother, Mark. Linda rolled down her window and waved at him. Amy Newman sat on the passenger side of the Camero. Martin's deal with the boy was: I'll make the car payments for you, but you have to pay for the insurance and gas and upkeep. It was an agreement that

31

both sides honored.

Mark lowered his window and smiled at the girls. Nearly everybody liked Mark. Except for Karl Steele and his bunch of near-thugs. Mark was too straight-arrow for them. He wasn't a prude or a preach, but he didn't drink and didn't do drugs, and if he gave his word, that was that. Like his sister, Mark was fair-skinned, with blonde hair and blue eyes. A handsome young man.

He told them about Jimmy Harold.

"You mean he just fell out and started having fits!" Jeanne asked.

"Yeah. And he was talking in a foreign language and yelling that the monsters were coming and he was burning up. And something else: you could really smell the smoke around him. It was strange."

For a reason she could not fathom, Susan suddenly shuddered.

"What's wrong with you?" Linda asked.

"I don't know. Mouse ran over my grave, I guess."

Linda got out of the truck and walked over to her brother. She stood between car and truck. "Have you been down to the fairgrounds, Mark?"

"No. Why go down there?"

"There's about a couple hundred people down there. All crowded up by the fence." She paused and her brother picked up on it.

"What's wrong, sis?"

"It's like I've been trying to tell you, Mark," Amy broke in. "Something weird is happening in this town. I can feel it."

"But it isn't anything tangible," Linda said. "But for some reason, I'm a little jumpy."

She expected Mark to laugh at her and was surprised when he did not. Even more surprised when he agreed with her. "I thought it was my imagination. I still think we're making more out of it than we should. You girls take it easy." He dropped the Camero into gear and rolled on.

Linda turned her head, looking at Jeanne. "What now?"

"I think we should go home."

"I'm with you."

Martin was asleep in five minutes, dropping into a gentle darkness.

Then the gentle darkness lifted its outer veil and the sleep became a chamber of horrors.

The man became frightened. He was being driven by a fear like none he had experienced before. Not even in 'Nam. Somebody, or some*thing*, was chasing him. Running after the boy, cursing as the boy ran through a long barn.

Boy?

Martin had mentally been torn from the present and hurled unwillingly back into time, his sleeping body separating from his mind; one rested while the other took him on a journey into terror.

He was no longer running. And he could see with perfect clarity. His senses, all of them, were working overtime. He was in a hay-filled stall. But how did he get there and what was that crying and those painful noises? Where were they coming from? That animal-like grunting.

The tow-headed little boy peeped through a crack in the wall of the horse stall in the livestock pavilion. He could see a girl with her dress up around her waist, the bodice all ripped open. Her tanned bare legs were spread wide, while a man, naked from the waist down—that was all Martin could see of him—was between her legs. He was hunching and grunting and saying all sorts of crazy things. And just to the left of that couple, another girl and guy were doing the same thing.

"You know you been wantin' this, Mary," the man closest to Martin said. It was not a mature voice. A young man's voice.

The girl turned her head and Martin recognized her. Mary Mahoney.

"Goddamn you!" Mary cursed the young man in a

33

husky voice. "Goddamn you all to hell! My daddy'll kill you for this."

The young man's voice hardened. "Shut your damn slutty mouth, girl! And keep your voice down, or I'll really hurt you."

Mary began to cry, the tears running down her cheeks and dripping onto the bales of hay.

Martin hunkered down in the hay-filled stall, the movement of his feet kicking up dust. He shifted positions until he could see the face of the other girl. June Ellis. Both Mary and June were in high school. Both of them about fifteen. But the boy could not see the faces of the young men.

But their voices sure were familiar to him.

"We gonna do this regular from now on," the other young man panted.

"My daddy'll cut you like a gelding!" June raised her voice.

That got her a hard open palm to the side of her head. She yelped and fell silent except for a low whimpering and the silent fall of tears.

"Your daddy ain't jack-shit!" the young man told her, his voice as hard and cruel as the forced act he was a part of. "Dirt farmer on rented land is all he is. Our daddies got papers on both your daddies. They own them! One word from us and your folks don't have nothing! You wanna see your daddy lose his farm?"

June said something that Martin could not make out.

"That's right," the young man told her, a cold, mean, smugness in his voice. "So you lay back and shut up."

Martin huddled in fright in the stall next to the couples, too scared to try to make a run for it.

But what was he doing in the stall? How did he get here? Then he remembered. He'd ridden a ride and had gotten real sick to his stomach. He'd gone into the far end of the long pavilion and had lain down on the hay. Gone to sleep. The late autumn warmth had lulled him gently. The grunting and panting had awakened him.

"No!" Mary suddenly cried out, real pain in her voice.

"I won't do that. You can't make me!"

Martin looked. He was making her do it, with a hard hand over her mouth to stifle her screaming. Martin crouched against the stall wall, the scene making him sick to his stomach. He trembled in fright.

The rape and perversion seemed, in his young mind, to go on for hours. But it was really maybe fifteen minutes—twenty minutes tops.

The sounds of grunting and cursing faded away. The girls continued their almost silent weeping. Martin peeked through the narrow crack and watched as the young men pulled on their jeans and buckled their belts. Then they bent over to tug on their boots.

And Martin knew both of them. He bit his lower lip in fright. They were both bullies. His own father called them rich trash.

Martin moved his feet. The dust puffed up from the hay. He sneezed violently, the dust particles setting him off like a small bomb.

"What the hell was that?" one of the young men yelled.

Martin left the stall as fast as his short-panted legs could carry him, running hard, fear making him strong and swift.

"Get the little son of a bitch!" the hard voice reached him. "And then break his neck!"

Martin ran and ran, but the longer legs of the older boys were closing the gap as they raced up the seemingly endless middle aisle of the livestock pavilion.

Martin glanced behind him. His feet slipped in a fresh manure pile. He crashed into a wall.

Martin was plunged into a painful darkness.

THREE

Who was shaking him? And why? What was going on?

"Daddy!" Linda's voice came through the fog of years past. "Wake up, daddy!"

He opened his eyes and looked into the face of his daughter. With a groan, Martin sat up in bed.

"What happened?" he managed to croak.

"You were yelling, daddy."

It all came back to him. Everything. His mind had finally, after thirty-four years, unlocked the suppression. "Well, it was a nightmare, baby." He looked at the clock by the bed. Nine-thirty. He had been asleep for only a few minutes. "Where's your mother?"

Something flickered in the girl's eyes, then was gone. "I don't know. We drove by and I noticed the car was gone. I had them drop me off. They said they'd be back in twenty minutes or so."

"Your mother is gone? No note? Nothing?" He slipped into a robe.

"Not that I can see. She probably drove down to the store for a book or something. You know mother."

I don't know whether I do or not, Martin thought. Here lately, I'm beginning to wonder. He shook his head. "I'm groggy."

"How about if I make you some coffee?"

"That would be very nice."

He had to tell somebody. And Linda and Martin had

37

always shared secrets, as had Martin and Mark. And she was a grown up girl for her age.

". . . and that's why I could never remember anything about the fairs and carnivals we used to have here," Martin wrapped it up for her.

"So all the rumors I've heard over the years are true?"

"Yes." He knew what rumors she was talking about; he'd heard the same ones himself as a kid.

"I guess for a little kid to see something that awful would be enough in itself to cause a memory shutdown. But it was probably that crashing into the wall that did it."

"Oh, it was. It's all come back to me now." He had made no further mention of his wife's absence and Linda had not brought it up. "I woke up in Ol' Doc Reynolds' office. Couldn't remember a thing. Doc had me sent immediately, that day, into the city and I stayed there for a long time. Skull fracture and neck injuries. Broke my jaw and knocked out some teeth. I was a mess."

"And by that time," Linda was putting it all together, "the trouble had happened between the carnival people and the townspeople, so you missed all that."

"Honey, I missed the next eight months, or so. Dad sent me on down to North Platte to stay with my aunt. Aunt Louise. I doubt if you remember her. You were just a little girl when she died." Linda shook her head. "I never did understand why he did that; and he never told me. Except to make it clear that it was for my own good. Of course, I know now why he did it: somehow he found out that the carnival people hadn't raped those girls and he was fearful for my life. Anyway, by the time I got back to Holland, the lid had been clamped down tight—nobody talking—and it stayed that way."

"What happened to those boys you saw raping the two girls?"

Martin had not told her any of the names of those involved. The two men were among the richest ranchers in the state and were just as thuggy and no-good as they had been as boys. He drained his coffee mug and said, "Well . . . that happened in mid-October. I didn't get back here until late August, the next year. By that time, their fathers had packed them both off to college and since nobody told me about the rapes, and I sure couldn't remember them . . . well, everything appeared all right to me. Except for the burned down fairgrounds' buildings. I learned about that later.''

"Do they still live here, dad?"

He hesitated. "This is between you and me, kiddo. If they found out I remembered and had told you—even now—they'd kill you."

She nodded her head in understanding. "I'm cool, dad."

"Yeah?" he chuckled. "That word still in use, huh?" He sighed. "Yes, they still live around this area. But they rarely come into town. Two, maybe three times a year, tops. But now I know why they hate me like they do. They've been thinking all these years that I would tell on them. They didn't know that I didn't remember a thing. I do recall some mighty evil looks I got from them when they'd come back home from college. Not that they went that long, they didn't. They both busted out within a year. Then I guess they got drafted. I don't really know what happened to them. I don't think I've seen them twenty-five times in that many years."

She looked at her father for a moment, her eyes serious. "What do you plan on doing about this?"

He leaned back in his chair. "I don't know, honey. I really don't know if there is anything I can do about it."

The woman in the girl took over. "What do you mean? Daddy, the men who raped those girls are both walking around free! And that's not right!"

Martin could but shrug his shoulders. "I know, baby. But I don't know what I can do about it after all these years. There is probably a statute of limitations on the crime. Besides, the girls—girls, hell! they're older than I am—have been content to stay quiet about it for almost thirty-five years . . ." He let that taper off into silence.

"OK. You're right, I guess. Now, what about these hallucinations of yours."

He had completely leveled with Linda. "What about them?"

"I think you should see somebody about them."

"Who? And for heaven's sake, why?"

"Daddy, you saw a lot of combat. I know you did. People talk. And you won an awful lot of medals. Maybe? . . ."

He smiled and laid a big hand on top of hers. "No, baby. I'm not suffering from a post-Vietnam syndrome, or anything even remotely related to that. I'm one of the lucky ones. I went over there, did my tours, did my job, and tried not to let it get to me. Yes, honey, I killed a lot of people. And I had friends who got killed. Good friends. I will not allow myself to think they died in vain. But unlike so many other 'Nam vets, I came back to a hero's welcome here in Holland. Parades and so forth. Just like Pete and Howie and Richard did. Your mother and I got married, and we settled right in."

A horn honked outside. Linda smiled and kissed her father. "I love you, daddy."

"And I love you, too, baby. Now take off. And not one word about this."

"Deal!"

"And we don't tell mother we know she took off somewhere, right?"

The girl's face hardened. "If you say so, daddy." The girl's voice was as hard as her expression.

She knows something, Martin thought. But do I want to know? "I say so."

"Right." She turned and was gone.

Martin went back to bed.

He didn't tell Gary about Alicia's disappearing act either. His wife had been asleep when Martin left the house that morning. But he did level with his best friend about everything else.

"Well, I'll just be damned! After all these years, and it just pops back into your consciousness. It happens that way sometimes. But I wonder what triggered the memory response?"

"Probably the sight of those carnival trucks. That's all I

can think of. Wouldn't you agree?"

"Yeah," he replied absently.

The men were at the Holland Country Club, talking in the club house before teeing off for their regular Saturday morning eighteen holes.

"How's the Harold boy?"

"As far as I can tell, fine. We're sending him down to Scottsbluff for some tests." He looked at his watch. "Should be pulling out about now. Martin? How come those carnival people pulled in almost a week before they're due to open the show?"

The sudden shift in conversation caught Martin totally off guard. "Why . . . I don't know. Haven't given it any thought. Why do you ask?"

Gary sighed heavily. "Martin, I like to think of myself as a reasonable man. A logical person. But . . . well, my fourteen-year-old was over at the teen center last night with some friends. He finally wanders in about two hours overdue. He tells me some bullshit about being drawn over to the fairgrounds. Naturally, Janet gives me the, 'See, I told you so,' bit. But I wasn't buying any of it. I came down pretty hard on the kid. Then I got to listening to some of the guys talk—before you got here this morning. Martin, every one of them said their kids came in late last night. One or two or three hours late. And they all had the same story to tell."

Martin was conscious of his pulse rate going up just a tad. "That something drew or pulled them all over to the fairgrounds?"

"That's it."

"What do you make of it?"

"Martin, let me run it down for you. First of all, you have two hideous hallucinations: your daughter turning into an old hag, and then Joyce's face becomes a pig, or something. The two hallucinations are about eight hours apart. Jimmy Harold goes into some sort of convulsions, seeing monsters coming out of a fire—they're after him— and then he starts speaking in tongues while the odor of smoke and charred wood lingers around him. Joyce and

41

Alicia and Janet felt some sort of overpowering urge to go to the fairgrounds. You have a dream—a true nightmare—that unlocks some bad memories, all of them associated with and centered around the fairgrounds and a carnival. And the young people of this town, many of them, come in late telling their parents some tale about being drawn or pulled to the fairgrounds. Martin, do you really want to play golf this morning?"

"No."

"What do you want to do?"

"The same thing you want to do, Gary: go over to the fairgrounds."

The fairgrounds hummed with activity, most of it coming from the townspeople working on their booths. Many of the carnival people were still inside their trailers and campers and vans.

"Do you remember what pavilion you were in when the rapes occurred?" Gary asked.

Martin waved his hand. "Over there, somewhere. But it doesn't make any difference now. All the original buildings are gone."

"I keep forgetting about that fire."

"Didn't your folks ever tell you anything about it?"

"No. And I asked several times. Last time when I was about fourteen, or so. My dad busted me up side my head. I called dad this morning and asked him point blank about it. He said he didn't remember and then hung up the phone."

Martin glanced at him. "Odd behavior. Do you remember anything at all about it?"

"Not really. You were seven and I was six. The memory is pretty damned vague. And it hasn't helped that no one ever talked about it."

"Have you considered that we may be trying to open a can of squirmy worms, Gary?"

"You mean about the men who really raped those girls?"

42

"Yes. If we say anything about it at all."

"What do you think?"

"I think I'll first talk to Eddie about any statute of limitations." He pointed to a row of newly constructed booths. "Look over there." The smell of fresh cut pine was in the air. "Those folks are from Alliance and Chadron. We're really pulling in some people for this thing."

Gary agreed. "I didn't think they would come from so far away."

"I didn't either." He looked around him. "I wonder when they're going to start putting up all the rides?"

That got him a grin from his friend. "Going to ride the Loop-the-Loop, Martin?"

"Not unless somebody holds a gun to my head and makes me get on it. I've never been much of a thrill-seeker, Gary. I did enough of that in 'Nam. A shrink might say that stems back to my getting sick on that ride years ago."

"Maybe. Maybe it just shows you have uncommon good sense. Why did you volunteer for that special outfit in Vietnam, Martin?"

"Good question." His smile was rather sad. "Maybe I just liked the funky-looking berets we wore."

"Damn, were you a green beret, too!"

"Oh, no. We wore tan berets. Some LRRP units just wore conventional headgear."

And as Gary knew he would, Martin changed the subject. His friend had been quite a hero in Vietnam, winning a lot of medals and being put in twice for the Congressional. But he never talked about the war. There was nothing in his house to even hint that he had served. He wasn't ashamed of going; Gary knew that. He just never talked about it.

"You like the rides, Gary?"

"I don't know. I've never had any overwhelming urge to get on one. I can't consciously remember ever going to a carnival. As you know, we never had another carnival in town after '54, and I never had the time in college. After my residency, it was straight back here and, we are sort of isolated here in Holland."

43

"A good and bad thing."

"Yes."

They rounded a corner of a long tent and came face to face with something out of a horror movie. Both of them pulled up short and startled.

"Jesus Christ!" Gary blurted.

Martin was too shocked to speak.

The men were face to snout with a human man with a dog's head: pointy, furry ears, long snout, human eyes, furry, clawed hands—paws really. The man-beast snarled in fright, jerked back, and quickly slipped into the shadowy interior of the big tent, closing the flap.

"What in God's name? . . ." Martin finally found his voice.

"Ralph Stanley McVee," the heavy voice came from behind them.

Both men turned.

"Known world-wide as the Dog Man," the stranger finished it. The tall man was dressed in dark clothing: dark suit, dark shoes, and dark turtleneck sweater. He wore extremely dark glasses. Martin wondered how he could see out of the things.

Martin cleared his throat. "I'm Martin Holland. This is Gary Tressalt. And you are? . . ."

"I am Nabo. I own this carnival; run this establishment." He pointed with a thick blunt finger to the long tent. "It is known as a Ten-in-One."

"I saw the trucks come in yesterday," Martin said. And then another thought flashed through his mind: I've seen this man before. I've seen all of this before. But that is impossible.

Then the thought was gone, as if neatly and quickly and deliberately excised from his mind.

His eyes touched the dark lenses of Nabo's glasses. The man's lips moved in some semblance of a smile. Martin didn't know if it was pleasant, or not. He thought the latter.

Gary looked at the closed flap of the tent, then back to Nabo. "He wears his make-up all the time?"

"It isn't make-up, friend. He was born that way. A cruel, vicious trick of nature. Ralph is actually quite intelligent and well-read. But due to the shape of his jaw, he finds speaking quite difficult—so he elects not to speak. To strangers, that is."

Gary thought about that for a few seconds. "His condition could have been corrected by surgery."

Again, Nabo's lips moved in what might have been a smile. Neither man could tell if the smile—if that's what it was—reached the man's eyes. Nabo shrugged his heavy shoulders. "He's approximately fifty years old. That type of corrective surgery was not performed back then."

"What do you mean by that? That he is *approximately* fifty years old?"

"He was found in a trash bin in New York City as a baby. The authorities first took him to the dog pound."

"That's hideous!" Martin said.

"That's the way it is outside these canvas walls, friend."

"Who named him?"

Again, Nabo shrugged. "Who knows? Who cares? A nurse, a cop, a doctor, a janitor. The important thing is that he has a home, here, with us. And here, with us, no one ridicules him."

"No one except the people who pay to see him," Gary contradicted.

"But that, friend, is a very small price to have to pay for enjoying a feeling of belonging that he could find no place else on earth. And, do not think the ridicule is all one-sided. Don't think that we—and I am as much a freak as anyone else here—don't find some enjoyment in watching the faces of those who ridicule us. Perverse is not something enjoyed only by those who think of themselves as normal."

Gary frowned at that. But he had to admit there was truth in what the man said.

"A Ten-in-One means that there are ten acts, or shows, under one tent?" Martin asked.

"How quick we are." Martin couldn't tell if the man was being sarcastic or merely condescending. "Yes. You are correct on all three counts."

That jarred Martin right down to his shoes. Was the man a mind reader? He was conscious of Gary looking at him strangely.

"Are you gentlemen officers of the law or some other officials of this town?" Nabo asked.

"I'm the mayor and Gary is one of the town's doctors."

"Ah! Well, then. A tour—grand is in the eyes of the beholder—" Nabo thought that amusing and chuckled for a few seconds "—Is certainly in order." He stepped to the canvas flap and pulled it open, toward him. A quiet dimness beckoned them from within. "Enter then. And welcome to Nabo's Ten-in-One, Mister Mayor and Mister Healer."

The men hesitated for a moment, then stepped inside.

A huge shadow fell across their path.

Alicia puttered around the house for a time, but a restlessness within her made the routine work irritating. She changed clothes and called Janet. Her friend was also experiencing the same type of restlessness.

"I was just about to call you, Alicia. I just hung up from a call from Joyce. I'll pick you up in about fifteen minutes. We'll do something."

It remained unspoken, but two of them knew what that something would turn out to be.

Janet picked her up in her Mercedes and together they drove over to Joyce's.

From there they went to the fairgrounds.

Linda and Susan and Jeanne got up very early, for them, and took their baths, then sat down on the bed to make plans for the day.

But no one had any ideas. And no one really wanted to go to the fairgrounds, either.

"Well, hell!" Susan said. "We can go over there just to see who's there, I guess. But I'm gonna tell you something:

that place spooks me."

Mark leaned against the counter in his father's hardware store. Business was off—way off. Hadn't been but a handful of people come in all morning. And that was unusual for a Saturday. Place was always jumping on a Saturday. People buying things for home fix-up and stuff like that.

But not today.

Something weird going on in town, he thought.

"Hope it's just my imagination," he muttered, and turned to straighten up a display rack.

And Jimmy Harold broke his restraints in the back of the ambulance, screamed once, and then died.

FOUR

A giant of a man blocked their way. To their eyes, the man looked to be about ten feet tall, with the weight to go with it. He was anything but skinny.

"Tiny," Nabo said gently. "These gentlemen are my guests. Doctor, Mayor, this is Tiny the Giant."

Both men noticed that Nabo did not remove his dark glasses. And both men wondered how he could see in the gloom of the tent.

Martin and Gary held out their hands. The giant of a man ignored the offering of friendship. He glared down at the men for a moment, his eyes burning with what both men accurately perceived as loathing and hatred. Tiny turned his back to them and stalked away, up the long tent, and into the darkness. For a man his size, both men noted, Tiny moved very gracefully.

"Tiny has never been known for his social graces," Nabo said, by way of explanation.

"Man like that could be very dangerous," Gary remarked. He was wondering what lay in the darkness at the end of the long tent.

"All men are dangerous, Doctor," Nabo replied. "But some of the most gentle men are big men. Tiny has never harmed a soul in any of his lives. He's a strick vegetarian; won't even hurt any type of animal. Can either of you say that?"

"What does he wear on his feet and how does he hold his pants up?" Gary asked, a touch of sarcasm in his voice.

"With a cloth belt and his sandals are not made from the

49

skins of beasts."

"Admirable, I suppose," Gary muttered.

Personally, Martin had always admired those types of people, but he kept his mouth shut on that subject and spoke on something else he had picked up from Nabo. "You said lives? Plural?"

Nabo's lips again curved in that strange smile, creasing the dark face. East Indian ancestry, Martin thought. "Tiny believes in reincarnation. As I do. Don't you?"

"No," Martin told him.

"Ummm. Well, we may get the chance to debate that subject at some later date. One never knows what the morrow will bring, does one? Are you gentlemen ready to view the men and women who offer themselves to the public's adoring eyes via this humble establishment?"

The front flap was suddenly jerked back. Bright sunlight flooded into the semi-gloom of the tent, the floor covered with fresh sawdust. Chief of Police Paul Kelson stood in the brightness.

"Mayor. Doc." His eyes touched Nabo. "Whoever you are. The station just got a call from the ambulance. That Harold boy just kicked the bucket."

Martin inwardly winced at the chief's casual expression of death.

"Damn!" the word exploded out of Gary's mouth. He started to ask "how?" but knew better than to ask Chief Kelson anything that might strain his brain. The man was a dope. "The boy will have to be taken to Harrisville for autopsy."

Kelson shook his head. "Got a rub there, Doc. The county coroner is on vacation. Out of town. You're the assistant coroner."

Gary came very close to telling the chief that he didn't need to be reminded of that. He didn't like Chief Kelson and almost always had to struggle to contain his dislike. And he knew that Martin did not care for the man, either. They had all gone to school together. Knew each other well. Kelson had been a bully in the first grade; a bully when he dropped out of school in the eleventh. And while

Kelson was careful not to step across that invisible line, both men knew the chief resented them, resented and was envious of their success and their station in life.

The only reason he was chief of police in Holland was because there was seldom any serious trouble. It was a small and isolated community. Strangers were spotted immediately. The only trouble came from the ranchhands who could be counted on to have their weekend brawls at one of the local honky-tonks. Kelson and his people would break it up. A brutal boy had grown into a brutal man. Kelson liked to hurt people. Most bullies do. And like most bullies, Kelson shared something else with his counterparts around the globe: he was cruel to animals, he was a very insecure man, and he was a coward at heart.

"So you told the driver to return to Holland?" Gary asked.

Kelson shook his head. "Oh, no, Doc. I wouldn't never do nothin' like that without askin' you first. I'd be steppin' out of my place. And I sure wouldn't want to do that."

Nabo smiled at the exchange.

Martin had to turn his head to hide his own smile. Kelson was no mental giant, but he sure knew how to stick the needle to people.

But Gary was better at it. He expelled breath and said, "Fine, Chief. That's good. A man should always know his place in the overall scheme of things."

Nabo ducked his head as his smile widened.

Kelson's eyes narrowed. He kept his mouth shut.

Gary said, "Tell the driver to bring the body back here. Take it to Miller's. I'll meet them there."

"Right, Doc. See you people." Kelson walked out of the tent, his back stiff with anger.

"A very angry and dangerous man," Nabo observed. "In this business, we see far too many of them and learn to recognize them quickly."

"I'm sure that's right, Mr. Nabo," Martin said. "If Kelson gives you any trouble, let me know."

Again, that slight smile. "I certainly shall."

Martin and Gary had not noticed as Tiny and the Dog

51

Man and Samson had gathered at the far end of the tent, standing in the dimness, watching and listening.

"We'll finish the tour later," Martin told him. "Thank you for your hospitality."

"You're quite welcome, your honor. Doctor. You both know your way out."

Nabo turned and walked away, into the dimness of the other end of the tent.

As the men reentered the sunlight, neither said it aloud, but both knew the other was glad to be outside of that tent. There had been, was still, something odd about that place. And not just the poor misshapen and grotesque souls who earned their living displaying their deformities and other physical and mental uniquenesses.

Something was strange about that dark place.

Neither man, at the time, knew how to put that feeling into words.

But it would come to them.

Soon.

They rounded the corner of the tent and stopped. "Now what in the hell are they doing out here?" Gary asked, a touch of annoyance in his voice.

Martin smiled at his friend. "What are *we* doing out here?"

"Good point." He waved at Janet and Joyce and Alicia.

The ladies walked over to join them. "Fancy meeting you two here," Janet said with a grin. Martin and Gary braced themselves for what they knew was coming. "Must be something terribly important for you semi-pro's to miss your golf game."

Gary and Martin never played with anyone else for a very simple reason: no one else wanted them as partners. They were, collectively or singularly, the worst golfers in the county. Possibly the state. Maybe the nation. They needed a computer to keep up with their scores.

"Very funny," Martin said. "Ha ha." But he was grinning. He jerked a thumb toward Gary. "He has to do an autopsy."

"I'm sorry, Gary," Alicia said. She had yet to meet her

husband's eyes. "Who is it?"

"The Harold boy just died."

"Died!" the women echoed, Janet adding, "But you said last night that he didn't appear to have anything seriously wrong with him."

"Yes. That's what I said, all right." Gary's voice held just a touch of weariness. Doctors-aren't-supposed-to-make-mistakes syndrome.

Janet touched his arm. "Sorry, honey."

He smiled at her. "I'll know the cause of death later on today. Hopefully." He looked at Martin. "You want me to drop you off somewhere? You left your car at home, remember?"

"Yeah. No, I'll stay out here and prowl around with the girls. Catch up with you later on. You'll be at Miller's?"

Gary glanced at his watch. "Time we get the body in and washed down . . . I'd say . . . I'll be there until late afternoon. Ever seen an autopsy?"

"No."

"Come on over. They're very enlightening."

"Thank you for the invitation. I shall do my best to avoid it."

Gary nodded his head and walked away, his mind on the upcoming work. Those watching him leave knew that he did not like to do autopsies. Especially on young people.

"So what's on the agenda, ladies?" Martin asked.

"What were you and Gary doing out here?" Alicia asked, for the first time meeting her husband's eyes.

Martin hesitated. He did not wish to tell the ladies about his memory-jogging dreams of the previous night. Not just yet. But the strange happenings around town? . . . "Truth time, gals?"

They nodded. Martin noticed a flush creeping up his wife's neck at his words. He wondered about that. Then he told them about the conversation he'd shared with Gary about the occurrences that had been taking place around town.

Janet nodded her head. "Gary was sure hot about Rich coming in so late last night, and that's a fact. Came down hard on him. But I wonder why he didn't tell me about the rest of the kids doing the same?"

"Gary?"

"Yes."

"He didn't know anything about it until this morning, out at the club. Come on, let's walk around some." He pointed to Nabo's Ten-in-One. "But stay out of that tent."

"Why?" his wife asked. "Is there a girlie show in there?"

Martin bit back a sharp reply and patiently told the women about the Ten-in-One.

Joyce giggled at that. Janet grimaced at her friend's reaction and said, "There must be something wrong with me. Poor misshapen people have never held any fascination for me."

Alicia looked to her right and put her hands on her hips. "Now what in the hell! . . ."

Linda, Jeanne, and Susan were walking toward them.

No one said anything about the absence of Joyce's daughter, Missy, from the group. Missy and the other three girls she'd palled around with since learning to walk had themselves a major falling-out some months back. Missy was running with another group, Karl Steele's bunch of thugs. Missy, so the rumors went, had turned into a sixteen year old tramp. For a time, all concerned thought Joyce was going to have some sort of breakdown. She worked her way out of it with a lot of help from friends. Missy, however, continued to allow the entire male student body of Holland High to use her body.

Joyce and Eddie's other child, seventeen-year-old Ed, was a fine young man, very studious and brainy. He had plans to attend the U of N next fall, and when the boy tried to explain to Martin what his major would be, he had lost Martin sometime during the first ten words.

Martin thought it had something to do with space. Or semi-conductors. Or something strange and beyond a normal being's comprehension. Martin finally had to admit to his own son—after buying the family a new station wagon—that he couldn't figure out how to set the buttons on the super-dooper computerized radio.

Took Mark about fifteen seconds to set them. All on rock stations—done with a grin.

Alicia looked at her daughter. "I thought you girls would still be sleeping?"

"We all woke up real early," Susan volunteered the astonishing news, since the girls were famous for staying in bed as long as their mothers would let them, on any given day.

"Real early meaning? . . ." Martin prompted.

"Around seven."

"Jesus," Janet breathed. "What is this world coming to?"

"We were by here last night," Linda said. "We saw the giant man. Have you seen him?"

"Yes!" Martin said quickly, a flash of annoyance surging through him. Why? he asked himself. He felt he knew. "That man is dangerous, kids. I don't think he likes people very much. Maybe he has reason not to. But you girls stay away from that tent over there." He pointed and explained why.

The girls picked up on his irritation. "Sure, dad," Linda assured him. "We were just going to walk around some. Is that all right?"

"Walking around is fine. Just stay together and don't go off by yourselves."

"OK if we tag along with you-all?" Susan asked, showing a lot of insight.

And it wasn't lost on Martin. He smiled at the con job. "That's fine. So come on, gang. Let's walk."

They had not walked fifty feet when Janet looked up and pointed in horror. The eyes of the group followed her finger.

A roustabout had slipped, high up on the skeletal frame of a ferris wheel. They watched in morbid fascination as he lost his one-handed hold and fell spinning to the ground. Suddenly, they were running to the site.

They stopped at the same time, staring in disbelief.

The man had picked himself up and was brushing the dust off his clothing.

"Are you all right?" Martin ran to him.

The man smiled. "Oh, yes. I landed just right, I suppose. Thanks for your concern." He turned and began climbing back up the frame of the ride.

"He must have fallen fifty or sixty feet!" Joyce said. "I saw him hit. He bounced and then landed on his feet like nothing happened."

"That's impossible." Susan summed it up. "Nobody falls that distance and just gets up and walks off. He fell at least three stories."

Nabo had watched it all through the flap of his Ten and One. He frowned. He'd have to tell his people to be more careful.

Lyle Steele stepped out of his house and looked over his holdings—that part of the ranch that he could see from his front porch. His spread extended all the way over into Wyoming. The Bar-S, one of the oldest ranches in the state. Only the Watson ranch, the Double-W, was older, and only by about a year or so. The Double-W bordered the Bar-S to the east, then cut north, meandering up into South Dakota.

The screen door banged shut behind the man. He didn't have to turn around. He knew who it was. His son, Karl. Had to be. Lyle's wife had left him years back; said she couldn't take anymore of her husband's womanizing and brutality. Took the girl and split. Lyle didn't know where they went. Didn't care either.

Without turning around, the father said, "You sure come in late last night, boy. Morning would be more like it."

"Big doings in town." Karl sucked noisily at a mug of coffee. Sounded like a hog at the trough.

"Yeah?" Lyle asked without interest. He seldom went into Holland. Maybe once a year, tops. He did all his shopping over in Wyoming. Bought all his cars and trucks and farm and ranch equipment and supplies outside of Holland. Lyle hated the town of Holland. Hated to hear the name of Holland. Despised Martin Holland. Only thing he liked about Martin Holland was his wife. Fine-lookin', classy woman. Uppity, though. Thought she was better than other folks.

"What's all the big doin's in Holland, boy?"

"The carnival's done come to town."

The man spun around so fast he startled the boy. The father's eyes were buggy. *"Carnival!"* he shouted the word.

"Yeah. Carnival. Like in rides and stuff. What's the matter with you? You look like you swallowed a bug."

"Don't get too lippy with me, boy. I can still take you down and don't you forget it."

The young man smiled at his father and set the coffee mug down on a wooden bench. "Maybe. Maybe not. But it'd be a tussle you'd not soon forget."

The father leaned up against the porch railing, his eyes taking in the size of his son. Both men were built like bulls, stocky and very strong. Both were quick, tough, and cruel men. Both were bullies.

"Yeah," the father spoke softly, and with some degree of pride in his voice. "I reckon it would at that."

Neither father nor son possessed one ounce of anything that could remotely be described as a socially redeeming quality. Certainly nothing of moral value. The father took what he wanted, by any method he felt he could get away with. And so did his son. The father had been forced, on more than one occasion, to buy or threaten or coerce his son out of trouble—just as his father had done for him. All to protect the good name of the family, of course. Both father and son held women in contempt, something to be used and then discarded. There was not one ounce of compassion in either of them.

"What's the name of this carnival, boy?"

Karl had to think about that some. He had a slight hangover from all the long necks he'd consumed the night before. But it'd been fun on the drive back to the ranch from Holland, trying to run over as many dogs and cats as he could; almost wrecked his truck a couple of times trying to squash them. Wouldn't have made no difference if he had: he had inherited money of his own to buy another one.

"I don't know," the young man finally said. "Didn't see no name. It's just a carnival."

The father shook away some very fleshy and enjoyable mental memories from years past. In a pavilion, he and Jim Watson and those two young gals. Then they'd had a good time with Pete and Frank Tressalt and a whole bunch of other folks—damn near the whole town—horsewhippin' and shootin' and finally burnin' all them carnival people alive. Other memories filled his head: screaming and running and burning human torches. That'd been pretty damn good fun, and it had covered his and Jim's tracks, too. Them gals had been too scared to open their mouths. As far as them dead people went—carnival trash was all they was—all dead and burned up. Them, and damn near everything and everyone connected with the carnival.

To Lyle's way of thinking, it was just too bad that Martin Holland hadn't burned up with the rest of them. And as far as them carnival people having the insight—as his own daddy had insisted—that wasn't nothing but a bunch of crap. Nobody had no insight; couldn't nobody see in the past or in the future. They was all burned up and dead and their ashes scattered. And don't no dead person ever come back to this earth.

Lyle had to grin when he thought of that fat lady in that sideshow—what was it called? Yeah, a Ten-in-One. Way she bubbled and crackled and popped and sizzled when the flames got all over her and she couldn't carry her fat ass and the fire ate her up. His grin widened when he thought about that stupid-lookin' Dog Man and the way he actually barked as the flames covered him.

Karl looked at his father, the man he admired most in the whole world. "What you grinnin' about?"

"Old times and better days, boy." The father took a closer look at his son. You sure are all duded up. You got you some little gal in town waitin' for you?"

Karl grinned. "Don't I always?"

"She got a name?"

"Missy Hudson."

"Ain't she the one who puts out for half the boys in high school?"

"She was. She ain't no more. She's just puttin' out for me, now."

"How old is she?"

"Sixteen."

"That's young, boy. And you close to legal age. I bailed you out too many times for you to forget that a stiff dick'll get you in trouble quicker than a gun."

"Her folks'd have to charge half a hundred 'fore they ever got to me."

"That's a fact." He punched his son on the arm.

He understood, remembering how he was at his son's age. "I might take me a ride into Holland. Look around some. Is it just a carnival, boy?"

Lyle never read the Holland weekly. And since he took no interest in anything connected with the town, he seldom paid any attention to anything he heard concerning the town of Holland.

"No, dad! It's a big fair. Gonna kick off official next Thursday."

That rang a mental bell. It kicked off on a Thursday years back, too. Made Lyle sorta feel funny. He shook that off. "A fair," the man repeated softly, remembering, despite himself, what his daddy had warned him of, over and over, just before he died. But Lyle hadn't paid any attention to it then, and he wasn't going to pay any attention to it now. Lyle didn't believe in that insight business. When you died, you was dead. That was that. "Well, now, don't that beat all? A fair's done come back to Holland."

Gary Tressalt began his lonely work on the body of Jimmy Harold. With the cassette/corder running, recording every move of his hands, announcing each cut just before he made it, the tape trapped each word. Gary made one long incision from throat to crotch, then side to side twice, the first cut just under the shoulders, across the chest, and then another cut just above the hips, across the lower abdomen. He peeled the flesh back and then used rib-spreaders to open the boy up wide and lock the cavity open.

The strong smell of flesh filled his nostrils.

The doctor stood and stared in total utter disbelief. He had done autopsies on burn victims before. But they had all been burned through and through. He knew what to expect from that. But this boy's outer skin showed no signs of burns. Inside, every organ: heart, lungs, liver, kidneys, everything had been cooked, and from first glance, cooked from the inside out.

Microwaved, the thought came to him.

Don't be stupid, Gary! he mentally berated himself, careful not to say anything aloud so the tape would catch him. There is a logical explanation for this. Just keep looking, you'll find it.

But the more he cut—and he knew he had to record his findings—the more evidence bore out his initial feelings: Jimmy Harold had been baked to death. Cooked. But only on the inside. Not on the outside.

Impossible.

Working swiftly and carefully, with a strange feeling of dread hanging around him, the tape machine running, Gary peeled off the skin from the head and took a small electric saw, opening the skull. Steam hissed odorously from the open skull. The brain had been cooked just like the other organs he had examined.

Gary vocally summed up his findings and tossed a sheet over the body, tucking it in tight and sliding the body back into the cooler. He locked the cooler and placed an official county coroner's seal on the front. He tossed his gown and mask into the hamper and his gloves went into the trash bin. After washing up, he told the young mortician that under no circumstances was the seal on the cooler to be broken.

He drove back to the fairgrounds and went looking

for Martin.

In the several hours he'd been gone, the place had filled up with people, workers, mostly, carnival and local. The sounds of sawing and hammering and the clink of wrenches on bolts filled the air as the rides went up and and the booths were assembled.

Martin glanced at him, surprise in his eyes. "You finished quickly, but I'm glad you're back."

"I think we have problems, Martin. I know I do."

"We both do." He told him about the roustabout falling from the top of the ferris wheel.

"And he just got up and walked off!"

"Yes."

"That's impossible, man!"

"We all saw it, Gary."

"What'd Nabo do?"

"Nothing. I haven't seen him. The guy just climbed back up on the ferris wheel and went back to work."

Gary looked up at the huge wheel. "Christ, Martin!" He pointed. "He fell from there?"

"Yes."

"That's . . . about five stories."

"Yes."

"Mystery on top of mystery. Where are the gals?"

"Over there." He pointed. "With the kids."

His wife waved to him and Gary returned the wave. The women were talking with several women who were setting up a Home Ec booth, part of the County Extension program.

"You finished with the boy, Gary?"

"Like I said: problems. I know this is distasteful for you, Martin; but I can't go to that fool Kelson with this, and I don't want to call Deputy Meadows just yet. I want your opinion first." He shrugged. You're a fully commissioned deputy sheriff, aren't you?"

"Yes. Is it that bad, Gary?"

"Worse than you can imagine. You feel right about leaving the women and kids out here?"

"Oh, sure. Must be several hundred townspeople here."

"Come on."

Martin almost gagged when Gary pulled back the sheet, exposing Jimmy Harold. The organs had been piled into the open cavity. Martin recovered and stared for a moment. "I saw a lot of broken-open bodies in 'Nam, Gary. But their insides didn't look like that!"

Gary dropped it on him. "He's been cooked, Martin. From all indications, cooked from the inside out."

The two friends stared at each other over the operating table. "Are you serious, Gary?"

"I wish I wasn't, believe that."

"Could it be, ah, is it possible that the body temperature got so high it did this?"

"No. These organs have been exposed to very intense heat."

"Then? . . ."

"I don't know. I spoke with the ambulance driver. He neither saw nor heard anything out of the ordinary. The only thing he said was that the boy didn't look strong enough to break his restraints."

"Audie Meadows or Kelson?"

"You know the answer to that one right off the mark, buddy."

Deputy Sheriff Audie Meadows stared at the body for a long moment, finally motioning Gary to cover the body. The deputy was young, only twenty-five, but with eight years experience as a cop. One year as dispatcher on the Holland P.D., one year on city patrol, and then off to the academy. Upon graduation, he joined the county sheriff's department. He was the lone deputy in the area, with hundreds of square miles of territory to cover.

"I, ah, don't know what charges I could bring, Dr. Tressalt," Audie finally spoke. "Or against who. I'll say this, though: Jimmy Harold was a no-good troublemaker. He won't be missed."

That rang a bell with Martin. "Is this the boy who terrorized Mrs. Stafford last year?"

"Yes, sir. And the same punk who's vandalized, stolen, and in general been in trouble all his life."

"I see," Gary said. "Well, I didn't have any charges in mind, Audie." He slid the body back into the cooler and shut the door.

It was rare for a town of Holland's size to have a refrigerated holding area for bodies. But since the town was so isolated, it had finally become a necessity.

Audie met the doctor's eyes, a puzzled look on his face. "I don't know what you mean, Doctor."

"Then I'll try to explain. What do you know about the fire and the killings that happened after an alleged double rape by carnival people here in Holland back in 1954?"

"Probably more than anybody else in town anywhere near my age. But that happened nine years before I was born."

Both Gary and Martin felt their ages suddenly rear up and slap them in the face. Gary said, "But there would be some records on it down at the sheriff's office in Harrisville, wouldn't there?"

"Not much, I'm afraid. You see, way it was told to me, the state police took over that investigation. They took over—so I'm told— because the sheriff at that time was from Holland—or this area—and his own brother was suspected of having something to do with the fire."

"Jim Watson's brother," Martin said. "Marshall Watson. Where is he now? Anybody know?"

"He disappeared a long time ago, sir," Audie informed them. "Several years before your daddy vanished."

"Then the state police would have all the records on the fire, right?"

"No, sir. They don't. For personal reasons, I wanted some information on that fire a couple of years back. I sent out an inquiry. Seems that most of the important files got misplaced or lost or whatever, probably when the state went to full computer some time back." The young deputy smiled. "At least that's the story was told to me."

Gary noted the deputy's smile. "But you don't believe that, right?"

"That's right. And neither does anyone else who would talk to me about it."

"And? . . ." Martin prompted.

The deputy shuffled his cowboy-booted feet.

"Come on, Audie. What is going on here?"

The deputy sighed. "You—neither of you—heard this from me, OK?"

"Agreed."

"Well, the state police investigator who worked on that carnival fire never thought the fire was an accident. He never thought it was carnival people who raped those unnamed girls. And I think he got awful close to the truth back in '70. Just before he was due to retire. You see, too much money had been spread about to cover a lot of those deaths. Big money; thousands and thousands of dollars. And it came from the Steele and Watson and Tressalt and Cameron and Clark ranches." He looked at Gary. "Sorry I had to be the one to tell you, Doctor."

Gary was shocked, ashen-faced for a moment. He shook his head and regained composure. "It doesn't come as much of a surprise, Audie. I know what my brothers are: no good. But that's still hard for me to say. Go on."

"The investigator was killed up in South Dakota."

"What was a Nebraska cop doing up in South Dakota?" Martin asked.

"Most who would talk about it don't believe he was in the Dakotas when he got killed. The opinion is that he was honing in on Jim Watson and Lyle Steele, and was on the Double-W spread to arrest them. Jim and Lyle killed him and then toted his body up into South Dakota and dumped it. Right at the base of Limestone Butte."

"All right," Gary said, his voice still a bit shaky. "I wouldn't put anything past Jim or Lyle. Or my brothers, for that matter," he added grimly. "But that doesn't explain about the missing files."

"To paraphrase one of our recent presidents," Audie said with a smile, "let me say this about that: Right after

64

the investigator got killed, murdered, a certain member of the patrol—who was about to get canned anyway—took early retirement and moved to Mexico. Down on the coast of Baja. He went out one morning fishing—this was about 1975—and his body was found late that afternoon."

"Now put all that together for us civilians," Gary requested.

"Well, the rogue cop who took early retirement was the one who lifted the files about the rapes and fire. Paid to do so and keep his mouth shut by certain ranchers in this area. Some people think they got tired of paying him and killed him."

"Was my father involved in that scheme, Audie?" Gary asked.

"No, sir. Frank and Pete were, probably."

"I can believe that."

"Do you think the ranchers killed him, Audie?" Martin asked.

"No, sir," the deputy replied softly.

Puzzled, Martin stared at him. "I don't understand. How was this ex-cop killed?"

"Well, sir, the ex-cop was found by some fishermen. He was sitting strapped in the fishing chair at the rear of his boat. He'd been cooked through and through. But there wasn't a sign of a fire on that boat."

FIVE

Since the deputy had leveled with Gary and Martin, the men did the same for him, telling him about the strange occurrences that had been taking place in town.

The trio had left the chemical smell of the autopsy room in the funeral home and were standing out front, by their cars.

"Well, I'll admit I wondered about all those people around the fence at the fairgrounds last night." He spat a dark stream of tobacco juice from his fresh chew. "And I'll confess something to you men: I think my daddy had something to do with the burning down of that carnival years back."

"Why do you say that," Gary asked.

"'Cause right before he died—started about two days before he passed—my daddy kept talking about the flames and how they were going to eat him up and he was goin' to burn forever. I kept telling him he was a good man, and that he wasn't goin' to Hell. He told me he'd already seen it. Said he had a part to play in it. I didn't know then what he meant by 'it.' I do now. He cried and cried and begged for forgiveness. Said he'd seen the hell-fires back thirty years before. That's what got me to digging into that so-called accidental fire. Daddy died in October, '84. I never saw a man that suffered so much. You remember it, Doctor Tressalt; you was there even though my daddy wouldn't let anybody except Old Doc Reynolds touch him. My daddy couldn't get enough to drink."

"I remember, Audie."

Martin wiped sweat from his forehead, even though the day was not that warm. "What was the date of his death, Audie?"

"My daddy died four years ago exactly come next Thursday."

Martin stood with Gary and watched the deputy drive off. Audie had told them he would be at the fairgrounds that night, just to keep an eye on things. Gary had smiled and said, "Sure you'll be looking at people. And that city patrol-person named Nicole'll be one of them, won't she?"

Audie had grinned boyishly and allowed as to how that was right.

Martin said they might join him. The deputy said that would be fine.

"Assuming that everything Audie said—including that bit about his father and the hell fires—is true, what has that got to do with the odd happenings occurring around town?" Gary asked.

"You don't believe in Hell, Gary?"

"I believe in a Hereafter. And I also believe in the supernatural."

Martin looked at him for a moment, his eyes unreadable. "Well, old friend, if you're waiting for me to say anything like the devil has arrived in Holland, you're going to be in for a long wait."

"I don't think this has anything to do with the devil, Martin."

"Then? . . ."

"Martin, without making myself appear to be a fool—and I'm not saying this has anything to do with what's been happening in town, let me tell you something, some . . . things I've seen over fifteen years of practicing medicine. I've seen people that I pronounced dead come back to life. Nearly every doctor in the world has seen that. I've seen people so eaten up with disease that I would have bet money they wouldn't last a month. But they're alive and well and walking around today. And I'll tell you something else—a couple of things: I've seen people hang on to life for just one reason: revenge! And many of them hung on long enough—against all odds—to get that revenge. And I've had patients who've died on me come back to life within two or three or four minutes and tell me about that dying—out of body experiences. And they were sent back. They actually crossed over and were sent back!''

"And you believe that?"

"Yes, I do."

Martin rubbed his chin. "Then . . . what are you trying to say, Gary? Or what are you telling me that's not getting through?"

"Martin, I'd like to find out who owns this carnival that's in town now. And who owned the carnival that was destroyed."

"Oh, come on, Gary!"

"No, Martin—no. I'm adamant about this. I think there is a connection. Call me a fool, think me a fool. Whatever. There is something going on here that we don't understand. Over the years, I've asked my father dozens of times about the fire. I told you this. I get nothing out of him. Martin, my dad may have had something to do with that fire."

"That's a terrible thing to say, Gary. Your father is a fine man."

"I know he is. And I know it's a rotten thing to say about him. But Audie believes my dad helped buy my brothers out of trouble. Martin, my dad, like so many people, can be easily led. He doesn't have much education; and I'm not making excuses for that. Never will you hear me excuse ignorance. Dad hunted and fished and bar-hopped with the good ol' boys all his life and in the process, turned out to be a wealthy man. But it wasn't because of his intelligence. It was luck and some hard work. And you know that as well as I do. We've been friends since birth, almost. Intelligent, educated people rarely join mobs, rarely take part in mindless violence. And,'' he said with a painful sigh, "I sure don't have to tell you about my brothers, do I?"

69

Martin shook his head. Coarse and crude and both of them wallowing in dumb. Pete and Frank Tressalt were ten and twelve years older than Gary. Together, they ran the Tressalt spread, the Snake-T.

"Gary, listen to me. So what if your father did have something to do with the fire? So what? How does that affect you? You haven't experienced any overwhelming pull to come to the fairgrounds, have you?"

"No. No, I haven't. But I'm . . . somehow a part of all this. I just know it. Listen to me, Martin. While I was working on that boy in there," he waved his hand toward the funeral home, "I got this mental flashback. Martin, I've been in Nabo's tent before. I know now. I was in there a long time ago. When I was six years old. Think about that day, Martin."

Martin's brow furrowed. He turned his head to one side and frowned. "Yeah. Wait just a damn minute. We *both* were on that ride when I got sick. I remember now."

"That's right. I recalled it, and now you do, too. I waited because I didn't want to say anything else in front of Audie. You said that you wanted to go somewhere and up-chuck—your exact words. I said I'd wait for you by the ferris wheel. But you never came back and my dad came and got me right after an accident of some sort. He took me home. That accident must have been you."

Martin nodded his head. "I guess so. But what's all this about Nabo's tent?"

"After you went over to the pavilion to throw up, I slipped around to the back of Nabo's tent and crawled in under the canvas. I was trying to see what was in there. But I couldn't see any of the so-called freaks because of the legs of the paying customers. But I'll tell you what I did see: I saw Nabo."

Linda told the others to go on; she wanted to retie her tennis shoes. She bent down on one knee, leaned a shoulder against a wood side-wall of a bally platform in front of a tent, and fell right through the wood.

Fall was not exactly correct: the girl seemed to dissolve into the wood. She fell spinning, almost endlessly, around and around in a slow descending circle.

She heard a voice calling out. "No, no! Not her. Not her."

"She's one of them!" the words came in a scream as her fall was halted and the girl seemed to float, suspended in darkness.

"You are wrong. She is not. Don't fight me on this."

Linda, strangely calm, could feel a kinship coming at her in almost tangible waves, while the single voice argued with the many voices that seemed to spring out of the darkness from all around her.

"It's time!"

"Let them know!"

"Let them join us. Now!"

"No!" the heavy voice commanded, and the abyss fell silent.

Linda willed herself to move, even locked in the dark void as she was. Her mouth opened in a silent scream as her eyes took in what lay below her.

She was gazing down into a huge, open, yawning pit, smoky from fires that seemed white hot. She knew some of the naked and horribly burned men and women that stood below her, screaming at her, shaking their clenched fists at her, shouting the most hideous of profanities at her.

"Silence!" the single voice roared, and the pit below her fell silent. "It is not yet time. We must wait."

The girl caught a glimpse of Frank and Pete Tressalt, naked on the hot coals, their flesh hanging in raw, bleeding strips from their bodies. She saw Jimmy Harold and Binkie and Missy and a lot of kids she went to school with, all naked and raw from the fires. The pit—and it kept changing in size—seemed to contain nearly everyone in Holland that she knew.

Then she saw herself. And she was . . . No. That couldn't be right.

She began spinning, but this time she was spinning upward. She called out, screamed out, held her hands out to . . .

She looked up into her mother's eyes.

"Are you all right, honey?" Alicia asked.

Linda cut her eyes, afraid to move any part of her body. She was on the ground, by the Home Ec booth, her mother placing cold wet cloths on her forehead.

"You fainted, Linda," her mother told her. "When you feel like you can stand, I'm going to take you home."

Linda nodded her head and closed her eyes. It must have all been a dream. A devil's nightmare.

Martin went to his mayor's offices and called his part-time secretary at her home, asking her if she knew anything about a contract between the town and the carnival. She told him where it was in the files. Martin made a copy of it—he couldn't recall ever seeing it before—and took it over to Eddie Hudson's office. Eddie was working on this Saturday afternoon.

"Can it be broken, Eddie." Martin laid the contract on the lawyer's desk.

Eddie looked up at him, questions in his eyes. He quickly scanned the document. "I'll get to the why of your question in a minute, Martin. But yes, almost any contract can be broken. Sure, we can break this contract, if the town of Holland wants to pay them a lot of money. And I'm talking about thousands and thousands of dollars. These people know, within a few percentage points, what they're going to pull in, based on the size of the town, how long it's been since a carnival played, so forth. Only way we could get out of it free would be if some act of God were to happen: flood, tornado, hurricane—something of that nature."

"All right. That answers one question. Now then. Eddie, I read that contract three times. There is not one word about where the show is home-based."

Eddie once more scanned it. "Ummm. Well, you're right. But . . . so?"

"They've got to have a home address. They've got to

72

have some sort of permanent mailing address."

"Well, yeah. You're right. It would sure seem so. But Martin, I didn't set this thing up. I'm the city attorney; but this is the first time I've laid eyes on this contract."

"What!"

"For a fact. Let me call Marie. She works part-time for the Chamber of Commerce. Took over when Mrs. Neal retired a couple of months ago." He spoke briefly with the woman and then hung up the phone, a very odd expression on his face.

"What's wrong, Eddie?"

"The initial correspondence is over at the Chamber offices. Says she'll meet us there. And Martin . . . she said the letter has your signature on it."

"My signature? Arranging to bring the carnival in here?"

"Yes."

"No way. I had nothing to do with it. I don't even know who did."

"One way to find out." Eddie stood up. "Let's go look at the letter."

The secretary, the lawyer, and the mayor all stood around the desk and stared at the letter.

The initial correspondence was dated February, 1954, and was signed by Martin Holland.

"That's my father's writing," Martin said. "See how he loops the N in Martin back to cross the T?"

"But you do the same, Martin," Eddie pointed out.

"Eddie, I was seven years old in 1954!"

Eddie shrugged.

Martin looked at the envelope which the secretary had wisely paper-clipped to the letter. The postmark was blurred and the stamp was missing. No return address.

"Stamp probably fell off in the mail," Eddie ventured. "You can see where it was cancelled."

Probably fell off from old age, Martin thought. But he kept that thought to himself. He could make out that the

73

letter had originally been mailed from West Virginia. He could not make out the name of the town.

But it was a starting place. Keeping his voice unemotional, Martin said, "Well, the carnival is here and the people are looking forward to the fair. Big event. But I sure would like to know who signed my name to that letter."

"Martin, that date is nothing more than a typo," the lawyer insisted. "An error. You probably signed the letter and just forgot about it. After all, it was nine months ago. I can't even remember what I had for breakfast yesterday."

Martin laughed along with Eddie and Marie, but he decided at least for the moment, not to level with his friend about his inner feelings. It had nothing to do with distrust; Martin just didn't want to appear to be a superstitious fool.

He made a copy of the letter and the front of the envelope, gave the copies to the secretary, and kept the originals. He thanked them both and went in search of Gary. He found the doctor at his offices, tending to an emergency.

"Girl went stiff as a board and started screaming about seeing monsters and burned-up people and about the fires coming to get her," Gary explained.

Martin had passed by a weeping mother in the waiting room, being consoled by a grim-faced man.

Martin looked first at the girl, then at Gary. "How is she now?"

"Appears to be fine. Very relaxed. Everything is normal. Shut that door behind you, please. Thanks." The door closed, Gary took Martin to one side. "I know now what Don was talking about. The girl was speaking in some language I never heard before. But it was not, or did not appear to be, mumbo jumbo. It was a real language, or so it appeared to me."

"This is getting out of hand, Gary."

"I agree. But what do we do?"

"I have an idea. Soon as the child is out of here we'll talk."

Gary returned to the examining table and motioned for

74

his nurse to come in. He smiled at the child. Mean look in her eyes, he thought, then put that thought out of his mind, chalking it up to mild paranoia. "How do you feel, Alma?"

"Oh, I feel fine, Doctor. I'm looking forward to going to the carnival. It's in town, you know?"

"Yes, I know." He questioned the girl for a moment, but she remembered nothing about her strange attack.

He had the girl sit up, move her extremities, and then walk around the room. He rechecked pulse and BP, and concluded she was fine and it was all right for her to go home.

"Oh, thank you, Doctor!" Alma said, her eyes very bright and very mean-looking. And this time Gary knew that it was not his imagination. "I'm looking forward to going to the carnival. It's in town, you know?"

Martin and Gary exchanged quick glances.

Gary told his nurse she could go on home and the child walked out to where her parents were waiting. After they'd hugged her, she said, "You know what I'd like to do?"

"What, honey?" the father asked.

"I'd like to go over to the fairgrounds and see the carnival. It's in town, you know?"

"Yes," the mother agreed. "The carnival is in town. Certainly. We'll go over there."

"What a great idea!" the father said. "Sure. The carnival is in town, you know?"

The three of them walked out the front door, all of them chatting gaily about the carnival being in town.

"I'll drive," the ten-year-old announced.

"Of course!" the father agreed, and handed her the keys. They went bouncing and lurching and weaving from side to side down the street, the girl barely able to see over the steering wheel.

Martin stared out the waiting room window, not believing what he had just heard and was now witnessing as the car wobbled out of sight.

Gary rubbed his face with his hands. "I think we have a problem, friend. That girl's eyes scared the hell out of me."

"More problems than you know, Gary." Martin told him about the contract and then showed him the letter.

Gary fingered the letter. "This paper is old, Martin."

"I know. And that is not my signature. That's dad's writing."

Gary nodded his head, looked at his friend, and waited. Martin pointed to the phone on the secretary's desk. "Can I use your phone to run up about five hundred dollars in long distance calls?"

Gary smiled wearily. "Go ahead. But the next time you come in for a hangnail, you're going to have one hell of a bill."

It took him almost two hours, but Martin finally struck paydirt. He had begun by calling all the major cities in West Virginia. He had thought about contacting the Mayors' offices or the Chambers of Commerce, then realized it was Saturday, and most would be closed. He called the local P.D.s or sheriff's departments, identifying himself as a county deputy sheriff—which he was—and his reason for calling was to try to locate a missing person, who was believed to be working in a carnival. He used the name of a buddy of his he'd served with in Vietnam, who Martin knew was currently living in Fresno, California.

Do you have a carnival based in your city?

By the time he'd gone through the cities over five thousand population, he'd consumed a pot of coffee and worn a blister on the tip of one finger. Then he started calling the towns under five thousand.

"Well, we did have one," a deputy finally spoke the welcome words. "But that was years ago. That carnival got all burned up in a fire out west somewhere. I had just started workin' as a deputy when that happened. Long time back, 'cause I'll be retirin' this year."

"Do you remember the name of the show?"

"Ahhh . . . no, I don't. Sorry. Oh, wait a minute. I do remember the name of the man who owned the show. I sure do."

Martin waited.

"He was a foreigner. Name of Nabob."

"Nabo, perhaps?"

"Yeah! You're right. That's what it was, all right. Nabo. Big fellow. Dressed all in black all the time. Nabo, it was."

"Was?"

"Oh, he's dead. Newspapers here played it up big. He used to give a lot of money to charities. Folks said he was a real nice fellow. But he burned up in that fire with the rest of his people, freaks and all."

"He didn't have any family?"

"One son. But he was just a baby when that Nabo died. Somebody adopted the kid and I don't have no idea what happened to him. I remember all that 'cause some fellow from the Nebraska Highway Patrol called about the fire . . . oh, twelve, fifteen years back. I don't really remember exact. Probably workin' on the same thing you don't want to tell me about. I understand. But about Nabo, I can't help you, except to tell you that he's dead."

Martin had taken down the name of the man he'd spoken with and the name of the town. He thanked the deputy and slowly hung up the phone.

He told Gary the news.

"Jesus God, I was right!"

"Now, just calm down, Gary."

But the news had jarred the doctor. He was visibly shaken. He tried three times to light his pipe, and finally, in frustration, he flung the unlit pipe across the room. He stared at Martin. "All right, all right, I'm calm. Now what?"

"You're about as calm as a Tasmanian Devil, Gary." Martin shook his head. "I don't know what. For sure, we've got to tell Audie. But I don't know what he can do." Martin smiled at his friend; he was not sharing Gary's ideas about this matter. But he was about to. In a matter of moments. "Is it against the law to return from the dead?"

Gary jumped to his feet. "Goddamnit, Martin!" he

77

yelled. "That isn't funny!"

"Sorry, Gary. Man, calm down. Look, what can we do about it? Let's just settle down and try to think this thing out rationally. Now then, the man who calls himself Nabo might well have taken the name just to keep the show going. Now, Gary, think about that before you let your imagination run wild on this thing."

"OK. But do you really think it's just someone who took the name?"

"It doesn't make any difference what I think. Let's stick with the facts we have and take it from there."

But the doctor wouldn't be put off that easily. "Do you believe it's just a person who kept the show going? Do you?"

A long expulsion of breath, followed by a minute shake of the head. "No, Gary. Despite all my talk of logic, I don't believe it."

"Then who do you think it is?"

"I don't know who it is!"

"Now who's getting excited?"

Martin refused to reply to that.

Gary stared at him.

"What do you want me to say, Gary? Do you want me to say that it is Nabo? All right. Maybe it is."

"But Nabo is *dead!*"

"Yes. Yes, I believe that, too."

"Then? . . ."

"Gary, do you have just the tiniest idea what the sheriff would say if we went to him with what we have? He'd call a judge and have us both committed for mental observation?"

"Not without several doctors agreeing to it," Gary automatically replied. He shook his head. "We have to do something, Martin."

"What, Gary? What? No one has broken any laws. I have a contract with a dead man's signature on it. I—" Martin paused, a very odd expression on his face. It came to him, and it did not come gently. Just the germ of an idea. Horrible. Impossible. Ridiculous. But there it was. He

78

paled. A thin trickle of sweat slid down one side of his face. The hand holding the contract began to tremble.

He laid the contract on the desk and steadied his shaking hands.

"What's wrong, Martin?"

Martin shook his head.

"You're not thinking that *your* father had anything to do with this . . . situation, are you? Or that he's . . . still alive?"

"No. No, to both your questions. Dad wasn't in the best of health when I left here for 'Nam. And he was almost fifty when I was born. My father is dead."

"Then why that strange look on your face?"

Martin picked up the contract. "It was never fulfilled, Gary. The carnival never got to play out its date. It's crazy, Gary; maybe I'm a little touched for saying it, thinking it. But maybe they've . . . come back to play out the contractual agreement. And you said it: Revenge."

Gary stared at him. He opened his mouth a couple of times but nothing came out. He cleared his throat and tried again. "I said, Martin, that people have died and have been revived. I said, Martin, people have hung onto life for revenge. I never said, Martin," his voice was almost at the screaming level, "that people can come back from the *grave!*"

Martin sat still and watched and listened as his friend cussed and stomped around the office, waving his arms and shouting. He let him wind down to a breathless, red-faced silence.

"Are you quite through now, Gary?"

Gary nodded, glaring at him, his chest heaving from the sudden exertions.

"Any lucid suggestions, Gary?"

"Call the state police!"

"You want the state cops in here on this? And tell them what? That we're dealing with some walking dead people?"

"Martin, get a grip on yourself."

"We don't have any proof, Gary!"

"Just get them in here and we'll lay out what we have for them."

"You're sure?"

"I sure am! And if you won't call them, I will."

"All right." Martin picked up the phone and dialed his home. Alicia told him about Linda fainting and about the horrible visions she'd experienced while out. Martin ground his teeth together and told his wife to stay home and to keep Linda there; under no circumstances were either of them to leave the house. He pressed the disconnect button and handed the phone to Gary, punching out the doctor's home number. Gary told his wife much the same and to keep the kids at home. He shook his head, wondering why he was feeling so strange.

"Jeanne stayed at the fairgrounds," Janet told him.

"Damn!" he cursed, then hung up the phone, leaving his wife holding a buzzing receiver and wondering what in the world was going on.

She pointed a finger at Karl Steele. "You better get out of my way, Karl!"

"I ain't doin' nothin,' Jeanne," the young man said, an arrogant smirk on his lips. "I'm just standin' here."

"Refusing to let me pass is what you're doing. Get out of my way."

She had gone to look for a restroom after the others had left, assuring them that she would be all right. Now, Robie Grant stood on Karl's left, Hal Evans to his right. Jeanne had the side of a livestock pavilion to her back, and the boys thought they had her trapped. But like a lot of country girls, Jeanne had been a tomboy all her life, and could scrap with the best of them. She had also been well-taught, by her father, which part of a boy's anatomy to kick when in trouble.

"You gonna let me by?" she asked, turning slightly, to face Hal. Hal Evans, she knew, was a beer-bellied coward.

He grinned at her; a nasty, knowing grin. "Let's have some fun first, Jeanne."

"What kind of fun?" Jeanne knew what kind of fun they had in mind. Lilly Johnson had found that out, and so had Betty Tullar, and no telling how many other girls too scared afterward to tell what had happened. But it was always the same: the boys' fathers bought them out, or the whole gang of them would threaten to testify that the girl was a willing partner. There was a lot of money in this part of the county, and little city law. Kelson could be easily bought.

"What kind of fun?" Jeanne demanded.

They were country boys, but too street wise to say the words out loud. Karl began working the zipper of his jeans up and down and grinning at her.

"All right," Jeanne said sweetly, one hand going to the top button of her blouse. The boys' eyes followed, lingering at her breasts. "I like to have fun. Who's going to be first?"

The trio laughed. Hal Evans stopped laughing abruptly when the toe of Jeanne's tennis shoe caught him smack in the groin. He dropped like a fat rock to the ground, screaming.

Jeanne darted past him and was clear, running full tilt, yelling as loudly as she could.

She ran around the pavilion and headed for the rapidly-growing city of tents and rides.

She ran right into a man all dressed in black. Looked up at him, fear on her face. She could not see his eyes behind the very dark sunglasses. But she could feel the enormous strength through his big hands. Looking down at her, his tanned face darkened and his jaw muscles bunched.

Jeanne had a quick feeling—and one she did not understand—that she was standing very close to hate.

Abruptly, the man released her and stepped back. "What's the matter, girl?"

And another odd feeling overcame her: he knew what was the matter. Jeanne caught her breath and pointed across the lot to the three young men, one of whom was lying on the ground. "Those three guys trapped me behind the pavilion—I was looking for a restroom. They

81

threatened to do . . . to . . . you know?"

"I suppose so," he said, a strange bitterness in his voice. Jeanne couldn't understand that. "Nothing ever changes in this dreadful place." She didn't understand that, either. He looked down at her. "Do you wish me to call the authorities?"

She shook her head. "I guess not. It would be their word against mine. And I've seen what happens in that situation. Besides, that boy in the stupid-looking cowboy hat with the feather in it is Karl Steele. His dad is rich. Lyle Steele. He'd just buy his kid out of it." Jeanne realized that she was probably talking too much with this carnival person . . . how did she know he was with the carnival? . . . she just did. But he sure was real easy to talk to.

"Their word against yours? Yes. I know that feeling as well." More bitterness in his voice. And something else, too.

Jeanne stood looking up at him. She suddenly realized that she was afraid of this man. She smiled at him. The smile was not returned. And there was an odor about him. Like something charred. But that thought vanished from her head as quickly as it had entered.

Several women came running over. The man gently pushed Jeanne toward them. "Ladies, those young hooligans over there by the pavilion were bothering this young lady. They frightened her very badly. I would not like for them to confront her again this day. Do any of you know her parents?"

They all did.

"Fine. Then I might suggest that one of you call her parents and ask that they come get her. Or if that is not possible, would one of you take her home?"

Jeanne smiled up at the man. He stared at her. She could not see his eyes behind the dark glasses. "Thank you, mister?"

"Nabo, girl. Just Nabo."

SIX

"I'm gonna whip Lyle Steele's ass!" Matt Potter said.

Jeanne's mother had not been at home, so the ladies, all local women, knowing Linda was the girl's best friend, took her to the Holland's. Matt had stormed in about an hour later, when he'd finally been tracked down and informed of the incident, his wife with him. Another couple in Martin and Alicia's circle of friends.

"Lyle didn't have anything to do with it," Matt's wife told him.

"Lyle has everything to do with it," Martin corrected. "However, I will agree that being an overbearing jerk is a family trait of the Steele family." He looked at Matt. "Sit down and calm down, Matt. And think about it. Lyle Steele is a bull of a man. He's spent his life fighting. When's the last time you had a fight—in high school? You might last one round with him. And I don't mean to be ugly by saying that. So don't go out and get yourself stomped."

Threatening to beat Lyle Steele to a pulp was something that Matt had to say, and everybody knew it. They also all knew that Martin was giving the man an acceptable out. The father blustered for a moment more and then sat down, sipping on a beer handed him by Alicia.

"Why'd you call us all over here, Martin?" Eddie asked. "I know it wasn't about Jeanne's . . . incident. I got the call before we knew anything about that."

Gary opened his mouth to speak just as the door bells chimed. Alicia opened the door and waved Chief Kelson inside. The chief had a wary look in his eyes. He was out of his element, and knew it; but he was also perversely enjoying this intrusion into the town of Holland's sanctum sanctorum.

"Real sorry to come in like this, folks," Kelson said, holding up a piece of paper. "But I got an arrest warrant charging Jeanne Potter with battery against Hal Evans. Where is the girl?"

"Let me see that!" Eddie jerked the warrant out of the man's hands, startling the chief.

Martin openly laughed at the charge. The red began creeping up the chief's neck. "Boys sure have changed over the years, haven't they?" He directed the question at no one in particular. "Chief, Jeanne is a minor child. I wouldn't press my luck on the validity of that warrant, or place my law enforcement career in Holland in jeopardy by trying to arrest her."

Kelson tried his best to look confused. He was anything but confused and most in the room knew it. Most also knew that Martin had just handed the man a very thinly-veiled threat. Kelson looked around the richly furnished den. Yeah, he was out of his element, and yeah, he knew it. Handling rowdy cowboys was one thing, foolin' with the kids of rich folks was something else.

"I still got the warrant, Mayor . . ."

"The fairgrounds, Chief, is outside of your jurisdiction," Eddie reminded the man. "That's county business."

"Oh, yeah. Say, you're right." Kelson had been just a little muddle-headed ever since yesterday. Thought he might be coming down with something. "So what do I do?"

"Let it cool for a few days and give me time to call the judge down at Harrisville," Martin took it. "Jeanne isn't going to run away."

The chief nodded, then walked to the door, opening it. He looked back at the group. Blinked a couple of times. "I think I'll just go over to the fairgrounds. The carnival's in town, you know?"

The chief stepped out into the late afternoon and closed

84

the door behind him.

"What an odd thing to say." Diane Potter looked at the closed door. "Well . . . not really. He's right. The carnival is in town, you know?"

Martin and Gary exchanged glances. Gary arched one eyebrow and reserved comment.

"Say, that's right!" Matt said. "The carnival is in town. By golly, this is going to be fun."

"Matt?" Martin gently spoke to the man.

"Yes, sir. The carnival's in town."

"Matt!"

The man jerked his head and looked at Martin. "Huh?"

"You want me to speak to Hal's father about this incident?"

"Huh? Oh, yeah. You do that, Martin."

"What's wrong with you, Matt?" Eddie asked, annoyance in his voice. He shook his head and cut his eyes to Martin. "Back to the issue at hand, Martin. I repeat, why are we here?"

Martin stood up. "Brace yourselves, people. The next few minutes are going to be interesting."

"To say the least," Gary muttered.

They gathered in Nabo's Ten-in-One. The Dog Man and a few others were not in attendance.

"You had one in your hands," Madame Rodenska said. "How did she feel?"

Nabo looked at the woman. "There was no evil in the girl! And the three young thugs screwed everything up . . . except what they were supposed to screw. Fools!"

"How did the other girl break through to the damned?" Slim asked.

"We're very close to the edge. We've got to bear that in mind and be very careful. What we're doing is very dangerous for us and those like us."

"The young girl who was affected this afternoon and taken to the doctor's office," a canvasman said. "She is not an innocent?"

"No. She carries the seed of evil within her. Remember, we cannot stop what has already been set in motion. So that means we are all going to have to be extra careful while we are here. It's taken us a long time to reach this point in our journey."

"The list in the book is long," Monroe reminded him. "And our time here is relatively short. "The list was compiled at great risk to—"

"Don't speak the name!" Nabo's order was sharp. He softened that with a smile. "Besides, even if we are discovered, what can anyone do?"

Tiny, towering above the rest, rumbled, "Kill them all! Give them all a taste of the flames. Let them all feel the pain and the helplessness of injustice. Our journey has been too long and too arduous to play favorites."

The others in the tent agreed . . . in various ways.

Lulu jumped around and hissed and grunted and filled the air with profanity.

Carlson swore in a language that had been dead for centuries, while at the darkened end of the long tent, the Geek laughed insanely.

Samson grunted and raised his mighty arms and clenched his big hands into fists and rumbled low in his throat.

"No!" Nabo silenced them all with the word. "Friends, listen to me: we cannot risk failure here. We must win. We've all witnessed those across the River who have no choice but to spend forever attempting in vain to undo the failures they committed or who simply sat back and allowed good to overcome evil without thought of interceding. The eons will roll while they suffer in timeless agony, the pain forever locked within them, while they burn outside—no hope ever of redemption. I will not allow us to become as they. Think about it."

Tiny glared at Nabo for a moment, then lowered his big head and sighed. "You are right, of course. And I was rude to those men this morning. The doctor and the mayor. I will try to play my role more convincingly. But my pain of remembrance is great. Almost overpowering at times."

Madame Rodenska walked to the giant of a man and put a small hand on his forearm. "As is all our pain, Tiny," she reminded him.

"The doctor does not know?"

"Not yet," Nabo said. "But soon."

"What a marvelous time we will have. It's so difficult to contain my emotions," the fortune teller said with a smile. "But the Master, speaking through Nabo, is right. We must wait." She met Nabo's gaze. "For here, time is both our friend and our enemy. We must all be very careful."

Dolly Darling sat in her special-made chair and wept silently, no tears falling, remembering the feel and the smell of her own flesh cooking while townspeople laughed at her. "Yes," she agreed. "I watched as your cards spoke to you last evening."

Madame Rodenska wore a worried look. "But the cards also told me that this Martin Holland is very dangerous. He is insighted, Nabo."

"I know. But he can be dealt with. We must be careful. So is it agreed?" Nabo asked.

"It is agreed," they all murmured.

"Go, friends," Nabo ordered. "And choose your method of revenge."

Eddie sat and looked at Martin as if the man had taken total leave of his senses. Alicia, Joyce, Janet, and Diane, wore stunned expressions on their faces. Gary held his empty coffee mug in his hands, staring into the emptiness of the still-warm mug. Audie Meadows had joined the group, coming over at Martin's call. The deputy sat uncomfortably on the sectional, wishing he could have a chew of tobacco, but not knowing where he'd spit.

Matt Potter sat speechless.

Eddie opened his mouth to speak. His wife shushed him. Startled him and slightly angering the man by saying, "I agree with Martin."

The lawyer jumped to his feet. "Now, wait just a minute!" He looked at his wife and shook his head. "Are you telling me that you agree that the carnival is, well, I mean, that the people out there are . . . *dead?*"

Not quite sure she could trust her voice to speak, she nodded her head.

Martin said, "Audie has agreed to ask a friend of his with the state police to come in and give us his opinion. From the criminal investigation division. The detective is starting on vacation Monday, so unless we so desire, there won't be any official word on any investigation going on in here."

"I think you've all lost your goddamn minds!" Eddie yelled.

The young people, all of them, including Mark, who had just come in from work, had been sent out into the back yard of the Holland house. The house was two-story, built by Martin's father back in the late '40's. It sat on a five acre tract of land, neat and well kept, but certainly not a house one might think of a millionaire many times over living in.

"Something's up for sure," Mark said, Eddie's shouting reaching them as they sat around the pool.

"I sure would like to know what Kelson was doing here a minute ago," Jeanne said. "That guy gives me the creeps."

"He gives everyone the creeps," Linda said. "If it wasn't for a few rich ranchers around here, he couldn't get a job night-herding."

"Yeah, and one who comes to mind is Lyle Steele," Rich added. He looked at Jeanne and laughed. "I wonder how Hal Evans is feeling about now?"

Everyone had a good laugh at that. Joyce and Eddie's brainy kid, Ed, saying, "Hal is going to be walking rather oddly for a couple of days. From what I hear, you really kicked him a good one, Jeanne."

Linda had told them all about her vision—if that's what it was, and it had sobered them all.

"Where's Missy, Ed?" Linda asked.

"My sister told mom and dad she wasn't about to come over here, and that they couldn't make her. Dad's just given up on her and mom is about ready to do the same."

Susan had slipped up to the window of the den and had been listening through an open window. She ran back to the group and took her seat. "Hal's dad swore out a warrant for your arrest, Jeanne."

The kids all spoke their opinions of that move, most quite profane.

"Hal's dad is just as disgusting as Hal is," Susan's brother, Rich, put in his two cents. "Everytime Lyle Steele or Jim Watson bends over, Halbert kisses their ass."

The kids all smiled, knowing what he said was true. Halbert was the attorney for Steele and Watson and two other big ranchers, the Flying C, Thomas Clark's spread, and the Circle DC, Dennis Cameron's spread. Those men, along with Martin Holland, were the five richest men in the county. If it wasn't for the ranch business, Halbert would go broke. He was a mean, petty little man, always on the edge of something either illegal or unethical.

Angry voices once more came from the house, the words muffled.

"What else did you hear, Susan?" Linda asked.

"You're not going to believe this; I was saving it for last."

She paused to heighten the suspense.

"Will you get it said!" Ed frowned at her.

"I'll bet it's got something to do with that carnival," Mark guessed. "Ever since it came to town, things have been flat weird."

"Eddie!" Martin's voice came out the open window. "Will you, please, just sit down and listen for one minute? I've never seen a lawyer yet who didn't want to talk all the time."

"Martin and my Dad believe all the people out at the carnival are dead," Susan dropped it.

"*Dead!*" Rich blurted.

"You mean like in ghosts!" Jeanne asked.

"They think they've come back for revenge; something about that fire a hundred years ago, or something."

"You're joking!" Mark said. "You can't be serious!

89

What are they going to do about it?" He wanted to laugh.

"I don't know. I slipped and was afraid the noise might attract attention. That's all I know."

"I bet you all one thing," Ed said. "I bet we all get orders to stay away from the fairgrounds."

He had no takers.

Gary had not told any of the group about Jimmy Harold's insides being cooked. Now he did, quietly and professionally. He told them about the young girl who went stiff as a board and talked in tongues. And about her parents strange behavior, and about Kelson's repeating the exact same phrase as the others had. And about the ten year old Alma driving off, her parents smiling and carefree while she almost ran off the road everytime she turned the wheel. He told them his suspicions about the people gathering at the fairgrounds, and then agreed with Martin's theory about the contract now being fulfilled.

For revenge.

"And now," Gary summed it up to a silent and very captive audience, if not all-believing, "almost to the day, Karl Steele and some of his trashy friends confront Jeanne in almost the same spot where those two girls were raped thirty-four years ago. Coincidence? No, people. I don't believe that for a minute."

"Let me break in here," Audie spoke for the first time. "What's this kid's name that you saw today, Doctor?"

"Alma Sessions. She had the meanest eyes I have ever seen on a child."

"Uh-huh," Audie leaned back. "That kid has been in trouble ever since she was old enough to crawl. Her parents have taken her to every shrink in three states at one time or another. You talk about some kids just being born bad? She's one, and her entire little group is just as bad. That shrink from the visiting mental health van, Dr. Lamply? He told me—off the record—that Alma practically oozed evil."

"And Jimmy Harold was a bad one, you said?" Martin looked at the deputy.

"One hundred percent."

"What are you getting at, Martin?" Eddie asked.

"I don't know, really. Something jumped into my head just then and went out as fast as it came in. I couldn't get a handle on it."

"I had a dream last night," Janet confessed. "More than a dream. A nightmare." She looked at her husband. "It was all so jumbled. That's why I was so restless. It kept switching around. First there was this open fiery pit, all filled with people that I knew from here in Holland. It was horrible! Then when I heard about Linda's . . . well, visions, I almost fainted. We shared the same nightmare. Then I was in this house of horrors, sort of, a wax museum thing. And again, they were people that I knew. But their faces were all burned and scarred and melted down . . ." She shuddered.

"The carnival has a wax museum and a house of horrors," Martin spoke softly. "I know. I was in them a long time ago."

"So was I," Gary added.

"Okay! Okay!" Eddie held up a hand. "I'm sorry, folks, but I am not convinced. I think you've all let your imaginations run away with you. You're going to have to show me some proof before I believe."

"You'll believe," Gary said, standing up and reaching for his jacket.

"Where are you going?" his wife asked.

"To see my father. And this time, he's going to give me some answers."

"I don't have to tell you a thing, boy!" the old man said. He stared at his son. Could it be? Dear God in heaven. Please—not all three of them!

Gary's mother sat on the front porch, saying nothing. His brothers were not present and Gary did not expect them to show while he was there. Pete and Frank did not like Gary and the feeling was shared mutually. His brothers thought Gary was smart-alec and uppity. Gary felt his brothers were ignorant and proud of it.

"Yes, you do, dad. I want the truth about that fire and what led up to it. Now, tell me!"

"You don't order me, boy!" His father twisted in his chair, and Gary could see that the old man's eyes were frightened. He experienced a strange sense of power from his father's fear.

"Then stop lying and hiding the truth from me, dad!" Gary shouted.

His mother flinched at the hard words.

They did not have to worry about being overheard. They could have emptied a pistol into the air and disturbed no one. The brothers lived miles away, and the old home place was located far outside of town.

"I told them young fellows in town not to get no carnival in here. I warned them. That's all them insight people was waitin' on. 'Course, they probably helped it along, too."

Gary blinked. "What young men? Who helped what along? And what do you mean by insight people?"

"That's all them carnival people been waitin' on. Tryin' to find that crack in the wall that can't no mortal person see. They just slipped right on through and here they are."

"Dad . . . have you been drinking?"

"Ain't had a drop in years. Ask your mother."

"What young men, dad?"

"Them young men that meet every week at the cafe for lunch. The Young Holland Club."

"They brought the carnival in?"

"The carnival come in on its own, boy. You can't tell a dead person what to do. The Young Holland Club just opened the crack in the wall."

Gary sighed. Rubbed his face. "Who, ah, suggested contacting the carnival?"

"Don't know."

"What did you mean by insight people?"

"The power, boy. Nabo had it. I knew that back in '54."

"Power?" Gary was silent for a moment. "Do you mean intuition, dad? Something like the ability to foretell the future?''

"Something like that. Yeah, I reckon that's it. Son, you're the first Tressalt to get past high school, and I'm proud of you for that. You got lots of sense. Now use that good sense and pack up your family and get gone from this area."

That shook Gary. He didn't know what he was expecting to hear from his father, but it wasn't that. He stared at the man. "Leave? Why?"

"'Cause they've come back for revenge, that's why." The man's words sounded weary, and touched with more than a note of fear.

"Dad, did you have anything, anything at all, to do with that fire back in 1954?''

"I suspected it was going to happen. No, that's a lie! I knew it was going to happen. I heard the talk right after we—me and Martin—found the boy all bloody in the pavilion. The girls were still in there. Tryin' to repair their torn dresses. They told us who raped them. But by then it was too late. Steele and Watson had done started spreadin' their lies. I took you right on home, right out to this house, and here you stayed with your mother. I went back to town and joined up with Martin. The doctor sent young Martin on to the city; told Martin he'd best stay. All hell was gonna bust loose. Sure did.''

"And you did nothing to stop the madness?''

"No.''

"Why?''

"Nothin' I could do, boy. Me or Martin or Doc Reynolds or none of the few of us with any reason left us. Fifteen hundred wild people, all liquored up and carryin' guns and ropes and whips. And the heavyweights eggin' them on.''

"The heavyweights?''

"Steele, Watson, Cameron, Clark. And the silly bastards who followed them.''

"Including my brothers, Pete and Frank?''

"Yeah.'' There was disgust in the man's voice. "Dumb shits!'' And I wonder, boy: Are you just like them. Oh,

93

God, don't let it be.

"Lyle Steele and Jim Watson raped the girls?"

"Yeah."

"Mary Mahoney and June Ellis?"

"Yeah."

"Why didn't the girls come forward with the truth?"

"The boys' daddies threatened them with death. The girls believed them."

"All right. I can believe that. Now what is all this talk about insight?"

"Nabo ain't . . . well, I don't think he was quite human even back then. He, and some of the others, they can see, sense, evil. They had, have, the power. Don't ask me how. I don't know. It's a death carnival, boy. They come to town, and people die."

"Dad, that's nonsense!"

"No, it ain't neither. I had a book about them. Your brother Pete took it and burned it. It was about this carnival that would come into town and see evil in people; the people would give their hearts to the devil."

"Where'd you get this book? There has to be more than one copy."

"Martin found it somewheres. I think you've probably figured out what happened to him. Boy, take your family and get gone from this area."

"No."

"Then I got to say that I sired three fools, then. Maybe you'll come to your senses before it's too late."

"Are you and mother leaving?"

"No. We wouldn't be allowed. It's just too late for us."

"Who would stop you?"

"Things."

"Things?"

But the old man would only shake his head.

"Things?" Gary persisted.

"That book Martin found, it told about shape-changers. I believe that too. Things."

Gary sighed heavily. "What really happened to Martin's dad?"

"Another dark spot on my mind. Lyle Steele and Jim Watson killed him. Years ago. Martin's dad still owned the paper back then. He was gonna open up that carnival fire story. Get some state people in here. Lyle and Jim knew they couldn't allow that. Their daddies were dead by then. So Lyle and Jim, along with Cameron and Clark, ambushed my old friend Martin. Killed him. Buried his truck—with him in it—up near the state line; bulldozed earth over the pit."

"God!" Gary muttered. The word felt nasty to his tongue. He didn't understand that. "Dad, why didn't you go to the police with this information?"

"I didn't know it then. By the time the talk began to filter out—night whispers—it was too late. Besides, there was no proof. Just talk. But it'll soon be over and done with. The carnival's done come back, and pretty soon, so will my old friend, Martin."

Gary's skin broke out in a cold sweat. He rubbed his arms. His jacket was no protection against the fear-sweat. He looked at his father, something akin to horror in his eyes. "Dad, what are you talking about?"

The old man's voice was soft, but charged with emotion. "I'll tell you what I'm talking about boy. Flames jumpin' five, six hundred feet into the air. People bein' burned alive, just for spite and sport. Runnin' with no way to escape. Flesh bubblin' and crackin'. Them poor animals that was a part of the show, screamin' in fear and agony as they burned up. And let me tell you about that man called Nabo. Man all dressed in black. Just standin' there in the middle of all the flames and fiery death, his arms folded crost his chest, them eyes of his burnin' just as hot as the flames." The man shuddered in his chair. "He didn't make a sound when the flames touched him. But his eyes! Them white eyes of his touched every man of us with hate and contempt. I had run down there to help, not to torch the place. But I was too late. Me and Martin got there 'bout the same time. We both seen your brothers, Pete and Frank, laughin' at the pain and sufferin' all around them, pushing people and animals back into the fires. It got so hot, me and Martin had to back off a good five hundred feet. The volunteers in the fire department was sprayin' water on the townspeople so's they could keep them poor carnival folks in the flames. Both me and Martin seen the bodies of some of the carnival folk that'd been hung. Stripped 'em nekked and horse-whipped 'em and then hung 'em. At that, I reckon they was the lucky ones; dead 'fore the flames burned them up.''

The father looked hard at the son. "And don't you kid yourself none about the good people of Holland, boy. There was over half the town down there. Little boys and girls and women and men took part in that night's awfulness. It was like a disease that spread with the wind; like a wildfire sweepin' crost the prairie. They was hundreds of townspeople and ranchhands and others took part in the evil of that night. And now they, and their offspring who hold the bad seed, well, they got to pay.''

Gary felt strangely elated. He wished he could have seen the fire. What a wonderful sight that must have been! Then all thoughts of that left him. "Dad . . . what you said about the carnival people coming back for revenge, back from the grave . . . that's impossible.''

"Sure it is, boy." The father stared at the son. "Impossible as we humans see the overall plan. But we don't know what's on the other side of that Dark River. But boy,'' he touched Gary's arm, "we're about to find out.''

SEVEN

The father and mother watched the son walk to his car.
"Just like his brothers," the old man whispered.

"No."

"Yeah, old woman. He's one of them. I don't know why
God punished us. But he did."

"We have to tell Martin. He's got to know. We have to
tell him."

"Can't, Mother. We can't do it. We'd be dead soon as we
set foot off this porch."

She sighed, knowing it was true.

"Don't come back here, boy!" his father called after him.
"I don't want to see you again." But he knew he would.
One more time. "Just get gone!"

Gary had mumbled something under his breath and
stumbled into his car.

He didn't even remember the drive back to Martin's
house. The confusing events of the visit to his parents had
been wiped from his mind.

Most of the others had left when he pulled into the
driveway at Martin's. He felt like it must be midnight, at
least. He looked at his watch. Seven-thirty. He walked
slowly up to the porch.

Martin met him on the porch, took one look at Gary's
almost gray face and quickly led him inside. He sat him
down on the couch and poured him a stiff snifter of
brandy. Gary slugged back at least half of the drink,
shuddered as the brandy impacted with his empty
stomach, and then leaned back, telling them everything

his father had said. Linda and Mark and Susan had gathered around, Gary Jr. was in the rec room, watching TV with Rich.

"Maybe they're shape-changers," Mark said. "I've read about them. The Indians believed strongly in them."

Linda and Susan fixed a platter of sandwiches and a pot of coffee. Gary shook his head at the offer of another drink and chose food and coffee instead.

"Then my memory was correct," Martin said. "It was Mary Mahoney and June Ellis in that pavilion."

"According to dad."

"Are we leaving town, daddy?" Susan asked.

"No. I think the very idea is ridiculous. Your grandpa was overreacting, that's all." His dad had told him to leave, hadn't he? He couldn't remember. "But I do want you kids to stay away from the fairgrounds until, or if, Martin and I can make some sense out of what's happening."

Martin wondered if he really believed his dad had been exaggerating or if he was merely saying that for the benefit of the kids?

"Now what, Gary?" his wife asked. "I'd be lying just a bit if I said this wasn't beginning to scare me. I feel like I want to start peeking into closets and looking under the bed."

"I second that motion," Linda said. Susan just looked plain scared.

Alicia looked dubious about the whole matter; but there was a strange smile on her face.

"Everybody just calm down," Gary told the group. "And don't discuss what you've heard tonight with anyone." He looked at Janet. "You stay here with Alicia and the kids, honey. Please. Soon as I rest a second, I'm going over to the fairgrounds with Martin. We're to meet Audie there."

"And do what?" Janet's voice was a bit on the shrill side.

"Watch the crowds and try to figure out what is happening around this town," Martin answered the question.

She opened her mouth to protest. The ringing of the phone closed it. Martin stilled the ringing. "All right, Audie. Yes. I'll tell him. I'll come over with him. See you in a few minutes." He turned to Gary. "Hank Rinder just stuck a pistol in his ear and pulled the trigger. Audie thinks it just happened. Hank left a note. Come on. I'll ride with you."

I CAN'T MAKE THAT THING LEAVE ME ALONE. I CAN'T MAKE IT GO AWAY. I'VE SAID I WAS SORRY. IT'S AWFUL. I BEEN ASHAMED OF WHAT I DONE THAT NIGHT FOR OVER THIRTY YEARS. I CAN'T TAKE IT NO MORE. THE WHOLE TOWN IS DOOMED TO BURN FOREVER IN THE PITS OF HELL FOR WHAT WE DONE. GOODBYE AND FORGIVE ME.

The note was signed Hank Rinder.

Martin sniffed the air. "Smells like wood smoke in here to me."

"Yeah," Audie agreed. "All mixed up with gunsmoke and something else I can't get a fix on. But there's too much gunsmoke for just the one head wound."

Gary was busy with the body. But when he had read that part about the "thing," he recalled his father's words and shuddered.

Martin had noticed and put a hand on his friend's shoulder.

"What thing is he talking about, Audie?" Martin asked, still trying to identify the third and still-elusive smell in the house. Martin thought then about the shape-changers. He shook that away, as best he could.

"Beats me, Mr. Holland." His eyes widened. "Look over there!" he pointed. "And over there and there. Those are bullet holes. Must be twenty or thirty of them in that wall. He sure was shooting at something."

"Real or imagined," Martin offered.

"It was real," Audie argued in defense of the dead Hank. "My father and Hank used to buddy together. Hank is the one who fought that bear off my dad over in Wyoming years back. Fought him off with nothing but an empty rifle. Swinging it like a club. Hank was a very brave man, Mr. Holland."

"Yeah," Martin's reply was desert dry. "I'm sure he was. I'm sure it takes a lot of courage to deliberately burn up men and women and children and helpless animals in a fire."

Gary stood up from the body, stepping between the two men before the exchange might turn physical—although he didn't think that was much of a possibility. Audie knew perfectly well that Martin was physically and emotionally capable of breaking him in many pieces and scattering the bones. "All right, Audie. How are you writing this up?"

Audie dropped his gaze from Martin's calm, steady eyes. "Well, I bagged his hands for residue testing just before you got here—as you can see. There is nothing missing in the house—that I can tell—or from the body. More than a hundred dollars in his wallet and he's still wearing his diamond ring and watch. I'd rule out robbery. I don't know anyone in this town who would kill Hank." He pointed to the pistol. "That's his gun fully loaded except for one round which was recently fired. I'd call it a self-inflicted gunshot wound to the head." He hitched at his gunbelt and looked up at the high ceiling of the old house. "Jesus Christ!" he yelled.

Martin and Gary looked up. It was the face of Hank Rinder, and it had been burned into the ceiling. The expression on the face was one of pure, blind terror.

The men stood frozen in shock for a moment. Gary was the first to react. He pushed Audie toward his camera, sitting on a table. "Get some pictures of that, Audie. Take several shots. Go on—do it!"

"How could that possibly? . . ." Martin said. He stood staring at the burned-in image on the ceiling.

Then the face began to slowly fade.

"Hurry, Audie!" Gary yelled. "We're losing it."

Gary fumbled with the 35mm and aimed it at the ceiling. He got off a series of shots before the face finally faded into nothing. The ceiling was bare, void of any burn marks.

Gary lowered the camera, still staring at the ceiling. "What? . . ." was all he could say.

"I don't know," Gary said. "But it was there. I saw it."

"So did I." Martin shifted positions, angling himself for a better look at the ceiling. But nothing was left of the face of Hank Rinder.

"Get away from me!" Audie screamed, pointing a shaking finger at Gary. Horror was stamped on the young man's face, his skin color ashen.

Gary stepped toward him. "What's the matter with you, Audie?"

"I'll kill you!" Audie yelled, his right hand dropped to the butt of his pistol. "I'll kill you if you don't leave me alone!"

Martin jerked the deputy's hand from his gun butt and slapped him, openhanded and hard, rocking Audie's head. Gary grabbed the other arm and together, they put the deputy on the floor and held him there.

After only a few seconds, Audie's eyes lost their wildness and he blinked, shifting his gaze from man to man. "I'm all right now." His voice was firm. "Really, I am. You can turn me loose."

They did, cautiously, and eased back, both men ready to grab the young man again. Audie sat up, an embarrassed smile on his lips.

"What happened to you?" Gary asked.

"I feel like an idiot, Doc! Your face, it was . . . no offense now . . . but your face was like, well, a wax person that was all melted. That's the best I can come up with. I mean you were some hard to look at. Scared me to pieces."

Martin glanced at Gary. "Just like my hallucinations. They jarred me, too."

"Thank goodness, I've been spared them."

"So far," Martin tossed cold water on that.

"Thanks. You're a real comfort to me."

The men helped Audie to his boots and Gary checked his pulse and BP. Both were high, but steadying down.

"About the face on the ceiling," Audie said. "I don't think I want to report that to Sheriff Grant just yet—personal reasons."

"I understand," Martin agreed. "Wise decision. But sooner or later, we're going to have to bring him into this thing."

"Yeah, I know. But let's make it later. First I want to get a hook on this thing."

The other men agreed, Gary saying, "Well, it happened outside the city limits, so the city cops don't have to be brought in."

"Gee!" Audie snapped his fingers. "I forgot. It was the city who called me on this thing."

"Where are they?" Martin looked around.

"I don't know. It's the first time I've remembered. What's wrong with me?"

"Who called you?"

"I . . . It was Jack."

A low whimpering drifted to the men. All three looked up. Cut their eyes to one another. The painful whimpering seemed to be coming from the second floor of the old house.

They listened, their breathing very shallow.

"Hank was a widower," Audie whispered. "Nobody lived here with him. And he almost never had company of any kind. His kids live far away. He never saw any ladies; swore off women years ago. Said he knew he'd never find one to take the place of Ethel."

The whimpering continued.

The men seemed mesmerized by the sound.

Martin broke the silence on the first floor. "That is not a child's whimpering."

"No," Gary agreed.

All three men continued to look up at the dark landing of the second floor.

"Leave me alone!" the voice sprang at them, the words slurry and difficult to understand. "Please don't hurt me no more." Then a scream ripped through the house, jarring the men standing on the ground floor, moving them into action.

They ran up the stairs, Audie in the lead, his pistol drawn.

The whimpering had changed into a low moaning that cut at the men's already raw nerves.

They began working their way up the darkened hall, pausing at each closed door, listening. They stopped at the next to the last door.

Audie sniffed the air. "What's that smell. Smells kind of sweet."

Gary and Martin knew what it was. They'd both smelled it before. Martin as a combat vet, Gary as a doctor.

"That's the smell of cooked human flesh," Martin told him.

Then Audie remembered that wreck he'd worked, where that drunk driver had plowed into the back of that station wagon, exploding both vehicles, trapping those in the station wagon, burning them alive.

"I can't stand the pain!" the voice wailed. "Oh, Sweet Baby Jesus—help me!"

Gary turned the door knob, pushing open the door. Darkness struck them, bringing with it the sickening odor of seared human flesh.

"Jack!" Audie called. "Jack, is that you. Where are you?"

A long wail of pure agony was the only reply, the screaming hanging in the air, reverberating around the musty-smelling room.

It came from a closed closet door.

The men stood for a moment, staring at the closed door, not wanting to open that door, but each knowing that it had to be.

Martin swallowed hard, shook his head to clear away the tension—it didn't work—and found the light switch, flooding the dusty room with brightness. He walked to the closed door, put his hand on the knob, hesitated for just a second, then turned the knob and jerked open the door.

Martin grunted in shock. Gary hissed his shaky feelings. Audie vomited on the floor.

It was Jack. What was left of him, that is. The man was naked, with only scraps of his uniform remaining, and that was burned into his flesh. His leather Sam Browne belt was partially intact; some of it seared and melted into his flesh. His lips were gone, burned away; his gums were bloody from the flames, the teeth stark white and bloody red. His hair was gone, his scalp a mass of bubbles and blisters. His ears only blackened stubs on the side of his head. His boots had melted into his feet and ankles and calves.

He could not close his eyes. The lids were burned away.

Audie cursed himself and regained his composure. Second time in his cop career that he'd puked. First time was years back. Thought he'd gotten over that. He knelt down in the open doorway, facing Jack, who was wedged into the closet space. Jack's stark white kneecaps were sticking out where the flesh had once been.

"Who did this, Jack?"

"Thing!" Jack pushed the word out of a raw throat and past where once his lips had been.

Martin and Gary exchanged glances. *Thing?*

"What kind of thing, Jack?" Audie questioned.

Jack tried to shift positions in the cramped closet. The movement brought a wild scream of agony from the man.

"Jack, listen to me." Audie scooted closer to the man. "What kind of thing?"

"Two of them!"

"Two things?"

"No . . . two Hank's." Jack took several painful breaths while the others exchanged glances. "Hank . . . called me. Come out and . . . talk to him. See this . . . monster. I . . . thought he was . . . drunk. Come on out later. Hank answered the door. But . . . wasn't Hank. Looked just like . . . Hank. Then I seen Hank . . . dead on the . . . floor. I turned to run. Thing got all over me. Flames burnin' me."

"How'd you get up here?"

"Don't know." The expelling of words almost exhausted the man. He leaned back against the wall. When

104

his back touched the rough wood, he squalled in pain.

"Two Hank Rinder's?" Audie looked confused.

"Twins. I . . . swear it."

Martin knelt down by the ruined man. "Jack, it's Martin Holland. Listen to me, Jack. It's important. Did you have anything to do with that carnival fire years ago. Did you, Jack?"

"Fire," he breathed. "I been on fire."

"We know, Jack. Think back years. The carnival that was in town. It was destroyed by fire. Did you have anything to do with that?"

"Yeah. Fire. All them freaks and trash. They all burned up, didn't they?"

"Yes, they did, Jack. Did you have anything at all to do with that?"

"Yeah." The reply was very weak. Fluids were oozing out of the man, from all over his tortured body. All those gathered around him knew that Jack did not have long to suffer . . . not in this world. "I was . . . fifteen. Runnin' with Lyle and Jim and that . . . crew. Ever'body in . . . town went crazy that night. I helped push them . . . people and animals back into the . . . fires. Helped horsewhip some . . . others. Was there when some others was . . . hung. Trash was all they was." His eyes opened wide, the charred and cracked crow's feet at the corners splitting open. Jack began wailing as a dark flapping shadow fell over the poorly lighted room.

The men looked up and around them. There was nothing in sight. But the shadow was real.

Jack lifted one hideously burned arm and pointed at Gary. "Get it away from me. Get away!" He screamed his fear. "Get—"

Jack tumbled over, half out of the closet, one side of his face pressing against the old carpet, one hand to his charred chest. Gary pushed Martin and Audie aside and knelt down beside the cooked cop. He quickly examined him and shook his head.

"He's gone. His heart probably quit on him."

The shadow flapped away; the men looked up, trying to

find the source of the dark flapping. But there was no sign of what might be causing it in the musty-smelling and dusty upstairs bedroom. They had no way of knowing what Jack had last seen as he exited this life. Whatever it was, they all, to a man, doubted it was Saint Peter welcoming him home.

"What was that flapping thing?" Audie asked, his voice shaky.

"I don't know," Martin was the first to respond to the question. "I'm not sure I want to know."

Gary said nothing. He was thinking about his father's words. *Things!*

"Well . . . it's murder, for sure," Audie stood up. "But who do I charge? How do we handle this? I don't want a panic in this town."

Martin took it. "We have no choice in the matter now. We have to include Kelson. But we don't have to tell all that we know, or have seen, or that we suspect."

"Suppress evidence? Why, Mr. Holland?"

"No, not evidence . . . if he asks for that evidence. Just the unverifiable things we've seen. Why? Because Kelson is stupid. Any stupid people have no imagination. What is, is. What is not, is not. And that is the bottom line with them."

"I agree," Gary said, rising to his feet and stretching. "We'll make no mention of what we saw or think we saw this night. We'll wait until that state investigator gets here and lay it all in his lap."

"Uh . . . there is one problem with that, people," Audie looked sort of guilty.

Martin looked at Audie. "What do you mean? He changed his mind about coming in?"

"No. It isn't a he—it's a she!" The men walked out into the hall.

"Well, I have no problem with that," Audie commented. "Let's get Kelson over here."

When the Holland chief of police had sufficiently

recovered from his shock to speak, he said, "Uh . . . Audie, how do you figure this?"

"Which body?" the better-trained and much more intelligent deputy sheriff asked drily.

"Uh . . . Jack."

"I don't know, Kelson." Audie had found Jack's city unit parked behind the house. And before the chief had arrived, all three men had wondered why the unit had been parked behind the house and not in the drive. "He was burned in or near this house."

"How you figure that?"

"Because he called me from here. Said he was here; just getting out of his unit."

"Ah! And there ain't no burnt place nowhere's in the house, right?"

"Not that I can find."

"Well . . ." Kelson took off his hat and scratched his head. "It's your case. You be sure and let me know how it comes out." He plopped his hat on his head and turned to leave.

"Where are you going, Kelson!" Audie asked, amazed at the man's lack of concern over two dead bodies, one of them his own man. His words stopped the man and turned him around.

"Why . . ." Kelson smiled, rather stupidly, "I'm goin' over to the fairgrounds, of course. The carnival's in town, you know?"

Gary had a long night facing him: by law, he had to perform autopsies on both men. He told Martin to ride on over to the fairgrounds with Audie and he'd see him in the morning. He didn't know whether he'd make church, or not. Probably not.

"Good God!" Audie muttered, as they drove up to the fairgrounds. "There must be five or six hundred people milling around outside the fence."

Martin cut his eyes to the deputy. "You have any overwhelming desire to join that crowd, Audie?"

107

"Hell, no!"

"Then the way I have it figured—and the odds are as much that I'm wrong as right—you aren't carrying the bad seed."

"Beg pardon, sir?" Audie parked the car and cut the engine.

"Give some thought to all those who have been affected so far."

The deputy pushed his hat back on his head and was silent for a moment. "All right. I'm with you now. Yeah. Everyone who's been touched by some weirdness, or who had died mysteriously, or is acting funny, was either connected directly with the fire, or else is just a total jerk."

"That's the way I see it."

"How can it be?"

"You believe in the supernatural, Audie?"

"I like to read books about it; see the movies. But do I actually believe in it?" He took a deep breath. "I don't know. Do you?"

"I guess it's possible," Martin's reply was guarded. "Is that what we have here? I don't know. I pray not. But all signs point to it. You want to get out and walk around some?"

"No. Not yet. Let's just sit here and watch the crowd; try to figure out what they're doing. What pulled them here. And what they're going to do. That's what's got me concerned."

But after fifteen minutes had passed, it became obvious that the crowd was doing nothing. And probably was not going to do anything. Most just stood at the fence and stared inside, at the darkened trucks and trailers and tents and concessions of the carnival.

The "why" of it remained an unanswered mystery.

And none of the crowd seemed to notice the sheriff's department car and the men inside.

"Damn!" Audie summed it up.

"Yeah." Martin pointed. "Kelson."

The man stood with several other of Holland's more thugy types, by the fence, just staring into the darkness.

108

As their eyes adjusted, they could pick out Ed and Joyce's daughter, Missy, and the gang of young men and women she ran with: Suzanne and Polly and Rose and Judy. Robie and Hal and Paul and Karl. And surprisingly, to both men, Binkie was with them.

"I hate to see that," Audie commented on the boy's presence. "Binkie has always been just a real nice kid. At least to my way of thinking."

"You know his parents well?"

"No. But sir, are you saying the sins of the parents are on the shoulders of their kids?"

Martin sighed heavily. "I don't know, Audie. I surely hope not. No!" he spoke firmly. "I don't believe any higher power would permit that."

"I pray you're right. 'Cause my daddy sure had something to do with that fire years back."

Martin nodded his head toward the row of young people. "Hal seems to have improved dramatically."

"Yeah. But you watch him. When he walks, he's real careful with it."

Both men shared a quiet chuckle at that. Both had had their bells rung a time or two.

A pickup truck rolled slowly by the sheriff's department unit: a pickup with chrome roll bars and fog lights and spotlights and running lights and six antennas. A power wench on the front, chrome bumpers and chrome running boards and twin chrome stacks up the side and smoked windows. A plate on the front bumper bluntly proclaimed: I'LL GIVE UP MY GUN WHEN THEY PRY IT FROM MY COLD DEAD FINGERS. The ever-present gun rack in the rear window, contained two rifles and a small animal trap. A sticker on the bumper read: NUC THEIR ASS AND TAKE THE GAS. A small sticker on the rear window warned: THIS VEHICLE PROTECTED BY SMITH & WESSON. The two men inside each wore forty-seven gallon hats with a feather a foot long protruding from each sombrero.

"Well, well," Audie muttered, sitting up straight in the seat. "Would you just take a look at who's come into town."

"I can tell *what* it is," Martin said. "But not *who* it is."

"Fellow driving is your old buddy, Lyle Steele. Other guy is Jim Watson."

Martin smiled at the "your old buddy" bit. Lyle Steele hated Martin and the feeling was mutual. "I don't think I've seen either of them in a year or more."

"For a fact, they don't get into Holland much." He cut his eyes at Martin. "And for a fact, neither one of them like you very much."

"It goes back a long way, Audie."

"So I hear. You are aware that Lyle had made the comment, many times, that he'd just love to kick your sissy ass."

Martin laughed aloud. Genuine laughter. "Oh, yes. I've heard it. But Audie, I've been back a good many years, and I'm real easy to find. Anytime Lyle is ready, I'm available."

The deputy grunted. "You really mean that, don't you, Mr. Holland?"

"Oh, yes."

"Then I'd better warn you. Lyle Steele is tough and snake-quick. I've seen him whip men half his age and in very good shape."

"Yes, I know that, too."

"Figured you might. Did you really whip Pete Tressalt some years back?"

"So the story goes."

"I guess it's true then. I heard you put the boots to him."

"He was annoying my wife. He became quite belligerent when I asked him to stop. He invited me outside the store and I accepted his invitation."

The deputy grinned. "And then you kicked his ribs loose and busted up his face."

"For a fact, I did. And I'd do it again if he ever crowded me. Pete, or anyone like him. I have no use for those types of people."

"Frank and Pete Tressalt are both losers. Dr. Tressalt, on the other hand, is a nice guy and an asset to the community. I have problems understanding things like that."

"Well, you live and learn," Martin replied.

The men waited and watched for another half an hour. Nothing out of the ordinary took place. But still, more and more people from town lined the fences that surrounded the fairgrounds: men, women, kids.

"They just stand and stare," Audie commented, shifting around behind the wheel. "But what are they staring at."

A thought came to Martin. "Maybe nothing. Maybe, and this is just a wild guess, maybe they were all called over here."

"How?"

"I don't know. Or the why of it, either."

Before Audie could reply to that—not that he had any firm response—a sharp knock on the passenger side of the unit startled both men. Martin turned and met the eyes of Lyle Steele. The rancher motioned for him to get out.

Martin stepped out into the night, facing the man. "Lyle."

"Holland. You part-time deputyin' now?" His words were slurred and he stank of whiskey.

"Every Holland in the past one hundred years has held a county commission, Lyle. Or are you too drunk to remember that?"

The rancher spat tobacco juice to one side. "I'd sure like to see you try to 'rrest me someday, Holland. That'd sure be the day you get your ass kicked."

"Not by the likes of you, Steele. And don't press your luck with me," Martin warned him. "My name isn't Mary Mahoney or June Ellis."

That stung the man. His head snapped back as if he'd been hit by a yellowjacket. His eyes became very bright. Jim Watson stiffened at Martin's words.

Not one person who lined the fences had turned around to see what was going on.

Audie was leaning against the fender of his unit, watching and listening to the exchange. He had been trying for two years to catch Karl Steele doing something—anything!—but he had better radio equipment in

111

his truck than the county had in their units, including the best scanner made, and the little punk seemed to know where Audie was at all times. But Audie kept hoping. But on this night, he tried to keep one eye on Jim Watson, not knowing what either man might try to do. He could smell the booze from both. And both men were unpredictable, mean as snakes in a fight.

"Huh?" Lyle recovered his composure and ignored Martin's remarks about the long-ago rape. "You take me in a fight, Holland? Not on your bes' day. And you sure ain't never gonna 'rrest me."

"Don't let your asshole overload your mouth, Steele," Audie vocally stepped between the two wealthy men. "Martin's commission is just as valid as mine. And in case you don't know, he voluntarily went through the academy and graduated in the top five of his class. Crowd him, and he can and will put you in jail just as quickly and just as legally as I would."

Lyle shifted his hard mean eyes to Audie. "You a smart-assed young pup, ain't you?"

"No," Audie stood his ground. "Just a deputy sheriff who is tired of listening to your ignorant bullshit and who isn't going to take any more mouth from you this night. And let me tell you something else, *Mister* Steele: you and Watson had best get back in that fancy truck of yours and hit the trail back to your ranches. Now I'm gonna give you ten minutes to get gone. I find you in town tonight, and I'll pull you over and run a breath and blood test on you. And then I'll toss you in jail—one way or the other—with enough knots on your head and tickets hanging around your red neck to keep you there. Now how's it gonna be?"

Lyle had always been able to either intimidate or just flat buy off all the other deputies Sheriff Grant had put in this part of the county. But he'd never had any luck with Audie Meadows. You couldn't buy him and he wouldn't back down from a grizzly. Big-ass sissy with a badge was all he was. At least that's what Lyle tried to make himself believe.

He shook his head. What was the matter with him?

112

What was he doing in this jerk town anyway. In the middle of the night. Lyle couldn't figure it. Just seemed the thing to do when he left the ranch, was all. Pick up Jim at his place and then turn north to raise some hell up in South Dakota. But oh, no! Something made him cut the wheel south, toward Holland. It was like something pulled him down here. But that was too stupid to even think about.

Jim Watson tugged at his friend's sleeve. "Come on, Lyle. Let's shake this place. They's other ways to handle this."

Lyle jerked his arm free of the clutching fingers. Thought for a moment. His eyes touched Martin's unwavering gaze. Shifted to Audie. "This ain't over," he warned. "For neither one of you. Bear that in mind. Cain't neither of you talk to me like I's some drifter. It ain't over." He stalked away into the night, his back stiff with anger, Jim Watson keeping pace with him.

Lyle gunned his engine like some kid in a hot rod.

Audie said, "If he spins out, I'm gonna bust him hard."

But Lyle drove away sedately, keeping well within the speed limit.

Not once had anyone from the fence turned around to see what was happening behind them.

Audie watched the taillights fade. When he spoke, his words were very soft. "I'll have to hurt that man someday, Martin."

"No, I don't think so," Martin contradicted.

"What do you mean?"

"I think *I'll* have to kill him."

EIGHT

Martin stepped out of church, his family with him. Linda headed for her brother's car for the ride back to the house. A pickup truck was all right, but a station wagon was the absolute pits!

It had not been a particularly inspiring sermon, Martin felt. He had been forced to struggle to keep his attention from wandering. The minister had rambled, having some trouble keeping his train of thought.

Martin wondered if it had been his imagination, for everyone else had seemed completely enthralled by the services. On the ride home, he asked Alicia about it.

"I thought it was an excellent sermon," his wife disagreed with him, as usual, of late. "I enjoyed it very much."

Martin sighed and offered no other comment.

"I wonder why Gary and Janet didn't make it this morning?"

"We checked back with Gary around midnight. He still had a lot of work to do with the bodies. I imagine he elected to sleep late." He glanced out the window. "Alicia, does the town seem unusually quiet to you?"

"Not more than on any other Sunday."

Naturally, Martin thought. We're going to have this out shortly, he made up his mind. I've got to find out what's bothering her. What's been bothering her for a long time.

Again he glanced out the window. Something was out of whack. Something was just not right.

The kids were going to the cafe to have lunch; Martin

watched as Mark cut off to head for the downtown area. Martin turned the other way and headed for Gary's.

"Must we?" his wife asked.

"I just want to check on Gary, that's all."

"Are you two sleeping together lately?" she spat that at him.

Martin lost his temper. "Sleeping is about all you and I have been doing together for the last few months."

She turned her face away and gazed out the window.

Martin cursed under his breath.

Susan answered the door on the first dong and waved them in. "Mom and dad are in the den. Where's Mark and Linda?"

"Having lunch at the cafe." Alicia managed a civil tone.

There were several drive-ins around town, and one chain-type fast food joint and an eatery at a local motel, but whenever anyone mentioned "the cafe," they meant the cafe at the Holland Hotel.

"Hey, Mom!" the girl yelled. "Okay if me and Rich go to the cafe and eat lunch with Mark and Linda?"

"As long as you take your little brother." Janet appeared out of the den."

"Chill out!" Susan muttered. "Oh, okay," she grinned. "Where is nerd?" She was referring to her eight-year-old brother, noisy and rambunctious Gary, Jr.

"I'll get him." Janet disappeared up the hallway.

Gary, Jr. came barreling up the hall and almost knocked Rich down in his haste to get outside. "Come straight back after lunch!" Gary called from the den.

"Right, dad!" Linda called over her shoulder as she was going out the door.

The silence was numbing.

"I love 'em all," Janet said with a smile. "But . . ."

Alicia managed to return the smile. "I know the feeling."

"I made a big pot of stew. The kids turned up their noses at it." Janet waved Martin and Alicia into the den. "How does it sound to you two?"

When Alicia didn't reply, Martin took it. "Delicious."

"I think I'll pass," Alicia said. "I'll take the car and go on home. Gary, will you run Martin back over to the house later?"

"Sure. We'll probably link up with Audie Meadows later on this afternoon. Might be back late."

"Oh, of course," Alicia's tone was very ugly as she looked at her husband. "Be sure and strap on your six-gun before you leave, partner!"

She turned around and walked out of the house.

"What was that all about?" Gary asked.

Martin shrugged. "Things have been a little strained between us lately. But I don't know why."

Gary looked at his wife. She shrugged and walked out of the den, heading for the kitchen.

"Something tells me she knows."

"Let it drop," Martin urged him. "No point in both of us getting the cold treatment. Whatever *it* is, it's coming to a head between us. We'll hash it out. I'm hoping it's nothing serious."

"Probably isn't. Let's eat. I'm hungry."

The cowboy was riding fence line, a lonely and boring but necessary job, when he suddenly reined up, not believing his ears.

What was that sound? He sat his saddle and listened very intently. It sounded like an old car or truck trying to crank up, but it was very faint. Just could hear it.

As a matter of fact, he thought, pushing his hat back on his head and grinning, it sounded like it was coming from under the ground, sort of a deep and hollow grinding like an old starter would make.

He chuckled at that. What a dumb thought. How stupid could you get?

But, he listened, there it was again. Now where was it coming from? He stood up in the stirrups, looking around him. Nothing or nobody in sight. Sure wasn't any truck for miles around.

And just how did he know it was a truck?

He scratched his head. Well . . . he just did. It was a truck. He'd bet on that. And an old one, at that.

The cowboy riding the horse with the Bar-S brand dismounted and ground-reined his horse. He stood for a moment. The grinding sounds of the old starter had stopped. Only the low sighing of the wind spoke to him in its invisible but audible way.

Even the wind sounded different.

"Now, just settle down," he muttered.

Then he heard the starter again.

Crazy! he thought. I'm going slap-dad nuts! The old starter grinding drifted to him. He walked around in a huge circle, gradually narrowing the circle, until the noise became the loudest. At that point, he got down on his hands and knees and pressed an ear to the ground.

Sweat beaded his forehead. Fear-sweat. There was no doubt about it. He was not imagining things. That was definitely the sounds of a starter.

And something else, too. All mixed up with that sound: someone calling out, followed by laughter. And he wasn't nuts either; that was really laughter and real words. But he couldn't make out the words. Something about coming home, or something like that.

Then it all stopped. The grinding of the starter, the laughter, the words. Just quit. Leaving nothing but the never-ceasing and lonely winds.

The cowboy looked down at his work-hardened hands. They were trembling. He got to his boots and looked around him. There was nothing out there. And it wasn't possible for a truck to be under the ground!

Well . . . maybe a truck could be under the earth, but there sure couldn't be anybody in it trying to start the thing!

The cowboy, a young man from Wyoming named Don Talbolt, pulled his hat low over his eyes and stood for a moment, pondering on this development. These were grasslands, leased from the government, and there wasn't even any roads running through this part of it. Nearest dirt road of any sort was a good ten, twelve miles away to

118

the west.

So what was going on?

He expelled pent-up breath. Well, whatever it was, it could just wait. Don walked back to his horse thinking what a good story it would make around a cookfire some night. A ghost truck. He'd have some fun with that. He climbed back into the saddle and pointed the dun's head toward the line shack. It was a good five miles back to the shack and he was hungry.

By the time he reached the cabin he was sharing with a cantankerous old puncher named Red, Don was so hungry he could have eaten a polecat.

Then he smelled something.

Whatever it was, it wasn't Red cookin' up a stew. This smelled terrible. Matter of fact, it just reared up and killed his appetite.

And the horses in the corral were all bunched up and scared, all wall-eyed with their ears laid back.

Don rode in closer and took a better look. Jesus Christ! All the windows had been knocked out of the cabin, and the front door was hanging open, hanging there by one hinge. And what in God's name was that thing hanging out of a front window.

Looked like a—

Oh, no!

Swallowing hard, Don dismounted. He opened the flap to his saddlebags and took out a pistol, checking to see if it was fully loaded. One empty, under the hammer. He dug down into the saddlebags and fished out a .44 magnum round and filled the empty.

His own horse was getting skittish as hell, wanting to get gone from the smell of death that lingered all around. And Don knew that's what the smell represented. He led the horse to the hitchrail and tied the reins securely.

Then he jerked back the hammer on the single-action .44 mag.

He walked up to the window where the object—he knew what it was—was hanging out. Don swallowed hard, again, and forced himself to look.

119

It was a leg. Or a part of a leg, with the boot still attached. The worn and faded denim was all torn and soaked with blood.

Don touched the boot with shaky fingers. He jumped back, almost falling, as the leg fell out of the broken window to land with a squishy thud on the ground. Don forced his eyes to look at the severed object. No, not severed. That was not a clean cut. The leg looked like it had been torn apart, ripped right out of the knee socket.

And it was Red's leg. No doubt about that. Don recognized the boot. But what could have done something like this? Nothing but a bear or some big ape would have the enormous strength to rip a man apart. There were no grizzlies around here, and for sure, there weren't any big apes.

Don walked slowly over to the broken door. Steeling his nerves, he forced himself to look inside the cabin.

He promptly puked up what was left of his breakfast.

There was blood everywhere. Dripping from the walls and the ceiling and off the battered old table. One of Red's arms was on one side of the room, the other arm, ripped out of the socket, was on the cook stove, clear across the big room.

Don couldn't immediately spot Red's other leg.

What to do?

He sure didn't want to step inside. Whoever—or whatever, he thought—might still be waiting there.

But he had to look.

"All right, you, come out of there with your hands up!" Don shouted.

Nothing.

He felt like a fool.

He took off his hat and dropped it on the ground beside the door, so as not to present too big a target (he'd seen them do that in cowboy movies), then slowly poked his head farther inside. He got the dry heaves as his eyes found Red's torso, headless, propped up against the far wall. The legless, headless, armless trunk was covered with blood.

Don could not help himself as his numbed and horrified

eyes settled on Red's head. It was sitting on the window ledge on the south side of the cabin. The eyes were wide and staring, still terrified in death, the mouth open in a silent scream.

Don screamed. His howl of fright spooked his own horse and caused a minor stampede in the corral. Don ran to the hitchrail just as his horse reared up, breaking one rein and trying to run. Don grabbed the horse's neck and talked to him, rubbing him and stroking the animal's neck, quietly soothing him, calming him. It stood, trembling in fear, not liking the blood-smell rolling in invisible waves from the cabin.

"I don't like it either," Don said, as he led the animal to the tack shed. There, he replaced the broken rein. He squatted down and had him a smoke, trying to calm his own badly jangled nerves. He quickly smoked the cigarette down to a butt and crushed it out under his boot, then he stood up, walked to a horse trough, and bathed his face and neck in the cool water. Back at his horse, he loosened the cinch and let the horse blow and drink, then he tightened it down, smiling as the horse puffed up, as usual. He waited until the animal blew and then tightened the cinch down right.

His hat was over there by the broken door, but he wasn't gonna go back there and get it. He swung into the saddle and lit out for the nearest phone, which was a good eight or ten miles off, over there at that farmer's house just off the county road.

The young cowboy could not recall ever being so rattled in all his life.

"When I called dad this morning, I asked him about that book he'd mentioned last night. No help. He couldn't remember who wrote it or what the title was. Martin, it may have been a book of fiction and dad just got confused." The strange stirring within Gary had ceased. For a time.

"Gary, what are we facing out there at the fairgrounds?"

121

Martin asked. "I've had a dozen changes of heart over the past twelve hours. I've flip-flopped my opinions so many times I feel like a mental yo-yo."

"Do you believe that's the original Nabo out there at the fairgrounds, Martin?"

"Yes. I know it's impossible, but yes, I do."

Gary experienced a numbness around his heart. Looking at his lifelong friend, he knew that Martin was experiencing the same sensation.

"What are you guys talking about?" Janet asked.

"If this investigator from the state is the best in the world, honey," her husband told her, "it still isn't going to solve anything."

"I don't understand that."

"There is nothing anyone can do," Gary tried to put it all into words. But he knew he'd failed.

"Will somebody, anybody, please explain?" Janet pleaded with the men.

Martin finally took it. "What is the investigator going to do, Janet? If Gary and I are correct in our assumptions, it's laughable to even consider bringing charges. How do you bring charges against a person, or a group of people, who, from all available evidence, have been dead for decades?"

Janet looked first at Martin, then at her husband. She shifted her gaze back to Martin and yelled, "But you just let your kids go off downtown to eat! Alone! And my kids are with them!"

"Janet . . ." Martin spread his hands, "what do you want us to do. Nabo had Jeanne in his hands yesterday and didn't harm her. He helped her. I'm not going to sit on my kids until I'm given a reason to do so."

Janet sat down on a hassock and put her face into her hands.

The waitress had taken their orders, grudgingly, and stalked away, muttering obscenities under her breath. She slammed the ticket down on the counter and said, "Fix this for the little turds over there!"

The kids exchanged looks at that but said nothing. They looked around the room while they waited for their lunch.

Two ministers traded curses for a moment and then resumed eating as if nothing had happened.

"Hey, you lazy bitch!" the cook shouted from the kitchen. "Here's the slop for the turds!"

More looks of amazement mingled with a bit of alarm were exchanged between Mark and Linda and Susan and Rich. Gary Jr. was enjoying it all immensely, grinning hugely.

The plates of food were tossed on the table. "And eat every lousy bit of it!" the waitress snarled at them.

"Place is weird!" Linda summed up the feelings of them all, except for Gary, who had grabbed up a chicken leg and was gnawing on it, his attention on the food, no longer interested in the antics of those in the dining room.

Rich cut his eyes, an uneasy expression on his face. "What's the matter with everybody?" He kept his voice low. "They're acting like they're half crazy, or drunk, or something."

"It's spooky," Susan said.

"At least that," Linda agreed. "I think we made a mistake coming here."

"Pass the ketchup," Gary said.

His sister looked at him. "On *chicken!*"

"You eat peanut butter and banana sandwiches," the boy fired back. "So gimme the ketchup."

Linda grimaced and handed the boy the ketchup bottle before the conversation could turn any worse.

"He has such a way with words," Susan said.

Linda nodded her head and cut her eyes just in time to see Mr. Morris, who owned a clothing store, lean across the table and give a backhand slap to the face of Mrs. Morris. The blow knocked the woman out of her chair and sent her to the floor.

"I can't believe this," Mark said, his mouth hanging open.

Mrs. Morris crawled to her feet, profanity rolling in

soiled waves from her mouth, her lip split and bleeding. She picked up her lunch plate, piled high with mashed potatoes and gravy, roast beef and green beans, and let her husband have it, right in the face. He toppled over backward and landed on the floor.

The kids stared.

"Kick him in the nuts, Sally!" a woman screamed. "That'll get the bastard's attention."

The husband of the woman who suggested a kick to the parts reached across the table and busted her right in the mouth.

The woman climbed to her feet, snarling at her husband, her mouth bloody. She picked up a metal serving tray and clanged him right on top of his bald dome, bending the tray around his bean and sending the man to the floor, stunned and bleeding.

The cafe erupted in a wild melee as everybody joined in, cursing and shouting and screaming with the first person they could find, in most cases, their spouse. Mashed potatoes and gravy and green beans and chicken fried steaks and roast beef and liver and onions were flying throughout the place. Mark grabbed up Gary Jr. and slung him over his shoulder, and the young people hit the air, getting outside just as a chair came crashing through the glass of the front door.

The young people were back at the Tressalt house in five minutes, happy to have a bowl of stew, and relating their adventures to their startled parents.

"What next?" Gary muttered, disgust in his voice.

Martin shook his head and looked at Gary. "You'll be busy this afternoon, patching up the wounded."

"If nothing else happens."

Janet answered the phone and listened for a moment, her face tightening. "Yes, right away." She hung up. "That was Audie Meadows, Gary. There's been a murder up on the north range of the Bar-S. He said he'd pick you and Martin up in five minutes."

*　　　*　　　*

124

"I still can't figure what got into Alicia today," Gary said, as they rolled toward the murder site in the sheriff's department's four-wheel drive Blazer. Audie drove, Gary in the front seat, Martin in the back.

"I have no idea. But that was the greasiest tone of voice I've heard from her in a while. At least since yesterday," he added.

Audie kept his mouth shut and concentrated on his driving. Half the town knew what was going on with Alicia, but he sure wasn't going to be the one to inform the husband.

"You two getting along all right?" Gary asked.

"No. I thought we were, but lately it's been a silent war zone around the house." Martin abruptly changed the subject. "Audie, do you know anything about this Red person?"

The deputy was glad for the switch. "Yes, sir. He's a good hand, but a sorry person."

"You want to elaborate on that?"

"Yes, sir. Red is, was, not a very nice person. One of those mean types that Lyle and Jim like to have around them all the time. A bully. Always picking fights with people. He was a cruel man—cruel to animals and to people. I just can't think of anything good to say about him. Most of the hands that Lyle and Jim hire are like that; same with Cameron and Clark. The only saloon that'll have them is one up in South Dakota. They've been barred from every joint in this county. They respect force, and that's it. Red will not be missed," Audie summed up the short eulogy for the dear departed Red, then added, "I don't even know the son of a bitch's last name."

"Sounds like you've had a couple of run-ins with him," Martin said, unable to hide his smile. Audie was not a man known for keeping his feelings under a bucket.

"Yes, sir. Exactly two. Last time I wore a slapjack out on his head. He had so many knots on his gourd when I got through with him he looked like a billy goat. I told him if I ever found him in Holland again, chances were real good that Miller over at the funeral home would be stuffin' him.

I guess he believed me. He never came back."

"The man who reported the incident?" Martin asked.

"A cowboy name of Don Talbolt. He was pretty shook up. Don's a nice guy, believe it or not. 'Bout my age. Got a good head on his shoulders. Don works for a year, saves his money, then goes back to school until his money runs out, then goes back to work. He's got three years toward his degree at the university at Laramie."

"What is he doing working for Lyle Steele?"

"I guess he needed a job. Steele does pay top wages."

A few miles farther up the road, they pulled into the drive of a small farm and Audie waved to Don to climb in. "I'll bring you back for your horse, Don." He introduced him to Gary and Martin.

"I called Mr. Steele, Audie. I thought he had a right to know."

"That's all right. If he's there ahead of us, tampering around with evidence, it'll give me an excuse to put him in jail."

Don glanced at Martin and smiled. "I figured you to have horns and a tail, Mr. Holland."

Martin had to laugh. "Not only does the boss dislike me, but it appears that most of his hands don't much care for me either."

"You got that right, sir," the young cowboy settled it. "But don't include me in that bunch. I knew I made a mistake within a week of signing on with that outfit."

They chatted for a few minutes and Martin formed an instant liking for the cowboy. His boots were worn and his shirt and jeans patched, but he was working and saving his money for an education. Martin made up his mind.

"What do you know about lumber, Don?"

"I spent a summer building houses. Roughing out and framing."

"You want to get away from the Bar-S?"

"I sure do!" There was considerable feeling in the short sentence. "I just don't like those fellows. There's something, well, cruel about them. And I hate that kid of Steele's."

126

"You're at the end of a long list, Don," Audie told him.

Martin stuck out his hand and surprised, the cowboy took it. "You want a job working for me at my lumber yard? I guarantee you I'll pay more than Lyle Steele."

"But you don't even know me, sir!"

"I make very quick judgments of people, Don. How about it?"

"You just hired yourself a hand, Mr. Holland."

"Fine. There's a couple of rooms behind the offices you can fix up and use. It'll be good to have someone on the premises at night to look after the place."

Don told them about the carnage at the cabin, ending with, "I can talk about it all day, but you won't believe it until you see it. And I can truthfully say that I hope I never see anything like it again."

Audie's stomach did a slow rollover at the young cowboy's depiction of the scene. All he had known prior to picking Don up was that there had been a murder.

"Like I said, Martin: you're gonna have to see it to believe it."

"How about tracks, Don?"

"None I picked up on. For sure no car or truck tracks. But to tell you all the truth, I really didn't spend a whole lot of time concerning myself with tracks—except for the ones I made gettin' away from that place."

"Robbery?" Gary inquired.

Don shook his head. "I don't think so. Some . . . wild beast did this. But I sure don't know what kind it might have been. Robbery? No, sir. My rifle and Red's rifle were still on the pegs. And I'd bought a new hat to wear to the fair Thursday night. Saved my money for it. A brand new Stetson. It was still in the box, by my bunk, the box all blood-splattered. I don't want it."

Martin was the first to ask the question that he suspected was on the minds of them all. "Was Red making plans to go to the carnival, Don?"

Don glanced at him. "That's an odd question, Mr. Holland. But it's sort of funny that you would ask it. I did mention the carnival to him and he near took my head off.

127

Told me not to ever mention nothing about no carnival to him again. Not ever again. Red was a surly man to begin with, but I thought I was gonna have to fight him that morning.''

"This might seem strange to you, Don," Audie said, "but bear with me. How about the rest of the hands—the older hands? How did they feel about the carnival coming to Holland?"

"Well . . . now that you mention it, that's sort of funny, too. Most of the men are a lot older than me. Most of them in their late forties or early fifties. Just like it is at the Watson spread. Very few young hands. But there wasn't any of them real happy about the carnival. Not that many would talk to me about it. I had to just sort of pick up on bits and pieces of conversation. I was the outsider at the ranch, if you know what I mean. I just did my job and kept to myself. I'm happy to get gone from that place, tell you the truth.''

They spotted the carrion birds when they were still miles from the line shack. The buzzards had already begun their slow death-circling. As they pulled up to the cabin, a few of the huge, grotesque-looking birds had begun to strut and wobble toward the house with the broken door and smashed windows and smell of death. One had his sharp eyes on the mangled and bloody leg outside the cabin.

The buzzards reluctantly flew off as the men shouted and waved their arms.

But they did not go far, rising ponderously into the air and resuming their slow circling high overhead, gliding effortlessly on the currents. They would wait, with the patience of a million years inbred.

Audie took one look inside and began taking pictures with his 35mm. He had instructed the others to stay back and don't screw up any tracks that might have been left. Finally, he reappeared in the broken doorway and waved the men in.

Don chose to remain outside, by the Blazer; he'd seen enough of the inside of that cabin. He never wanted to look at it again.

Martin stayed by the door, looking in. He'd seen worse in 'Nam, and since he had not known the dead man, and probably wouldn't have liked him had he known him—based on Audie's summation of the man's character—he could view the carnage with some degree of detachment. But still, it was not pleasant.

"Mr. Holland," Don called, pointing. "Mr. Steele comin' in."

Martin stepped away from the door and walked to the Blazer, looking out over the vast emptiness of the grasslands. Lyle was hotrodding his fancy pickup, gunning it toward the cabin, several more trucks right behind him, coming up fast.

Audie stepped out of the cabin and his face was hard with anger. "That arrogant, dumb son of a—!" He stepped directly into the path of Lyle's pickup. When the dust had settled, he said, "Now back the trucks up about five hundred feet, Steele, and stay with them. No telling what evidence you've ruined now."

Lyle stepped out of his truck, grinning arrogantly, several of his hands with him, their hands balled into fists, ready for a fight.

"I told you they'd come a day, Meadows," Lyle said. "And today is that day."

"I don't have time to chat with the likes of you, Steele. I've got a dead body in the cabin, I'm trying to reconstruct the scene, and as for you, get moving or I'll arrest you for interference with an officer of the law."

Steele stepped closer. "You don't give orders on this land, Meadows."

Martin reached inside the Blazer and came out with a sawed-off twelve gauge shotgun. He shucked a round into the chamber and things got real quiet, real quick.

Martin said, "I carried one of these often when I was in 'Nam—and used it. Take my word for it, boys: they make a real mess out of a man's belly."

The Bar-S hands, to a man, stopped dead in their tracks, and then slowly began backing up.

Lyle looked at the shotgun, then lifted his eyes to meet Martin's steady gaze. "You a real hot-shot with a gun in your hands, ain't you, Holland?"

Right then, at that moment, Martin reached the breaking point. The past few days had been confusing, frightening, and in most cases, unpleasant. As far as he was concerned, as illogical as it seemed—even though he was convinced it was true—everything that had been happening was due in no small part to Lyle Steele and his partner, Jim Watson. He laid the shotgun on the hood of the Blazer and walked over to Lyle.

When he came within swinging distance, Martin decked the man.

NINE

While a stunned and surprised Lyle Steele was flat on his back on the ground, Martin took off his sunglasses and watch and handed them to Audie, who was standing with his mouth open at the suddenness of Martin's attack and his following calmness.

"This won't take long," Martin told him, then turned and clubbed Lyle on the side of the head just as the man was trying to get up.

Lyle hit the ground again. He shook his head, roared like an angry bull, and tried to grab Martin around the knees, to bring him down.

That move got him a knee in the face. Martin felt the man's nose give under the impact and Lyle's hands lose their grip from his legs.

Martin stepped back and gave the man an opportunity to get to his boots, and that was not something that Martin was noted for doing. But he wanted to whip the man at his own game. It was intensely personal and a bit on the childish side, he knew, but it was something he wanted. Martin's hands were balled into big, flat-knuckled fists, held chest high, moving in tight little circles. He felt good. Felt the adrenaline surging within him. He was looking forward to this scrap.

But he was not so smug as to feel he would come out of it unscathed. Lyle was quick and tough, and Martin would have to be ready for anything.

While Martin had not done the type of heavy physical work that Lyle had done all his life, Martin nevertheless was in excellent shape for a man just over forty. His was a naturally heavy musculature, and he kept in shape by using the small gym he'd built in his basement and by running several miles every day, no matter what the weather. He had never backed down from a fight in his life.

And had lost few of them.

With blood leaking from his bent beak, Lyle charged Martin, both fists swinging. Martin took a hard pop to his belly and it stung. That was followed by a left to the side of his head and that hurt, too. Lyle could punch; give the man his due.

But so could Martin, who was taller and had a longer reach than Lyle, and he gave the man a combo—a left and a right to the head—just to remind him. Then he stepped in and planted a right fist to the man's heart, staggering him. Martin stepped in closer and caught a fist on the jaw, snapping his head back and loosening a tooth for him. He spat out a glob of blood. Sensing premature victory, Lyle closed with him and Martin gave him a kick to the kneecap that brought a yelp of pain. Martin backhanded the man and stepped in, swinging.

The men stood close and slugged it out, both of them drawing blood from the other. Martin's lip was cut and bleeding and there was a cut on his cheek—and his head hurt, as well—but for every punch Lyle landed, Martin landed two, always a punishing body blow followed by a blast to the head that jarred the rancher. The blows were telling on Steele. His eyes were closing and his face was battered and bruised and bleeding.

Martin tangled his shoes with the man's boots and brought Lyle down to the dust. Martin clubbed him on the back of the neck as he went down, then stepped back, catching his breath and allowing the rancher to slowly get to his feet.

"I'll kill you, Holland!" Lyle panted, as the blood leaked out of his mouth.

Martin laughed at him and taunted him. "You've done a piss-poor job of it so far, Steele."

Lyle's face darkened with hate and rage and he swung, leaving himself wide open. Martin stepped inside as he started his punch chest high, planting it directly on the side of the rancher's jaw.

Lyle Steele hit the dirt and did not move.

Martin pointed a finger at the knot of hands, gathering around and staring in disbelief at their fallen boss. "I got a couple of more rounds left in me if anybody else wants to waltz."

Audie stepped forward, as did Don and Gary, the doctor holding a broken axe handle in his hand.

"That's it!" Dick Mason barked the orders. Dick was foreman of the Bar-S and not a man to trifle with. He looked at Martin and smiled faintly as his eyes twinkled with rough humor. "It's over, Mr. Holland. The boss opened the dance and now he's paid the caller. It's over and done with."

Martin let his fists fall to his side. He smiled at the foreman. "Deal." He looked at the Bar-S hands. "Couple of you men take your boss back to the ranch. The rest of you scatter. Dick, stay for a moment, if you will please."

The Bar-S hands, to a man, didn't like Martin, but they did as he ordered, picking up Lyle—who was still unconscious—and carried him to his truck. Martin Holland might be a town fellow who wore a suit and tie, but he could sure fight. And by God, there wasn't no backdown in him.

But all knew, including Martin, that this was by no means the end of it.

Dick Mason had come into this part of the country from up Montana way, and he came highly respected as a ranch foreman. He was married, with children, and was neither a hard drinker nor a womanizer. He simply did his job and did it well.

While Martin washed his face and neck and soaked his hands in a horse trough, Dick took a look inside the cabin and then walked to the outside of the tack room where Martin was waiting.

"You're a wahoo, Mr. Holland. But I figured that from

133

the git-go."

"Oh?"

"Yeah. It's in the eyes, Mr. Holland . . ."

"Call me Martin, please."

"All right, Martin," the foreman said easily. "It's all in the eyes and the bearing of a man. Worst whippin' I ever got, and it landed me in the hospital, was from a man a lot like you. Suit and tie and such. Every time you knocked Lyle down this day, it took a lot for you not to step up and kick his face in, didn't it?"

"Sure did."

"I thought as much; and I'll keep that in mind. Anyway, them ol' boys that just left here, they won't like you any better than they did before you whipped the boss, but they'll walk light around you. Now then, what about all that mess in the line shack?"

"You don't seem too torn-up about Red's death."

"Red was a ornery, no-good. Left up to me, I'd have fired him and about ninety percent of the other hands on the Bar-S first day. That answer your question?"

"For a fact." He waved Dick to a wooden box and Martin sat down on the side of the trough. "Dick, you want to hear a rather bizarre story?"

"I'd rather hear a tale than have to fight you!"

Dick shifted around on the box and fished in his vest pocket for a cigarette. He lit up, then shoved his hat back on his head. "Martin, that's the weirdest tale I believe I've ever heard in all my life."

"I know. And I wouldn't blame you a bit if you sat back and laughed in my face."

The foreman sighed. "No . . . I won't do that. 'Cause what you just told me makes some sense . . . in a way. Ever since news of that carnival comin' into town hit the ranch, tempers have been stretched tight, and the hands—the older ones—are behaving, well, funny."

"Some of them have been with the Bar-S and the Double-W all their lives. More than a few were born right there on the spreads. They're almost all local people."

Dick agreed. "And they might have had something to do with that carnival fire years back—is that what you're getting at?"

Martin nodded his head and spat out a glob of blood from a cut inside his mouth. "The sorry bastard can throw a punch, I'll give him that."

Dick chuckled and then sobered. "Lyle Steele will not forget this day, Martin. Tattoo that on your arm and keep a good eye on your back trail. And tell your kids to be careful. Lyle isn't wrapped too tight and neither is that punk kid of his. Both of them are as crazy as road lizards."

"If you feel that way, Dick, why do you work for Lyle?"

"Money. Pure and simple. He's a jackasss, but he pays top wages. Provides me and the family with a nice house, all utilities paid, and gives me a good bonus at year's end." He smiled. "I have a master's degree in Agri-business, Martin. I not only run the ranch operation, but I run the farming end of it too. Couple more years, and I'll be able to head on back to Montana and add to my little spread up there."

"And Lyle Steele can go to hell."

"That's probably not quite as strong as what I'll tell him when that day comes."

And Martin had made yet another friend that day.

Gary and Audie and Don joined them. Don told the foreman he was quitting and Dick congratulated him on finally showing some good sense.

Gary said, "I can tell you only this about Red's death: nothing human did it."

The foreman sighed audibly. "I think I'll send the wife and kids back up to Montana for a week or so. Be on the safe side. She's been wantin' to see her mother anyway."

"No tracks that I can pick up," Audie informed them. "Horse or vehicle or foot. Nothing." He shook his head. "I've got to call the sheriff about this. Too much has happened for him to be left out in the cold and uninformed." He walked back to his Blazer to call in to the Holland P.D. They would relay to the county seat. From this point, almost eighty miles away.

"You need me anymore, Deputy?" Dick called.

135

Audie stopped and turned around. "No. This'll do it, Dick. Thanks for sticking around. And, Dick, keep this under your hat, OK?"

"No sweat. Audie, when you find out if any of, well, the theory you all share is true, or not true, let me know, will you?"

"I think you'll know, Dick," Martin took it. "I think we're all going to know at just about the same time. Will you be coming into town for the fair?"

"I think I'd better."

"Then I'll see you there. Stop by the house for a drink."

"I'll do that."

After the foreman of the Bar-S had left, Don said, "I forgot to tell you all something. I don't know whether this has anything at all to do with this . . . murder, but I can tell you it was just about the oddest thing I ever had happen to me."

He told them about hearing, or thinking he was hearing, the truck starter grinding and the moaning and the voice calling out about coming home, or wanting to come home, or something like that, way out to hell and gone in the empty grasslands.

Martin and Gary exchanged quick glances, each one thinking about Martin's dad, murdered and buried, truck and all, up near the state line.

Martin shook his head, absolutely refusing to accept that. "No."

Don looked at him. "Beg pardon, sir?"

"Nothing. It isn't important." But he couldn't turn loose of it. "Don, do you think you could find this place again?"

"Well . . . I could probably get you to within fifty yards of it, I guess." He looked at the men. Tried to grin; didn't quite make it. "Ah, people, you guys don't think, I mean, you, ah, don't think that there's anything to what I just said, do you?"

"We'll brief you on that later, Don," Gary told him. "How about your horse and your gear at the ranch?"

"I'll pick up some things in town. I don't want nothing

136

out of that cabin, and feelings are going to be kind of hard against me at the ranch. I'd as soon avoid the ranch. We'll turn the horse loose. It'll find its way home. But the saddle is mine."

"We'll stop on the way back. How about any wages due you?"

"Dick will see that I get them. Don't worry about that. He's arrow-straight."

"There are sheets and blankets stored at the yard, Don," Martin told him. "Pick out a company truck and use it as your own. The bedding will have to be laundered. Place not far from the yard. And Don, whatever we tell you on the way back to town, and what you've seen out here, don't repeat any of it, okay?"

He nodded his understanding just as Audie walked back to the group.

"I got Miller's coming out to body bag the pieces." He looked at Gary. "You'll want an autopsy."

Gary nodded. "What about Sheriff Grant?"

"Out of town. Gone to some law enforcement seminar out of state. Chief deputy's gone to Florida to pick up a prisoner. Left this morning. I didn't say anything to the chief investigator about what's happened up here; except to tell him there'd been a murder. No details. Maybe I should have. But I didn't."

"Perhaps that's for the best," Gary agreed. "Hell, who would believe us? Anyway, when is this state investigator coming in?"

"She'll probably check in late this afternoon or early evening. I got her a room at the motel. Name is McClain. Frenchy McClain. And she's good. Knows her business. She's quick and tough. Dropped the hammer on two people over the years. Killed both of them."

"There's aren't many women with the state police, are there?" Don asked.

Audie grinned. "Not *any* like Frenchy. She's a knock-out. You'll see."

*   *   *

Monday morning.

Martin had run his miles and done his exercises. Back at the house, he had showered and changed clothes and was sitting on the front porch, drinking coffee and watching the sun unfold the new day. But he couldn't make the term "nice morning" fit. It was a different kind of morning. One that Martin didn't like but could not put a finger on the *why* of that feeling. He struggled to find a word that fit it. Tainted, came to him. There was a flatness to the dawning. He had noticed it while running. The dogs were not barking and playing and running along with him as many of them did. They lay under or on the porches, silently watching him as he jogged past. They were not unfriendly . . . that was not the mood Martin felt from the animals. Wary, was more like it. Suspicious. Like they could sense some . . . dreadful thing about to enter and alter their lives. Only a fool believed that animals could not sense an approaching storm or a bad change in the weather.

And they were sure sensing something this day.

Gary had spent several hours Sunday afternoon patching up the men and women involved in the hotel fracas and he had later told Martin that the people could remember absolutely nothing about it. They were alternately astonished or outright indignant and disbelieving when he told them what had happened.

A strangeness was overtaking the town. And Martin could not help but connect *deadly* with it.

Don Talbolt had his quarters as clean and neat as that much-talked-about pin, and was settling right in.

And Alicia was furious at Martin for, as she had put it, "Getting into a fist-fight like some common cowhand in a drunken barroom brawl."

Martin had laughed at her—at first.

Alicia had always been a tad on the snooty side, but of late, she had become almost unbearable with her haughtiness. There were things—and Martin would agree with her in most instances—that decent people just did not engage in. And brawling was one of them. Only the lowest

138

classes beat each other about the head and shoulders with their fists. According to Alicia.

Martin wasn't particularly worried about Alicia's newest opinion of him. She'd either get over it or she wouldn't. But she had irritated him last night by harping about the fight. It seemed to Martin that she was deliberately trying to bring something to a head; but he couldn't imagine what. She kept complaining about what other people might think about his fighting Lyle Steele. Martin had finally told her to shut up about it.

She had then puffed up like a spreading adder and ordered him to leave their bedroom and sleep in the guest room. Martin had looked at her and told her if she wanted to sleep alone then she could leave the room.

Which she had promptly done, stalking out in a cold, silent huff.

He had not seen her that morning. But out of pure spite—amazing how delicious-feeling it was—he had dressed in old jeans and old worn—but comfortable—cowboy boots, and denim western shirt with a frayed collar and cuffs. He knew, of course, how she despised seeing him in that kind of attire.

It was very childish, and he knew it. But he gleefully did it anyway. And to make matters worse—to Alicia's mind, when she did see him that morning—he had gone down to the basement storage room and found his battered old Stetson hat. It was now tilted back on his head.

Now was one of those rare moments when he wished he'd gotten a tattoo in the Army.

It promised, he thought with a smile, to be a very interesting morning.

Those words would return to haunt him.

The kids were up and moving around; he could hear them talking in low tones in the house. They probably would not tarry this morning, having heard their parents quarrel the night before, something they rarely did. But, Martin recollected, over the past six or eight months, their quarreling had taken on a seriousness and bitterness. They had quarreled more in the past half year than in all

139

the previous married years combined.

Martin waved at a neighborhood teenager passing by on her way to school. It was to be a short school week in Holland. School would be dismissed at noon Wednesday, enabling the kids to put the final touches on their fair projects.

The word "final" seemed to stick in Martin's mind. Odd.

Mark and Linda joined him on the porch, Mark with a cup of coffee and Linda with a Coke. His daughter took in her father's slightly swollen lip, the bruise and cut on the side of his face, and his battered hands.

"Mom's up," she informed him, then cut her eyes to her brother.

"That's nice. How is your mother this morning?"

"In a bad mood," his son told him. "I said good morning and I thought she was going to look out the window to check it."

Martin laughed. He stopped laughing when Linda said, "She's packing, dad. I don't know what she's planning on doing."

There was something in his daughter's tone and in both his kids' eyes that told Martin they both did indeed know what was going on. He didn't pursue it. He nodded his head and dug in his pocket, handing the kids some bills, not looking to check the denominations. "Go get you some breakfast at the Dog's Puddle, or whatever that place is called where you kids hang out."

She laughed at him. "It's Chicken & Dog, dad!"

"Whatever."

Linda studied him, checking out his clothing and hat. "You mind if I say something, dad?"

"You probably will anyway. You both got your mother's good looks and my mouth."

She grinned. "You look funky!"

"What is this, Alicia?"

She glanced up from her packing. Martin stood in the

140

doorway to their bedroom. *Theirs,* but for how long? Martin thought.

"I'm moving my things down the hall." Her tone was very cool. She studied his attire through decidedly hostile eyes, her gaze finally settling on his old hat. "Good God, Martin! You look positively dreadful."

"Thank you." He wondered if dreadful and funky lay on the same plane. "How long is this change in sleeping habits going to last?"

"I don't know, Martin. And that is a totally honest answer."

"You want to talk about it?"

"We have. Over and over. It doesn't seem to do any good."

That confused him. He wasn't certain what she was talking about. "This—" He waved his hand at the pile of clothing on the bed, "—is rather sudden, isn't it?"

"No. Not really. If you'd paid attention to details you would have known that it's been building for quite some time."

"I knew something was bothering you. But I didn't know it was this serious. Could have fooled me."

The look she gave him shook him right down to his old cowboy boots. It told him that she had been fooling him, and for some time. "Well. I . . . see."

"I rather doubt it, Martin. Your sensitivity level is rather low."

"What does that mean?"

"There isn't another man." She said it quickly. Too quickly to suit Martin.

"Another woman?" he tried a joke.

"Don't be *disgusting!*" she snapped back.

He stepped into the room, pushed aside the pile of blouses, and sat down on the bed. "Maybe you need a vacation, Alicia. Might be a good time for it. Name your spot. I'll take care of the kids."

"Oh, you'd like that, wouldn't you?"

With a sigh and a shake of his head, he said, "Alicia, what do you mean by that?"

141

"Read anything into it you like."

"My God, the possibilities are endless. Alicia, do you feel all right?"

She turned, facing him squarely. "I think, Martin, that I feel better than I have in years. And I should have done this years ago, I suppose. But the children . . ." She let that drift off. "Anyway, the children are old enough to understand this and to take it all well enough."

"Wait a minute!" Martin almost shouted the words. "Just hold on. Correct me if I'm wrong. But the way I'm reading this is you're going to walk right past the guest room and out the front door. Now you tell me if I'm reading something into this scenario that isn't there?"

"That last sentence is very apropos, Martin."

"What?"

"You know very well what my major was in college, Martin."

He got it then. How could he have ever forgotten? "Oh, no!" he said wearily.

"Yes." The one word held enough frost to ruin a spring garden. "That's the very way you've summed up my feelings for years. And quite frankly, Martin, I'm tired of it."

A line from *Gone With The Wind* sprang into Martin's head. The very last line.

Alicia had majored in drama at the university. But she was just not a good actress.

"Honey," Martin said patiently, thinking this was all covered ground, "I told you years ago, when you came up with this little theatre idea, that I'd back you."

"I have money of my own, Martin!" she popped at him. "I don't need your money. What I needed was your personal support, and you did not give it to me."

What you wanted was for me to tell you you were another Faye Dunaway, and baby, you ain't. "Alicia! I'm not an actor. I'm a businessman, with a lot of businesses in this area to look after. Not to mention a ranch and farm operation down in Colorado, a mine and mineral—"

She cut the air with a curt slash of her hand. "Enough!"

she shouted at him. "I don't need to be reminded of your great wealth, Martin. Great wealth!" she said contemptuously, her eyes sweeping him. He could feel the scorn from across the room and wondered if what was taking place in town had anything to do with this? "You look like some saddlebum."

He couldn't help it; a smile played around his lips. "I can say with all honesty, Alicia, that I dressed just for you."

"I certainly don't doubt that!" she came right back at him. "And to me, that is just another indication of your tastelessness and your utter lack of respect and support for me."

Martin got a little hot under his battered hat at that. "Alicia, I told you when you started this theatre group thing it would flop. This town is simply not big enough to support it. Or cultured enough, for that matter; and it hurts me to say that. This is cowboy country. Honey, you know that I enjoy the plays and the opera and the ballet on PBS—we've always watched them together. But I am not an *actor!*" He flung his arms wide, wincing slightly at the pain from Steele's blows that he'd blocked with his arms. "And I will not make a fool of myself by wandering around on stage, wearing a mini-skirt and carrying a wooden sword and yelling, *Et tu, Brute!*"

The look in her eyes summed it all up. That, and a whole lot more.

And Martin could not believe it; did not want to believe it. There had to be some other explanation. Something else behind it all. "Alicia, what are you holding back from me? Why not get it all out into the open, now, and let's talk it out."

She sighed and shook her head. "Because you just can't, or won't, see it, Martin."

"Well, obviously I don't. That's why I'm requesting we talk about it."

"You're not going to like it, and believe this or not, I don't want to hurt you. I want us to be friends."

The kiss of death from a woman's mouth, Martin

143

recalled. Anytime a woman says, "Oh, but I do want us to be friends," hang it up, find your shoes, and start looking for the door. "Uh-huh. Right," was all he could trust himself to say at that moment.

"Martin, you are perfectly content to remain exactly as you are." She arched an eyebrow as she eyeballed his bruised face. "Perhaps even to regress some. But I, on the other hand, wish to grow. Now . . . don't sit there all dressed up in your cowboy clothes and look so startled. You know it's true. We've discussed this very thing time after time, and you haven't made any effort to change."

And, he was forced silently to admit, they had discussed it. But he had never taken her threats of leaving seriously.

"All right, Alicia. So say it. Are you leaving, or not?"

"You really want to press the issue, don't you, Martin?"

He shrugged. "Why drag it out? If you've made up your mind, so be it."

"Very well. Perhaps that is for the best. Mark can remain here. I shall take Linda, of course."

That got Martin hot. He pointed a finger at her. "You walk out that door, the kids stay right here, with me! For when you walk, with your only reason for doing so some unfulfilled, middle-aged theatrical urgings, that is desertion on your part, just any ol' way you want to cut it. Now you hear me well, Alicia. You want a nasty court fight that I guarantee will last well past Linda's eighteenth birthday, you just try to take her. You push me on this and I'll have Linda on a plane bound for a girl's school in Europe in the *morning!*" He shouted the last, rising from the bed, his bulk huge in the bedroom and his bruised face flushed with anger.

"How dare you threaten me!"

"Oh, I'm not threatening you, honey. Not at all. I'm just telling you the cold, hard, cruel facts of how all this is going to be."

"I see." Her voice was hushed. "Well. Do I walk over to my parents' old homeplace, or will you allow me to take the station wagon?"

Martin knew then that he had, at least for the moment,

won. Alicia did not like confrontation. And, he felt guilty even thinking it, he knew that she was slightly afraid of him when he lost his temper. Even though he had never given her the slightest reason to think he would do physical harm to her.

"Don't be ridiculous, Alicia. Take the car. Keep it. Take anything in this house that is yours, or was," he said sarcastically, "ours."

The sarcasm was not lost on her. Her mouth tightened and her eyes narrowed. He knew that she knew that when he made a decision, there was no turning back. That if she walked, keep walking. For that was the end of it.

She said nothing.

"Take anything you want except the kids. But get it all out and be clear of here today, Alicia. I'll arrange for a couple of hands to help you and get some company trucks over here. And I'll have a man to open up and air out your parents' old place. Now you tell me firm, right up front: is this what you want?"

"Can't we be civil?"

"Just answer the question."

"You seem to be doing all the talking, Martin. Carry on."

"That's no answer from you. And you're still holding back from me. I don't like that one bit. I have never lied to you. Nor has there ever been another woman. Not even in 'Nam. I always assumed I was getting the same kind of respect from you. Now I'm not so sure of that. Is there another man, Alicia?"

She stood in the room, holding a folded blouse, saying nothing. Aloud, that is. But the silence told it all.

"Say it, Alicia. Is this what you want?"

This time there was no hesitation. "Yes, Martin. I think that it's best."

He picked up the phone.

And nearly eighteen years of marriage went down the drain.

TEN

Martin left the house just seconds after arranging for the men to come help his wife move her things out and to have another man open up her parents' old home just a few blocks away. Martin checked in at his mayor's offices, did some paperwork, and then spent most of the rest of the morning at his business offices. His people—who had all heard the story about the fight with Steele—took in his bruised face and slightly swollen hands and the cut on his lip, and said nothing.

After about an hour of the silence and of feeling the curious looks of his office staff, Martin glanced up, a smile forming on his lips, and yelled through the open door to his office, "Well, at least I whipped the bastard!"

That broke the tension and after the laughter died down, work flowed smoothly.

Martin, from his glassed office, would study his people from time to time. They all appeared normal—at least for now.

At 11:30, unable to keep his mind on his work, he packed it in and went home, fixing a couple of sandwiches and a big glass of milk, taking his lunch into the den.

Alicia had been busy. She had cleaned out her closets and taken what furniture she'd wanted, moving everything over to her parents' old place, which had been deserted ever since the death of her mother, several years back.

Martin sighed heavily. He did not look forward to telling the kids.

The day was pleasant and Martin had left the front door

147

open. The slamming of a car door turned his head. He could tell by the fast footsteps up the walk that it was Gary.

"Martin?" the doctor called from the front porch, through the screen door.

"Come on in, Gary!"

The doctor entered and looked around him, his eyes picking up on the few pieces of missing furniture and the assorted bric-a-brac Alicia had taken with her. He muttered something terribly obscene under his breath and said, "I almost called the man who told me about this a liar. Glad I didn't."

"Small town, buddy. News travels fast. It's true, as you can see. You had lunch?"

"No. Janet's over with Alicia, at the old homeplace. Been helping her get settled in. I've been busy patching up a few more of those who were involved in that hotel fight yesterday. None of them remember a thing about it. Damn place is getting stranger and stranger."

"I won't argue that. Fix yourself something to eat and join me. We still have some planning to do. Alicia and me splitting the sheets aside, the problems that faced us yesterday—the town, the carnival—are still with us. And I'm just as confused as ever."

Gary fixed a sandwich and poured a glass of milk, joining his friend in the den. "I won't press you to talk about you and Alicia, Martin. But whenever you're ready, I'm here."

Martin chewed reflectively for a moment. "Tell you the truth, Gary—and this is going to sound awfully stupid on my part—I don't really know what happened. Right before I went to work—and yes, I went dressed like this— Linda called me funky-looking and Alicia said I looked positively dreadful . . ."

"Your reaction to that?" Gary was studying his friend closely.

". . . No reaction. Anyway, Alicia said that she guessed love had died somewhere along the way. She said that she felt I was holding her back." He arched an eyebrow, looking at his friend. "The actress bit."

148

Gary groaned. "Oh, no, Martin! Even Janet, her best friend all her life, will tell you that Alicia is a terrible actess."

"Oh, I know. Anyway, she said that I was stagnant; and she was angry because I refused to take part in the theatre group." Martin laughed. "Hell, I can't sing, I can't dance, and I sure can't act." He sobered and shrugged. "I guess it's all going to hit me later on. But right now, all I'm feeling is terrible about having to tell the kids."

Then Gary took some of the load off his shoulders. "They already know, Martin. Right after I was told, Susan called me from school. The kids know, and they're taking it well, Susan said. And—" He paused.

"And . . . what?"

"Well, reading between the lines of Susan's comments, I got the impression they both knew it was coming."

Martin nodded, not terribly surprised. "I'll talk to them later about it." He frowned. "Small town. Well, maybe I'll get to the bottom of it all someday. Have you seen Audie today?"

"He called earlier. Said he and that state man, ah, woman, were going out to the cabin where Red was killed. He said they'd be here, at your place, about 12:30. I said I'd close at noon and meet them here. I got so busy I forgot to call you. And all that took place before I learned about you and Alicia. I'm sorry. You want to postpone the meeting?"

"No. Forget it. No harm done. It might be the best thing for me, get my mind off my troubles for a time." He glanced at his watch. "They should be coming along at any moment, now."

"I have to hand it to you, Martin. You're taking this situation a lot better than I would. And I mean that."

"Well, maybe I'm in some sort of mild mental shock, or something like that. Perhaps later on I'll throw a tantrum or get drunk or do something equally stupid—but I doubt it. You want to hear a truth, Gary?"

"Lay it on me."

"My overriding, or primary emotion is, so far, pure

149

relief. Just before you got here, I was realizing that what Alicia said was true. But unknowing to her, and to me, until this morning, was the fact that it was working both ways. Actually, we are complete opposites, wouldn't you say?"

"Yeah. I guess you're right." Gary eyeballed Martin's attire for a moment and then busted out laughing.

"What's the matter with you?"

"Martin . . . you do look funky!"

And Martin instantly regretted his funkiness when he met Sgt. Frenchy McClain. The emotion came as quite a surprise to him. Then he realized that the relief he had spoken of was real. He realized with a slight jar, that Alicia had been right all the way down the line: theirs had turned into a marriage of routine and convenience.

And he also realized that unless he wanted to go celibate—which he sure didn't—he was back in the dating game. And that realization was real.

Martin pegged Frenchy as in her early to mid-thirties. Short black hair as shiny as sunlight off a raven's wing. Deep blue eyes. About five-five, a great figure. Perhaps a touch of Latin or Indian in her veins.

"You have a lovely home, Mr. Holland," Frenchy said. If his manner of dress shocked or amused her, her eyes did not show it.

"It's Martin. And thank you. The house is a bit bare, I'm afraid. My wife just left me this morning."

That shocked her. She blinked and stared at him for a moment. "Then we've sure picked a rotten time to meet with you, Martin."

He waved that off. "Not really." He looked at Audie. "You should have warned her."

"I didn't know myself until right now! We've spent all morning out at Red's cabin and then over at Hank's house. I'm sorry, Mr. Holland."

"It happens, Audie. But at least it was an amiable parting of the ways. More or less," he added drily as he met Frenchy's eyes. "Have you had lunch?"

"No. But—"

Martin held up a hand. "I'll fix some sandwiches and put on a pot of coffee. Then we'll get down to business. Please, both of you, make yourself comfortable."

"I'll help with lunch," Frenchy volunteered.

"That would be . . . nice." Martin looked into the deep blues. "Yes. Thank you."

"How you feelin', Boss?" a hand asked.

"Not worth a good goddamn!" Lyle snapped. His words were slurry, spoken through swollen, puffy lips. He sat on the front porch of his ranchhouse, leaning against a pillow, easing his battered ribs on that side. Nothing was broken, but he sure hurt. One eye was still closed and his face was swollen and cut and bruised. His nose, while not broken, was sore as a boil.

The ranchhand didn't know what to do or how to respond to that.

"Forget it, Ned," Lyle told him—as close as the hand would ever get to an apology from his boss. "None of it was your fault." He wasn't about to say it right out loud, but that Martin Holland could hit like the kick of a mule. "Ned? Tell the boys that Thursday is gonna be a day off for everybody. We'll leave early, all of us, and head into Holland. We're gonna make sure that this fair is one that ever'body is gonna remember. And the treats is on me. Pass the word."

Ned grinned. "Yes, sir!"

Lyle leaned back and mentally wallowed in his dark hatred for Martin Holland. He had a plan to get back at Martin for the beating he'd taken at his hands. And it was through Martin's daughter, or into Martin's daughter was a better way of looking at it. And after Lyle got through with her, he'd give her to his men for some fun.

He chuckled softly. He couldn't laugh too much. His ribs hurt.

Jim Watson was, like Clark and Cameron were doing,

151

informing his men that Thursday was going to be a holiday for everybody. They were all, en mass, going to the Holland Fair. Free booze for everybody, as much as they wanted.

By God! Jim thought, I'll show that Martin Holland a thing or two—always did want to get into Alicia Holland's pants. And it'd be one more good excuse to get away from his own old lady and them squallin' useless kids.

"Are you going to take me to the fair, Jim?" his wife asked from the screen door of the front porch.

"No!"

Fine, she thought. While you're at the fair, I'll just take me a tippy-toe over to Joe Carroll's spread and have me a good old time. More fun than riding the ferris wheel anyway.

No truer words had she ever thought.

Alma Sessions, the little girl who had been stricken with seizures and the unknown tongue a couple of days back, thought she just about had it all figured out. If she could get the Dennison girl to take just one more step, and she put just enough power behind the playground swing, the seat should catch the girl right in the face. All the others in her little circle of friends, Bette and Virginia and David and Norm, all thought that would be a fun thing to see and do.

"Oh, Shirley!" Alma called sweetly. "Look here!"

Alma had shoved the seat just as the last word left her mouth. The wooden seat caught Shirley flush in the mouth and knocked her sprawling, busting several teeth and smashing her lips. She fell to the hard-packed earth of the playground, half-knocked out, bleeding and crying.

Alma and her friends thought it all hysterically funny.

Down at Matt's Meat Market, Matt Horton whistled as he worked, preparing an order. Of fresh ground pork.

"Where's your wife, Matt?" the customer asked. "I

haven't seen her around for a couple of days."

"Oh, she took a little vacation. Gone to visit some friends down in Texas. She's had nerve problems for years, you know. This last attack, well—" He smiled with his back to the customer, "—might say she just went all to pieces."

"I'm real sorry to hear that, Matt. When you talk to her, give her my best, will you?"

"I sure will do that. And you might say a little prayer over her . . . at supper. She'd like that." He wrapped the pork and handed it over the counter.

"I'll sure do that little thing, Matt. Sure will. You take it easy now."

"Thank you."

When the front door had closed, Matt stepped into his freezer and moved a couple of sides of beef. And there hung his darlin' Ruth. Naked, frozen, blue, from a meat hook. She was minus part of one leg. Everybody that had taken advantage of Matt's sausage specials that day would find their sausage tasting just a tad sweeter than usual. Matt told them it was his secret combination of spices and herbs.

He reached down and tickled his blue baby's toes. On the leg that remained, that is. "This little piggy went to market, this little piggy stayed home!"

Matt laughed and laughed, his breath frosty white in the freezer.

Then he picked up a meat cleaver and buried the blade in his wife's head.

"Old bag!" he said, just as the buzzer sounded, signaling that someone had entered his shop. He rearranged the sides of beef and stepped back into his shop, carefully closing the door. "Hello, Mrs. Johnson!" Matt called cheerfully. "Come for some of that good fresh seasoned pork I have on special?"

Chief Kelson watched as patrol-person Nicole Jordan bent over, her uniform pants stretching tight. He licked his lips and felt himself become aroused. "Nicole, baby, did anyone ever tell you that you got the finest-lookin' ass in this whole county?"

She straightened up, amazement mirrored in her face and eyes. She knew that Kelson was just about as crude as they come, but she thought they'd straightened all that out a year or so back.

She turned, facing him, brushing back a lock of auburn hair. "Have you lost your mind, Chief?"

"Nope." He grinned at her. She could smell his bad breath clear across the room. "But I got me a hard-on that you wouldn't believe, baby."

"How'd you like a sexual harassment suit filed against you, Paul?" Nicole's face was crimson, and she could feel the heat of it.

He laughed at her. "Your word against mine, baby. Aw, come on, Nicole. What's a little lovin' between friends?"

She slammed the file drawer shut and stalked out of the office, Kelson's laughter following her. She slammed the door and got into a city unit, driving off, thinking: What is happening in this town?

Old Doc Reynolds sat in his office chair and stared out the window. He was not open for business and had a pretty strong feeling that he would never reopen. But he enjoyed sitting in his chair and gazing out at the quiet neighborhood where he'd practiced medicine for more than fifty years.

Today was not a good day, he thought. And tomorrow will be even worse. And the next day and so on until the town finally looked the devil right in the eyes. All anybody ever had to do to learn about Nabo's Show of Shows was to come to him—he knew. But no one ever did, and he didn't expect them to. Until it was too late.

Just an old country doctor.

Who had the insight.

His old friend Martin had the insight, too. He knew he was going to die that day—came by and told Doc Reynolds so. He wasn't afraid to die. Death is something we all have to face, he'd said, and quite calmly too. It was the way he was going to die that had bothered him. The two men had sat and talked for a long time about various things. Talked without ever mentioning that each knew the other had the insight, and knew that insighted people, once gone, did not necessarily step through that misty veil and paddle placidly across that Dark River.

Insighted people, and others with a strong will, had a habit of returning to settle old scores.

Doc Reynolds turned in his creaky old wooden desk chair, thinking: Like that carnival in town had just returned. To the date. He smiled grimly, remembering. He'd been a young buck of only fifty, still full of piss and vinegar when that awful night had erupted. He could still see those flames leaping up into a dark and seemingly angry sky. Could still hear the cries of those being burned alive, heard and was shamed by the pitiful cries of the helpless animals as the flames turned their hair-coats into pyres.

He and Martin and Tressalt had gotten there too late to be of much help.

Except to witness the horror of it all.

And to never forget.

Now the carnival was back. And very soon, within a couple of days, the doctor felt, the town was going to pay for that terrible night. The aura of vengeance was an almost tangible thing. Every time Reynolds stepped out onto his front porch he could feel it.

Old Doc Reynolds knew the invisible, silently choking, almost claustrophobic sensation very well. And he also knew the message it carried, as it floated throughout the town, wrapping an invisible, stinking shroud around the town and its people.

To those few who possess the insight, the message was plain and frightening.

Death.

*   *   *

155

The group was still at it when Mark and Linda returned from school. Martin excused himself and went upstairs with his children, to Mark's room.

He sat down on the bed and spread his big hands. "What can I say, kids? Except to say that it came as a shock to me and I'm very, very sorry."

"It didn't come as any shock to either of us," his daughter bluntly informed him. She jerked a thumb toward her brother. "We've seen it coming for about a year. Maybe longer."

Martin stared at first one kid, then the other. "How come I didn't see it?"

Sister looked at brother. Mark took it. "Maybe, dad, there's that old saying about being too close to the forest to see the trees." He sighed and shook his head, looked at his sister and received a slight nod. "Dad, if I tell you something, will you promise not to get all nuts and beat the hell out of somebody else?" He grinned boyishly. "Not that Lyle Steele didn't need it."

Martin chuckled and nodded his head. "I give you my word, son."

"Mother's been seeing Mr. Hanson for about a year." The boy seemed relieved to have it out into the light.

Martin understood that the knowledge must have been a mental burden for both his kids. And the husband and father waited for the hot, wild rage to fill him. It did not come, and he was grateful for that. He slowly expelled his breath. "She told me there was no other man. Tell you the truth, I didn't believe her."

"Maybe it's been platonic so far?" Linda suggested, but her tone read that she didn't believe that anymore than she believed pigs could sing.

Martin left that alone. "I wonder why Gary didn't tell me about it?"

"I doubt that he knew, dad," Mark said. "Very few people did know. But you can bet all the people in that little theatre bunch knew about it."

"Yeah," Martin agreed, and that pissed him off. Mike Hanson taught English Lit and doubled as assistant band

156

director at the high school. Big worker in and supporter of the Holland theatre group. The scattered pieces of the sudden and unexpected departure of his wife were beginning to come into place in Martin's head. He rose from the bed.

"You two change clothes and get you something to eat, if you're hungry, and then come down to the den and join us. I want you both to talk with Audie and with Sergeant McClain."

"Sergeant McClain that dark-haired fox?" his son asked with a smile.

Embarrassed, Martin opened the bedroom door. "I wouldn't know about that 'fox' bit, son."

"Sure you wouldn't, dad," his son needled him. "I guess that means you're over the hill."

Chuckling, Martin closed the door on his kids' laughter and rejoined the group in the den. He sat down and looked at Gary. "They're taking it better than I am, Gary. Did you know about Alicia and Mike Hanson?"

The doctor almost dropped his pipe. "Mike Hanson! That wimp? Are you serious?"

"Apparently so. The kids knew. They seemed to think that everyone connected with the Holland theatre group knew all about it. Said it's been going on for about a year. Linda said that maybe it was platonic. But from the tone of her voice, she doesn't believe it anymore than I do. Probably saying that to make me feel better."

Frenchy and Audie stayed out of it, Frenchy studying some notes and Audie gazing at the ceiling.

Gary's face tightened in anger. "And you can bet that Janet knew all about it as well. I'll tell you one thing. When I get home, I'm going to have a little chat with Janet about this matter. I will never be convinced that Alicia didn't confide in Janet about it. I'll find out."

"That won't help matters, Gary."

"It doesn't matter! I don't like for something like this to rear up and hit me in the face out of the blue. I really resent it."

Martin shook his head, conscious that Frenchy was

157

looking at him. "Forget it, Gary. Men share secrets with other men, women share secrets with other women. It's over, and I've got to accept that it's all for the best. I didn't even get angry when the kids told me about it. I got hot about the whole town knowing it, though." He met Frenchy's eyes. "Is Frenchy your real name?"

"Oh, yes. My dad had a weird sense of humor. It was either that or the terrible name my mother picked out."

"Oh?"

"Yes. Penelope."

ELEVEN

Martin was the closest to the den phone. He stilled the ringing, listened for a moment, then said, "Okay, right." He hung up, turning to Gary. "There's been an accident at the school playgrounds. It appears that Alma Sessions deliberately hit the Dennison girl with a swing board. Doctor Rhodes is out of pocket. The school nurse is taking the girl to your offices."

Audie grunted. "Alma Sessions," he said, disgust in his voice.

Frenchy looked at him, a curious light in her eyes.

Gary stood up. "On my way." He paused. "Alma Sessions?"

"Yeah."

"How interesting."

After Gary had left, Frenchy asked, "What's all this about Alma Sessions?"

Martin explained about the girl's seizure and then about her speaking in tongues and about the strange behavior of Alma and her parents.

"That is a bad kid," Linda tossed in. "I mean, a real little creep."

Frenchy looked at her. "You want to explain that?"

"She's bad, that's all. Likes to torture animals, if she can catch them. She set one little boy on fire. The flames were put out before a lot of damage was done; but he'll carry scars all his life . . ."

"How come you didn't tell me that, Audie?" Martin asked.

159

"She's a juvenile. Those records are sealed. You can't release the name for print or broadcast of a juvenile charged with a crime. Stupid law."

"I agree," Linda said. "And *I'm* a juvenile. Anyway, that whole group that runs with Alma is bad. They're nothing but a younger, smaller version of Karl Steele and his thugs, and you can't get much lower than that."

Audie again nodded his agreement.

"You men were right," Frenchy said. "There is definitely a pattern emerging." She looked at Martin. "I hate to toss gasoline on a fire, or even the coals, but I have to ask you something."

"Ask away."

"Your wife."

"What about her?"

"Her behavior. Do you think it's connected, somehow, with all these strange occurrences. I don't think I said that right."

"I know what you mean. I don't know, Frenchy. Alicia was reluctant to admit to any pulling toward the fairground. But I think she was. I know several of her friends were."

"But you, personally, experienced no such pull?"

"No. None."

"I had a weird feeling the first night they were in town," Audie said. "The carnival, I mean. But it wasn't pulling at me to come over there. More like, well, a feeling of dread. Something like that. Confusion, I'd have to add to it."

Frenchy stared at him, but didn't pursue the confusion bit. She looked at Linda and Mark. "Either of you feel any sort of compulsion to go to the fairgrounds?"

They shook their heads.

"Any of your close friends?"

Again, a negative response.

"You mentioned a pattern, Frenchy," Audie said. "Let's see how close it is to ours."

"Yes. Well, this . . . peculiar behavior, at least the deadly form of it, seems to be striking only those whose character is, well, not of the best, so to speak. Red, like

Hank Rinder, had something to do with the carnival fire thirty-odd years ago. The Harold boy was a punk; Alma Sessions is a little no-good. But how about the behavior in the cafe? That doesn't make any sense.'' She looked at Linda. "Tell me again what your friend Jeanne told you this Nabo person said to her after she'd explained what the boys had done.''

"He said that nothing ever changes in this dreadful place.''

Frenchy nodded her head. Expelled a long sigh. "I've worked on some weird cases in my eleven years, but this one is shaping up to be the oddest of them all. All right, people, here is what I have so far: Sam Nabo died in a fire right here in Holland back in 1954. That's firm. He died and was positively identified. Nearly *everybody* connected with the carnival died that night . . . or two or three days later, from burns, gunshot wounds, stabbings, what-have-you. According to what I've been able to find out, sixteen people actually survived that fire; but that figure is coming out of the heads of state investigators—all of them now retired—who worked the fire back in '54. We have a few records of it, of course, but damn few, and not all of them gone because of some rogue cop who light-fingered them years ago. That fire was a long time ago, and a lot can happen to paper in almost thirty-five years.

"Now then, I prowled around the fairgrounds this morning. Early. Taking down the license numbers of cars and trucks. Haven't any of you noticed the age of the vehicles and the plates on them?''

No one had paid that much attention.

Then Martin remembered that strange sensation of his: the hearing of 1950's music, seeing the old cars, all models manufactured back in the '40s and '50s. He told the group about it.

Frenchy asked if anyone else had experienced anything like it?

No one had.

"Strange," she said with another sigh. "Anyway, every vehicle belonging to the carnival can be classified as an antique. And the license plates all ran out back in '54 to '55."

"I am ashamed of myself for not noticing that," Audie said, then snapped his fingers. "Wait a minute! I just remembered this. I wasn't even in town the day the carnival began arriving. I was gonna jump all over Dr. Rhodes' case for sending me way out to Harrisville on some wild goose hunt about a child abuse case he said he had. Said it had to be done that day; a kid's life was in danger. I got down there, and nobody knew what I was talking about. No such people lived there. I felt like a fool."

"Don Rhodes sent you down there?" Martin beat Frenchy to the question.

"Sure did. I was gone all day looking for those people. Who don't exist. And I was some hot about that. I made me a mental note to get all up in his face about it. But it just now came back to me."

Frenchy punched a finger in the deputy's direction. "Audie, get me everything you can on this doctor. Get on the horn now, please."

"I'm gone. See you people." He left the house.

"Stranger and stranger," Martin said. "Getting back to the carnival trucks and cars—why wouldn't some highway cop or local cop or deputy have stopped them somewhere along the way?"

The sergeant sighed and rubbed her hands together. Chuckling softly, the laughter void of any sort of humor, she said, "Well, folks . . . maybe the route they took is not one that's on any highway map."

Linda shuddered and Mark put his arm around his sister's shoulders.

"Let's don't jump off into the unknown just yet," Martin said with a caution he did not feel. "However . . ." he let that wander off.

"Yeah," Frenchy agreed with him. "That's one reason I don't want to call this in and ask for official help just yet. It's difficult enough for a woman to make it in this business. I don't want to be made to look like some fool.

162

Now you know the second reason."

Nobody said anything for a moment. Frenchy took a sip of coffee and continued. "Audie has been doing some legwork on his own. He's a fine cop. Since the carnival people have been in town, they have not purchased one single item of food in this town. And they have not, as near as he could tell, left the fairgrounds area. Not once. Audie has been observing them through long lenses at various times over the past two days. Nobody eats. Nobody appears to drink—anything. The carnival has several kinds of animal acts with them: elephants, horses, tigers, lions, monkeys, baboons . . . the animals don't eat or drink or defecate. The fair people, locally, put in a dozen porta-potties. They have never been used by anyone connected with the carnival—that Audie has observed. You with me so far?"

"Interesting little tidbits," Martin said. He glanced up. Audie was standing in the door. "What are we dealing with here?"

"People who aren't human," the deputy said, entering the den and taking his seat. He looked at Frenchy. "I got the ball rolling. But the computer at headquarters doesn't have anything on Don Rhodes—not our Don Rhodes, anyway—not under that name or physical description. I gave him a warning ticket for speeding a couple of weeks ago. Still had his driver's license and plates. He doesn't like me very much. The computer is working on the latest. It'll be awhile."

"I didn't expect him to be in there," Frenchy said, glancing at Martin. "You have a funny look on your face."

He didn't reply. He picked up the phone at his elbow and called his offices. "Mary? Martin Holland. Your husband belongs to the Young Holland Club, doesn't he? Yes. Good. Fine organization. Look, could you give him a call and ask him if he remembers what member originally brought up the idea of bringing in a carnival? Oh, you do? I . . . see. Thank you, Mary. No. Just curious, that's all." He slowly hung up the phone.

"Who recommended the carnival?" Audie was first with

163

the question.

"Dr. Don Rhodes. And I just remembered something else about the good doctor and his pretty wife, Colleen. She told Alicia they were both from West Virginia."

"Bingo!" Frenchy said. "That's where Nabo's Show of Shows was home-based, right? It's going to be interesting to see the package on Dr. Rhodes."

Martin nodded his head. "Let's sum up what we have, Frenchy."

"All right. Since the moment the carnival began arriving in town, some rather, well, bizarre happenings have taken place. Several deaths. Wild nightmarish hallucinations. The townspeople in a brawl that none of them can remember. The preacher's sermons are rambling and disjointed. Don Talbolt hears voices and what appears to be a car or truck trying to start, in the middle of grasslands; the sounds seems to be coming from under the ground. Violence is on the upswing in town. I drove by the fairgrounds last night—must have been five or six hundred people just milling around outside the fence. Others just standing and staring into the darkness.

"Okay. Let's add it up and see what we can get a warrant on." Again, she chuckled, and again, it was totally void of mirth. "I can see it now: 'Oh, Mr. County D.A. I'd like to have some warrants for a bunch of people who don't eat or drink. What have they done? Well . . . nothing, really. They're traveling in classic cars and trucks and it appears they have driven a couple of thousand miles with license tags that expired back in 1955 or so. Based where, sir? Oh . . . well, they're not based anywhere, sir. Not on this earth. You see, it seems they all died back in '54.'"

The laughter was strained, but still felt good to them all. It helped to drain off the tension that had been building.

"So we have nothing to take to court?" Martin asked.

"Well, Audie could go down there and write a bunch of tickets. But that would tip our hand to them that we know something dirty is going on. Or is something dirty going on? We have no proof that anyone connected with the carnival is responsible for any of the deaths or bizarre happenings in town."

"So we're back to square one?" Mark asked.

"Not necessarily. We feel the carnival people are up to something; we just don't know how they're doing it."

"So how much time do we have, Miss Frenchy?" Mark asked.

"Just Frenchy, Mark. How much time? Well, let's add it all up. The carnival was torched back in '54. On a Thursday night. Beatings, shootings, stabbings, whippings. A mob went berserk—as mobs usually do. That was the opening day of the fair. Now then, we're all in agreement that, as impossible as it seems, or is, the carnival is back. The same carnival, the same people. To do what? I don't know. My guess would be—and I'm hoping this is all a bad dream and I'm going to wake up in my bed back in Alliance—revenge. So how much time do we have?"

Linda took it. "Until Thursday night. Whatever is going to happen, will happen then."

"The main thrust will happen then. But it's already beginning to happen," Martin said.

Frenchy put dark eyes on the man. "I agree. And the events are going to intensify as the week progresses."

"I believe that, too."

"While we were riding around today, Audie and I worked out some possibilities. They seem to fit in this craziness. We think. Audie, who killed Hank Rinder?"

"Nabo. He deals in fire."

"Who killed Red?"

"Samson. The strong man."

"How?"

"I don't know."

"So what's next?"

"That's anybody's guess. But I agree with Martin, adding this: Unless we can stop it, it's going to get much worse."

"How do we stop them?"

"Confront them and hope for the best."

Frenchy met the eyes of all in the den. "That's it, people."

"What would we gain by confronting Nabo?" Martin asked.

"Probably nothing," Frenchy replied. "And we just might be putting our own lives on the line, and in the end, accomplish nothing. Remember this: If what we think is true, they have nothing to lose."

Martin looked at his children. "Both of you stay away from the fairgrounds. Tell Jeanne and Susan the same. Mark, tell Amy."

"Don't you worry," Linda assured him. "The fairgrounds is off-limits."

"Is there anyone you can trust to call in on this thing?" Audie asked Frenchy.

"I don't know. Maybe. But not now. Like I said, I can't get on the horn and call for back-up based solely on the assumption that we're dealing with a bunch of . . . ghosts! I—" She cocked her head to one side and listened. "What is that sound?"

They all listened as the very faint sounds of music drifted to them.

"That's a . . . calliope," Martin spoke after a few seconds. "I haven't heard one of those in years."

"It's beautiful," Linda said. "But, something else, too."

"It's . . ." Frenchy paused, listening.

"Haunting," Martin finished it.

When Gary returned to the Holland house, his wife and Susan came with him. Gary Jr. stayed home with his brother, Rich. Susan and Linda went upstairs, Gary and Janet joined the group. Janet's eyes were red and puffy and all could see that she had been crying.

"I knew about them seeing each other, Martin," Janet admitted. "But Alicia told me they were only friends. I believed her. She'd never lied to me before."

A car pulling up and the door slamming closed the

166

conversation on any further discussion concerning Alicia.

"Hi, Nicole," Mark's voice came through the screen door.

"Mark. Is Audie here?"

"Right inside. Join the crowd."

The men stood up as the city patrol-person stepped into the house. Martin waved her into the den, introduced her to Frenchy—Nicole wore a puzzled look as the sergeant from the state police was introduced—then said, "Is something wrong, Nicole?"

"Other than everybody in this town acting flaky, no, sir. Audie, if you're busy, I can catch you later."

The deputy glanced at Frenchy. "Sit down, Nicole," she said. "I think we'd better talk."

The first purple shadows of night began settling quietly over the community. Nicole had gone with Audie and Frenchy. Gary and Janet had gone home. Martin sat with his son on the front porch of the house and watched the twilight gradually turn into darkness. Gary and Martin had called and personally spoken with their friends, warning them of the danger they felt was all around them.

The reception had not been cordial.

Of the friends they had called, only Eddie and Joyce Gilmer had believed them. Matt and Diane Potter had openly laughed at the warnings. Milt and Pat had listened, not doing a very good job of suppressing the snickers, and then told Martin he'd been working too hard and to take some time off and relax.

But among some of the disbelievers' children, it was a different story. Jeanne had packed a bag and was spending a few days with Linda.

"It's weird at my house," she told Linda, who would later tell her father. "Mom and Dad said they didn't care what I did. They were going to have a party—Milt and Pat are coming over—and they were all going to get drunk."

"That is weird," Linda agreed.

"Dad?" Mark asked.

"Ummm?"

"Why'd mom do what she did?"

"I guess love died, son. It died on both sides. She claims I took her for granted, and maybe I did. She claims I wasn't supportive of her, and I guess I wasn't. Not in the way she would have liked. Love just doesn't bloom and keep on flourishing all by itself. Two people have to work at it. I guess we let the flowers die, son."

"You should have been a writer, dad."

"I sure am no actor, son."

"Neither is mother."

"I don't know, boy. She did a pretty good job of fooling me."

"You trusted her."

"Yes."

"Would you take her back, dad?"

Martin had given that some thought. More than a little thought. He was tempted to say yes, to make his son feel better. Then the mental image of his wife on the floor, making love with Mike Hanson—Alicia had finally leveled with him—entered his mind.

"No, Mark. I wouldn't."

The boy stood up. "I wouldn't either." He walked back into the house, a very angry and hurt young man.

Martin noticed that it had gotten very dark, very quickly.

Johnny Davis made his move at full dark. With a little help from a silent voice inside his head. He climbed over the high fence of the fairgrounds and slipped toward a big canvas and wood concern with the sign: HOUSE OF MIRRORS on the front. He'd always heard about them places but he'd never been inside one. He'd always heard they was weird. Tonight he was gonna find out.

Twenty-one year old Johnny Davis was one of those types that if someone were to hand him a million dollars, cash, and tell him it was all his, if he'd just straighten up and fly right, he would grin, promise to stop his various criminal activities, and then take the money and go out and promptly break into the first house he came to and attack anyone who might be in there.

But Johnny Davis's days of being an evil punk were about to come to a rather reflective halt.

Johnny turned in the darkness and gasped for breath when he bumped into a tall man all dressed in black. Even wore black sunglasses.

"May I be of assistance?" Nabo asked.

"Ah . . ." Johnny managed to gasp. "No. No, I was just lookin' around, that's all."

"Really? I was under the distinct impression you were very interested in going inside the house of mirrors."

"Oh, yeah?" How did this big sucker know that?

"Yes. Would you like to visit the house of mirrors? No charge, of course."

"Ah . . . sure. No charge?"

"No charge."

"How do I get in there?"

"How were you planning to enter?"

"I was gonna sli—" Sucker almost trapped me, Johnny thought.

"No need to do that, friend," Nabo told him, smiling. "Just walk right in and let your eyes drink in sights that you have never before experienced. Let your imagination run wild; let your mind take you on flights of fancy." He held out his arm, fingers pointing toward the darkened entrance of the house of mirrors.

"Don't mind if I do." Johnny stepped toward the dark entrance and walked up a short flight of wooden steps. He stepped inside.

The canvas flap closed with a soft whisper behind him. He paused for a moment, trying to get his bearings. Hard to do. Kinda spooky in here, he thought. And dark, too.

Soft lights suddenly muted the darkness. And for the first time in his life, Johnny Davis was impressed by something other than his ability to make life miserable for almost anyone who had the misfortune to come in contact with him. His impressed state lasted about as long as any promise he'd ever made.

He looked at his distorted image in the mirror.

Something gave him a sharp goose in the behind.

Johnny let out a squall and jumped about a foot in the air.

"What the—" he said, settling down, looking around him. Nothing but what appeared to be about a zillion of his own reflections: fat, skinny, short, tall, pin-headed, squat-headed. You name it, it was there.

"Who goosed me?" he demanded.

Who goosed me—who goosed me—who goosed me? his words came echoing back to him.

"Shut up!" Johnny yelled.

Shut up—shut up—shut up! his words were again hurled back into his face.

"What a stupid place!" Johnny mumbled, some of his original fascination gone with the house of mirrors.

Johnny walked on and ran right into a wall of reflecting glass.

Johnny was rapidly losing his patience and his interest in this wacky place.

"I'm gettin' out of here!" He turned and ran into a wall of mirrors. He shoved at them. They would not yield. He turned, took two steps in the reflecting maze and hit another bank of polished glass.

Johnny's heart was hammering and his blood pressure soaring as overwhelming fear and more than a touch of claustrophobia hit him hard, numbing him, turning his mind into pudding.

"Lemmie outta here!" he yelled.

His words returned to haunt and taunt him. But they were all different in tone. It was his voice, but it was all mixed up with something else. Sounded like a whole bunch of people crying and screaming.

Johnny got down on his hands and knees and tried to crawl out of the crazy place. But he couldn't find his way out. Everytime he'd round a corner, he'd bump his head on another mirror. He was so scared spittle was leaking out of his mouth.

170

"Momma!" Johnny squalled.

Momma couldn't help him. No one could help him. Johnny Davis's future was in the hands of a group who knew no fear of after-life retribution.

Johnny finally found a place where he could lie down fully stretched out on the wooden walkway. He fought his fear, and got it under control. He willed with all his might for his heart to stop its mad pounding and his breathing to even out. His panicked gasping lessened. Gradually he regained most of his composure, telling himself it was all just a trick. The mirrors were only creating illusions and if he kept his wits about him, he could get out of this crazy place.

Johnny crawled slowly to his knees and looked around him. He blinked at the sight before his startled and lusting eyes. The most beautiful girl he had ever seen was standing a few feet away from him. And she didn't have a stitch of clothes on. Nekkid as a jaybird. Looked like she was maybe twelve or thirteen. Just the kind of girl Johnny liked.

A composite of all of those he had molested over the years.

"Aren't I lovely?" she asked, her voice as pure as silver bells.

"You bet!" Johnny whispered. He reached out to touch her. His fingers touched glass. "Lemmie feel you, baby."

"Would you like to touch my body? All the soft secret places?"

"Oh, yes!"

"Do you want to make love to me?"

"Do I ever! I got a hard-on that you wouldn't believe, baby."

And he did. He unzipped his jeans, revealing himself to the young girl.

"That's very nice," she complimented him, licking her lips. "I bet that would feel good."

"Right on!"

Then she began to fade from view.

"Wait a minute!" Johnny shouted. "Hey, baby! You

171

forgot about me."

The young girl reappeared in all her young beauty. "Yes?"

Johnny pointed to his aroused flesh. "What about this?"

The girl gently caressed her breasts then held out her hand. "Come to me," she urged.

"Whatever you want." Johnny got up and immediately walked into a mirror, banging himself against the reflecting glass.

The young girl stepped forward and reached through the glass to grasp his jutting hardness. Impossible! But Jesus God and Mary! her hand was icy cold.

Johnny gasped at the cold touch and tried to pull away. But the hand that gripped him held him firmly. Smiling at him she squeezed. Pain surged through Johnny and he screamed in pain.

She smiled at him and Johnny no longer thought she was beautiful. Her eyes were wild-looking. And when did her lips become so blood-red?

The girl began pulling him against the cold shining surface. Harder and harder until he could not bear the pain. He beat his fists against the mirror and suddenly both hands penetrated the thick glass without breaking the mirror.

Again, impossible! Johnny's pain-numbed mind managed to produce that thought.

More pain than he ever imagined filled him as something began gnawing at the flesh of his hands and wrists. His howling was monster-hideous as his flesh pushed through the polished barrier and slowly entered an acid-like sheathing that gripped and sucked at him. Felt like a thousand needle-sharp teeth were gnawing at him.

Johnny screamed and begged and cried and howled as the unseen and unknown—whatever it was—behind the entrapping mirror devoured his flesh.

He could feel the blood pouring down his legs.

His feet slipped into the yawning depths behind the mirror, and Johnny knew terror at its purest as his boots were torn from his feet and something began gnawing through his skin.

He willingly succumbed to the blackness of unconsciousness. He did not feel the flesh-ripping and bone-crushing agony as he went whirling into a wild vortex. He did not feel his savaged body hit the ground, his blood splattering.

"Who found him?" Martin asked Audie.

"Mr. Bradshaw. Said he heard a thump in his back yard and came outside to check it out. That's when he found . . . what was left of Johnny."

The group had gathered at the morgue. Martin met the eyes of Gary. "This might be a stupid question, Gary. What killed him?"

"You can take your choice, buddy! First of all, it appears that every bone in his body is broken. It's like he was dropped from a thousand feet in the air. But all this other . . ." He waved his hand at the broken and smashed body of the young man. "That was done somewhere else. But *what* did it? Something literally ate his flesh. And it was human; no doubt about that. Look at the teeth marks on his belly."

Martin was silent for a moment. "Ever seen a Geek, Gary?"

"I don't even know what a Geek is."

"That's a sideshow attraction for those with a strong stomach or a depraved mind—or both. A geek is a sick person, who tears the heads off of live chickens and drinks the blood. Eats live rabbits."

"And people actually *pay* to see something like that?" Frenchy asked.

"They did before animal rights groups got involved and put a stop to it. That was back in the '50s, I believe. The early '50s."

"Yekk!" she spat out the word as if it tasted bad. "What type of person was this Johnny Davis, Audie?"

"A low-life. Child molester. Brought up a half dozen

times for it; never convicted. Thief, vandal, arsonist. He is, was, a real jerk." He met the eyes of the others, gathered around the blood-soaked table. "Fits the pattern, doesn't he?"

Johnny Davis's eyes were still open in shocked death, staring at only God knew what. Or Satan. Gary flipped the sheet over the ravaged and broken body and then stored Johnny in a refrigerated vault. The group walked outside the funeral home.

"I think," Audie spoke softly, "it's time to run this bunch out of town. What do you people think about that?"

"I agree with you," Gary said.

"I got a hunch, people," Martin dashed cold water on that suggestion. "I got a hunch that the townspeople wouldn't let us do that."

"What do you mean?" Frenchy asked.

"I think we waited too long to act. Don't ask me how I know that. I don't. It's just a hunch."

Gary paused in the lighting of his pipe. "How do we find out?"

"First let's check the weak links. Any suggestions, Nicole?"

"You know who I'll suggest."

"You're gonna do *what?*" Chief Kelson yelled at them from the front porch of his house.

"We're going to run the carnival out of town, Chief," Martin repeated. "And we'd like your help in doing it. Don't you think that's a good idea?"

"Absolutely, no! What I think is that you're a pure-dee nut, Mayor. And you ain't gonna get my help in hay-rassin' them good people out at the fairgrounds." He pointed a finger at Martin. "You just try it, Mayor. You just try. And by God, I'll stop you."

"All right, Kelson, all right. Settle down. I was just getting your opinion on it. Calm down."

Kelson stomped back into the house, slamming the door.

174

"This is making me very uneasy, friend," Gary said.

"It's scaring the hell out of me!" Nicole stated. She stepped close to Audie and the deputy didn't seem to mind putting his arm around her waist. He couldn't hide his grin.

The move didn't escape Martin's eyes. "Never miss an opportunity," he muttered.

The group drove to the home of a local schoolteacher. She screamed at Martin when he suggested ordering the carnival out of town.

Audie voiced his amazement. "Mrs. Carlson is one of the most level-headed people I know."

"She still is," Martin said. "Or will be again as soon as the carnival leaves town."

"Maybe," Gary said. "But in what condition they'll leave the town is what concerns me."

Martin chose not to reply to that.

They drove on. A man threatened to sic his dog on Martin if he didn't leave his property. Another threatened to get his shotgun. A lady cursed him. Several teenagers jeered him and shot him the bird.

"Let's try something else," Martin suggested.

The two-car caravan, Martin in the lead, drove outside of town and kept going for several miles. Martin finally signaled that he was pulling over.

"Now what was all that about?" Gary asked.

"I wanted to see if they'd let us leave."

"*They* meaning? . . ." Frenchy asked.

"Nabo and his people. Obviously they don't care what we do."

"I . . . don't understand this," Nicole said. "Surely we're not the only ones in this whole town who are unaffected by this . . . thing?"

"I can't answer that, Nicole. Or if we are, why we are." A thought came to him. "Satan does love a good game, or so I'm told."

"Now what does that mean, Martin?" Gary's tone was impatient.

"Let's go back to the house. Talk this town out."

They called off the impromptu canvassing of homes

and returned to Martin's house. Linda and Susan made coffee and they all gathered on the huge front porch, telling Janet and the kids about the evening's surprises.

"Everyone you talked with was indignant about your suggestion?" Janet asked.

"To a person. Male and female. Adults and kids. Even Mr. Noble got hot under the collar about it. And you remember I told you he's the one who was against the carnival coming in—just a few days ago."

"Let me tell you what the kids just told me about Matt and Diane and Milt and Pat," Janet said. She informed the gathering.

Gary blinked. "Drunk? Party?"

"That's what they said."

The group sat in silence and mentally digested that for a moment.

Frenchy broke the silence. "Whoever 'they' might be," she said, as the night wound around them, "they sure are clever. The carnival people, that is. They've got it all tied up as neat and pretty as a Christmas package."

"Maybe not," Martin said.

"You know something we need to know?" Gary asked.

"A hunch. A guess. We're all pretty much agreed that the carnival came in here for revenge. But just suppose there is another force at work that the carnival doesn't know about."

"What do you mean, dad?" Mark asked. "What kind of force?"

"Satan." He tossed it out and waited for someone to pick it up. When no one did, he said, "What if, unknowing to the carnies, Satan saw a golden opportunity for some mischief and stepped in, say, as the carnival passed from the afterlife to the present?"

"Why would he do that?" Janet asked.

"Why not?" Martin countered. "Just think, with the state of the nation, the world, being what it is, Old Nick must be getting bored. People are voluntarily, willingly, rushing headlong into Hell, without Satan having to do a thing. God is struggling, people. The Almighty is in a war for survival.

"So the Devil sees a chance to further hasten things along down the dark path, right here in good ol' Holland, Nebraska. As God is All-Seeing, so is Old Nick. As the carnival slides out from the other side, he just sends some of his minions with it. Perhaps they're even a part of the carnival. Probably so. It might even be Nabo, but something tells me it isn't." He cut his eyes to Jeanne. "What did you feel when he had his hands on you, Jeanne?"

"Compassion. Regret. Sorrow," the girl answered.

"But wouldn't he know, dad?" Linda asked. "I mean, he's a part of the . . . well, other side."

"Not necessarily, baby. None of us knows what really lies on the other side of life. Our faith teaches us that there is a Heaven and a Hell. And nothing in between. Other religions teach that there is a middle ground. Still others claim there are levels of afterlife. No one really knows."

"It must have been a treacherous journey getting back here," Audie spoke, directing the statement at no one in particular.

"Not if you have outside help," Martin replied.

"And not knowing that you do," Frenchy added.

"Yes."

"Assuming that you're right in this . . . Satan theory," Gary mused aloud. "That means that we don't know who in town is on what side—right?"

"That's the way I see it."

"You mean that we might be . . . all alone in this thing?" Nicole asked.

"Quite possibly."

"Why, dad?" Mark asked. "Why us and not somebody else?"

"I can't answer that, son."

"Who can, dad?" Linda asked.

"God."

"I can't speak for the group," Audie said. "But I don't recall ever having anything except a one-sided conversation with God."

"Maybe He is telling us right now," Jeanne spoke softly. "Maybe this is His way of telling us the direction He wants us to take. Maybe that's why He spared us. Anybody thought of that?"

Out of the mouths of babes, Martin thought. "You just might be right, Jeanne. No, I hadn't thought of it in that way."

The sounds of music drifted to them, and they all recognized the tune as one almost always played as the merry-go-round whirled. *Oomm-paa-paa oomm-paa-paa,* over and over and over.

"I get the weirdest feeling that somebody, or something is listening to every word we say," Susan broke the silence. Her eyes were fixed in the direction of the fairgrounds. "Whether it's the ears of good or evil, I don't know."

"I'm not afraid of Mr. Nabo," Jeanne said. "Not one little bit."

The music stopped. The night grew silent.

"I don't know whether I am, or not," Audie admitted. "But I'm sure scared of something, and I don't know what. I don't know what we're up against. I'll fight a man. But how do you fight something when you can't even see it? Or know, really, what *it* is?"

The calliope began its lonely pumping, and Martin had to smile ruefully. The tune was "The Long And Winding Road."

BOOK TWO

To every man upon this earth
Death cometh soon or late;
And how can man die better
Than facing fearful odds
For the ashes of his fathers,
And the temples of his gods?

—Thomas Babington,
Lord Macaulay

ONE

Tuesday.

Martin had never liked to sleep alone. On the rare times that he had gone on business trips without his wife, he had never slept well, and this first night at home with Alicia gone was a miserable one.

He finally got to sleep about three o'clock in the morning and was so tired when he did sleep, he awakened with that loggy, heavy feeling, extremely cranky.

He checked on the kids, making sure they were up and getting ready for school—although he had some doubts about whether they should go, or not, he finally left it up to them—then went back to bed and didn't wake up until ten.

He took a long, very hot, soapy, steamy shower, shaved carefully, and dressed in his normal conservative style. He fixed a light breakfast and while eating, called the sheriff's substation. No answer. He closed the front door—few people in Holland ever locked doors—and drove downtown to his business offices.

As soon as he entered the place he sensed something all out of whack.

"Mary," he spoke to the woman.

"Mr. Holland. We are going to close at noon Thursday, aren't we? The carnival is in town, you know?"

"We'll be closed all day Thursday, Mary," Martin informed her. "We won't reopen until Monday morning."

"That's so nice of you, Mr. Holland," Edith told him from the desk opposite Mary. "The carnival is in town,

181

you know?"

"Yes, Edith, I know."

Edith stood up and the others in the office did the same. Then they all sang "For He's A Jolly Good Fellow." Martin stood, not knowing what to expect next.

As if on some invisible cue, his office personnel sat down and resumed their work.

Thinking some dark thoughts, Martin retreated to his office. He did some routine paper work but his mind was not on it. He would occasionally lift his eyes to gaze at his office staff, at their work stations, the computer screens blinking in various colors. If one met his eyes, they would smile, but their eyes looked odd and their movements were jerky.

Eerie was the word that came to Martin's mind.

They were doing their work, but it seemed to Martin it was all rote.

He gave up on his paper work and drove over to Gary's office. There was not one single car in the parking lot. And Gary usually stayed very busy.

"What you see is what you get, Buddy," the doctor informed him, spreading his hands. "Not a patient all morning. Not one. And my nurses and receptionist all called in sick."

"My office crew is behaving as though the wicked witch just cast a spell on them," Martin replied. "Oddest thing I've ever seen. I had to get out of there. You want to close up and prowl the town?"

"Might as well. I've read every magazine in the place. And you know what? The patients are right. The magazines are boring!"

Gary rode with Martin, their first stop the sheriff's substation.

"I called in," Frenchy told them. "I wrestled with my better judgment half the night. I told my people what I felt I could tell them without being labeled some sort of nut. I canceled my leave; I'm back on the job."

"So you have some help coming in?" Gary asked.

She shook her head. "Not anytime soon. We've had a

blow-up with some paramilitary groups. So far, it's a standoff; but any extra personnel are a couple of hundred miles east of here. I was told to handle this situation; work with the sheriff's office and the local police departments. I didn't know whether to laugh or cry at that, with one deputy and one city cop still lucid.''

"You seen Nicole this morning, Audie?''

"Yeah. She just left here. Said the situation over at the P.D. is awful. The guys are functioning, but that's just about it.''

They sat in the sheriff's substation for a moment, looking at each other. Finally, Martin suggested, ''Let's check out the high school, people.''

"I am just thrilled about the upcoming fair, Mayor. It's going to be such fun—I just know it. The carnival's in town, you know?''

"Yes, Bob. I know.'' Martin wanted to grab the man and slap him. The principal's eyes were dull and he spoke in a monotone. ''Bob, do you have any objections to our walking around the building?''

"Oh, no, Mayor. Not at all. I shall be in my office if you need me. I'm experimenting on how to make a better paper plane. I made one just a moment ago that sailed almost twenty-five feet.'' He smiled happily.

"That's . . . nice, Bob. Very good. You keep at it and we'll just walk around.''

"Oh, I shall.'' The principal winked at Frenchy, and returned to his office, pausing every few feet to do a little dance step.

"Bob Peterson was one of the toughest teachers I ever had,'' Audie whispered as the office door closed. ''This is weird.''

"And getting worse,'' Gary added.

They walked up the hall, stopping at a classroom and looking in. The kids were sitting at their desks, most of them erect, staring straight ahead. The teacher was at her desk, looking out the window. No one was reading or writing. Most were just sitting and staring. But a half dozen young people were talking loudly and profanely.

"I got an idea," Martin said. "Watch." He jerked open the classroom door.

The teacher instantly began lecturing, most of the kids writing in notebooks.

Martin stepped back and closed the door. The lecturing stopped, the writing ceased. Teacher and most pupils stared as before.

Martin glanced at Gary. "Find our kids, Gary. Get them out of here. Tell them to go home and stay there. Would you go with him, Audie?"

Doctor and deputy began searching.

"They're sure not cognizant of what's happening around them," Frenchy stated. "They're in some sort of protective cocoon. The insanity, the spell, whatever, is not touching them. That's the best I can come up with."

"I'll accept it. I sure don't have any better explanation for it."

They walked on, looking into classrooms as they passed by. Conditions were the same in every classroom: a few rowdies, male and female, were fully cognizant and engaged in sexual play, while the majority seemed to be in a catatonic state. Martin and Frenchy linked up with Gary and Audie and the kids.

"It was like a dream, dad," Mark told his father. "I looked up and Deputy Meadows was shaking me. I don't even remember walking into the school this morning."

"I do," Linda said grimly. But would not elaborate further.

"Let's get out of this madhouse!" Gary said, pushing Rich and Susan in front of him. "You two go straight home. I'll go over to the elementary and get your brother. And there better not be any hanky-panky going on over there, or somebody's going to get hurt!"

He was moving toward the door before anybody could stop him.

Martin glanced at Audie. "Find Ed Hudson and Jeanne Potter. We'll meet you outside the building."

184

Waiting by their cars, Martin noticed that Frenchy had a worried look on her face. "Want to share that concern with me?"

"Yeah. So I insist on help coming in and just looking over the situation here. How much would you like to bet that everything would be normal the instant they arrived?"

"No bet." He looked at his daughter. "Now you tell me what went on in there."

"Yes, sir. I remember John Stacker trying to touch me. I kept pushing his hands away. But it was like everything was in slow motion. It was a real effort for me to lift my hands."

"I shall remember the name John Stacker," Martin said tightly.

"No, dad," Mark spoke up, his voice edged with anger. "You leave John to me. I've been looking for an excuse to whip his ass ever since I caught him trying to cut my tires."

"You're welcome to him. But watch him. Word I get is that he's just like his dad: a street fighter. He could come up with a knife."

Son met the father's eyes. "Sounds like you've had trouble with his dad."

"A long time ago, in high school. I whipped him then, I can put him down now if I have to."

Within the school building, bells started ringing, and moments later, kids began pouring out of the old two-story school.

"Now what—" Martin muttered.

Mark grabbed a boy by the arm as he passed by the little group. "Steve . . . what's up, man?"

Steve looked at him through eyes that seemed lifeless. "School's out, man. Nothin' doin' 'til next Monday. Turn me loose or I'll kill you." He said the last with no more emotion than if he were ordering a burger and fries.

Mark slowly withdrew his hand. Steve turned and walked on.

"Steve?" Mark called.

Steve walked on without acknowledging the call.

185

"I'm not liking this," Linda said. Frenchy put an arm around the girl's shoulders.

Cars roared away. School buses rumbled into life and began transporting kids out into the county. In five minutes, the school yard was very nearly deserted. Martin and the others watched as Bob Peterson walked out of the building and ambled over to the flagpole. He unzipped his pants, and urinated on the pole, and then strolled off. Then he got into his car and drove off.

"Insanity!" Frenchy said, and that was the only comment concerning the principal's strange behavior. They waited until Audie came out with Jeanne and Ed.

Jeanne's face was crimson. "They're screwing on the desks in there!" she blurted. "All the teachers have gone nuts!"

"Screwing isn't all they're doing," Ed said. Even his ears were flaming crimson.

"That's sure the truth," Audie confirmed. His face was beet-red. "Man, it's wild in there."

The explanation clicked on like a bulb in Martin's head. "The constraints on personal inhibitions are no longer in place," he spoke his thoughts aloud. "People are doing what they want to do, when they want to do it. Social and moral codes no longer matter. But that doesn't make them our enemies . . . I think."

"I don't know what to think," Frenchy admitted. "I'm totally out of my league. I can deal with thieves and murderers and dopers and the like . . . but this?" She shook her head.

"Everybody go to my house," Martin said. "I've got to see a man."

"Nabo?" Frenchy asked. Martin nodded. "I'll go with you. And that is not a request."

"I felt it would be you," Nabo said with that strange smile.

The three of them sat on wooden chairs, outside Nabo's Ten-in-One. The fairgrounds appeared normal, with

186

citizens working on booths, men bringing in prize cattle and sheep and hogs, and ladies putting the final touches on various projects.

And to Martin's eyes, they did not appear to be working as automatons.

"They aren't," Nabo replied aloud to the unspoken thought.

Martin did not question how the man could see into his mind. Frenchy said nothing, not understanding what was going on.

Martin explained.

Frenchy looked first at Martin, then stared at Nabo, something akin to horror in her eyes.

"You have nothing to fear from me," Nabo assured her. He turned his head to look at Martin. "Neither of you."

Martin met his own reflection in the dark lenses. "Maybe not. But Nabo . . . what would you have us all do?"

"Go home. Stay there. Do not attend the opening of the fair."

"But you know that I will."

Nabo shrugged. "You've been warned. If you choose to ignore the warning, then so be it." A faint smile played around his lips. Like a man who had baited a trap and won.

"I'm not going to sit back and allow you to destroy this town, Nabo."

"Who said I was going to destroy the town? A few of its citizens, perhaps. But in either case, you couldn't stop me. Forces are at work that neither of you understand. So stay away."

"Innocent people are going to be killed, hurt."

Nabo laughed, and it was not a pleasant laugh. "Innocent? Oh, no, Mr. Mayor. I assure you, no innocents will be harmed."

No one noticed as the Dog Man slipped quietly to the flap of the tent to listen. There was a very strange expression on his canine face. His ears were perked up, listening intently.

187

"Perhaps not by you, Nabo," Martin was saying. "But surely you are much more aware than I of Satan's presence."

"The Dark One is everywhere on earth, friend. At all times. So there is no need to be unduly alarmed by his presence here."

Frenchy tried to light a cigarette. Her hands were shaking so badly she finally had to give up.

"They're bad for you anyway," Nabo said with a slight smile.

"I don't believe this!" she slung the words from her mouth. "I'm sitting here talking to a dead man!"

"Dead is relative, young lady," Nabo once again smiled that strange curving of the lips. "I've been dead many times."

Frenchy rolled her eyes. "This is crazy!" She got up from her chair and walked a short distance away.

"How can you be so sure your power is stronger than Satan's power, Nabo?" Martin asked.

"I can't. It isn't. But the Dark One will take only those who choose to follow him. The strong-willed will survive. Therefore, your community will be the better for it."

A small wave of suspicion touched Martin. Nabo spoke of Satan with too much familiarity. Could it be? . . . "Isn't that rather cold-blooded?"

"Not at all. It's reality."

Martin tried a guess. "You've done this before, in other places?"

Nabo again smiled. "Of course."

The Dog Man frowned at the lie, wondering why Nabo would say something like that when it wasn't true? But . . . maybe he had. The Dog Man, Balo, and JoJo had only recently crossed the Dark River and once more linked up with Nabo. None of them were really sure what had gone on during the before. Or for that matter, how many *befores* there had been in Nabo's life. Or lives.

"I am told about a book . . ."

"Yes." Nabo's response was impatiently given. "It is unimportant."

"I repeat, Nabo: I will not allow you to do this thing."

"And I repeat, Mr. Mayor: You cannot stop me. You can only put yourself and your family and friends in the path of great harm."

Martin sighed. "All right. Tell me this: who killed Red?"

"Samson."

"Who killed Hank Rinder?"

"I put him out of his misery. Along with the officer who happened to blunder in."

"But there were two Hank Rinders."

Nabo chuckled and Martin sat, watching as a metamorphosis began taking place. Nabo became a monk, a soldier, a knight in armor. Martin cut his eyes to the busy people, some of them not twenty-five feet away. No one was paying any attention. He looked at Frenchy, standing just to his right. Her face mirrored her fascinated horror.

Martin returned his gaze to Nabo. The man had resumed his shape, sitting on the wooden chair, that strange smile on his lips.

Martin opened his mouth to speak. Fear closed his throat. He waited a moment, feeling his throat muscles ease. "Past lives?"

"Yes. The creature I became at the Rinder house was something from far back in time, long before humankind emerged from the caves." He laughed aloud, softly. "Back when all things were."

Frenchy and Martin waited for him to explain that. Nabo did not.

Frenchy put a hand on Martin's shoulder. "You're admitting all this? Knowing I'm with the state police?"

Again, he chuckled. "My dear child, what can you do? Arrest us? That's laughable. Bring in help? All right. But bear this in mind: their deaths will be on your head. Think about that."

The Dog Man fought back a low growl in his throat. He had been assured—they all had—that no innocents would be harmed.

"You sorry son of a—!" Frenchy muttered.

189

Nabo shrugged his muscular shoulders. "I'm overcome with emotion at your dilemma. But at least I'm being honest with you both."

I wonder, Martin thought, averting his eyes from the dark lenses. I just wonder about that. It's too easy. The man is just too open and too honest about impending destruction. "What if we did bring in help?" he once more looked at Nabo. "Suppose I called the governor and he sent in the . . . well, national guard! Hundreds of troops?"

"The innocent among them would live. The rest would die."

Sure, Martin thought, staring at the dark lenses, bring in an atomic bomb—what difference would it make?

"Now you're beginning to understand, friend."

"I'm not your friend!"

"But you're not my enemy, either. A pity that we cannot be friends, for I would then be allowed to tell you so much."

Martin stared into the dark lenses. It was like looking into twin mini-screens. He watched as ages rolled in war and fury and peace and love.

Martin blinked.

The scenes were no more. His own reflection stared back at him.

Nabo smiled at him. "See what you're missing, Mr. Mayor?"

"I know of two very important things I'm retaining by not accepting your offer of so-called enlightenment."

"Oh?"

"My sanity and my faith."

TWO

Tuesday evening.

"I was there," Frenchy backed up Martin's story. "I know what I saw and heard."

The group had been enlarged by two: Eddie and Joyce Hudson. Neither of them had seen Missy since the night before. Ed had seen his sister getting into Karl Steele's truck after school had been dismissed early that day. He had mentioned that to his father, but not his personal thoughts: that his sister was probably into some pot and heavy stuff with Karl's dad out at the ranch.

The group sat on the front porch, drinking coffee or iced teas. Gary said, "So Nabo admitted that Satan was present?"

"In a manner of speaking, yes. He was also very glib about only the unworthy ones being harmed. Those of strong faith would not be."

"But I don't even go to church!" Nicole said. "I was raised a Catholic, but broke away years ago. I was just a kid."

"I was raised a Baptist," Audie spoke up. "But I haven't been inside a church in five or six years."

Martin stirred on the porch. "If you're looking at me for an explanation, you're going to be disappointed. I don't have the answers."

"There has got to be something we can do!" Joyce looked at her small gathering of friends. "I can't believe we're just sitting here allowing this to happen."

"What would you suggest, babe?" her husband asked

191

her. "Short of a miracle, that is."

She opened her mouth. Closed it. She knew she must not protest too much. She had been warned.

"There hasn't been a vehicle of any type pass by here in over an hour," Linda said. "Where is everybody?"

"On one side or the other," Martin answered her. "The question is: where does that leave us?"

"Stuck in the middle," Gary said softly. "Not knowing what to do about the situation."

The sounds of the calliope began again, cutting the night, and as before, it was taunting in its haunting melody.

Martin opened his eyes and lay very still for a moment, trying to determine what had brought him out of a very troubled sleep.

His sleep had been filled with a babble of voices, hollow-sounding and very far away. And his father's face kept appearing and fading, appearing and fading.

He glanced at the luminous numbers of the clock on the nightstand. Two o'clock.

Despite a lot of misgivings on his part, everyone had decided to go back home for the night. Only Jeanne was staying over.

Martin lay very still and listened. He could detect nothing out of the ordinary. Perhaps it had been his nightmares that had awakened him.

He quietly slipped out of bed, shoving his feet into house slippers and putting on a robe, belting it. He looked back at the nightstand, hesitated, then walked over to it, taking a 9mm autoloader out of the top drawer. He jacked a round into the chamber, put the hammer down, and the weapon became double-action, safer than carrying it cocked and locked. He walked to his closed bedroom door and stood for a moment, listening.

He could still hear the voices. Faint and muted. Many voices; a babble. Coming from downstairs. So he hadn't dreamed it after all.

He quietly opened the door and stepped out onto the carpeted hallway. He knew where every squeak was and avoided them as he made his way up the hall, looking in on the kids as he passed their bedrooms. They were all asleep. Jeanne was lying on top of the covers, her short nightie hiked up around her hips, her legs slightly spread. A very lovely young lady. Martin stared, then realized what he was doing and backed out, closing the door, angry at himself for his feelings.

"No need to be!" the voice popped into his head.

Martin stopped dead in the hall, looking around him. The voice had sounded so real.

But he was alone in the hall.

Or was he?

He looked up and down the darkness.

"She's almost seventeen years old, Martin," the voice whispered. "A young woman. And she likes you. Wants you. I know she does. I know her secret thoughts."

"Nabo?" Martin whispered.

"If you wish. Of course."

"You're not Nabo."

"I am, I am! I said I was. Martin," the voice became soothing. "How long has it been since you stroked young virgin flesh?"

Jeanne's half-nude body as he had seen her on the bed entered Martin's head. He could not drive it away. He tried. He could not.

"She'd like for you to be the first, Martin. I know. Look up the hall, Martin."

Martin turned his head. Jeanne was standing by the bedroom door. She smiled at him and pulled her nightie over her head, dropping it on the floor. She smiled provocatively.

"Go to her, Martin," the voice urged in a sly whisper. Martin could still hear the faint babble of voices. "She wants you, Martin."

Jeanne licked her lips and held out one small hand to him.

Martin stepped toward her.

The girl's pale golden flesh beckoned him on. He was close enough to hear her hard breathing.

He reached out to touch her skin

"No, son!" another voice boomed inside his head. "No. Don't do it."

His father's voice.

"Do it!" the other voice urged. It did sound like Nabo's voice. "Don't be a fool. Who would know that you had her? Take her, Martin. Now!"

"But I raised you better than that, Martin," the other voice was knowing.

Martin lifted the 9mm, muzzle pointed toward the ceiling, and pulled the trigger twice.

The booming was enormous in the quiet house. Jeanne's mouth dropped open and she stood for a moment staring at Martin, then became aware of her nakedness. With a cry of shock and disbelief, the girl ran back into the bedroom, almost knocking Linda down before she could jump into bed and pull the covers up.

Mark and Linda rushed into the hall, to stand staring at their father.

Martin leaned against the wall for a moment, collecting his thoughts. Briefly, he told his kids what had taken place. "Be very careful," he cautioned them. "Satan is trying us. Just like he's probably done everybody in this town. Fight him with everything you've got. Find your Bibles, carry them with you, read them, take strength from them."

"And the second voice?" Linda asked.

"Your Grandfather Holland."

Mark's eyes were wide. "But? . . ."

"I don't know, son."

"That grinding sound that Don Talbolt heard out in the grasslands." Linda's eyes searched his face. "That's where Grandpa is supposed to be buried, isn't it?"

Martin nodded his head, not quite trusting his voice.

"Grandpa?" Mark whispered.

"I don't know, son. I'm just as confused as you are. I don't know what to think or what to believe."

Linda touched his arm. "I was dreaming that I heard voices, dad."

"You weren't dreaming. I heard them myself. You two go on back to bed. There is absolutely no telling what daylight will bring."

The kids back in bed, Martin stood in the hall, looking up at the twin bullet holes in the ceiling. "What next?" he muttered.

He wasn't sure he was all that anxious to find out.

Wednesday morning.

His kids had never so openly disobeyed him. He sat and stared at them at the breakfast table, not knowing whether to be proud or angry or a combination of both.

"I don't think you kids are fully aware of what you're saying," Martin finally spoke. He cut his eyes to Jeanne. "And that goes for you, too."

"I'm not afraid, Mr. Holland. Maybe I should be, but I'm not. And as far as us being kids, maybe so. But Mark is almost eighteen. Linda and I are almost seventeen. I think we should have some say in what happens to us."

"I talked to Amy a few minutes ago," Mark said. "Her folks are acting weird. She's scared. Her dad is coming on to her. If you know what I mean. She wanted to know if she could come over here and stay." He looked at his father, defiance in his eyes. "I told her I'd be over to get her."

"It's a big house, son. Of course, she's welcome. Take a close look at her parents while you're over there. Tell me how they're behaving."

"Yes, sir."

"Fine. All right, ki . . . young ladies and young man," he corrected that with a smile. "Ground rules. I'm not going to restrict you to this house. Not yet. For I don't know what's going to happen. But when you leave, you leave in a group. Now, Mark, I saw you put your pistol under the seat of your car this morning. Do you really think it's come to that?"

"I don't know, Dad. But you always say it was Mr. Colt

who made everybody equal."

"Yes. I did say that, didn't I?" the father's reply was very dry. "All right, son. Keep it in your car. I taught you to respect firearms, and you do. You all stay away from the fairgrounds. I don't know about Thursday—yet. You're all back in this house by nightfall. Understood?"

The rules were agreed upon.

"The three of you go get Amy. I'll take care of the dishes."

By the time he had put the dishes in the dishwasher and turned it on, the doorbell donged. Frenchy. He waved her in and poured her coffee.

"Anything new this morning?" he asked.

"Town is very quiet. Very few people stirring about. A lot of businesses are closed."

He told her about the voices during the night. He did not tell her about his experience with Jeanne.

Frenchy wore a troubled look on her face.

"Share it with me?" Martin asked.

"You want me to call for back-up?"

"Do you want their deaths on your conscience for the rest of your life?"

"No."

"You answered your own question, then."

"Martin, I am not accustomed to this helpless feeling. I do not know what to do!"

"Can I say something without making you angry?"

"Try me."

"There is nothing holding you here, Frenchy. No reason for you to put your life, or your sanity, on the line. I certainly wouldn't think badly of you if you should choose to leave."

She tried a smile and made it. "Cops are naturally nosy, Martin. Besides, when I requested to come off leave, I was ordered to stay here. So there needn't be any further discussion about whether I stay or go. I'm staying."

Their eyes locked, and remained so. With a smile, Martin said, "I'm . . . glad."

"Good." She let it remain at that. Time would take care

of the rest of it, if there was to be any "rest of it." "Okay. So what's on the agenda for today?"

"I don't know. I've never been in this kind of box before. I'm damned if I do, and damned if I don't. Figuratively speaking, that is."

"Let's hope."

"Yeah. Look, there is no point in returning to the fairgrounds. Nabo has made it clear we can't stop him and he has no intention of backing away from his . . . vendetta —if that's really what it is. We've tried in a manner of speaking, to warn the townspeople. That was a waste of time. We've agreed that if we leave and try to tell our story outside of Holland, one: no one is going to believe us; and two: if we did manage to convince someone, Nabo would somehow arrange for things to return to normal for as long as the outsiders remained. Are we agreed on that?"

"Agreed."

"So we wait it out and see what the fair opening brings. But, I think it's best if we wait in a group. This is a huge home, with a lot of rooms. I'll suggest it to Gary. What do you think?"

"I agree with you. But give me your reasons."

He told her about Jeanne.

She frowned. "That was close. Too close. Your father's voice stopped you? Okay, Martin. Safety in numbers."

Martin called his lumber shed and got Don on the phone. "I'm the only one showed up today, Mr. Holland."

"That doesn't surprise me, Don." He told him to pack a few things and get over to the house.

"On my way."

"What a strange little group," Frenchy remarked. "So diverse. A doctor and his wife, a lawyer and his wife, a businessman, a cowboy, a handful of cops, and some kids. Where is the common denominator for us to have been spared?"

"My kids asked me that. I've tried to come up with some answers. I can't. But I know this: for the kids' sake, I've got to see their mother and try to convince her to come back. Not to me," he quickly added, "but for her own safety. I'll

197

do that when the kids get back." He explained where they'd gone.

"You want me to wait here for them, Martin?"

"I would appreciate it."

Martin parked outside the old home and sat in his pickup for a moment, looking at the place. He did not want to walk up there and face Alicia. Mike Hanson's car was in the driveway. And it had that look of having been there for more than a few hours. With a sigh, he cut the engine and got out.

The front door opened on the second ring. Alicia stood looking at him. Her hair was a mess and her mouth was puffy. She stank of sex. She did not invite him in.

Martin got the distinct impression he was looking at a lost soul. He had no idea where that thought had come from, only that it had. "Are you well, Alicia?"

"What business is that of yours?"

Martin scratched his head. "Okay. Sorry I asked. Alicia, look, something is wrong in this town. Surely you feel it? I'd like for you to come home, for the sake of the kids. Bring Mike, if you'd like. I—"

She hissed at him like a big cat and slammed the door in his face.

He stood for a moment on the porch, fighting a mixture of anger and frustration. A man and a woman were sitting on their front porch, in the house next to Alicia's. They both laughed at him. Martin cut across the yard and walked up to them. He had known the couple all his life.

"You find something amusing in all of this?" he asked them.

"I reckon your wife got fed-up with you and got herself a young buck with some stayin' power," the man told him, his eyes shining with undisguised viciousness.

The laughter of the man and woman followed him as he drove away.

He could not understand what was happening in his town.

He drove over to Gary's. It was easy to see that the doctor and his wife had been quarreling.

"I pick a bad time?" Martin asked.

"Not really."

"Not really is right," Janet said. "I want the kids to leave town and he wants them to stay."

That's odd, Martin thought. Then decided to keep his mouth out of his friend's family business. He told them about his encounter with Alicia.

Gary, oddly, had nothing to say about it. "Forget her," the doctor's wife told him.

"Consider it done."

"We can look after squirt," Susan said, taking her father's side, a defiant set to her chin. "Me and Rich. Mother wants to stay with Dad. Is that so bad or wrong?"

Janet spread her hands. "I give up."

Martin voiced his thoughts about them all staying over at his place.

"You're probably right," his friend agreed. He looked at his wife. She nodded her head in agreement. "Okay, Martin. We'll pack up some clothes and food and meet you over there."

"You want me to call Joyce and Eddie?" Janet asked.

"Yeah. That'd be fine. Thanks. I'll see you all in a few minutes." He noticed that Janet's face was pale and her hands were trembling. He winked at her. "Hang in there, kid. We'll make it. We'll put some twenty-year-old rock music on the stereo and have a party."

She smiled at him. "Like old college times, huh, Martin?"

"Why not?"

Janet's smile faded. "I have to tell you, Martin. Alicia called me earlier this morning. She invited me over. Said we could have a threesome."

If there was any feeling left in Martin for his wife, it died right then. He nodded his head and left the house. He suddenly had a very bad taste in his mouth.

He drove to the downtown business area. Most stores were closed; what few remained open were doing no business. He almost stopped at Matt's Meat Market for some fresh meat, then changed his mind and drove on past. He drove to his own business offices. The doors were locked. A car pulled into the drive and Martin turned around. Nicole and Audie, in the S.O.'s unit.

"Eerie, isn't it, Mr. Holland?" Nicole asked from the passenger side.

"At least that." Martin told them about staying at his place. Both agreed and said they'd meet him there later on.

Martin stood for a moment outside his offices after Audie had driven away. Some kids passed in a car. One girl leaned out the window and cursed at him.

On impulse, Martin screamed profanities back, feeling rather childish doing so.

The car stopped and backed up. Two young men got out and walked up to Martin. "I think you're looking for trouble, old man!" one told him.

Martin took one step forward and flattened the young man, then backhanded the second, knocking him spinning.

"You sorry old fool!" the girl squalled at him.

One young man tried to get to his feet and Martin kicked him squarely in the butt, just as hard as he could kick. The guy went rolling over into the street, hollering in pain.

"We'll get you!" the kid with the bloody mouth yelled. "We'll get you."

Martin walked to his pickup and pulled away. He drove to his pastor's house and parked, getting out and walking up to the front door.

The kids had followed him, picking up a couple more carloads of troublemakers on the way. They drove by, shouting and cursing and hurling threats at him.

Martin ignored them and rang the bell. The door opened. Martin stood for a few seconds, shocked by the appearance of the man. "Reverend Alridge?" he asked, finally finding his voice.

The man stank of whiskey. Dirt-lines were evident on his throat and face. His clothing was rumpled and stained.

The pastor stared at him through rummy eyes.

"Well . . ." He swayed unsteadily on his feet. "If it isn't the mayor, Martin Holland, his honor. Come on in. Have a drink with me."

Martin stepped into the house. It smelled like Martin had always imagined a whore house might smell.

"I don't care for a drink, Reverend Alridge. And I'll stand, thank you. Pastor, what's wrong with you?"

The preacher slopped some booze into a glass, spilling most of it on the carpet, ". . . wrong with me? I'm tired, my boy. I've come to the realization that if you can't beat 'em, join 'em."

"By 'them,' you mean? . . ."

A girl about sixteen or seventeen walked past the archway separating living room from hall. She was naked. She was the daughter of a church deacon. She looked at Martin and winked.

Martin's face tightened. "Well, Pastor, you've been having a good time, I see."

"What business is that of yours?" the preacher yelled at Martin. "For thirty years I've been banging my head against the wall, trying to save lost souls. I'm tired of trying to live up to a standard that no one else will even attempt to reach. Oh, they'll give you lip-service—plenty of that. And the lies! Thirty years of lies. I'm tired of it." He slopped more booze into his glass. Eyeballed Martin. "Why'd you come over here, Martin?"

Martin felt like an idiot saying it. "To warn you that Satan is all around us."

The preacher laughed at him. "Oh, really! Are you just now figuring that out? Yes, he's all around us. And I can't fight him alone—don't know who to trust—so I quit trying."

Martin slapped the drink out of the man's hand and then backhanded the preacher across the mouth, staggering the man. He slapped him again, this time knocking him down. He jerked the man to his feet, while the girl jumped around, yelling filth at him. Martin popped her on the side of the face and the girl ran out of the room. He shoved the preacher into the hall and toward the bathroom, then tossed the drunken man of God into the shower stall and turned the water on full force, full cold. Yelling, the preacher tried to crawl out. Martin back-handed him again.

"You keep your drunk butt in there until you're sober, Ned. I'll put on some coffee and make some breakfast." Martin found the naked girl in the kitchen, her eyes wide with fear. "Get your clothes on and get out of here!" he yelled at her.

Seconds later, he saw the girl racing across the back yard. He heard water pressure change and looked up the hall. Steam was coming out of the open door of the bathroom.

He fixed coffee and started bacon frying, then wondered where Mrs. Alridge was. He went looking for her, searching all the rooms. But she was not in the house. Back in the kitchen he placed the bacon on a paper towel to drain and broke the eggs. Out of the corner of his eyes, he saw his pastor, a towel wrapped around him, pad up the hallway to a bedroom. A few minutes later, dressed, the man entered the kitchen. He wasn't full sober, but a lot more so than he had been just moments past.

"The girl?" Ned asked.

"I sent her packing."

"God help me, she's been after me for a month. I didn't understand why a seventeen-year-old girl would want a man in his mid-fifties. Of course, I now do."

Martin waited.

"It was all planned out in advance by Satan. You probably don't realize the problems this town has been experiencing over the past few weeks, Martin. But the town's preachers do; we've discussed it, our ranks dwindling as the ministers fell by the wayside, one by one."

"That's why you said you couldn't do it alone?"

"Yes."

Martin set the breakfast plate in front of the man and poured them both coffee. Ned Alridge looked up, pleading in his eyes. "I feel like such an old fool, Martin! It's the carnival, isn't it?''

"Yes. Don't be too hard on yourself, Ned. You're only human. Where is Alice?''

"I sent her to California. She has a sister and a brother out there. I did have a few lucid moments before I gave in to temptation.''

"You did that . . . when you saw this thing coming?''

"Yes. Sunday afternoon. My sermon Sunday morning frightened me. Those weren't my words coming out of my mouth. I didn't write that sermon. It came straight out of *Hell!* Then, after that altercation at the hotel cafe, I knew that my worst fears were real, and not imagined. Sunday night, I went again to see the town's ministers. I was so frightened, Martin. They laughed at me. They were drinking. I ran back here, and found the girl naked. Then, all of a sudden, I just thought: Why fight it? I'm alone. I gave in to temptation.''

"Why didn't you call me, Ned?''

"I didn't know who to call. Who to trust. I just felt that I was alone.''

"You're not alone. There are a few of us who are still fighting. More eggs?''

"Yes, please. If you don't mind. This is the first time I've eaten in . . .'' He looked up, a puzzled expression on his face. "I don't remember when I last ate. I don't even remember where I got the whiskey.''

"I'm sure that was the easy part, once Satan's helpers had you beaten down.'' While Martin fixed more breakfast, he brought the preacher up to date, leaving nothing out.

"Incredible!'' Ned said with a shake of his head. "I've only been here five years, Martin. I've never even heard about the fire. Of course, it all ties in. What about this Nabo person?''

"He's too slick, too glib. I think he's playing me along—me and the few others.''

"Why?''

"Because, for whatever reason, or reasons, he can't pull us into his trap.''

"And you don't know why that is?"

"I don't have a clue, Ned."

"But you have a plan?"

"No plan, Ned. None at all. All we're doing is taking it minute by minute. But we are gathering at my house for the duration. Will you join us?"

"Thank you, I will."

THREE

Ned Alridge had gone to his church and picked up a dozen Bibles, then joined Martin at the Holland house. The pastor was shocked at the few people who had gathered.

"This is it?" he questioned, after being introduced to Frenchy.

"As near as we can tell, Ned," Martin confirmed.

The pastor glanced at Frenchy. "And you don't intend to call in for help?"

"What kind of help would I call for, Pastor? And would you like to be responsible for sending a half dozen cops to their deaths?"

"No, of course not. I see what you mean. And I quite agree with you." He sighed, looking around him. "I did some thinking on the short drive over here. First lucid thoughts I've experienced in several days. I don't have a battle plan for the simple reason that I don't know how the war is going to be fought. I'd like to hear some comments on that."

"How about the other ministers in town?" Janet asked.

"As of a few days ago, they had gone over to the other side. But we can try again. Perhaps if Martin is as, ah, forceful with them as he was with me, a few might come around."

Martin cut his eyes to Audie and Nicole. They got the message. "We'll check on them." They left the house.

The group fell silent, sitting and looking at one another. Gary Jr. was the only one missing. He was in the basement rec room, watching TV.

Don Talbolt sat off to one side, looking uncomfortable in his patched jeans and boots. "You know what's wrong?" he broke the silence. "There isn't a dog barking. Not a bird singing. There isn't a sound to be heard in this town."

The group listened. The cowboy was right. Not even a breath of breeze stirred the outside.

Don walked to an open window and looked out. When he spoke, his words brought out a cold fear-sweat on the others. "It's like everybody else in town is dead, but nobody's told them yet."

"They were . . . blunt with us," Nicole informed the group. "I can't recall ever seeing ministers behave in quite that manner."

"What did the Reverend Masters have to say?" Ned asked.

"He asked Nicole if she'd like to—! I get the picture," Audie said.

"How quaint," Ned muttered. "Did you see Father Bastian?"

"He's out of town for a few days. Some conference in Omaha."

"I'm at a loss as to how to fight this thing," the minister admitted. "I've never faced anything like this before."

"Neither have any of us," Gary told him. "I don't know what to do."

"We do what any combat vet will tell you is the hardest thing of them all," Martin said. "We wait."

They began circling the house at full dark, adults and kids, male and female. They hooted and called and shouted obscenities at those inside the huge home.

"How many you think?" Gary asked.

"Couple of hundred," Martin replied. "Most of the town may be under this . . . spell, but that bunch out there is the town's less desirable element. I've already picked out a dozen that I've had run-ins with over the years."

"I'd like to kill them all!" Mark said, clutching a shotgun and speaking through tight lips.

"Just calm yourself and put that shotgun back in the gun cabinet, boy," his father told him. Mark hesitated. "Do it, boy!"

Mark stalked back into the den. Gary looked at Martin. "Have you thought that it might come to that? Have you given that any thought at all?"

"Yes. But I hope it won't come to that. Listen, Gary, there has to be something to break this . . . evil . . . whatever it is. There has to be something. I don't want to have to hurt anybody."

All that changed with Linda's wild screaming from the back porch.

Martin tore through the house, grabbing up a poker from the fireplace set as he ran past it. His daughter was naked from the waist up, her blouse and bra ripped from her. Two men that Martin knew only by face and reputation were trying to pull the girl off the porch.

With a wild cry of parental rage, Martin swung the poker. The heavy metal impacted with skull and the man dropped like an anvil, his head split open. Gary jerked Linda back from the edge of the porch and hurled her into the arms of Frenchy and Janet just as Martin drove the end of the poker into the throat of the second man.

He tried to scream; only a horrible bubbling sound coming from his mouth. He kicked his feet and pounded the grass with his fists as life began to leave him.

The mob was still out there, but they were silent, disbelieving. Martin tossed the bloody poker onto the kitchen table and stalked into the den, muttering dark curses as he walked. He opened the gun cabinet and jerked out a Mini-14, inserting a full twenty-round clip into the belly of the weapon.

"I've had it!" he snarled.

"Martin—no!" Ned yelled.

Martin ignored the man as he walked through the house, toward the back porch. He was just jacking in a round when his son tackled him, bringing the bigger man down on the kitchen floor, sending table and chairs spinning around the room.

"Dad! No, Dad!"

Gary jerked up the .223 and handed it to a very startled Janet, who looked at the weapon as if her husband had just handed her a squirming snake.

"I'll kill you Godless bastards!" Martin roared, fighting his friends as Audie grabbed one arm and Don grabbed the other. "Turn me loose!"

Together, they managed to pin the big man to the floor. Gary scooped up a pan full of dishwater from the sink and doused his friend.

Martin sputtered and blubbered and shook his head. "Enough is enough!"

"Sure is," Audie said. "You got me, too."

"All right," Martin said. "It's under control. Let me up."

"Now, settle down," Gary warned him. "We don't need anymore dead men in the back yard."

"The mob?"

"They're all gone, Mr. Holland!" Amy called from the front room. "I saw them carry off those two men. They looked dead."

Martin sat up on the wet floor and rubbed his face. "How's Linda?"

"Scared. Shook up. But otherwise all right," Eddie told him. "Joyce took her upstairs." He didn't tell Martin—thought he might have imagined it—but it looked to him like his wife and Linda were smiling at each other.

"All my fine and noble words didn't last long, did they?" Martin got to his feet, almost slipping on the wet floor.

"Your daughter wasn't being attacked when you said them. Something like that has a habit of changing things very quickly."

Martin took the .233 from Janet and pulled the clip from it. He looked out the kitchen window. "They're all gone. But I wonder for how long?"

*　　　*　　　*

The mob did not return that night. Guards were posted on both floors of the house, with each person standing a very boring and uneventful two-hour lookout.

Martin slept well, if lightly, and was shaken awake by Gary. "You gotta see this, buddy. It's weird."

He sat up and glanced at the clock on the bedside table. 7:00.

"What's that noise?" Martin asked, pulling on his pants.

"It's street traffic. Everything appears to be normal. The paper was delivered about forty-five minutes ago. People are out, jogging, riding bikes, just like normal. And Martin? . . ."

Martin stood up and slipped his shirt inside his pants. "What?"

"Alicia is downstairs."

"Alicia," Martin greeted her.

She was perfectly groomed and immaculately dressed, just like the Alicia of old. She smiled at him and held out her hand. Martin took it briefly. "Darling. I'm so sorry for my behavior yesterday. Please forgive me. You will, won't you?"

"Ah . . ." He let her hand drop. "Of course, Alicia. What brings you over this early?"

"Why darling . . ." She smiled at him with her mouth. Her eyes were dead-looking. Scary, the word came to Martin. "Today is the opening day of the fair. You have to make a speech. I want us to go together. Appearances, you know? We've had our differences, but we can put them aside for this day, can't we?"

"Why . . . ah, sure, Alicia. That would be nice." He cut his eyes to Gary. His friend shrugged his shoulders.

Alicia looked around her. "You naughty boy, you! You've been having a party without me." Her eyes settled on Frenchy. "And who is this?"

"Sgt. Frenchy McClain of the Nebraska State Police."

"Oh, really? You must tell me about it sometime.

209

Something to do with the children, I'm sure."

"The children are fine, Alicia. It's a long story."

She waved that off. "And a boring one, I'm sure." She looked at a diamond wristwatch. "Why don't you pick me up about elevenish, Martin. At my place. We'll ride over to the fairgrounds together."

"All right, Alicia. I'll see you then."

She smiled sweetly and looked at Gary. Martin could have sworn she winked at him, and he returned the wink. No. Impossible.

Martin glanced at Audie who had just entered the room. "Audie?"

"I just drove downtown, Martin. Everything is normal. The gas stations are open, grocery stores are open. Everything is running as usual. I saw a couple of the guys who were in the mob around here last night. They acted like nothing had happened. I asked if there was any excitement last night and they said no. I didn't push it any further."

"Nothing about the men who were killed?"

"Not a peep. It's like nothing has happened."

"You think it's over?" Joyce asked.

Martin shook his head. "No. I think it's just the quiet before the storm. I think we're all being suckered."

"Do we go to the fair, Dad?" Mark asked.

"I . . . don't know. I don't know what to do." He met the eyes of all in the room. "Let's vote on it."

Only Jeanne and Janet and Amy voted not to go to the fairgrounds.

"You want to stay here and take care of the kids?" Gary asked his wife, more than a touch of irritation in the question. Again, Martin felt that odd.

She shook her head. "No way am I staying alone. I think Gary will be safer in a crowd than here."

Martin found the equipment he'd been issued by the Holland County Sheriff's Department years back, after he'd graduated from the eight-week academy course. He found his .38 Colt Commander, loaded a clip full, jacked a round into the chamber, and replaced the round, filling the clip full. Easing the hammer down, he laid the autoloader aside. He slipped into the shoulder holster rig, after finally figuring out how to untangle and work the straps and buckles and elasticized rig. His sport coat concealed the .38. He put two full clips into his jacket pockets and then inspected himself in the mirror. As long as he kept the jacket unbuttoned, the gun bulge was not that noticeable.

Wild thoughts filled his head: Maybe he should cut some sharpened stakes and take them instead. To pierce the heart of the Undead.

"Oh, come on, Martin!" he muttered. But he wasn't all that certain the idea was a bad one.

He tried to laugh at the idea of carrying around sharpened stakes in his golf bag. The laugh didn't quite make it.

He checked his watch. He still had about a half an hour before picking up Alicia. And he wasn't looking forward to that, either.

He looked in on the kids. First Mark, who was ready to go, then the girls, who were still primping. For whom, Martin had no idea.

"It makes us feel better," his daughter told him.

"Right. Now listen, gang," he cautioned them. "One solid group unless otherwise suggested. No one is going to forcibly split us up, understood?"

It was understood.

Downstairs, he handed Gary a Colt Diamondback, two and a half inch barrel, and a handful of rounds.

"I haven't fired a pistol in twenty years, Martin," the doctor told him.

"It'll come back to you." He looked at Eddie. The lawyer patted his hip pocket.

"Snub-nose. If I tried real hard, I could maybe hit that wall over there."

"Not exactly the A-Team," Martin said with a smile.

"I'm going to pick up Alicia," Martin told the group.

"Wish me luck. Let's all meet at the speaker's platform just before noon."

He looked at the faces of his friends. New and old. Strained faces; worried eyes. The expression one of uncertainty. He stepped out onto the front porch and paused for a moment. Everything appeared normal. Kids were playing in the soft fall air. Cars moving up and down the street. People waving at one another and stopping to chat. But there wasn't a dog in sight and none could be heard. Not one bird flew or sang.

"They've got more sense than we have," Martin muttered, as he stepped off the porch and walked to his pickup, wondering if Alicia was going to pitch a fit about riding in a truck?

She didn't have a word to say about it. She began chattering like a magpie when she opened the door and didn't shut up during the entire ride.

"I'm so excited, Martin. We're going to have a Shakespearean pavilion. And we'll be putting on a production every afternoon and evening. And guess what? I'm starring!"

"That's nice, Alicia."

"Thank you. I knew you'd be thrilled. Now you must come see me perform, Martin."

"Oh, I will."

Martin would steal glances at her from time to time. Her eyes were dead. Totally lifeless. And her conversation seemed to be mechanical; there was no voice inflection. He decided to take a chance.

When she paused for a breath, he said, "Alicia, you have a snake on your shoulder."

"That's nice. I think I'll make a marvelous Lady Macbeth, don't you, Martin?"

"Just wonderful, Alicia. Dear, there is a great big spider in your hair."

"That's nice. Did you know that Pat Gilmer is going to be in the play, too? The first production will be this evening, Martin. Now do try your best to attend. You won't be disappointed."

"I'll do my best, Alicia." Martin turned into the fairgrounds and found a parking place close to the front gate, backing the truck in for a faster getaway—just in case. "Here we are, Alicia."

"Yes. That's right. Here we are." She began clapping her hands. "Patty cake, patty cake, baker's man." She got out of the truck and smiled at him through the open window. "Straighten your tie, Martin. Remember, you are the mayor."

"Yes. I'll remember."

"I'll be listening to your speech, Martin. Ta-ta!"

He watched her walk off. Knew that person was not the Alicia he had known for most of his life.

He had detected something . . . evil about her during the short ride. And that had frightened him more than he wanted to admit.

Martin felt sick to his stomach and his palms were sweaty. The shoulder holster rig was chafing his skin and he was perspiring under the leather.

And he was scared. Just plain scared. Should he go back to the house and get the others and get out of this crazy place?

He knew that wouldn't do any good. Gary was firm that he was staying. So was Eddie.

He got out of the truck and walked toward the midway, his eyes moving. The fairgrounds was filling up rapidly. He spotted Pete and Frank Tressalt. Lyle Steele and Jim Watson. Tom Clark and Dennis Cameron. All their hands were in attendance, and they all appeared to have been drinking.

He saw Missy Hudson with Karl Steele and his gang of thugs. Martin paused when he saw Dick Mason walking toward him.

"Morning, Dick."

The men shook hands. "I got so wrapped up here I forgot to come by your place, Martin." He looked around him and shook his head. "It's all out of whack, Martin. It's a beautiful day, and the people are all behaving normally. But something is wrong. I feel it."

213

He told the man about the one-sided conversation with his wife.

"Weird! I'm glad I sent my family out of the state. You seen Lyle?"

"From a distance."

"He's got something up his sleeve. I don't know what it is, but you can bet it's not pleasant."

"I'm sure. Dick, you didn't by any chance bring a change of clothing with you, did you?"

"As a matter of fact, I did. Why?"

He explained about them all staying at his house and invited the foreman to join them.

"That's a good idea. I guess. I appreciate the offer. Thanks."

Martin caught sight of his kids. "There's my group, Dick. Come on."

Introductions made, Gary said, "It's about time for you to kick this thing off, Martin. I just wish I was sure we're doing the right thing."

"I had a burst of second thoughts a few minutes ago," Martin admitted. "I guess, Gary, I'm doing the only thing I know to do."

"How do you feel after killing those two men last night, Martin?" Ned asked.

That shook the foreman. "Say . . . *what?*"

Frenchy explained. And it was obvious to all that her feelings toward Martin had turned from friendly to something a lot deeper.

The foreman looked at Martin, realizing there was a lot of tempered steel in the man.

"I did what I had to do," Martin assured the minister. Martin glanced at his watch and with a sigh, said, "Let's get this show on the road." He walked toward the speaker's stand.

The high school band was tuning up.

The town council was already seated on the platform. And Martin was very dubious about turning his back to them.

With a sigh, Martin climbed the short flight of steps and

took his place behind the rostrum.

Then he looked out over the crowd and came very close to losing his breakfast.

Carnival people were all mixed in with the townies, and their faces had changed, along with many of the townspeople.

Martin's personal, unspoken and unshared suspicions had become reality.

He was staring out at a mixed crowd of innocents and demons; at men and women he had grown up with, whose features had changed into grotesque hideousness. Perhaps one out of every ten townspeople had changed into something from the pits of Hell. They stood grinning up at him, their faces piggy-snouts and snake heads, twisted ape features and half-human grotesqueness. They were the faces of monsters and creatures that defied description.

Martin struggled to keep a scream from passing his lips. He closed his eyes for a moment. When he opened them, the faces of townspeople and carnies looked up at him. No monsters or demons or hideousness among them. No hellish creatures.

But he knew he had not imagined it, not after meeting the dark lenses of Nabo, standing with his arms folded, in the front row, smiling at Martin.

Then he met the eyes of Alicia, and wanted to run screaming from the platform as her face changed into a huge horrible reptilian object. Her tongue danced out of forever-smiling lips, forked and red. Mike Hanson stood beside her, his head replaced with that of a goat. There was Lyle Steele standing behind Mike, the rancher's skin all rotted.

Chief Kelson stood in the center of the crowd, his head now as pointed as a pin, his ears elfin, his eyes large round black circles set in a face that was barely recognizable as his own.

Again, Martin blinked. The hideousness vanished and the crowd was filled with familiar faces, all staring up at him, waiting for him to begin.

Martin got through his short speech, not remembering a

215

word he'd said, and rejoined his friends.

"Let's get out of here," Eddie suggested.

They moved several hundred yards away from the speaker's platform.

"I wanna ride the rides!" Gary Jr. hollered.

They were standing next to the merry-go-round. "The merry-go-round," Gary said. "Go with him, Susan. And stay with him. Don't let him out of your sight."

"Gary!" Janet protested.

"Don't worry. He'll be all right."

Frenchy met Martin's eyes and he lifted one eyebrow, then nodded at his own kids. The young people trooped off, Gary, Jr. in tow.

Nabo suddenly appeared at their side. "Not a very inspiring speech, Mayor. Are you ill?"

Martin turned, meeting the mocking smile with a grim expression. "I feel fine, Nabo. Or should I call you the Devil?"

Nabo laughed. "Oh, no, my dear man. Nothing so dramatic as that." He turned his head to look at Ned. "You have more willpower than I gave you credit for possessing, Preacher."

The pastor stood his ground and met the dark lenses and the evil behind them. "Thanks to a lot of help from Martin."

"Ummm," Nabo said. Martin could feel the eyes return to him. Nabo lifted his arm and looked at his watch. "Seven and one half hours, Mr. Mayor."

"Until what, Nabo?"

"Hell, its fury and our revenge."

"You planted some seeds thirty-four years ago, didn't you, Nabo? Among the townspeople?"

"Actually, no," the man surprised him by saying. "I did not. I was a Christian then, as were many of the people in the carnival. It took a fire to convince us that being a Christian among so-called Christians was not the way. Shall I say that, ah, after our untimely demise, most of us struck a deal."

"With the Devil."

216

"You don't seem surprised to hear that."

"I guess I'm not. I put it together a couple of days ago. But it did startle me to see so many townspeople take the form of . . . creatures."

"Their kind is in every community, Mr. Mayor. But a catalyst is needed to bring them to the fore, so to speak."

"I see. So I suppose that I am looking at that catalyst?"

Nabo bowed slightly. "At your service, Mr. Mayor." He turned to leave.

"Wait a minute!" Martin's sharp words stopped him and turned the man around.

Nabo stepped close to Martin. The eyes behind the dark lenses seemed to radiate evil. The smile on the lips was mocking. "Yes, Mr. Mayor?"

"You just walk away?"

"What would you have me do?"

"Tell us what we're up against. What do we do?"

Nabo chuckled. "Why . . . enjoy the shows, Mr. Mayor. It's carnival time."

FOUR

To a stranger, the mood would have seemed festive. Music from the rides was joyous and the mixture of food smells, from cotton candy to hot dogs, hamburgers, popcorn and candied apples scented the air. The laughter of the young and the young at heart—evil as both groups might be—was everywhere.

Martin and his little group stood in a tight knot and stared grimly at the midway.

"Nabo said seven and a half hours," Frenchy said. "By my watch that reads eight o'clock this evening and the lid blows off."

"I guess that's what time it blew off back in '54," Eddie replied. "Do we just stand here and go down with the ship, so to speak?"

"I for one still do not understand, like Janet, why we all just don't leave?" Joyce's voice was surprisingly calm. "Will somebody please explain that to me?" Martin could detect no fear in her voice and wondered about that.

"Where would we go?" her husband told her. "And what would we do or say once we got there? Like Martin said: no one would believe us. We'd have to come back. This is our home. Every dime we own in the world is tied up right here. Nearly every investment we have is right here in Holland. And Joyce, do you want to go off and leave Missy? Or try to force her to leave with us?"

"We could try to do that, I suppose," Joyce said, without one ounce of conviction in her voice.

"I demand to know why I cannot leave these grounds!"

a woman's scared and shrill voice reached the group. They turned as one, watching a woman from out of town argue with Chief Kelson, who was blocking the main gate. They also noticed that the gate was closed and locked.

"Now we know why that expensive eight foot high chainlink fence was put up," Janet said.

"We can't get out of this crazy place!" Janet said, a definite edge to her voice.

Two carnival workers moved swiftly toward the woman as the artificial laughter from the crazy house was turned up, pumping through the outside loudspeakers. Martin and his group watched as the carnival workers, roughnecks from the look of them, led the woman away. She screamed and struggled to free herself. Nobody else seemed to notice.

Audie started to move toward the woman. Martin's hand stopped him. "No. It may be a set-up to separate us."

"And if it isn't?" Nicole asked.

"Then I made a mistake."

"It's wild! It's crazy! It's fun!" the loudspeakers blared from the crazy house. "Come one, come all. Bring the entire family."

"I've got nineteen .38 rounds that says no one is going to keep me in here against my will," Martin said grimly.

"I have six in my gun and twelve in my pocket," Eddie said.

"Same here." Gary looked at the tent where the men had taken the woman. He looked over at the merry-go-round. The kids were safe, watching his son ride the wooden horses as the music played. No one noticed the strange smile on his lips. Or on the faces of two others in the group.

"I've got a shotgun and a rifle in my truck," Dick spoke, his tanned face hard. "And a couple of boxes of rounds for each. Any time you folks opt for a bust-out, we'll bust out."

"You have a short gun, Dick?" Martin asked.

"Under the seat."

"Let's get it. The rest of you stay put and keep an eye on

the kids."

The men walked over to the foreman's truck and Dick unlocked the door, getting his pistol. He jacked a round into the government model .45 and refilled the clip up to six. He eased the hammer down and tucked the big autoloader behind his belt. "Now I feel some better." His smile was tight.

Together, they walked over to Chief Kelson, standing by the closed and locked gate. The pinhead, Martin recalled. "What happened to the woman who wanted to leave here, Kelson?"

"What woman?" the chief replied, a very faint smile playing around his thick wet lips.

"Fun! Fun! Fun for everyone!" the loudspeakers called, the words overriding the too-loud music. "Bring the entire family to the house of mirrors."

"The woman those carnival workers led away from this spot! Now give me an answer."

Kelson grinned at him. His breath was very bad. "Now, settle down, Mayor. Why don't you just run along and enjoy yourself. I can promise you that it's gonna get real interesting around here 'fore long."

"Maybe I don't want to run along, Kelson. Maybe I'd like to leave and go home. What then?"

"Why, sir, you and your friends can leave just any old time you like. Ain't nobody gonna stop you. You wanna leave now?"

Martin stared at him until the chief dropped his gaze. He muttered something under his breath about a long walk home.

"What did you say, Kelson?"

One of the city patrolmen laughed.

Martin's eyes followed the chief's turned head. All four tires on his pickup were flat. He looked up the line to Dick's pickup, the foreman's eyes following. A kid was running away from the truck, a knife in his hand. All the tires on Dick's truck had been cut.

"Bastard!" Dick muttered. He took Martin's arm and led him away from the gate, away from the now openly laughing city cops and the grinning Kelson. Just as he was about to speak, his eyes caught movement in the top chair of the ferris wheel. He pointed.

"Oh, no!" Martin breathed, lifting his eyes to the uppermost gondola.

A young man was standing up in the swaying gondola, waving his arms and shouting. "Look at me! Look at me! I can fly! Watch me fly!"

A crowd had gathered by the ferris wheel. "Jump, jump, jump!" they chanted.

"I can fly!" the young man shouted.

"Look at Nabo," Martin said, cutting his eyes.

The man in black stood apart from the crowd, his arms folded across his chest. He was staring up at the young man in the swaying car, high in the air. Nabo was smiling.

The young man began flapping his arms like a large featherless bird. He began cawing like a crow. Then he stepped out of the gondola and dropped like a brick. He turned twice, slowly spinning downward in the warm festive air.

He landed on the concrete lip of a permanent fair building. His head exploded, showering blood and brains all over the people standing closeby. The crowd all began laughing and joking at the sight.

Alicia ran up to Martin, her face flushed nearly out of breath. "Isn't that great, Martin? What a wonderful act. I've never seen anything like it. Have you?"

Martin stared at her for a moment. "Act? Alicia, that kid is dead!"

"Don't be such a silly-willy!" she tossed her head. "It's all staged by the carnival."

"Oh, lord!" Dick said, horror and revulsion in the words.

Matt Horton was kneeling by the broken and bloody body of the young man. The butcher had a plastic spoon in one hand and was dipping out brains from the shattered skull, eating them.

Gary pushed through the laughing, shouting, joking crowd, all of them looking with evil glee in their eyes at the

222

ruined body on the ground. He joined Martin and Dick.

"Isn't that hysterical, Gary?" Alicia asked. "I wonder how they do that?"

She laughed and walked off.

"Get the kids," Martin said. "We're getting out of this place. I was wrong. We should never have come."

Eddie had just walked up. "Guess again, buddy. Take a look over at the gate."

Twenty-five or thirty men were blocking the gate, all of them armed with rifles or shotguns.

"We could take a few of them out," Dick said. "But none of us would survive it."

The kids had joined the group. "Now what, Dad?" Mark asked.

Several "I should have's" entered Martin's head. I should have taken Alicia and the kids and left town. I should have called in state police reinforcements. I should have paid closer attention to what was going on in this town.

He felt the weight of defeat try to settle on his shoulders. He shrugged it off. "We fill up on hamburgers and hot dogs and then get to the farthest part of the fairgrounds. As soon as it's dark, we go over the fence. Is that agreeable with everybody?"

It was.

Nabo met them as they walked toward a large refreshment booth. "It won't do you any good," he informed Martin.

Martin knew exactly what the man was talking about. But he had to ask. "What won't?"

"Bunkering yourselves in some isolated part of the grounds. There is a lot of resentment toward you and your friends—among a certain segment of the community. They'll get you. It's only a matter of time. And bear in mind, Mr. Mayor: In all fairness, I did warn you to stay away."

"Why did you? Did you know I would ingore the warning?"

"No. Oh . . . perhaps it's because with you and your group, I sensed a bitter fight."

223

"Tell me the point of this, Nabo. I cannot see it."

The man smiled that strange curving of the lips. "It's only a game, Mr. Mayor. A fun game."

Nicole stared at the man. "A boy jumping off a ferris wheel is a game to you? Killing is a game to you?"

"Of course. And you people think Satan doesn't have a sense of humor. Shame on you!"

No one knew how to reply to that. Dick Mason stood and stared at the carnival man, his mouth open. He had one thought: kill this bastard!

Then it finally sank in: But the guy is already dead!

"Why don't you people go have a good time?" Nabo suggested brightly. "There will be isolated incidents during the afternoon, but nothing for any of you to really concern yourselves with. Nothing . . ." he smiled, ". . . drastic is going to happen to any of you until tonight. Go. Enjoy your last day on this earth."

"You're crazy!" Frenchy told him. "Go . . . *enjoy* ourselves?"

Nabo turned his head to stare a her. "I must take my leave now. I must prepare for what the night will bring. Yes, enjoy yourselves, people. That's what a carnival is for." He walked away, losing himself in the large milling crowd.

A scream of pain turned their heads. "My God!" Susan cried, pointing toward a concession. "Look!"

It was a dart-throwing concession. Bust three balloons and win a prize. But there were no balloons to break. A woman had been lashed to a makeshift backboard, and she had already been impaled by half a dozen of the sharp-pointed feathered missiles. Blood was running down her face and neck.

"Help me!" she screamed, her eyes on a laughing, jeering man standing in the crowd. "Jim, for God's sake. Help me!"

Her husband laughed.

Her tortured eyes found a teenage boy and girl standing by the man called Jim. "Help me, son!"

The boy and the girl spat at their mother.

The crowd snickered. A ranchhand took aim and let his dart fly, striking the woman in the stomach. She screamed in pain.

Dick stepped up to the man just as he was picking up another dart. The foreman balled a big right hand into a fist and busted the cowboy in the mouth, dropping him to the ground like a rock. Martin and Eddie had moved behind the concession, working at the ropes that bound the woman. They could hear the crowd turning ugly, shouting hate at Dick and the others.

"It's all just in fun, you bastards!" a man yelled. "You get away here and let us have some fun or we'll kill you."

The ropes came loose just as several men and women charged around the tent and attacked Martin and Eddie. Martin threw up his arm in time to block a wildly thrown punch. Crossing with his left, he hit the man on the jaw, knocking him back, then drew his arm back and drove his elbow into the mouth of another attacker.

Eddie gasped in shock as he pulled the woman out of the rear of the concession. Someone had thrown their final darts, one catching the woman in the eye, and the other directly in the temple. She was kicking in death spasms.

"Eddie!" Martin shouted, struggling with a large woman and finally doubling her over by driving his fist into her stomach. "Let her go. We've got to get back to the others."

"Grab the girl!" a man yelled. "Let's have some fun with the kid."

"You leave my sister alone!" Gary Jr. yelled, and kicked the first man he saw right in the kneecap. The man yelped in pain and grabbed for his knee. Gary Jr. balled his fist and hit the man on the nose, bloodying it.

"Kill him!" another man yelled. Audie stepped into the melee and smashed the man in the face with a tent stake he'd jerked from the ground.

Martin and Eddie jerked up stakes and tore the tent ropes from them, then waded into the crowd, the heavy stakes clogging off of heads and shoulders and backs.

Martin could see no sign of Linda or Joyce or Gary. And

he thought that strange.

Suddenly, and with no warning, the crowd veered off and began moving in another direction, leaving Martin and his group standing alone by the tent, wondering what in the world happened.

Susan said as much, looking around her as one of the men who had been screaming and cursing at her a moment past, smiled and tipped his hat and spoke to her.

"Let's get out of here," Dick suggested.

The group left the midway, moving into the maze of cars, trucks, campers and trailers. There they stopped and looked behind them. They had not been followed.

Martin quickly counted heads. They were all together. He cut his eyes. Nabo was standing a few yards away, smiling at them.

"Oh, you're in real trouble, now!" he called. "You should not have interfered."

"What did you think we would do?" Frenchy asked. "Just stand by and watch the torture without acting?"

"You're very attractive, Miss. It's a real pity that you're so dumb."

Without hesitating, Martin reached inside his jacket and pulled out the Colt Commander. He jacked the hammer back and shot the carnival man in the chest.

Nabo smiled. "Finally got a reaction from you. I was wondering when that might occur."

They could all see where the slug had struck the man in the center of his chest. They had all heard the bullet tear through him, rip out the back, and clang off the metal of a bob-truck.

Nabo smiled at them.

Susan picked up a rock and threw it at the man, striking him in the face. The rock did no damage. Nabo laughed at them.

"You'll pay for that," he said.

"Ghoul!" Gary Jr. yelled at him.

"And you as well," Nabo looked at the boy.

Then he vanished.

"What the—" Dick muttered, blinking his eyes.

226

"Where are Susan and Gary?" Janet yelled, turning in a slow circle.

The group looked around.

Susan and Gary Jr. were missing.

They were in total darkness. Susan felt for her brother's hand and found it. "Hold on to me, squirt. Let's figure out where we are."

"I gotta pee!"

"Don't think about it. Grab onto my belt. That's it. Now hold on tight and don't let go."

With both her hands free, Susan felt around her. Her hands found a smooth surface, on both sides of her. Glass. They were in a small corridor.

Gary felt with his free hand. Felt like glass. "We're in a glass house, Susie!"

Something began pulling at the boy. He yelled in fright. "Something's got me, Susie!"

"Hold on, Gary."

He felt his small fingers slipping from the leather of her belt.

"Susie!"

Then he was gone.

"Gary!"

Darkness and silence.

The silence remained. The darkness slowly became pocked with soft light, the light reflecting off of mirrors. Many mirrors. Susan knew then where she was. The house of mirrors. She calmed herself, forcing her mind to slow down, to think rationally. If there was a way in, there had to be a way out. Problem was, finding it.

She deliberately did not allow herself to think about how they—she—had gotten to this place.

No, it was they. But where was her brother? She heard movement from behind the mirror.

Gary stood in a house of horrors. Monsters all around him. His heart was beating so fast he really thought it might explode. The monsters were all great grotesque-

227

looking things.

He forced himself to calm down, close his eyes, and take several deep breaths. He opened his eyes. The monsters were still there, but they hadn't moved or snarled or growled or anything. He poked one in the belly. It did nothing.

Gary felt better. "Fake," he muttered. But he knew it wasn't fake that he had been separated from his sister by some kind of magic.

Black magic. Or so he guessed, although he really wasn't sure exactly what that meant.

Was he scared? You bet he was!

Then he heard a giggling. But it wasn't a very nice giggling. Evil, the word came to him. More giggling. He knew that giggling. He'd heard it before. Alma Sessions. That little creep.

"You crummy jerk!" another voice penetrated the near-darkness. "Now you gonna get what's comin' to you."

Gary knew that voice too. That dumb David that ran with Alma, Norm, Bette and Virginia. They were all really bad.

"I'll kick your butt, David!" Gary called, his voice carrying through the semi-gloom of the house of horrors. All fake horrors. Gary had to keep believing that. Fake, nothing but fake.

Then Davy told him what they were going to do to him. Gary was petrified. He kept his mouth shut and quietly slipped to the wooden floor. On his belly, he looked under a horrible hairy beast-thing. That really wasn't real. Thing was on a metal stand of some sort. Wires running to it. Big fake was all it was. He had to keep reminding himself of that. Sure looked scary.

Gary could see the tennis-shoe clad feet of Alma and her punky gang. They were standing in a small corridor that ran behind the lines and rows of fake monsters. Could he slip under the hairy things? He thought so. But first thing was to get Alma and her gang out of there.

Easing his small one-blade pocket knife out of his jeans, Gary opened the lock-back blade and silently slipped under the hairy beast and worked his way closer to the feet of Alma and her gang. Maybe, the thought came to him, he could jab her in the foot so she couldn't walk—or something.

"Gary?" he heard Virginia call. She was as bad as Alma. Maybe worse. She liked to hurt animals. "Gary, you better answer me."

Gary remained still and silent.

"Little brat is gone!" Alma said, anger in her voice. "He tricked us. Come on. Let's get over to the monster side."

When the feet were gone, Gary slipped all the way under the hairy beast on the stand and rolled to the canvas next to the corridor. He cut a slit into the canvas and peeked out. He could see some of the nutty-acting people on the midway. But another tent blocked most of his view. He tried to remember what was next to the horror house.

The house of mirrors! Sure. That's where they'd been. That's what he'd felt while he was standing behind his sister.

And that's where Susan was right now, he'd bet. He had to get over there. He had a knife. He could help his sister get free.

"The little creep is gone!" Alma's voice came to him. "But that ain't possible. The front door is blocked."

"Maybe they lied?" Norm asked.

Gary didn't wait to hear the reply. He slipped through the slit in the canvas and dropped to the ground, running across the short strip of grass to the next tent. He climbed up on the wooden walk-ramp outside the tent and cut a long slit into the canvas, then slipped into a maze of reflecting gaze.

Gary stood for a moment, startled by the many reflections of himself, all distorted. He listened for any sound.

"Stop it!" his sister's voice, low and muffled, came to him. "You're hurting me!" That was followed by a moan and a slap. His sister cried out in pain.

But where was she?

All Gary could see was his own reflection, about ten

zillion times.

He thought he heard footsteps behind him. He started to turn around just as a hard hand clamped over his mouth, cutting off his yelp of fright as strong arms jerked the boy off his feet.

Frenchy stepped in and blocked Gary's path. "It won't do anybody any good for you to go off half-cocked, Doctor. Just calm down. We'll find your kids."

"All right," Gary said agreeably. Too agreeably, it seemed to Frenchy. Had they been her kids she would have been climbing the walls and screaming.

She cut her eyes. Martin had noticed it as well.

He shrugged.

"Where did they go?" Janet's voice was edged with hysteria. "They couldn't have just disappeared. That isn't possible."

"Don't bet on that, Janet," Ned Alridge's voice was calm. "It's just now getting through to me that we're really dealing with the supernatural. We'd all better acknowledge that and act accordingly, by accepting that anything is possible."

Dick was looking at Gary as if he could see something that no one else could see. The man is taking the disappearance of his kids just too calmly, the foreman was thinking. He looked at Linda. She was seemingly unconcerned about the vanishing act of her best friend. Something is all wrong here. But what? And why did no one come to investigate the loud booming of Martin's Colt Commander.

Something is very wrong within this group.

But he didn't know what.

"What are we going to do!" Janet persisted.

"Relax, honey," her husband told her, about as much emotion in his voice as telling a patient that a shot isn't going to hurt.

"I'll go look for them," Rich volunteered.

"You stay put," Martin told him. "Let's just all calm

230

down for a few minutes and try to think this thing out."

The breath was hot and stinking and whiskey-smelling on Gary's neck. But the little boy kept his wits about him after just a few seconds of panic. Like he'd seen done on the TV, he palmed his knife, hiding the blade from unfriendly eyes. His assailant cuffed him on the side of the head, bringing a yelp of pain from the boy.

But I still got my knife! Gary thought. You big drunk bully! You'll see.

"You don't open your mouth, you little brat!" the man's voice hissed. "You gonna get to see your sister git hers."

The man pushed on a mirror and the glass opened, moving inward. Gary looked at his sister in the dim light, half naked on the floor, and moaning like she was in pain.

His captor dropped him to the floor, on his feet, and slapped the boy on the side of the head, bringing involuntary tears to his eyes. "You behave, you little punk!"

Gary spun around, driving the blade of his knife into the man's lower belly. He stabbed him three times and then ducked as the man screamed and tried to hit him. Gary darted under the blow and stabbed the man again.

Gary ran to his sister just as the man between her legs was crawling up on one knee, cursing. Gary drove the blade into the man's face. With a cry of pain, the rapist jerked backward, both hands to his face. Gary stepped over his sister's bare legs and drove the blade into the man's throat. He gurgled in pain as his blood squirted. He fell back, the blade pulling free.

Susan jerked on her jeans and fastened her belt just as her brother was slashing a hole in the canvas. The kids jumped to the ground and hit it running.

"Somebody grab them!" a woman yelled, pointing at the running kids from her spot on the midway.

Gary and Eddie appeared between concessions. Gary had the Diamondback in his hand and a very odd expression on his face. He leveled the pistol and shot the

231

woman in the head. Her feet left the sawdust and she fell in a boneless heap, a hole in her head.

Eddie said some very uncomplimentary things about life in general and certain types of people in particular just as the kids ran past him.

But no one on the midway paid any attention to the dead woman with a bloody hole in her head or to the doctor with the smoking gun in his hand.

"Fun! Fun! Fun!" the loudspeakers blared the message. "Come one and come all to the fun house. It's crazy, friends. Bring the entire family. Fun! Fun! Fun!"

Gary looked at the loudspeakers, grimaced, and then ran to join his family.

"That was Mrs. Jamison you killed, Gary," his wife told him, one arm around Susan. Rich had Gary by the hand.

"She was expendable," he replied. "Come on. Let's go."

"Where?" She looked at his face. There was a very strange look in his eyes. And that expendable bit was a very odd thing for him to say.

His smile was not pleasant. He turned and walked away.

FIVE

Nabo suddenly popped up in the middle of their group, startling them all. He smiled at them. "Oh, good moves, people!" he complimented them. "Very good. Showed a lot of initiative on your part. This is going to be such an exciting evening."

"You son of a bitch!" Janet cursed him. "Look what you've done to my daughter. You think it's exciting and fun."

"People are only doing what they have always wanted to do, Mrs. Doctor. Like the old song, 'Anything Goes.'"

"But you could stop it!"

"*Au contraire,* Mrs. Doctor. I cannot. I am powerless to stop them. It is completely out of my hands."

Janet was trembling with rage. She turned away from the evil smug face. She wanted to slap him.

"Then who can stop it?" Ned demanded.

Nabo smiled at him. "You are a man of the cloth and have to ask that, Preacher? Your god and my god can stop it. That's who. Why don't you ask your god to intervene? That should be good for a laugh."

Ned stared at the man for a moment, his expression grim. "Perhaps I shall. But bear this in mind, worshipper of the devil: my god works in strange ways."

"Then He'd better get off His ass and start working," Nabo replied. "For your time is growing short."

Then he was gone.

The group looked around them for some trace of the man. There was none.

"Let's walk the fence," Dick suggested. "Surely they can't be guarding the entire length of it."

"One man with a rifle every hundred yards or so would be sufficient," Martin said.

"Yeah," the foreman said glumly. "I already thought of that."

And that was the way it turned out. And the men were on the outside of the fence, behind cars and trucks, reasonably safe from any gunshots that might come from inside the fenced area.

Gary had never said one word about his daughter being molested, and his lack of concern was beginning to irritate Martin.

As they walked, Gary, Linda and Joyce in the rear of the group, Martin asked, "Did you know the man who raped you, Susan?"

"Just his face. I think he works for some ranch. I'd never seen the other man. Mr. Holland? What's wrong with my father?"

"I don't know, honey. I was about to ask you the same question about Linda."

"And Mrs. Hudson?"

Martin nodded.

"They sure are acting weird, I know that."

"I agree."

The group had walked about half the fenced area, and were now behind a livestock pavilion, and the irony of that had not escaped Martin.

"Listen to them," Rich said, disgust in his voice. "They're in there talking about the price of cattle and breeding stock and so forth. Like nothing has happened. It's like . . . we don't exist, or something."

They stopped to rest under a huge old tree.

"I sort of understand *what* is happening," Janet said, "but not the *why* of it."

"Perhaps there is no why of it," Ned said with a tired sigh. "Although I'm sure there was to begin with. From what you've all told me, revenge was originally the why of it. But I believe that probably got lost along the way as this

234

Nabo and his people made their pact with Satan. I'm no expert on the supernatural, folks. I'll admit that I never really believed in it. We always left exorcisms and the like to the Catholics. Somebody remind me, if we get out of this situation, to apologize to the first priest I see."

"We'll get out of it, Ned," Martin said, with more assurance than he felt.

"There has to be a why to it, Reverend Alridge," Jeanne said.

"Not necessarily, child. While, as I said, I'm no expert on the supernatural, I do come with some degree of expertise on the subject of Satan. He's the great destroyer. The ruiner. Creator of havoc. Nabo was right. It's nothing more than a game to the Dark One. Tweaking the nose of God. That's all this is. There is nothing more to it."

"A game," Amy spoke softly, as she held Mark's hand.

"I'm afraid so, child," the pastor told her. "All in the blink of an eye," he whispered.

"And when they're finished here in Holland? . . ." Eddie asked.

Ned shrugged. "Who knows. Who is to say that even should we survive, we'd remember any of what has happened? I can't say. You'd have to ask either God or Satan about that."

"Why us, Pastor?" Dick asked. "Why were we . . . spared, for the want of a better word? I'm certainly not a religious man."

"It was for a reason. Of that I'm sure. But the specific reason? . . . I don't know."

The ferris wheel was slowly making its circles, music from the midway reached them along with shouts and shrieks of laughter. But the laughter was darkened with an evil sound.

"Mr. Holland?" Susan touched his arm.

Martin cut his eyes.

"The carnival people haven't done anything that obvious, and I don't think they're going to. Do you see what I mean?"

"I'm not sure I do, honey."

"Well, if—*when*—we get out of this, what can we say for sure that the carnival people have done? That we could prove or that anybody would believe? They haven't done anything that I've seen. It's all been townspeople. I don't think the carnival people are going to destroy the town. I think they're going to sit back and let the townspeople do it. So if the cops were to come in while all this was going on, Nabo and his people are clear. It would just be sort of a reverse play on what happened back thirty-odd years ago. You see what I mean?"

"I think she's right, Martin," Eddie spoke.

He nodded, cutting his eyes to Gary, sitting with Joyce and Linda. They all three had odd expressions on their faces, and a strange look in their eyes.

Joyce met his eyes and smiled at him. But it was not a pleasant smile.

What was going on? "One thing for sure: Nabo can't afford to have us talking when it's all over. He's got to get rid of us."

"Kill us, Mr. Holland?" Jeanne asked.

"Maybe not," Ned broke in.

Eyes turned toward the preacher. "Would you explain that, Ned?" Janet asked.

"Not if he could convert us. The devil would much rather do that than see us dead. That would be a much greater victory for him. And wager on this: the Dark One will really increase the pressure on us as the night closes in. Divide and conquer, I should imagine."

"I think you're right." Dick met the man's eyes. "But there has to be something we can do."

"Oh, there is." Ned took out a small pocket Bible and opened it. "I would suggest prayer for starters."

Audie and Nicole had gone boldly onto the midway and returned with armloads of hamburgers and Cokes.

"No one bothered us," Audie said, passing out the hamburgers as Nicole handed around the large Cokes. "In a manner of speaking."

"People would look at us or stop us and chat like it was old times," Nicole said, before Audie could elaborate on his last remark. "But I didn't know what they were talking about half the time. They were talking about things and people and events that I never heard of."

"What do you mean?" Eddie asked.

"Well . . . Mr. Harris kept talking about a basketball game between Holland and Chadron and about the big fight afterward."

"That was in '59," Martin said. "I remember it. What else?"

"Well, he kept using terms like 'groovy' and 'neat' and 'cool' and 'hip.' And he asked me if I was going to the sock hop this evening." She looked at Martin. "Mr. Holland—what is a sock hop?"

"It's a dance. Usually held on a basketball court. You take off your shoes so you won't scar up the floor. Dance in your socks."

"Oh, yeah. I've seen that in the movies. I—" She stopped as Gary and Joyce both started snapping their fingers and singing "The Boy From New York City."

"What is that?" Audie asked.

"A song that was popular back when we were in high school," Martin told him. "Back in '64 or '65—somewhere along there."

"They look stupid!" Rich summed it up, watching his father and Joyce.

Gary and Joyce shifted vocal gears and began singing the old Dave Clark Five hit "Bits and Pieces."

"I don't get this," Frenchy muttered. "And I don't think I like it either."

Nicole shook her head. "That guy that jumped off the ferris wheel? He's still laying out in the open, gathering flies. And the woman that Dr. Tressalt shot is still in the middle of the midway."

"And nobody is paying any attention to them?" Martin asked.

"No one." Nicole grimaced. "And they're beginning to smell."

"I saw Lyle Steele," Audie spoke to Martin. "He told me to give you a message." He cut his eyes to Linda, snapping her fingers to the song Gary and Joyce were singing.

"Say it, Audie."

"Well . . ."

"Go ahead, Audie. The whole message. Intact. I told you the other night that I thought I'd have to kill Lyle someday. Just give me a good excuse to do it."

The deputy sighed. "Okay. He said that at first he was gonna screw your daughter and then give her to his men for a good old time. But something better has come up for you."

Martin's brow furrowed. "What is he talking about?"

"I don't know, sir."

"Susan," Martin asked, "just before you were taken away, did you feel anything strange at all?"

"No, sir. Nothing. And I've thought about that. One second I was with the group, the next second me and squirt were in that dark place."

"Hey!" Jeanne said. "Where's Don?" She looked around her. "He was right here a second ago."

They all looked around them. All but Linda, Joyce and Gary. The three of them were sitting and looking at each other in total silence.

The young cowboy was gone.

"I just handed him a couple of hamburgers!" Nicole said. "He was eating one."

Don was standing amid some of the strangest creatures he had ever seen in his life. Tiny towered over him, while Samson stood looking at him as though he would like to break every bone in the young man's body. Which he would cheerfully do if Nabo would cut him loose.

"A gentleman's agreement, young man?" Nabo asked with a smile.

Don looked around him. He had no idea where he was or how he had gotten there. "What kind of deal and how did I get wherever I am?"

"You are neither here nor there, young man," Nabo told him. "You are in limbo."

"I don't understand."

"You are behind the veil. You are between lives. For the moment, you are neither dead nor alive. Is that explanation sufficient?"

"I guess. What do you want?"

"Oh, I think you know."

Don lifted his right hand. Still had his hamburger, half eaten. He smiled and offered it to the man. "Care for a bite?"

"Don't be absurd!"

"Just thought I'd ask." He took a bite of the hamburger. It was tasteless. He looked at the sandwich. "What's wrong here?"

"You may experience only what I wish you to experience. And I assure you, pain is not an option."

He recalled Ned's words. "I won't sell my soul to the devil or betray my friends, if that's what you're suggesting."

"Don't be too hasty, young man. I would suggest you give it careful thought."

Don started to tell the man to shove it. But the words would not form on his tongue.

Nabo suddenly became angry. "Interference! Why?" he shouted.

Don couldn't understand who or what he was talking about. Or talking to.

The dark lenses of Nabo's glasses turned to the young man. "How would you like to spend eternity listening to your flesh burn, and living in the most excruciating pain you could possibly imagine . . . forever!"

"That would probably be unpleasant. But I don't think my God will allow that to happen."

Nabo spat in his face.

Don met the man's eyes. Or lenses. He was scared, but refused to let Nabo see the fear. "I may not be the most religious man in the world, Nabob, or whatever your name is, but I try to be a good person. I'm kind to people, I'm kind to animals. I don't even like to brand stock. And I was raised in the church. You want to hear me sing

'Onward Christian Soldiers'?''

"What?"

Don started singing as loudly as he could. Lot of echo in this place.

"Enough!" Nabo shouted. "The words are offensive to me."

Don kept singing.

Nabo slapped him across the face, bloodying Don's lips, silencing him. "I should have Samson tear your arms out of the sockets and then throw you back to your friends. How would you like that?"

"I wouldn't," Don replied honestly. "You always have to have others to fight your battles and do your dirty work for you?"

"I should tear your tongue from your mouth. You're a fool!"

Don didn't try to argue that. Maybe he was. He looked first at Samson, then at the giant, Tiny. The hate in their eyes chilled him. Scared him. But this came to him: If Nabo was going to do something, why didn't he just do it and stop talking about it?

He met Nabo's dark lenses and wondered if the man could read his thoughts?

Nabo smiled as he walked around and around the young man. Don didn't know where he was, but it was weird, no doubt about that. All black and foul-looking. But shiny enough to see. Dead silent and dark as hell. Then the thought came to him: Maybe that's where he was. Hell.

"No, no, you idiot!" Nabo snapped at him. "You are not in Hell."

That did spook Don. But confirmed his suspicions. Nabo could see into his mind.

"The entire town," Nabo said, disgust dripping like slime from his cruel mouth. "I have the entire village in the palm of my hand; a total victory—except for your little group. You're ruining everything!" he roared, spittle spraying Don's face. The man's breath was stinking. Smelled like . . .

. . . the grave.

Don forced himself to keep his expression as bland as possible and figured the best thing he could do was keep his mouth shut.

Nabo shouted threats at him. Told him what he could do, the most hideous of things. Nabo circled the young man, screaming threats and curses at him, seemingly never taking a breath.

Or course not, Don thought. Why should he have to? The man is dead.

"Let me gouge his eyes out," Sam rumbled, "before you send him back."

"Yes!" Tiny said, smiling cruelly. "Let's all enjoy listening to him scream."

Nabo shook his head. "That would only serve to solidify the group. He pointed a thick finger at Don. "But the night shall change it all. You Christians will probably survive the light, but not the dark. Go!" he screamed.

Don slid on his face and chest and belly and came to an abrupt halt, his head in Jeanne's lap. His face was cut and bleeding from the crashing impact with the ground. But he still clutched the mashed hamburger. Maggots crawled from the wrapper. Feeling them crawling on his flesh, Don jerked his hand back. Martin kicked the hamburger away.

Jeanne yelped in surprise as his head landed in her lap. She fought back her surge of fear and helped to roll him over on his back. He was scared and disoriented and looked to be in shock.

Gary, Joyce and Linda had gone for a walk, ignoring the warnings from Martin and the others. Susan wet a cloth from a nearby outside hydrant while Martin took the young man's pulse.

"Fast but very strong," he said.

Don tried to sit up. "I'm all right."

Jeanne pulled his head back down. "You stay still for a minute." She took the cloth and bathed Don's face. The cuts were minor, already closing.

"Where did you come from?" Amy asked, a trembling in her voice.

241

Don cleared his throat a couple of times. "From a meeting with Nabo and some of the weirdest-looking people I have ever seen. Big giant of a man and a huge, muscle-bound guy. I got the feeling there were others there that I didn't see."

"Tiny and Samson," Martin told him, watching as his daughter, Gary and Joyce returned. They did not seem at all interested in Don's return. "But where were you, Don?"

"I don't know." Don sat up and took a sip of Coke from a cup Jeanne handed him. He told them what he could remember about his journey—and return. And about Nabo's anger at his remark that God would not allow Nabo to send him to burn forever.

"Interesting," Ned spoke. "Very interesting. Our prayers might have been answered in a small way. And you say it was black?"

"Real black. So black it was shiny. That's how I could see."

"Mayor!" came the shout. "There you are. I've been looking all over for you."

"Please," Don muttered. "No more surprises for a few minutes—please?"

"Relax," Martin patted his shoulder. "It's old Doc Reynolds."

They watched as the old man walked toward them, leaning heavily on his cane. He came around the side of the livestock pavilion.

Martin stood up and greeted the man. "How'd you get in here, Doc?"

"I walked in through the front gate. How else?"

"But the gate is closed, locked and guarded, inside and out!" Audie said.

"I noticed that when I got inside," the old doctor told them. "But from the outside it doesn't appear that way."

"How? . . ." Amy opened her mouth.

Doc Reynolds waved a hand, silencing her. He motioned for Martin to walk with him. They moved a few yards away from the group.

"Listen to me, Martin. None of you are in a normal

situation here, so don't try to rationalize it as such. You must realize that you're facing the living dead, and act accordingly."

"And they are acting on orders from the devil?"

"Probably."

"You took a terrible chance in coming here, Doc."

"I'm almost ninety years old, Martin. I have no fear of death. Listen to me: I have the insight. Your father has the insight. Yes, *has*. He is not truly dead—not yet. He's been waiting for this. He'll be back very soon. Brace yourself for that. The sight will not be pleasant. Now, Martin . . . you also have the gift. You must bring it to the fore and use it against Nabo and his people."

"But I . . ." Martin wet suddenly dry lips. "The insight," he whispered. "Last week, on main street, I thought I saw time revert back to the 1950's. A little while ago, Audie and Nicole mentioned the people on the midway talking about events that happened years ago like it was just yesterday." He almost said he also saw his daughter change into a demonic-looking hag. He was conscious of Doc's eyes on him.

"Yes, Martin. I'm sorry to have to say that you are right on all counts."

Martin realized the man could see his thoughts. He remembered the night of the party, when Joyce's face changed into that horrible piggy-looking thing . . . and he thought of Audie, the night Hank Rinder was killed, when the deputy had seen Gary change into something not of this earth.

Martin stared at the old man.

"Yes, Martin. Right again. And again, I'm sorry about it."

"But? . . ."

"They are what they are, Martin. They cannot change. So you must be very careful and ready for anything at all times. Do you understand?"

"What you're saying—thinking—is monstrous!"

"I am truly sorry, Martin. But that is the way it is." The old man sighed painfully. "Martin, when you bring your gift to the fore, it will be something you will have to live with all your remaining days. And it can be dangerous. Your mind can destroy people. Always remember that."

The old man turned away.

"Where are you going, Doc?"

"To try to buy you some time to prepare yourself, and then to meet my old friend, your father." He chuckled oddly. "It's going to be quite a ride, son."

Martin didn't have the foggiest idea what kind of ride the old man was talking about, or even if the old man was telling the truth—but he strongly suspected the latter was all true.

Martin thought of his daughter, his best friend, and a woman he had gone all the way through school with.

The doctor read his thoughts. "Yes, Martin. Yes."

"You've known for? . . ."

"Since the birth of you all. I delivered you all. And no, you weren't born with a veil over your face or anything like that. I just knew. You are all perfectly normal-appearing babies, with all your fingers and toes."

"Why didn't you tell me before about Gary and the others?'

"I didn't think the condition would ever surface. Your father didn't want me to mention it to you. We talked about it the day before he was murdered. Anyway, would you have believed me?"

Martin shook his head. "I don't know. Alicia? . . ."

"Of course."

"How can I be sure you're telling me the truth?"

The old man smiled. "You know, Martin. You're sure." His words were soft and sad. "And now you have a job to do. How you do it is up to you."

"You want me to? . . ." He could not bring himself to say the words.

"Yes. There is no other way. You have no choice in the matter. If not . . ."

Martin could read the old man's thoughts clearly. Death. Betrayal. Savagery. Torture. Acts so depraved and hideous no human nor animal would do them.

"My daughter, Gary, Joyce . . . all the others I saw today from the speaker's platform . . . they've known since birth?"

"No. It takes someone like Nabo to bring it out. There are hundreds, thousands, of these types scattered throughout the world. Most of them, I suppose, live normal lives and when they die . . . go to hell, I guess. I really don't know. I don't know if they even have a soul, Martin. So little is known about them."

"My son?"

"Part of you."

"Linda?"

"Just like your wife."

"No hope?"

"None."

"Gary?"

"Like his brothers. Only able to disguise it far better. Joyce is the devil's own. Watch her."

"Jesus God!"

"I hate to be sacrilegious, but if I was going to call on anybody for help, I'd add Michael to that list if I were you."

"God's mercenary."

"And now, son of my old friend, so are you." The old man turned and walked away, slowly and painfully, toward the crowded midway. Filled with evil. Walking toward his death.

"Go with God, Doc," Martin muttered, as some of his group gathered around him.

"What was that all about?" Eddie asked.

"I'm not sure," Martin lied, looking at Gary. "I think the old man has become very senile. Gary?" he forced himself to look at his friend.

"Oh, I quite agree. He's been around the bend for years."

Gary Tressalt's handsome face had changed to a hideous mass of sores. Martin forced his expression to remain calm, as he stared at his lifelong friend.

He cut his eyes to his daughter. His beautiful Linda. She

245

was anything but beautiful. She had changed into a dreadful-looking old hag, with rotting lips and long greenish teeth. Her face was warted and hairy and her hands were gnarled claws.

Martin looked at Joyce. She was unbearably ugly. Pig snout and long curved teeth. Just as he remembered her from the party.

Everyone else appeared to be normal. Martin felt Dick's eyes on him. The foreman had sensed something was very, very wrong. But he was keeping his mouth closed about it for the moment.

Martin glanced at Ned. The pastor, like Dick, felt something was wrong.

Martin wished he could have spoken more with Doc Reynolds. He wished a lot of things. None of them, he knew, would ever come true. Conditions would never return to normal—not the normal he had once known. Not ever. He looked at his own half eaten lunch, still in the wrapper. He felt nauseous as he struggled to maintain his composure.

What to do?

He tried to tell himself he didn't know. But the lie fell flat.

How to do the act?

Easy. Just reach inside his jacket, take out his gun, and kill the demons while they were still in human form.

How did he know he could do that?

He didn't know how. He just knew.

Could he destroy them with his gift of insight? He didn't know.

Kill them, Martin! the words boomed inside his head.

But he couldn't do it. Not without more proof. How could Reynolds think he could destroy his own daughter? His best friend?

"What's wrong, Dad?" his son asked. "Other than the obvious, that is?"

Do it, Martin! a voice urged him. *Kill them all. It's your only chance. Kill them! Do it now, man!*

"I'm just trying to think of a way out of this jam, son." I

246

saw Gary kill that woman. Sure. Solidify his position with us, I suppose. Same with allowing the men to rape his daughter.

"I think the night will be better for us," Gary finally spoke. Was that a deliberate blandness in his voice? Martin thought it was; couldn't be sure. Couldn't be sure of anything. "I think we should just take it easy and stay out of sight until full dark. Then maybe we can make our move."

"Yeah, I agree with that," Joyce said. "Let's wait until night. Stay together."

Martin wondered where the three of them had gone during their walk. He looked at his daughter. "How about you, baby?"

"I think Gary is right." Gary! She had never called him Gary in her life. "I think we should just hang around here until dark."

"All right," Martin agreed.

"Fun! Fun! Fun!" the loudspeakers blared. "Come one, come all to the crazy house! It's wild and crazy, folks. I guarantee it."

Nabo's laughter rang out over the fairgrounds.

SIX

Dick took Martin's arm and led him to one side, away from the others. "What's going on, Martin? That old doctor was saying things to you with his eyes . . . and you were understanding them."

The foreman recoiled as if he'd been hit with a club when Martin told him. Then he remembered his own suspicions about Gary and Linda. "Oh, no! Do you believe the old man, Martin?"

"Yes. Keep your voice down. I guess I believe him, Dick. I don't want to. But they changed right before my eyes a moment ago. You remember they were the three who wanted us to stay here until dark."

"Yeah. But your own daughter, man! Is there no hope for her?"

"No. None. Not according to Doc Reynolds. And, yeah . . . I believe him."

"I don't know what I'd do."

"I'm numb. I'm doing my best not to dwell on it. But it's all beginning to fit, Dick. It's all coming together. My mind's been working overtime the past few minutes. As the carnival pulled into town, rolled through, the sight of Linda's, well . . . like creatures, I suppose, brother and sister demons, whatever, was too much for her to contain. She changed right in front of my eyes, not knowing I had this . . . insight gift. Same with Joyce. Obviously, Audie possesses some degree of it as well. We all might, for that matter. I think that's the bond that holds us. You have it. You all saw the creatures while I was making my speech."

"Yes. Maybe that's it. What are you going to do, Martin?"

"I don't know—yet. Obviously, even though I know I should, I can't just take Doc's word. They've got to make some move against me—us—before I'd feel comfortable reacting. I . . . I just really prefer not thinking about it."

"I understand. Who else do you plan to tell?"

"I haven't even thought about that."

"You have to tell the others, Martin. You can't endanger them by your silence."

"I know," he said with a sigh. "I don't want to tell the kids just yet. And certainly not Eddie. I'll try to prepare him a little at a time. Even though we don't have much time. He's liable to go wild. No telling what he might do. To me."

"At first. And then to his wife."

"Yes."

The foreman was thoughtful for a moment. "I have a question: why didn't Gary, Joyce and Linda change with the others while you were making your speech?"

"I can't answer that. I don't know. Maybe they did and you just didn't notice them. I couldn't see them from where I was."

"Come to think of it . . . could you see any of us?"

"No. You were all standing off to my left side, out of sight. Why?"

"Joyce and Gary and your daughter stood behind the main group. But I didn't think anything strange about it at the time."

Martin nodded his head. "Doc also said that my father would be back. I refuse to accept that. My father has been dead for years."

"Murdered and buried in his truck somewhere out in the grasslands, so the story goes."

"Yes."

"That sound that Don heard? . . ."

"My mind will not accept that, Dick. I'm having a hard enough time dealing with what we're facing now."

"I don't think we've seen anything yet."

Martin rubbed his face with his hands. "Unfortunately, Dick, I think you're right."

Far out in the grasslands, the starter was once more grinding, pulling juice from the old battery. It sounded very weak in the warm fall air. But this time there was nothing around to hear it. Animals had deserted the area; birds had soared far away from the site. Where the cattle had grazed, they had sensed something wrong and moved on, several miles away, not even taking time to feed as they moved.

The area was deserted. And except for the sound of the old truck starter, as silent as death; as still as the damp confines of a musty grave.

The battery sounded very weak now. Sounded as though a few more seconds of grinding and it would be as dead as the passenger in the cab of the truck had been for years. Until now.

Then the engine caught, sputtered, faded, and finally roared into life. Blue smoke began rising from out of the ground. The earth began to tremble. The engine revved up. A crack appeared in the earth's surface. More smoke poured out of the ground as the engine and transmission strained. A spinning sound was heard as the old tires, rotted and flattened, dug into the cool inner earth. A high whining noise came from underground. The crack on the surface widened. Earth fell away from the crack and the top of the rusted cab was exposed.

The earth trembled as the nose of the truck appeared from the widening hole; the front tires—more rim than tire—rose out of the earth, exposing the chrome grill of the old truck. The man behind the wheel grinned his death-smile as the truck lurched from the hole and rattled and banged onto the flat surface of the grasslands.

What remained of the man slowly opened the door and stepped out of the cab. His flesh had been mummified to a wrinkled and deep brown. His hair and fingernails had grown during his period of death. The hair, a yellowish

251

gray hung over his ears and down his neck. The fingernails were at least an inch long, pale against the leather-like skin. He stretched and a smile of pleasure crossed his face as his old joints cracked; mini-firecrackers on the grasslands. His smile broadened, exposing yellowed dentures.

"Aahhh!" the sound came from his slowly opening mouth, the dentures clacking together with the exclamation.

He got back behind the wheel and dropped the truck into gear, moving out slowly, lurching and bumping and rattling and banging toward the road he hoped was still there.

As his son was sitting behind the livestock pavilion, wondering what might be coming next at the group, the long-dead father in the rusted old pickup truck, rolling along on rotting rubber and rims, slowed as he pulled onto the road and paused for a moment, getting his bearings. Yeah, Joe Carrol's place was just a few miles up ahead. Joe Carrol was as sorry as Jim Watson and Lyle Steele. The old man laughed drily, dust and dirt flying from his mouth. He'd just stop and pay Joe a friendly visit.

Well, he mentally amended that . . . he'd pay him a visit. Friendly was up for grabs.

Laughing, he rattled up the road.

As the death truck smoked and banged toward the ranchhouse, Billie Watson and Joe Carrol had polished off a pint of booze and were now coming out of their clothes on the way to the bedroom. They fell on the bed in a naked tangle of hot flesh.

They both heard the rattle-bang of the old truck, but heard it dimly, the metallic clanging scarcely penetrating the heat of passion.

Joe Carrol had been with the bunch of men who had kidnapped, tortured and finally killed Martin Holland all those years back.

Those thoughts were in the old man's dusty brain as he climbed the steps to the ranch house. The dogs that usually lay on the porch had left in a silent hurry as they sensed what manner of creature was in the cab of the truck. The hounds were a mile away and still moving as the leather-like hand closed on the doorknob and pushed the front door open.

He smiled his grim reaper smile. His skin stretching in a whispering sound, the old bones popping, he walked through the house, picking up a poker from the fireplace; then he stood unobserved for a moment in the open bedroom door.

He worked his tongue around in his dusty mouth, until he was sure the words would form and pass his lips. "Joe Carrol!" he finally croaked.

Billie turned her head and screamed in Joe's ear.

Her eyes rolled back in her head and she passed out under Joe just as Martin proceeded to beat in Joe's head with the poker. The old man tossed the gory poker to the floor and lurched back out to his truck, rattle-banging and clattering on toward the town of Holland. He hummed tunelessly as he drove, smiling, thinking how interesting the night was going to be.

Martin glanced at his watch, wondering if the afternoon was ever going to end. He and Frenchy had walked the rest of the fence line, and Martin had told her of Doc Reynolds' warning.

"You don't seem surprised."

She shook her head. "I'm not, really. If we can accept any of this . . . outrageousness, we can accept that friends can be a part of the other side." She paused in her speech. "I'm sorry about Linda. Very inadequate words, I know."

"It's odd. But I can't bring to mind's eye how pretty she was. All I can see is that horrible demonic face I witnessed."

"Keep that in mind, Martin. That will make it easier . . . when the time comes." Again, she paused. "Do you want me to? . . ."

She let that dangle.

Before he could reply, the carnival strong man, Samson,

253

stepped out from between a row of vehicles. He was wearing a cowboy hat that was much too small for his huge head. He grinned at the man and woman.

"Five will get you ten that's Don's hat," Martin said, taking Frenchy's arm, making her continue walking.

"He looks grotesque."

"I can't hate him, Frenchy. I can't hate any of them. I don't feel sorry for them. But I can't hate them personally. I can hate what they stand for, but not them."

She glanced at him. "What an odd thing to say."

"Not really. Think about it. They were not evil people when they were killed. Everything points to them being pretty nice people, really. The townspeople killed them, and did it horribly. I don't know how they changed; became what they are. But I know why."

They walked on past Samson. The huge man made no attempt to approach them. He watched them walk by and then turned his back and strolled off in the other direction.

"Revenge," she finished it for him. "But that doesn't excuse them from aligning with Satan." She shook her head. "Those words seem so odd on my tongue."

"No, it doesn't. Of course not. But the thought keeps returning to me; I wonder if all of them are aligned with the devil?"

Ralph Stanley McVee, known as the Dog Man, met in the darkness at the rear of the Ten-in-One with Balo, JoJo and Baboo.

"We've been tricked," he said, the words forming awkwardly on his long animal-like tongue.

Balo stroked the sixteen foot long King and nodded her head. "I suspected that a few days ago. But we're trapped."

"I want my vengeance," Baboo said, his face grim. "That is my right. But I will take no part in the deaths of innocent people."

"I think Dolly has made up her mind," JoJo spoke, his long ape-like arms dangling to his knees. "She has

254

accepted Nabo's god and is not to be trusted."

"That is not the point," the Dog Man persisted. "The point is: do we assist the small group fighting Nabo, or do we wreak our vengeance and then do nothing more?"

A wild, pain-filled shriek of horror ripped through the canvas. The sounds of breaking bones and the slurping and smacking of wet lips reached the small group meeting in the long tent.

Just behind the tent, the Geek had broken the back of a man and was busy ripping long strips of flesh from the living being and stuffing them into his mouth.

The Dog Man cocked his canine head and listened. "That is not an innocent," he finally spoke. "But as the dusk approaches, and night falls, the innocents will suffer just like the guilty."

"I say we cannot permit it," Balo said. "While none of us will ever attain Heaven, we have been promised protection from Hell. If we do nothing, we might lose that protection."

"Nabo is not sure of us," Baboo cautioned the others. "Someone is always watching us. I observed Jake following me earlier."

"Slim was watching me," Balo said.

"It will be easier when the night comes," the Dog Man told them. "It is agreed then? We help the small group?"

It was agreed.

"But they have traitors among them," JoJo warned. "And I am not sure they know that."

"They know," the Dog Man yapped the words. "The mayor possesses the gift."

"I wonder if he knows the danger he is in?"

"If he doesn't, he won't live to see the night."

"There's been another death on the midway," Nicole told them when they returned from their walk. "Audie and me found what was left of Mister Coleman. Looks like somebody ate his flesh."

"The Geek," Martin guessed accurately. "I've been

255

getting strange messages in my head. I told Frenchy about it. That's why we returned so soon. But they're very confusing messages.'' He looked at the deputy and the city cop. ''Frenchy has something to tell you. While she's doing that, I'll speak to the others.'' His eyes swept the area where his group had been waiting. ''Where's Gary, Joyce and my . . . daughter?''

Audie caught the hesitation; said nothing about it. ''They got up and walked away right after you and Frenchy left. They didn't say where they were going. Martin? What's up now?'' Ned had joined them, listening.

Martin looked at his watch. Four o'clock. About two and a half hours to dusk. ''Frenchy will bring you up to date while I'm speaking to the others. God help us all, I hope Doc Reynolds was wrong, but I know he wasn't.'' He walked away, moving to his son's side.

''Brace yourselves, people,'' Frenchy told them. ''This is going to be hard to take.''

Martin met the eyes of the kids. Mark, Rich, Jeanne, Susan, Amy, Ed. Gary Jr. was curled up on the ground beside his mother, both of them napping. Don was stretched out on the ground; Martin could not tell if he was awake or asleep. Eddie was sitting with his back to the group, some distance away. Martin stared at the man's head and was shaken when Eddie's thoughts entered his head. Shaken not only by his ability to read another's thoughts, but by the savagery in his friend's mind: Eddie believed his wife was having an affair with Gary, and it was in his mind to kill them both.

He averted his eyes from Eddie's head and returned his gaze to the young people ''What I'm about to say is going to be very hard for you to accept, gang.'' He met his son's eyes. ''Especially you, son.'' He looked at Susan. ''And for you, honey. But . . .''

''I looked at my father about half an hour ago, Mr. Holland,'' Susan interrupted him, her voice low. ''But it wasn't my father I was seeing. I don't know what it was. Whatever it was, it was horrible. Demon-like. I couldn't see it in Joyce and Linda, but I could feel it. That's it, isn't it?"

Martin did not trust his voice. He nodded his head and cut his eyes to his son.

"The daughter is like the mother and the son is like the father, right, dad?" Mark asked.

Martin found his voice. "Yes, son. I'm afraid so."

"Me, Sis and Gary?" Rich asked, a touch of fear in the question.

"You're not affected." He leveled with the kids about what he'd seen while on the speaker's platform. About Alicia, Mike Hanson, Matt Horton, Chief Kelson. The townspeople who were the devil's own in disguise. He told them every word that Doc Reynolds had said to him.

"Grandpa is coming . . . back?" Mark asked.

"Yes. According to Doc Reynolds. After all this," he waved his hand at the carnival midway, "I think anything is possible." He looked at the kids and marveled at the way they were taking it. Or was it that they really did not understand? He rejected that. They knew. But like the adults, they had deliberately numbed their minds. "I'll ask Ned to speak to Eddie."

"I'll tell mother," Susan volunteered.

"I'll tell Don," Jeanne said.

Martin hid a smile. Young romance in the midst of fear and death. Well, he thought, she could do a lot worse than Don Talbolt. "All right, kids. You hang in there. We'll make it."

"We don't have a choice," his son summed it up.

An hour later, Martin knew that his daughter, his best friend, and Joyce would not be back. They had deserted the group, their families, to join their true kind. It made things much easier to Martin's way of thinking. He walked over to Eddie and sat down on the ground beside the lawyer.

"I was married to that . . . *creature*," he spat out the last. "Loved her. I don't think I'll ever feel clean again."

"Believe me, Eddie, I do know the feeling."

257

The lawyer cut his eyes and tried a smile that almost made it. "Yeah, I guess you do at that, Martin. We've both lost a wife and a kid."

"You can't be sure about Missy, Eddie."

"Don't try to con a good lawyer, buddy. We both know her soul is as black as a coal mine. It's amazing to me that we're all taking this as well as we are. It's tough on young Ed, though."

Martin kept silent, letting the man talk it out of his system.

"What do you figure our odds, Martin?"

"Fifty-fifty," he replied honestly. "Maybe not that much. But I have the strangest feeling that I'm getting more and more powerful—mentally."

"You really read my thoughts awhile back?"

"Yes."

"I don't think that is a gift I'd want." He cut his eyes. "Powerful, how?"

"In all ways. I know now why it's called insight. I can see fear, joy, distrust, uncertainty. And I'm getting the feeling that I can destroy with this gift. Strange term for it, I guess."

The attorney looked at his watch. "Getting down to the wire, buddy."

"Not long."

Frenchy joined them. "Have you noticed the subtle change in the noise coming from the midway?"

They listened, with Eddie saying, "I can't tell any difference."

Martin nodded his head. "It's grown impatient, angry— no, sullen. Yes, a definite change in the crowd." With his eyes on Frenchy, he added, "You do have the gift."

"I guess." She shrugged it off. "If I do, I never knew it before now."

"Nor did I. You feel brave?"

"Not particularly. What do you have in mind?"

"Taking a walk. Let's size things up before it gets full dark."

*　　　*　　　*

Martin Holland rattle-banged along on the pavement, the rotted rubber long since thrown off the rims. The rims were kicking up sparks on the concrete as he rolled along at a stately 25 MPH. One leathery arm was hanging out the window, his bony right hand on the steering wheel. He was still many miles away from the town of Holland. But he wasn't worried; he'd get there in plenty of time to help his son and a few of his old friends. By now, he felt, his son would have learned he had the gift, and would be experimenting with it. And the father knew the son would soon discover how dangerous it was. He only hoped he learned it in time.

And, although the second mental request was not nearly so important as the first, the man hoped he got to the Holland fairgrounds in time to see his son put the gift to work.

SEVEN

Over the objections of the others, Frenchy and Martin went for a walk along the midway. Both of them were armed, with the pistols concealed. They were shocked at the change of attitude of the people who milled around on the midway. Fights were breaking out every few yards, men fighting men, women fighting women, and men fighting women. The crowds pushed and shoved and cussed. They saw two women holding a man down on the ground, forcing him to eat huge wedges of cherry pie.

"Tell me my pie is no good, huh, you son of a bitch!" a woman swore at him. She drew back and slugged the man on the jaw. The second woman knee-tackled another man and brought him down, straddling him, sitting on his chest, and hitting him in the face with both fists.

"And they're not even married," Martin tried a joke.

Frenchy chuckled until her eyes drifted to a dark space between two concessions. A body of a young man lay on the ground, naked and bloody.

Frenchy walked over to the body and knelt down, touching his dead flesh. "Still warm. This wasn't done that long ago."

"Sure wasn't," Linda's voice came from behind Martin.

He turned to face his daughter. Blood was splattered all over her clothes.

She laughed at the expression on her father's face.

Martin backhanded her, knocking the girl flat on her back in the sawdust.

A man who worked just up the street from Martin's

261

hardware store began screaming curses at Martin, charging at him with a club in his hand.

Frenchy's .357 barked once, the slug striking the cursing man in the neck, turning him around like a bloody human top on the midway. He danced for a few seconds, then fell to the sawdust, a gaping hole in one side of his neck.

Linda had scrambled off, but not before Martin had watched the girl almost begin her demonic metamorphosis. She had crawled off into the darkness before the change could be completed.

Sudden hate almost consumed the man, heating his blood to a blinding fever. He turned and saw Jim Watson looking at him, grinning, his face melting into a hideous mask. The words that rolled from the beast-like mouth forever damned the man. "We're one with the devil, Holland." The laughter was tinged with evil from the darkest places of Hell.

Martin felt a trembling take hold of him as his eyes bored into Satan's own.

Jim Watson began changing back to human form as flames licked at him, the fire coming from out of the air. Martin's eyes changed into yellow embers as Frenchy stood back and watched the crowds vacate the area. Within seconds there was no one within a hundred yards of the three of them. And one of them was a rolling mass of flames. Howling came from within the lashing flames; a screaming like nothing she had ever heard before.

"That's enough, Martin!" she yelled at him.

Martin's eyes changed. His trembling ceased. Jim Watson fell to the earth and sawdust and sizzled and bubbled and kicked as whatever sort of life was in him died yet another death.

Frenchy grabbed Martin by the arm and literally shoved him out of the main midway, to the darkness between concessions. She pushed him behind the concessions and toward the livestock pavilions.

"I'm all right," he finally spoke. "You can turn me loose, Frenchy! Can you believe that I did that back there? I just thought it and it happened!"

"It couldn't have happened to a more deserving . . . creature. I can assure you of that. How do you feel?"

"Drained. Tired. But I'm recovering fast."

"He admitted he was the devil's own. I wonder if he has known that all along?"

"I doubt it. Doc told me that someone like Nabo has to come along; that brings it out. Old Doc. I forgot about him. Did you see him on the midway?"

"No. Where was it he said he was going?"

"To buy us a little time and to meet my father. He said something about a ride. I don't know what he was talking about."

"I hope he's all right. He sounds like a very brave old man."

Doc Reynolds brought his heavy cane down on the head of a man and smiled in satisfaction as the man dropped to the earth, his skull caved in. Doc took a closer look at the man. He had delivered him forty-odd years back.

"Trash," the old man muttered, as he stepped back into the darkness between concessions. "And didn't have to be." After more than a half century of practicing medicine, Old Doc Reynolds was as knowledgeable about human nature as most psychiatrists: he had seen the best and the worst. The dead man was no demon, but he was just as bad: he would follow anyone with a half-baked idea—just as long as that idea involved violence against some decent person.

Doc glanced at his watch. His old friend Martin should be coming along in about an hour, and Doc wanted to be sure to stay alive long enough to see him.

He looked up and down the midway; what he could see of it from his hiding place in the darkness. His smile was grim. He had guessed correctly: most of the people were resting, gathering strength for the destruction they would wreak between the hours of eight and midnight. Just like back in '54. It was being repeated almost to the second.

Movement at the far end of the midway caught his eyes.

He squinted, trying to make out who it was walking up the deserted midway. He softly cursed under his breath.

Old man Tressalt, and from the way he walked, he looked like he'd fallen off the wagon and taken him several good snootfulls of hooch. As he drew closer, Doc could see the pistol shoved down in the man's pants. "No!" Doc whispered softly.

"Gary! Pete! Frank!" the father shouted, his voice carrying over the now-softened voices of the midway. "I know what you are, boys. Come out here and face me. Damn you all to the pits of Hell—come out here."

The music from the empty rides stopped. No loud-speakers blared. The old man stood alone on the midway.

Doc didn't know where all the people could have gone to. Only that they were gone.

All but the carnies. Those manning the concessions stood or sat and watched as the old man began walking slowly up the midway. Doc could see that their faces were no longer of a human form. They were dreadful looking creatures. Their laughter was demonic as the slobber leaked from fanged mouths and dripped over animal lips. They snarled at Tressalt and pointed clawed fingers at the old man.

"Spawns of Hell!" Tressalt shouted at the creatures behind the game concessions. "Filth of Satan!"

The creatures hooted, snarled, and howled at the man.

Gary, Pete and Frank stepped out onto the midway, about a hundred feet from their father. They stood looking at him.

"Your dear mother passed away this afternoon, boys. But not before she told me about her suspicions of all of you. It didn't come as much of a surprise. Only you, Gary. That was something I could not believe. Now I guess I don't have much choice in the matter do I?"

His sons stood in the center of the sawdust midway and stared at him.

Martin, Frenchy, Dick and Ned had slipped back to the midway after hearing the music fade. They stood in the shadows, listening and watching.

It was Frenchy who first noticed the slight white movement at the very end of the midway, just before the concessions began. She pointed it out.

"I don't know what it is," Ned whispered. "I can't make out anything except a blur."

Frank, Pete and Gary had not moved; continued to stare at their father.

Martin Holland, behind the wheel of the rusted old pickup truck, was clatter-banging his way closer to the fairgrounds. Only a few more miles.

Billie Watson had awakened from her swoon and managed to push the bloody, battered body of Jim Carrol off her. She had run screaming, naked, into the late afternoon, blind and mindless with fear.

Joyce was only a few yards away from Eddie, who was sitting by himself, away from the main group behind the livestock pavilion. Her daughter, Missy, was with her, both of them on hands and knees, inching closer to husband and father.

"I left your mother in her bed," Tressalt told his sons. "I dressed her in her favorite white gown and folded her hands across her chest; put her little Bible under her hands. Them hands loved you boys. Changed your diapers, bathed you, held you and loved you."

"Why don't you shut your old trap, you stupid old man?" Pete yelled to his father.

Martin cringed at the hateful verbal venom in the son's tone.

The father slowly shook his head. "Filth. I sired filth. I don't know why I was punished. Probably never will. But I sired monsters."

He stepped toward his sons.

"Behind his back," Ned whispered. "Stuck in his belt."

"What is it?" Dick returned the low tone.

"A stake. The pistol and that drunk act was just for show. He intends to kill one with the stake."

The white object seemed to float a few yards closer to the lighted midway. Still too far away for anyone to clearly see.

But Old Doc Reynolds knew what it was. Tressalt's wife.

Doc swallowed hard. He couldn't be sure what side the old woman was on. He remained very still in the shadows.

Martin silently prayed that the old man would kill Gary. Martin didn't want to have to be the one who did it.

Then he felt guilty about the thought. The feeling of guilt passed very quickly as Gary shouted, "So the old pious bitch is dead? Well, good! I thought she'd never kick off."

"Pitiful," the father said, his voice strong but sad. "And to think that you were always her favorite."

Eddie never made a sound as the long-bladed dagger slipped between his ribs and tore into his heart. Mother and daughter stretched the man out on the ground. Missy knelt down and kissed her father on the lips.

His eyes opened. Blinked rapidly a couple of times.

"Sleep," Missy whispered. "Sleep until we call."

Joyce and Missy slipped back into the shadows.

The elder Tressalt moved closer to his sons. Only a short distance separated them now.

"What do you want, old man?" Frank sneered at his father.

"I wanted to say goodbye to you boys. That's all."

"Goodbye?" Pete questioned. "You ain't goin' no-where. Except to the grave."

"Oh, I know that. I've made my peace with God." He had been watching the bright white object move closer. Watched it with dread circling and squeezing his heart.

"Something has frightened the demons away," Frenchy whispered, her eyes sweeping the concessions. "They're all gone. Look."

The game booths were empty. Still brightly lighted, but vacant.

Tressalt took another step toward his sons. The shimmering wavy object behind the three men moved silently closer.

Frank stepped out to meet his father. His face had

266

changed, turning beast-like. Spittle leaked from his mouth. His jaw had swelled with the transformation. Fang-like teeth protruded over his lips.

Tressalt put both hands behind his back and smiled at Frank. "I got to say it, boy: you sure are ugly."

Roaring, Frank jumped at his father, springing at him with the agility of a great animal. The old man pulled the stake from behind his belt and stood his ground. His son impaled himself on the point. He screamed, blood and pus spraying from his fanged mouth just as the wraith-like object wrapped its near-translucence around Pete.

Gary ran away, howling and ducking between concessions, just as Frank grabbed his father's throat in one clawed hand and squeezed and jerked, almost decapitating the old man.

Father and son fell to the ground, both dying, as good and evil struggled even unto death. One cursing, the other mouthing silent prayers in his pain.

Pete was screaming in an agonizing rage as the whiteness squeezed tighter. The white soon became stained with crimson as blood dripped from the cloth folds and mother and son sank to the sawdust covered ground of the near-deserted midway.

The righteous wraith increased the pressure and Pete's howling filled the brightly colored night. The top of his head exploded.

Tressalt and son lay still on the midway, the father's right hand still gripping the heavy stake protruding from the son's chest, the point penetrating and ruining the devil's heart. All signs of the demon within the man had disappeared.

Mother and son lay in a bloody pile on the sawdust. The woman had assumed human form; the son, with intestines forced out of his mouth by the pressure, lay with his arms around his mother.

Old Doc Reynolds, on one side of the midway, and Martin and his group on the other side, watched as the concessionaires, in human form, returned to their booths and began calling out their patter, urging those who had drifted back onto the midway to come and try their luck.

The ferris wheel and merry-go-round began slowly turning and revolving. The music began playing. The night was soon filled with the sounds of false gaiety.

"Come one, come all!" the loudspeakers blared. "It's fun time! It's a good time for all. The carnival is in town!"

EIGHT

The people paid no attention to the bodies lying in bloody heaps on the midway. They stepped around them or over them as the crowds milled up and down. They played the games, won prizes and then promptly tossed the teddy bears, plaster chickens, ducks and horses to the sawdust and moved on to the next concession.

Martin and Frenchy slipped around to the Shakespearean Pavilion in time to hear Alicia mouth some lines in a deadly monotone. Then they watched in numbed horror as she calmly stabbed a young man to death: a real knife, real blood, real death.

The crowd applauded politely and yelled for more. Alicia bowed gracefully while stagehands shoved the bloody body to the center of the stage. Nabo's Geek ran out onto the stage with a knife and began cutting off strips of human flesh, stuffing them into his grinning, foolish mouth while the crowds went wild at his antics.

Alicia screamed obscenities at them. They paid no attention to her. She stalked off the stage in a huff, Mike Hanson mincing along behind her, his robes dragging on the rough wooden floor.

Martin felt eyes on him. He turned his head. Nabo was standing across the large room, smiling at him.

Martin felt the man's thoughts barge into his head: *Enjoying yourself, Mr. Mayor?*

Not particularly.

What a pity. What can I do to liven up your evening?

Leave town.

Sorry.

Release the townspeople from this . . . trance you have them under.

I have them under nothing. Whatever they have become, they have done so willingly. I thought by now you would have guessed that.

Are you saying that the residents of this town are inherently evil?

But of course! Well, not all of them. And not just this town, but all towns. Just one of the reasons I chose to follow in the footsteps of the Dark One. Heaven is going to be so boring. One will have to wander for days just to find another soul to talk with.

I don't believe that!

Oh, I think you do, Mr. Mayor. You'd be a fool not to believe it. And you are not a fool. Having some mortal being proclaim himself a minister and then mouth some sanctimonious words about being washed in the blood and fully forgiven forever is bullshit—and you know that. I've read it in your thoughts. You know, as I know, that one must practice your religion. Live it. Try with all one's might. Talk to these people you've known all your life, Mr. Mayor. I have them under no spell. They are doing exactly what they wish to do.

Nabo turned and walked away, out of the pavilion.

"I heard it," Frenchy said.

"You believe it?"

"Yes. It's discouraging, but I believe his words."

A man started to walk past them. Martin grabbed the man's arm. His barber. "Chuck! Listen to me. Look at me. Why are you doing this? Come with us and fight this thing."

"I'm free, Martin!" the man shouted. "Free, I tell you. It's grand. Now turn me loose before I kill you." That was said with absolutely no emotion.

Martin dropped his hand from the man's arm.

"Thank you," the barber said politely, and walked out of the pavilion. By the door, without warning, he knocked a young man down and began kicking him on the head. "I

270

hate that long hair! I done told you for years I hate that long hair." He proceeded to kick the young man to death while those around him nodded their heads in agreement.

"Good, Chuck!" one said.

"Awright!" another yelled.

"Let's get out of here," Frenchy suggested.

They edged through the crowd and ducked out a back door. A group of men blocked their way.

"How about some lovin', baby?" one asked, grinning at Frenchy.

"Back off, David," Martin told him. "And do it right now."

"Make me, Holland!" David popped back. He reached out and tried to fondle Frenchy's flesh.

She slugged him on the jaw and the men surged forward, overwhelming the pair, knocking them down to the earth. Martin tried to get his hand under his jacket, to the Colt Commander. He was pinned helpless. Just before a hard fist slammed into his jaw, he heard the unmistakable voice of Nabo.

"Cover his eyes, and keep them covered."

A hard burst of pain filled his head, dropping him into darkness.

The old pickup truck sputtered and shuddered and sparked to a metallic halt. The leathery shell of a man behind the wheel cast his eyes over the gauges. Out of gas. He looked around him; found the dark outline of a house a few hundred yards away, off to his left. He lurched toward the house. Dogs heard his staggering shuffling footsteps, lifted their heads, sniffed the air, and took off, loping across the land, without even a glance back or a single bark.

The shell of a man found a five gallon gas can, filled it from a farm tank, and laboriously carried the heavy can back to his truck. He slopped some gas in the tank, then lifted the hood and poured a small amount into the carburetor. He ground the starter until the old engine roared into life. Raking the gears, the truck rattle-banged and sparked on down the road. He still had about five miles to go. And he knew that once there, he couldn't just barge onto the midway. He had to find his old buddy, Doc, and the two of them had to make a plan.

He drove on through the night.

"Something's happened to them," Audie said. "I feel it in my guts."

Shrieks of sudden laughter sprang from the midway. The joyous sounds were coming from the entire length of the brightly lighted strip of rides and games.

"Explain that." Dick jerked a thumb toward the midway.

"The news just reached them that Martin and Frenchy have been taken," Don said.

"I agree with you," Ned's words were followed by a sigh.

"Now what?" Janet asked.

The adults looked at each other. No one had anything to say.

"Something is wrong with Dad," Ed spoke in a whisper. "He hasn't moved in a long time. And I think that's blood under him."

The kids cut their eyes, Jeanne saying, "That stain sure wasn't there the last time I looked at him."

Eddie smiled wide in his ordered sleep. The kids stared. The man's teeth were fanged.

Ed put his face in his hands and began silently weeping.

Susan touched his arm. "We got to tell the others. We got to, Ed."

The boy nodded.

Susan slipped to the knot of adults and spoke softly.

"Dear God!" Ned was the first to whisper a comment.

"Keep that in mind," Nicole said, picking up one of the iron tent stakes the men had been carrying. "Somebody get Gary Jr. Don't let him see this."

*   *   *

"Anybody heard from Frenchy?" the Watch Commander asked, replacing the phone in its cradle.

No one had.

"Wattsford tried a half dozen times today to get through to Holland. I've tried every fifteen minutes since I came on. No dice. Okay. A couple of you guys get over there and check it out. I've telexed the sheriff's office at Harrisville. They haven't been able to contact their substation in Holland all day. They're antsy about it. The local P.D. won't respond to radio or wire. What was Frenchy working on over there?"

"She was pretty vague about it, Captain," a sergeant told him. "But she did say she was investigating a sudden rash of brutal murders that might be connected to some sort of Satanic thing."

"I don't like the sound of that. Not one little bit. I want four people over there as quickly as possible. Two cars. Stay in radio contact at all times. Take whatever gear you feel you might need. If you people are out of radio contact for more than half an hour at any given time, I'm coming in full force. Take off!"

Martin was coming, and he was close. Doc could feel it. But he hadn't been idle while he waited. He had used his heavy cane a half dozen times, bashing whatever head came close enough to his spot in the shadows. Bodies littered the ground around him.

And the old doctor knew, sensed, that Young Martin had been seized by the Dark Forces. He tried to bring to fore his third eye. But he was old, very old, and his powers were not what they used to be. And he was also tired. His joints aching from the unaccustomed exertion. He knew he should do something; but he didn't know what, or how.

He was very concerned about young Martin.

Martin brought himself to full consciousness before he opened his eyes. He still couldn't see. Then he remembered Nabo's voice, ordering his eyes to be covered. His hands were tied behind his back, and done very skillfully, by someone who knew knots.

"When are we goin' to have our way with the Mexican-lookin' chick?" a man asked.

"Nabo says he wants the mayor to be awake so's he can listen to the gal getting it."

"You reckon Holland is shammin'?"

"Naw. I've seen guys stay out for more'un an hour after bein' popped on the jaw like Lyle hit Holland. He'll come around."

"What we gonna do with him after we do the Mex?"

"Nabo says we gonna burn him—slow."

So it had been Lyle who'd hit him, Martin thought. One more he owed the rancher.

Very carefully, he moved his head, trying to hook the cloth over his eyes on some splinter or nail. He succeeded in scratching his jaw until he could feel the blood run. So much for that idea.

"I'm gonna piss. Be back in a minute."

Martin heard a chair push back and footsteps walk across a board floor. The boards rattled. A tent floor perhaps? Maybe. The footsteps paused in front of him and a hand shook his shoulder roughly.

"No dice, Smith. He's still out cold."

Smith grunted.

One left in the room. If I'm going to do something, it better be now. He pushed his bound hands backward a few inches and touched a support of the knock-together frame. Has to be a hinge here somewhere, he thought. He moved his hands and found metal. Just above that, a nail protruded through. Lifting his hands, Martin began working at the ropes, rubbing them against the nail point. A few strands parted, then a few more. He worked faster. A few more strands of the rope parted and Martin strained against his bonds. Something gave and his left wrist pulled free. He shook his right hand free and worked his hands open and closed, bringing circulation back to numbed fingers.

He could clearly hear the carnival sounds just outside the tent. A door opened and the floor shook with the sounds of footsteps.

"I still got the itch just thinkin' 'bout that Mex bitch, Smith."

"Well, you better control yourself 'til Nabo gives the word."

Martin put voices with faces. Smith ran the gas station/convenience store just outside of town. The other man was George something-or-the-other. A carpenter who came to town with a roofing crew after a bad storm several years back and then stayed. Not a very good carpenter, Martin recalled.

George walked over to him and once more put a hand on Martin's shoulder. Martin grabbed the wrist and clamped down, at the same time turning and twisting like an alligator, his other hand jerking the blindfold off his face.

He rolled to his knees, then his feet, using brute strength to bring George with him. Facing the man, Martin drove his fist into the man's belly as he propelled him across the room, both of them crashing into Smith. Martin released George, grabbed up a straight-backed wooden chair and smashed it over Smith's head and neck. Smith dropped like a brick. Martin went to work on George.

He hit him three times in the face: the jaw, the mouth, the nose. George hit the floor. Martin grabbed a gun out of Smith's belt: his own Colt Commander, then quickly fanned Smith, finding a .44 magnum and a pocketful of cartridges.

He stood over the men. Smith was out cold, his head at a funny angle. Martin knelt down beside the man. Smith's neck appeared to be broken.

He placed the muzzle of the .44 mag against George's face and the man's eyes widened. "Frenchy—where is she?"

"The Mex gal?"

"If that's how you choose to describe her, yes."

"What'll you gimme if I tell you?"

Martin removed the .44 and stood up. Then he kicked George in the face. Teeth splintered and rolled around the floor. George tried to put his hands to his ruined mouth. Martin stomped on one hand before he got it to his face. The fingers and knuckles cracked under the leather.

"Where is she?"

"Tiny's watching her," George managed to blubber through mashed and bloody lips. "Nabo's trailer by the Ten-in-One. I hope they kill you!"

Martin knelt down, picked up a leg of the broken chair, and conked George on his noggin, the hickory whanging under the impact.

His Colt in leather, Martin shoved the .44 behind his belt and kept the hickory club. He opened the door and came face to face with Dr. Rhodes.

The doctor's face changed into a mask of hate and he opened his mouth to yell just as Martin brought his hickory club down on the man's head.

Using the man's belt, he bound his wrists and tore off a piece of canvas to double the bond and to tie his feet and gag his mouth.

Sticking the club behind his belt, he picked up the smaller man and slung him over his shoulder. He carried him to a trailer and rolled him under it. If the doctor got away, it just couldn't be helped; Martin had more important things to do.

Staying behind the midway, Martin ran to the Ten-in-One. He stopped when he had the silver trailer in sight and worked a tent stake out of the ground, scraping the dirt off the end. If Tiny was in the trailer, Martin was going to do his best to ram the stake through his heart.

Martin almost jumped out of his shoes when fingers touched his arm.

He swung the stake and would have killed his son had not Mark ducked.

"Easy, Dad! It's me. Boy, you're quick!"

"For an old dude." Martin tried a grin. "Where are the others?"

"Out looking for Miss Frenchy."

"Find them and tell them to get Dr. Rhodes." He told his son where he'd stashed the doctor. "I'll get Frenchy and meet you all back behind the livestock pavilion. For some reason I can't fathom, I get the feeling that's the safest spot for us."

"That's what Reverend Alridge said, too. Dad, Mr. Hudson's one of them. Nicole tried to drive a stake through his chest, but he rolled away and ran off. He's out here somewhere."

"Wonderful," Martin said wearily.

"I can't do it," the Dog Man told Balo. "I had the club in my hands and still could not strike the man. Even though I know he helped set the fires that killed us."

"I, too, could not kill," Baboo said. "I found an evil man and could not drive the knife into his heart. What is wrong with us?"

"I think perhaps we are only permitted to do harm to our own kind," JoJo suggested.

"But we are not like *them!*" Balo said. "I don't understand what you mean?"

"I think I understand," the Dog Man whined the words, then licked his chops.

"Explain it to me," Balo urged him.

"And to me," Baboo added. "We came for revenge and now find we cannot attain it."

"We are not a part of the Dark One's forces here in Holland," Ralph Stanley McVee spoke slowly, so he could be understood. "But we are alike in one respect: we are all dead!"

NINE

Martin made his way to the trailer, moving silently between the trucks and trailers. He had spotted movement outside the trailer where Frenchy was supposed to be held. It wasn't the giant, Tiny. Nearly there, Martin crouched down beside a pickup truck and listened as another man walked up.

"How's the woman, Jake?"

"Tiny is with her, Monroe. Holland?"

"As far as I know, he's still out. I'll check on him soon as I leave here. I don't understand what Nabo is waiting on."

"He's worried about something. He didn't tell me what. Monroe? Be careful. I don't understand all my feelings."

"What's that supposed to mean?"

"There is a presence here that is foreign to me. I don't like it."

"What kind of presence are you talking about, Jake?"

The road manager hesitated. Martin could see and hear them clearly. "A strong presence that is working to defeat us. The old doctor with the third eye has been on the grounds for hours. He's killed many times. Yet no one makes any effort to stop him. The old man and his wife penetrated the screen with ease. Our brothers and sisters in the town made themselves known too soon. Things are not going well and I feel they'll only worsen. I feel there is a possibility we could all be destroyed here."

"That's nonsense, Jake! There is no indication of any representative of God here. God does not interfere in earthly matters. Those are the rules and you know it. Calm yourself. We'll be gone by midnight, our mission concluded. I'm going to check on Holland."

Jake opened the door to the trailer and stepped inside, closing the door behind him. Monroe walked to the spot where Martin was crouching and paused. He turned around and looked back at the trailer.

Martin drove the iron stake into the man's back, putting all his strength behind it. Monroe gasped just once as the point tore through his heart and rammed out his chest. He fell face down onto the earth. Martin stood and waited for the human form to leave the man, and a beast to take his place. But there was no transformation. The human form remained.

Not understanding what was taking place, Martin hesitated, and then gripped the stake and worked it back and forth to loosen it. He pulled the iron stake free of the man. Nothing happened. The man remained in very dead human form.

"What the—" he whispered.

"Most of them are not demons," the woman's voice came from behind him.

Martin spun around. Balo stood before him, her huge python wrapped around her. The Dog Man was with her in the darkness.

Martin was tired, his head hurt, and he was confused. "Now what?"

"Only Nabo and perhaps thirty percent of the other carnival people are the devil's own," the Dog Man said, speaking very slowly so Martin could understand him. "Unfortunately for you, Tiny is among that demonic percent. You cannot defeat him alone with that bloody stake. He will kill you."

"I have to try."

"No. Stay here. We will rescue your lady friend. Be alert, Mayor. You have more to fear from your own townspeople than from the living dead."

"I don't understand the point of all this . . . tragedy. I don't understand why you're helping me."

"So we can go home and live in peace," Balo told him.

The Dog Man and Balo walked away, toward the trailer, leaving a very confused Martin holding a bloody stake in his hand and standing over a dead man. He sensed movement behind him and turned.

"Relax, Mr. Mayor," Baboo told him. "You have no reason to fear me or JoJo. We may only harm our own kind."

A thump came from within the trailer. The door was literally torn from its hinges as Tiny charged out into the night, lumbering away into the darkness, shouting curses as he ran.

Jake fell out of the open doorway, King wrapped around the man. The road manager was wailing as the coils tightened around him. The python's big head struck at the man's neck again and again, the teeth puncturing the neck with each strike. Jake slumped to the ground as the sounds of his bones cracking reached Martin. The wailing abruptly ceased.

Balo stepped out of the trailer, Frenchy behind her. Martin walked to her and put his arms around the woman.

"You mind if I kiss a cop?" he asked.

"Not as long as the cop is me."

"You don't have time for that," JoJo cautioned them. "There is danger all around you. If you can survive the next few hours, you might live to see the dawning. And I stress *might*."

"Good luck," Ralph Stanley McVee yapped.

The four carnies vanished as silently as they had appeared.

"I'm more confused now than I was before," Martin said, still holding Frenchy in his arms.

"Martin . . . while I do like what we're doing, can we make kissy-kissy some other time? Right now, let's get out of here."

They walked toward the end of the midway, and there, stopped in shock and horror.

Alma Sessions was standing with a crowd around her. She was holding her mother's head, by the hair, in one hand, her father's head, by one ear, in her other hand. The crowd was applauding her.

"Oh, good show, Alma!" Alicia gushed while Mike Hanson clapped his hands and grinned.

"Really neat, Alma!" Binkie yelled. "I love the look on their faces."

Mr. and Mrs. Sessions wore looks of confusion and pain, their mouths open in that last hot moment of agony. Alma's clothing was blood-splattered.

"How'd you do it, Alma?" Hal Evans asked.

"With my daddy's electric saw. The one he uses to cut off limbs and stuff," she proudly stated, grinning. "I caught Daddy taking a nap and Mommy drinking coffee in the kitchen."

"Let's stick 'em up on poles!" Karl Steele yelled. "So's everybody can see 'em."

Martin and Frenchy slipped away while the crowd looked for poles.

The music from the midway began anew; the oom-pa-pa of the merry-go-round was unnaturally loud in the deadly and dangerous night. The pair skirted the midway and made their way to the far end, closest to the livestock pavilion.

"Martin!" the voice called. "Over here. It's Doc."

Both turned, eyes searching the gloom behind the midway, and saw Reynolds.

They walked to the old man, leaning on his cane. "I had to leave the center of the carnival," Doc told them. "It was getting too crowded with folks I conked on the head."

Martin brought the doctor up to date.

"Really getting cranked up good," Doc said. He glanced at his watch. "By now, the sheriff's department has tried to contact Audie a dozen times and can't reach him. If I know Sheriff Grant, and I do, I delivered him, he'll have called the state police and asked for their help. So people are on their way in. What me and your dad have to do, son, is get on over to the main highway and stop the cops, warn them what they're getting into. So you have to get me over that damned fence. Can you do that?"

"My . . . dad?"

"Yeah. He'll be here any minute now. I got to keep him from just blasting on in here."

Frenchy walked to a pickup truck and opened the tool box, rummaging around until she found wire cutters. She rejoined Martin and Doc Reynolds. "We can get you through the fence with these. But how about the guards on the other side?"

"That's up to you folks."

"We'll have to . . . kill them, Doc," Martin told him.

Reynolds shrugged. "They're lost anyway. There might be a few who come to their senses before this is over; but not many. This is not time to be squeamish, boy. Can you handle it?"

"Anything that will help bring this town back to normal."

"It'll never be normal, boy. Not ever again. Don't even think that. We have Nabo running scared, and there is a chance you and your little bunch will come out of this alive. I didn't think so for a time. Now I do . . ."

Martin opened his mouth and Doc told him to close it and listen. "Even if you win, Martin . . . you haven't won much. Think about it. You just try to bring charges against any of these people. You think there is a jury in the world who would convict solely on your word that the accused are really demons in disguise? Not a chance, my boy. The authorities would stick your butt in a crazy house and leave you there—forever! Now, I'm not going to make it, son. I'm going back with your dad. We've got a lot of jibber-jabberin' to do. Years of catching up. If you come out of this alive, Martin, don't stay in this town. Get out. I've seen the way you and this good lookin' heifer have been makin' moo-eyes at each other. That's fine. Sure beats what you were married to. And I say 'were' 'cause you're gonna have to kill your wife, boy. And your daughter. You. No one else. Now get me over that fence, people. I got to meet a man and bring this shindig to a head."

There was still plenty to say as the three of them made their way to the fence; but no one spoke.

"Git away from this fence!" a man ordered, stepping out from behind a car.

Martin lifted the .44 mag and shot as he'd been trained to do: just like pointing your finger. He'd never fired a .44 magnum before but had a pretty good idea of what the recoil would be like. It was tough in his hand, but not nearly as tough as what the slug did to the guard.

His aim was deadly accurate, the bullet taking the guard in the center of his chest.

A second man appeared and Martin put one round in the man's belly as Frenchy was working at the fence, cutting a hole for Doc Reynolds to slip through.

Doc looked back at them. "Now is the time for you to save yourselves, people."

"No dice, Doc," Martin told him. "Frenchy?"

"I always was a sucker for the underdog," she replied.

"See you people in the Middle Level," Doc said with a smile.

"How about Heaven, Doc?" Martin asked.

"Not for us, son." He looked at Frenchy. "Not for you, either, pretty lady. Martin here has a third eye. And you're probably too randy in the sack to suit the pious types manning the Pearly Gates. Bye, folks."

The old man went walking calmly up the road, leaning on his cane, his step still spry for his age.

Martin reloaded the .44 mag. "Randy in the sack?" He said with a smile.

"Think you can handle it?"

"I plan to try."

Before she could reply, the sound of footsteps behind them turned Martin and Frenchy around. Cowboys from Jim Watson's Double-W spread. They held clubs and iron stakes in their hands.

There was no evidence of any demons among them. Just drunked-up and willingly evil.

"Now you get yours, rich man," one told Martin.

"It doesn't have to be this way, boys," Martin tried to talk them out of it. "You can shake this thing. Try hard. Think of God, of Jesus and Mary."

"Shut up, Mayor. Your time is up!" a cowboy sneered.

Martin shot him in the face with the mag just as Frenchy's Colt Python began barking and sparking in the night.

Martin and Frenchy took off running before the echoes of the last shot was swallowed by the music from the brightly lighted midway. They left a half dozen cowboys dead or dying on the ground.

"I have an idea!" Martin said, panting the words as they ran.

Frenchy glanced over her shoulder and slowed. "We're not being followed. What's your idea?"

They stopped, catching their breath. "Getting little Gary out of this mess."

She looked at him. "Drop the other shoe, buddy."

"And you with him."

"Now look, I—"

"No, Frenchy. Think about it. If Doc is right, and some troopers are on the way, we've got to get you out of here and to your car. It's radio-equipped, isn't it?"

"Well . . . yes."

"So? I figure we can bust you through the back gate."

They reloaded as they spoke. "All right, Martin. Let's go get him out of here."

Dick slipped back to his truck and got his long guns out, giving the shotgun to Mark and the rifle to Ed. Frenchy had found a van with the keys hung on the sun visor. It would do.

Martin looked at Ned. "You want to go, Ned?"

"Reason says yes. But I think my obligation is here, Martin. I'll stay."

"All right, kids," Martin told the young people. "In you go. Get them to the house, Frenchy, and arm yourselves with everything I've got in there." He winked at the pale face of Janet. "Hang in there. Good luck to you all."

Frenchy leaned out the window and kissed him while Mark grinned at them both, then she dropped the van into gear and moved out. Dick and Audie and Don were in position at the back gate.

Martin glanced at Nicole. "What'd you do with Dr. Rhodes?"

"Taped his mouth shut and handcuffed him to a steel bull cage behind the pavilion. He'll keep."

"He have anything to say?"

"Lots of cuss words. Said we might win this round, but the fight would never be over."

"Essentially what Doc Reynolds said." It was odd to his mind, but Martin was experiencing no fear. He did not have the vaguest idea what the next moment might bring, but he felt he was up to facing it and beating it. He looked at his watch. It had stopped. "What time is it, somebody?"

"I've got fifteen past nine," Ned said.

"Same here," Nicole agreed.

"That's what time I have. But the second hand isn't working."

All the watches had stopped at the same time.

"What's it mean?" Nicole asked.

All the music on the midway had ceased. It was as quiet as a tomb.

The calliope began playing.

"I'm not familiar with that tune," Nicole said. "What is it?"

"Brook Benton sang it years ago," Martin told her. "The title is: 'It's Just A Matter of Time.'"

TEN

Nebraska State Troopers Davidson and Walton, in the lead vehicle, slowed and stopped at the sight several hundred yards up the road from them. Troopers Malvern and King, in the second car pulled up alongside and stopped. All of them stared at the slow-moving vehicle, clashing and crashing along, throwing up sparks.

"That truck doesn't have a tire on it!" King finally blurted.

"That thing is ridiculous!" Sergeant Davidson said, dropping his unit in gear and moving out. He pulled up behind the rusted old pickup.

"It's got plates on it," Walton said, staring hard. "But I can't make them out."

Davidson clicked on his bar-lights. The truck made no attempt to slow down or pull over.

Davidson hit the siren. Nothing. The truck kept on trucking and throwing up sparks.

Davidson turned off the siren and clicked on his outside speakers. "You in the truck. This is the state police. Pull that vehicle over."

A leathery-looking arm flopped out the driver's side window and waved at the cops, then made a motion indicating the cops should follow him.

"Black fellow, maybe?" Davidson asked.

"Or Indian," Walton suggested. "Gray hair hanging down to his shoulders. And he doesn't appear to be wearing a shirt."

Their radio squawked. "What is that thing?" Malvern asked.

Walton took it. "We don't know . . . yet."

"Tell him we're going to pull around and block the road," Davidson told him. "Have him close it up."

Walton took a closer look at the man behind the wheel as they drove past. Sweat beaded his forehead as the . . . *thing* behind the wheel grinned at him. "Ah . . . Gene?" he spoke softly.

"What?"

"Ah . . . that ain't nothing human behind the wheel."

"What are you talking about?" Davidson had centered his car in the highway and slowed, forcing the pickup truck behind to do the same. He stopped dead and so did the pickup. In more ways than one.

"Brace yourself," Walton muttered.

"You in the pickup truck!" Malvern spoke through his bar speaker. "Turn off your lights."

The one light that still burned on the pickup was cut off.

"Get out of your vehicle," Malvern ordered.

The pickup truck door opened. A rotted shoe touched the pavement. The trousers were rotted and just hanging on the leathery, bony body. The man wore no shirt. Holland grinned at the cops.

"Jesus Christ!" Malvern hissed.

"You boys gather around," Holland spoke, his dentures clicking and clacking.

"What's the smell?" King asked, crouching behind his door.

"The grave," Malvern replied. "Look at him! You! What's your name?"

"Martin Holland the third. Lyle Steele and Jim Watson and Joe Carrol and half a dozen more tortured me and killed me years ago. See the scars where they burned me?" He pointed to his bare chest. "I got my billfold in my back pocket if you doubt who I am."

Sergeant Davidson's hands were trembling. He remembered when a guy named Martin Holland disappeared.

His first year on the patrol. He stood up from behind his open door and walked to the man, stopping a safe distance away. The stench was awful. He didn't want to even think what he was thinking. But he was. The guy sure looked dead! "Take your driver's license out of your wallet and put it on the hood of that . . . truck."

"Sure, sonny." The old man fumbled in his back pocket, dust and dirt falling out when he removed the rotting leather.

"Where have you been, man!" King asked, his eyes on the dirt.

"Buried." His dentures rattled with the word.

"Back up," Davidson ordered.

When Martin backed up, so did Malvern and King.

Davidson picked up the tattered license. Put his flashlight beam on it. Put the license back down. Quickly. "This license has been expired for years!"

"I haven't been doing a lot of driving over the years, boy," Martin told him.

"Ah . . . What have you been doing?" Davidson asked. He felt like a total fool.

"Waiting."

"Waiting? For what?"

"For the carnival to come to town."

"The . . . carnival?"

"That's right, sonny. Now you just get out of my way, because I'm going to the carnival."

The van reached the back gate and the engine went dead. It would not crank. The guards outside the gate stood in a group and stared. Dick and his bunch left their hiding places and walked to the van. "Get over to Martin and tell him to forget the diversion," he told Audie. "Something's all wrong." He glanced at his watch. Fifteen past nine. Seemed to him that it had been fifteen past nine for an hour.

"It's dead," Frenchy said, getting out of the van. "The entire electrical system just went out." She glanced at her watch. "My watch has stopped too. I know it's later than 9:15."

Everyone's watch read 9:15.

Martin strolled up. He had walked right through the crowded midway. Not one person had tried to stop him or to harm him in any way. "Before anybody asks—no, I don't understand what is going on. Audie, you and Nicole go get Dr. Rhodes. It's time we asked him some questions."

The ferris wheel continued its endless circles, as did the merry-go-round. Happy music played in the background. Shouts and laughter came from the midway. The group waited in silence until Dr. Rhodes was pushed up to the useless van.

Martin lifted a long metal tent stake. "I want answers, Rhodes. Fast and straight answers. What is your connection with the carnival?"

The doctor looked at the stake and smiled. "I am Nabo's son."

"Rhodes is the name given you by the family who adopted you?"

"That is correct."

"Why did you come to Holland to set up your practice?"

"My true father told me to come here."

"Nabo?"

"That is correct."

"Why did you smile when you saw this stake?"

"Because I am a mortal being. Driving a stake through my heart would be an overkill, Mayor."

Martin didn't believe him for a second. But he didn't vocally pursue his doubts. He tried to see into the man's mind. He could not. "The truth about the carnival coming here, Rhodes."

"Revenge."

Martin didn't believe that either. There had to be more. "All those happy lies Nabo mouthed about his being a Christian before the fire . . . that's just what it was and is, right, lies?"

"Of course. My true father was very heavily into Satanic

290

worship; was building a carnival of and for the Dark Master. He had managed to convert most of the people. Oh, and yes, Mr. Mayor, he knows he has traitors in his midst."

"Why are you so willing to tell us this?"

"Time has stopped, Mr. Mayor. We are neither here nor there, in a manner of speaking. Any who enter, may not leave."

"Enter? You mean the fairgrounds?"

"The town, Mr. Mayor. The entire town."

"The point of it, Rhodes? What's the point?"

The doctor shrugged. "I don't understand the question."

"All this confusion and suffering and pain and death, man! Why?"

"It's a game, Mr. Mayor. The game has been played for thousands of years. It will continue to be played as long as worlds exist."

"Then we are not alone? Earth, I mean."

"Don't be absurd! Of course not. I personally have not seen them, but I believe."

"Are you afraid of death, Rhodes?"

"Not in the least. I have been assured that I will never truly die. So why should I be afraid of it?"

"Your wife?"

"What about her?"

"She is . . . like you?"

"Certainly!"

"Where is she?"

Rhodes smiled and shook his head. "Safe, Mr. Mayor. Ready to resume should I not return in this . . . well, shall we say . . . *form*." He cut his eyes, looking at Frenchy, shaking her head. "Oh, yes, Miss Detective, you're quite right in your thinking. The outcome will never be judged in any court of law. You see, you can't beat us, so why not join with us?"

"Jesus Christ!" Martin said.

"How offensive!" Rhodes grimaced.

"You would be no good to us as a bargaining chip, would you, Rhodes?"

"No, Mr. Mayor. So the best thing for you to do is to turn me loose."

Martin drove the stake into the man's body, bringing it up through his stomach, ramming it up with all the strength he could muster, which was considerable. The movement was so quick the doctor did not even have the time to scream before the long iron stake pierced his heart, the point driving through and exiting out the back of his head.

Rhodes fell backward, his hands clutching the haft of the stake. He lay on the ground and jerked in death spasms, his face changing as his body cooled. He died as he really was: a monster, a demonic being, a creature from Hell.

"Lies!" Martin was the first to speak. "All lies. They seem unable to speak the truth."

"Do you believe his saying that time has stopped, Dad?" Mark asked.

"Yes. That much I do believe. But I don't know what it means . . . other than what he said. And I don't know how much of that to believe."

"I do know this," Frenchy said. "I'm tired. And I wish if any of my people were going to show, they'd hurry up and do it."

Sergeant Davidson didn't trust any of what he had to say over the radio. So at a closed-for-the-night combination grocery store and gas station, he used the pay phone to call in to his troop HQ. The state police cars, one in front and one in back of Holland's rattle-bang old pickup truck, had forced the man to stop with them.

Davidson got his watch commander on the line and brought him up to date. There was a very long pause from HQ.

"You feel all right, Gene? You maybe got a fever or something like that?"

"I feel fine, sir."

"You been drinking, Gene?"

"No! I'm telling you what I saw. We got Martin Holland the third sandwiched in between our cars. He's driving the strangest looking truck you ever saw in your life!"

"Gene! Martin Holland the third's been dead for nearly twenty years! I knew him well. He was a friend of my dad's."

"Well, he looks like he's been dead for nearly twenty years, too!" Davidson hollered.

"All right, all right! You boys go on into town and wait for me. I'm 'coptering in. What's that deputy's name there?"

"Audie Meadows."

"Audie Meadows!" Holland hollered from the edge of the porch, almost scaring the crap out of Gene Davidson. He hadn't heard him come up. "His dad helped set that fire."

"Who's that?" the watch commander asked.

"Will you shut up old man!" Gene yelled.

"Don't tell me to shut up, Davidson!" the watch commander hollered.

"Not you, Captain! For Christ's sake. Martin Holland the third."

"Martin Holland the third has been dead for nearly twenty years, Gene!"

"I'm looking at him, Captain."

"Give me that phone, squirt," Holland clacked his dentures and jerked the phone from Gene's hand. "Who is this?" he demanded.

"Capt. Bob Mayfield. Nebraska Highway Patrol. Who is this?"

"Corncob Mayfield's boy?"

"Ah . . . yes. How did you know that?"

"Me and Corncob chased tail all over the western end of Nebraska back in the '20's and early '30's, boy. We done square dances from Ogallala to Valentine. He played the fiddle and I picked the git-tar. He met your mamma—God rest her soul—in Kilgore. I was best man at their wedding. They honeymooned at my summer house in the Rockies.

Now you tell me what you used to call me, boy?"

Another long pause from the troop's HQ. "Uncle Marty?" The voice was a whisper.

"Damn tootin'. What's left of me. Who taught you how to shoot a short gun, boy? Who taught you how to tie a fly right? Huh?"

"But you're . . . *dead!*"

"Sort of. But now I'm back. And I ain't got that long to stay. How quick can you get over here, boy?"

"Forty minutes, tops."

"Do it. But don't go into Holland proper. Not 'til I brief you on what you're up against. We'll meet you on the east end of town. Now get crackin', Bobtail!"

"Yes, sir!"

The old man hung up the phone and turned to Davidson. "I used to call him Bobtail. Come on, boy, let's get this show on the road. The carnival's in town!"

"Yes, sir," Mr. Holland. Whatever you say."

The four of them appeared out of the night. "I will stay with the small child," Balo said. "No harm will come to him with me here."

"Aw right!" Gary Jr. yelled from the van. "Can I play with your snake?"

Balo smiled and slid the snake into the van. Janet got out the other side much quicker than she got in. The others bailed out the rear as King slithered into the seat beside the boy. "If he starts getting a grip on you with his tail, let me know," Balo told the boy. "But he probably won't. Just stroke him every now and then."

"They're waiting for you all on the midway," the Dog Man barked. "You have to face them, for none of you can get out of this warp. To put it quite bluntly . . ." he had slowed his speech so all could understand, ". . . you have to win to leave."

"If we don't win?" Frenchy asked, one eye on the van with the snake in it.

"You'll be locked in this time-frame forever. You can

never leave."

"And you? . . ." Martin asked.

"We'll be here with you," JoJo told him.

"And that is not a prospect I relish," Baboo summed it up.

"Come on!" the call came out of the night.

"Lyle Steele," Dick said with a grunt.

The midway fell silent.

The calliope started pumping and snorting and wheezing.

"He sure has got a weird sense of humor," Ned said.

"Why do you say that, sir?" Jeanne asked.

"That's the theme music from an old TV series, child, 'Mission Impossible.'"

ELEVEN

Nabo knew his son was dead. And dead with a finality that was forever. Curse this place! he silently demanded. This game was supposed to have been easy. It had turned out to be anything but. The stupid do-gooders seemed to be leading a charmed life, immune to anything and everything Nabo threw at them. He should never have brought JoJo, Balo, Baboo and the Dog Man with him. But how was he to know they would turn against him? And with Balo and that snake guarding the boy, Nabo knew he could hang that up. And he also knew that even if he won, his victory would be a shallow one. The allotted time was over.

The taste of defeat left a copper-like taste on his tongue.

Nabo sat in the truck that housed the calliope and cursed God, Jesus, Mary, Joseph, and anything even remotely connected with them.

If he won? *If!*

He slammed his thick fingers down on the keys, producing a harsh, discordant note.

Everything had turned sour for him. Victory would be very nearly meaningless now. The townspeople who backed him were doomed to the Pits anyway. His Master wanted Christians—true Christians. Not this ragtag rabble of mealy-mouthed hypocrites who thought that just because they attended some church that would guarantee them entrance to . . . to . . . that *place.*

Nabo refused to even think the word Heaven. It was so offensive to him.

And now his last true flesh and blood was dead. Killed by Martin Holland. It just proved—again—that God loves His warriors. The genuine article. But, Nabo smiled grimly, he knew that Martin Holland would never attain the highest level. But that was little consolation, because Martin Holland wouldn't like that level anyway. That was reserved for the really wimpy types—to Nabo's way of thinking.

What to do?

Great men had pondered that very question for eons. And Nabo certainly felt himself to be a very great man. His Master had said he was on the same plane as that other great man, Hitler. Nabo had swelled with pride at that.

His fingers gently touched the keys and played the "Horst Wessel Lied." Beautiful.

What to do?

What to do?

The midway was silent, except for the sounds of the calliope. Still. Empty. Brilliantly lighted but without sound. As motionless as the fly-covered dead bodies that lay on the sawdust.

Balo sat with Gary Jr. in the van, King coiled and resting in the back seat. Gary Jr. was sleeping.

JoJo and Baboo and the Dog Man had slipped off into the darkness.

Martin, Frenchy and the others of his group were squatting on the grass, talking quietly.

And Dr. Reynolds was standing in the middle of the road, just inside the city limits sign. He had heard the rattle-bang of the tireless pickup truck long before he caught sight of it. When the vehicles came into view, he held up his hand, forcing them to stop on the other side of the city limits' marker.

"Hi, there, you old geezer!" Holland squalled and clacked, sticking his head out of the truck.

"Look who's calling whom old!" Reynolds returned the yell. "You look like death warmed over." Then he cackled at his own humor, slapping his knee. He pointed his cane at Sergeant Davidson. "You boys just stay where you are for the time being. Come on in, Holland."

Before the troopers could stop him, Holland had slammed the old truck into gear and cut around the lead patrol car, crossing over. He parked by Reynolds and got out.

The old doctor stuck out his hand. Holland shook his head. "Best you don't touch me, Doc. What I got is terminal. If you know what I mean."

"I hate to tell you what you look like, Holland."

"It'll all change as we cross over for the last time." Holland stared at his old friend. "You made up your mind that you're going with me, huh?"

"It's time, I think."

The troopers stood and listened, not really understanding what was taking place between the two men. But they all had a pretty good idea . . . and it wasn't thrilling any of them.

"My boy's held his own, hey, Doc?"

"He's done more than his share. You lost a granddaughter and a daughter-in-law, though."

"I felt it while I was in that hole.

"Corncob Mayfield's boy will be along shortly," Holland said. "He's a bigshot with the patrol now. I figure we'd wait and brief them all at once."

Sergeant Davidson took a step toward the two men.

"Hold it, boy!" Doc Reynolds shouted at him. "You just stop right there. You pass that invisible line, and you can't get back out."

"Listen to him, hardhead!" Holland clacked, holding up a warning hand. "We lose this fight, and we just might lose it, you're in here forever. You'll never die, never rest. You'll just *be* here. Think about it."

Sergeant Davidson stood very still.

"That's better. Now don't come any closer."

"Can you come out of there, mister?" Davidson asked Reynolds.

"Nope."

"Why?"

"Because you're really not talking to me, son, that's why."

Davidson muttered a few obscenities under his breath. He walked around in a tight little circle for a few seconds. Then he lost his temper. "I have put up with just about all of this insanity I'm going to take. I don't know what kind of stunt you're trying to pull. But don't lay any more of it on me. This is all some sort of big joke you old coots are putting down. And I don't appreciate it. I ought to run you both into a cell and you can sit in there and see how funny it is."

"You married, Sergeant?" Doc Reynolds asked.

"Not anymore. Divorced."

"Any kids?"

"One. Haven't seen the girl in years. She took her to California and got remarried. Why all these questions?"

"You know where your daughter is?"

"No. She planned it that way. I spent a fortune on investigators; never could find her."

"So you don't have much to lose, do you, Sergeant?"

"Just my life."

"What kind of weapons do you have in that car?"

"You name it, mister. What's all this talk leading to?"

"You think this is a joke, Sergeant? Well, you just get all your gear on, and step on in here. But if you elect to do that, don't say I didn't warn you."

Davidson hesitated, then walked to the rear of his car.

"Sarge? . . ." Walton said.

"No!" Davidson was adamant. "Something . . . funky is going on in there. I don't kow what. But we got a highway cop in there, and I for one am going in and see about her."

"Frenchy is all right," Doc told them. "She's got a lot of brass on her butt, boys. She and Martin Holland . . ." he jerked a thumb, ". . . his son, have been making goo-goo eyes at each other ever since the boy found out his wife was a demon."

Davidson fixed a jaundiced gaze at the doctor. "His wife

is a *what?*"

"The devil's own. A shape-changer. And Martin, like us, has a third eye."

"Where is it, under his hat!"

Nobody laughed at the try at humor.

Davidson took off his shirt and slipped into body armor, then put his shirt back on. He laid aside his revolver and slipped into a harness that contained a sixteen shot 9mm and half a dozen full clips. He loaded up with shotgun shells and clips for an M-16. Then he turned to face the other troopers.

"I am making this a direct order, boys. You are all, all of you, to remain on this side of that city limits sign and wait for Captain Mayfield. Is that understood?"

It was.

"Sergeant," Reynolds said. "How many walkie-talkies did you and your men bring with you?"

"We each have one."

"Turn one on, set it right, and then toss it to me. I want you to see what you're letting yourself in for."

Walkie talkie in hand, Reynolds backed up until he was nearly out of voice range. He keyed the hand set and spoke into it. He could not be heard nor could he receive transmissions from any of the cops.

Doc walked back to the invisible line. "You see what I mean, Sergeant?"

"I see it. But I don't understand it. I'm coming in."

Doc and Holland shrugged, Doc saying, "Your choice."

The sergeant stepped up to the invisible line and stopped. His men could see him, Doc and Holland could see him. But he could see none of them. They all watched as panic etched his broad face.

"It isn't too late, Sergeant," Doc called. "You can still change your mind. What do you see where you are?"

"Nothing." Davidson forced his voice to remain calm. "It's black. But shiny, sort of. Where am I?"

"You're very close to truth in that last remark. And you're running out of time. Make your choice and do it quickly."

Davidson stepped into the town limits of Holland. He was once more visible. He shook his head and blinked a couple of times. "What happens if I try to step back out?"

"You can't. You don't exist. You'll lose your form and eventually you'd be forced back in."

"Well," the sergeant stepped up to the men, "I guess I'm in for the duration."

"You certainly are," came the reply.

"See them?" Dick whispered.

"I see them," Martin said. "Lyle's leading the bunch."

Dick peered through the darkness, his eyes on the rear of the little group, all spread out behind the livestock pavilion. Mark held the shotgun taken from Dick's truck, Ed the .30-30 lever-action rifle. They were good kids. They would stand.

A chant rose from the large crowd massed together in the night, some one hundred yards from the beleaguered little group of Chosen Ones . . . although none among them knew why they personally had been spared.

"What are they saying, Don?" Jeanne asked, kneeling very close to the young cowboy.

"I can't make it out."

It sounded to Martin as though they were chanting "Torandie." But that made no sense. He listened more intently, and was then able to separate the words.

Torture and die!"

"Hear it now, Ned?" he called softly.

"Unfortunately, yes. Martin? I do not profess to have the courage of my Savior. I will not allow them to take me alive."

"You can't be sure how deep your well of courage is, Ned. Besides, they're not taking anyone, alive or dead."

"You have more faith than I, my friend."

"No. I just know what I can do, that's all."

Martin stared at the high dry grass just in front of the maddened, chanting group. He felt a cold rage take control of him. His eyes changed, burning yellow-amber. The grass exploded in flames, clearly illuminating those who had chosen to follow the calling of the Dark One.

The fires spread just as a slight breeze whipped up, driving the flames toward the knot of evil, pushing them back toward the fence line and away from the livestock pavilion.

Martin maintained his deadly gaze and the flames licked upward, hotly kissing the cool night air as the lethal yellow danced in fury, pushed on by a power that was being applied but not understood by the user.

A man ran from the group, trying to escape into the darkness at the edge of the flames. Ed lifted the rifle to his shoulder, took his time, and squeezed off a round. The man flung his arms into the air and pitched forward on his face, dying without a sound.

Ed swallowed hard and levered the empty brass out and a fresh round into the .30-30.

No one complimented the boy on his accuracy, even though if there ever was a time to kill, that time was upon them.

Sweat was beading Martin's head as his unblinking eyes continued to ignite and push the fires toward the now totally panicked mob of men and women. The crowd now had their backs to the fence, with some trying to climb the fence. Their weight collapsed the chainlink, ripping out several sections. But it was too late, their clothing burst into flames, spreading upward to fire their hair. The screaming overrode the happy sounds of the midway. The smell of cooked flesh drifted back to Martin and his group.

Martin closed his eyes and let his mind rest. Frenchy came to his side and with a handkerchief, wiped the thin rivers of sweat from his face.

"I think we could make it now, Martin," she said. "The fence has about a fifty foot gap in it."

The fire had reached several vehicles parked outside the grounds, with guards crouched behind them. The gas tanks blew, sending flames rolling into the night sky and knocking human torches clear across the road, where those still alive kicked and screamed their way into death and into the scaly, pusy, flesh-rotted arms of what awaited them . . . forever.

"You go, Frenchy. Take the kids. I have to stay."

"I'll be right here with you. How do you feel?"

"A little weak. But just like before, recovering very fast."

"You're not as pale and trembly as you were the first time you did this."

He smiled at her. "I'm getting the hang of it, I guess."

She stared at him. "What am I thinking, Martin?"

He looked into her eyes. "That your feelings are very confused about some ol' boy."

"They are that, ol' boy."

Martin slipped his arm around her and pulled her to him, kissing her gently. Not a lustful or demanding kiss. More a kiss of affection and assurance.

"Dad!" Mark called. "What do we do, now? Nabo is walking toward us."

TWELVE

Walton had heard the call from the helicopter pilot and using the two patrol cars, their headlights illuminated a landing pad in a parking lot not far from the city limits sign. And the invisible line that separated life from death.

Walton hurriedly briefed Mayfield on the walk from the 'copter.

If Mayfield was startled, he did not show it. "Gene stepped inside this line?"

"Yes, sir."

"And when he did, his walkie-talkie stopped working?"

"Yes, sir."

Walton stopped the parade of cops just inside the safe line.

"Gene!" Mayfield called. "You're a fool!"

"Yes, sir."

"But you're also a very brave man."

"If I'm so brave, how come my knees are knocking together, Captain?"

Mayfield smiled. No one had noticed that the Captain of Nebraska Highway Patrol was dressed in urban combat gear, from his bloused boots to the battle harness and the Uzi slung over his shoulder. He turned to a lieutenant.

"Take care of things, Norton." Then he walked to a patrol car, cranked it up, and drove over the line, joining his sergeant.

"Now, who's the fool, Captain?" Davidson asked, as Mayfield got out of the car.

"I suppose that will remain to be seen, Gene." He

looked at Holland. "Uncle Marty."

"Bobtail. That was a stupid stunt you just pulled, boy. You can't get out." His dentures clacked and clicked and whistled.

"First store we come to, I'm gonna get you some Poli-Grip, Uncle Marty. That clacking is gonna drive us all crazy."

"We don't have the time for that, boy. Me and Doc got to go in my truck. And don't ask me why; you wouldn't understand."

"I don't understand *any* of this!"

"You will."

"I'll take your word for that. Coming in, we saw a lot of flames over at the fairgrounds. Can you explain that, Uncle Marty, Doc?"

Doc Reynolds took it. "That was probably Martin Holland using his gift to defend his little group."

"His . . . gift?"

"He has a third eye. Some call it the insight. He's only just discovered the power. Don't get in his way when he's using it."

"I will, ah, do my best to avoid this . . . third eye." Wherever he keeps it, Mayfield thought.

"He keeps it in his mind, smart-ass," Doc told the man. "And watch what you think. He can look into your head as easily as I can."

"I'm gonna kill that son of a bitch!" a woman hollered. "You just watch me."

Heads turned and most of the eyes widened in horror as a naked woman, minus one arm and one leg came clopping up the street. She had tied a stick of stove wood around the stump of the missing leg. She also had a meat cleaver buried right in the middle of her head.

And carried another meat cleaver in her one remaining hand.

"Ruth Horton," Doc said, as the woman clopped and staggered over to them.

Mayfield and Davidson stepped closer to the patrol car as the woman staggered up against the rusted old pickup truck.

306

"Ruth," Doc said. "You'll be wanting a ride to the fairgrounds, I suppose?"

"Absolutely right!" she bellowed. Her flesh was unnaturally white in the gloom.

"Climb in!" Holland told her. "In the back."

Doc looked at him. "Thank you for that, at least."

Ruth fell into the bed of the truck.

The two old men, each on the opposite sides of the line of life and death, moved toward the truck.

"Wait a minute!" Mayfield found his voice. "What about us?"

"My suggestion is that you stand clear until it's over," Doc told him. "One way or the other. 'Course, that's up to you boys."

The old men got into the truck and Holland fired it off. Blue smoke poured and the truck went sparking and lurching and rattle-banging off in the general direction of the fairgrounds.

The sergeant looked at the captain. "Do we follow them?"

"Can we get out of the fairgrounds area?"

"According to Doc, we can."

"Let's prowl the town for a few minutes. This Martin Holland fellow seems to be holding his own over there. Besides, I still don't know what we're up against. You?"

"You got part of it right, Captain."

Mark, unknown to the adults, had made a side trip to the sportsmen's section of a pavilion during their search for Frenchy. There he had picked up a crossbow and a leather quiver filled with bolts. He had given them to Amy for safekeeping and forgotten about it. Now he remembered.

"The crossbow—what'd you do with it, Amy?" he whispered.

She pointed. "Laid it right over there."

"Get it for me. I don't want to leave this position."

The girl was back in half a minute, handing the powerful weapon to her boyfriend. "What are you going to do, Mark? Do you think you can kill that awful man with an arrow?"

"No. But we're being set up. Some men are slipping up on us. On Nabo's left side. One of them is Dr. Tressalt, I think. Get Jeanne off to one side. Tell her about Dr. Tressalt and then take Rich as far to the other side of the circle as you can get him. You know why."

"I don't want to leave you, Mark."

"Go on, Amy," he said gently, then kissed her. "I don't want Rich to see me kill his dad." If I can do it, that is, the boy thought.

The girl reluctantly moved away.

Mark set the bow-string and cranked it back until he could not turn the crank another turn. He set the bolt in place.

"Mr. Mayor!" Nabo called. "Are you there, friend?"

"I'm here," Martin spoke just loud enough to be heard. "But I'm sure not your friend."

"What a pity that you hold such hate in your heart."

"Yeah, I'm all torn up about it, Nabo."

The man in black laughed in the still fiery night; the smell of burning tires and human flesh was strong by the fence line.

"Can you kill him, Martin?" Ned whispered.

"No. I don't think so, Ned. I don't know if anything can kill him." Martin's eyes were fixed on Nabo. He had not noticed the men slipping up, edging closer in the tall grass. "What do you want, Nabo?"

"More than a modicum of civility on your part would be much appreciated, Mayor."

"Sorry for my bluntness, Nabo." Martin's tone overflowed with sarcasm. "You might say that I've been under a bit of stress lately."

"Your apology is noted and accepted." Then he surprised them all by saying, "You've won a few rounds, you know?"

"No, I didn't know that at all."

"Well, it's a small victory, to be sure. Your little . . . group has managed to demoralize the townspeople. You've really taken a toll this night."

"Music to my ears."

"No doubt. But you still can't get out of town. For that matter," he added with acid-like bitterness in his voice, leaving no doubt in Martin's mind abot his truthfulness, "neither can I."

"And? . . ."

"Compromise."

"Make a deal with the devil? I don't think so, Nabo."

"Hear me out, Martin. Don't be too hasty with your rejection. I alone know what can happen. You don't."

Martin waited.

"I'm taking your silence as an indication that you will at least hear me out. That's good. Are you a gambler?"

"I enjoy a friendly game of penny-ante poker, yes."

Nabo cursed under his breath. The man was definitely a goody-two-shoes type. But he knew that there had to be a fatal flaw somewhere within him. The trick was in finding it.

"We're both winners in this game. You realize that, don't you, Martin?"

"No, I don't. Get to the point."

Gary had slipped closer, very much in range of Mark's crossbow. Still, he waited, the crossbow at the ready.

"Forget the wager, then," Nabo's tone held a note of weariness. "You obviously are no sport."

Mark lifted the crossbow to his shoulder.

"Let me tell you a truth, Martin," Nabo spoke. "I can destroy this town. The only reason I don't do that is because I have no desire to live among rubble and ruin."

"You're telling me that you are trapped in here just as we are?"

His sigh was audible over the distance. "Yes, Martin, this is what I'm saying."

"And this . . . condition could go on forever?"

"That is correct."

"I find that unacceptable."

"I thought you might."

Martin thought about that for a moment. "How?"

"How . . . what?"

"How can that be?"

"Because you are not. Let me explain. Your scientists, when they spoke of time warps, were closer to the truth than even they realized. You're not really in a warp, but that will suffice."

"A whole town cannot just . . . vanish, Nabo."

"The town has not vanished. You have not vanished. But your soul is gone. Your being. Your molecular make-up has been altered. Are you beginning to understand?"

"You might say that those beings still present outside of this warp are merely our clones," Ed spoke from the edge of the circle.

"Ah!" Nabo's voice held a note of satisfaction. "The young man is not one hundred percent accurate, but he is very close. Yes. That will do. Thank you, young man."

"We are the souls and those that should remain visible are merely shells, Mr. Holland," Ed added it up.

"Oh, I do so enjoy an intelligent mortal!" Nabo cried. "Especially one so young. How would you like to be the most famous scientist in all the world, young man?"

"I only have to make a deal with the devil, right?" Ed asked.

"Crudely put, young man. But . . . yes."

"Sorry. But I'm not interested."

Janet spotted Gary in the dim light from the fading fires and the midway. The doctor was in the middle of his metamorphosis, his face that of a horrible beast. Janet screamed just as Mark triggered the crossbow. His aim was true, the bolt taking the creature directly in the center of his chest. The transformation continued as death began flapping its wings and cawing the demon home.

Nabo looked with disgust in his eyes at the thrashing doctor with a bloody bolt piercing his chest, driving deep into the black heart. He cut his lens covered eyes to the boy with the crossbow in his hands.

Mark had cranked the string in place and inserted another bolt, holding the stock to his shoulder, his finger on the trigger.

"They were too impatient," Nabo said with a sigh. "We

could have had it all. But they could not contain themselves." He cut his eyes to Martin. "You won't deal, you won't gamble, and you won't compromise?"

"That's the size of it, Nabo." Behind him, Frenchy was trying to comfort the sobbing Janet.

"Well . . . I'll still beat you, Mr. Mayor. But it will be a hollow victory for me." He half turned, then once more faced Martin. "You're quite a man, Martin. As a matter of fact, each person in your group is quite unique. Unfortunately for me."

He turned and walked slowly into the gloom. Then, once again, he paused and turned around. "You know where you and your group must meet me to bring an end to this, don't you?"

"I've had a feeling about that," Martin called. He pointed to the midway.

"That is correct, friend. Fun for one and all." He laughed in the night. "The carnival is in town."

THIRTEEN

Mayfield slowed and stopped in the middle of the street. "Look over there." He pointed. "Couple sitting on the front porch. Let's walk over and see what they have to say."

Davidson reluctantly nodded his head and both men got out of the car. They carried their weapons slung and set on full automatic. The middle-aged man and woman watched them approach. They said nothing. Mayfield and Davidson both noticed that the man and woman's eyes were very strange looking. They were both dressed in formal wear. Very outdated formal wear.

"Good evening," Mayfield said.

"Hubert and I are going to the prom in a few minutes," the woman replied.

"The . . . prom?" Mayfield asked.

"Yes," the woman said.

Hubert grinned. He looked like an idiot, sitting on the porch dresed in white sport coat that he could not button across his big belly. He had taken house paint and painted his shoes white. A pink carnation—made of paper—was pinned onto his lapel. His trousers were black. The woman was dressed in a formal that looked as though it had been packed away in a trunk for thirty years. Her hair was done up in '50s style.

"Ah . . ." Mayfield cleared his throat. "Isn't it a bit late to go to the prom?"

"Not at all," Hubert replied. "Some friends are coming to pick us up at 9:15. Oh! There they are now."

Both troopers looked around. No other car in sight. They glanced at their watches. Blinked when the hands read 9:15. But both knew it was a lot later than that. More like 11:30.

"Aren't you boys going to the prom?" she asked. "Don't you have dates?"

"Ah . . . no!" Davidson told her. "We . . . ah, have to work. Yeah, that's it."

"What a drag. Totally uncool. Bye now."

Hubert did a bop step on the sidewalk while the woman was engaged in conversation with somebody, or something, that neither cop could see.

"Well, pooh on you!" the woman said. "We'll just walk to the gym. Come, Hubert."

Both cops heard the sounds of a car pulling away, tires squalling on the pavement. Music from the 1950s was filling the air. But there was no other car in sight.

"Holy mackerel!" Mayfield found his voice.

"What next, Captain?"

"Follow them. But I have a hunch I know where they're going."

"To the fairgrounds?"

Mayfield nodded his head. "Yeah. Come on. Let's go find Frenchy."

"What's the matter, Dad?" Mark asked, walking up to his father. "You have a funny look on your face."

"Nabo lied. Again." The others gathered around.

Frenchy said, "The midway is deserted. Where has everybody gone? And what do you mean, Nabo lied?"

"The man who jumped off the ferris wheel, the woman who died with that dart in her head. The men Doc Reynolds killed and those I killed. Those men and women who burned to death just a few moments ago . . ."

"All right. What about them?" Dick asked.

"We may be locked inside this . . . whatever it is surrounding the town . . . but we're all very much human and intact. You can't kill a soul by fire or with a club or

314

knife or gun. Nabo lied."

The calliope began playing a tune from out of the 1950s, "Johnny B. Goode." Jeanne pointed to the midway.

"They're dancing over there!"

"If you call that dancing," Mark said.

"What is that silly stuff?" Amy asked.

"It's called the bop," Martin informed the young people.

"Gross!" Jeanne offered her opinion.

"Totally primitive," Susan said.

Martin looked at Don. "You got anything to add to that, boy?"

Don wisely played the diplomat. "I always sort of liked it, myself."

Dick chuckled. "I told you the boy was no fool, Martin."

"Now that I think some on it," Ned said, "I agree with you, Martin." He held up a cut finger. "I snagged my finger on a broken bottle not twenty minutes ago. That's real blood. So we're real, whole people."

"But he must have told us all that for some reason," Janet said, her voice soft in the night. She had not looked at the body of her dead husband once since Mark had put the crossbow bolt through his heart.

"Either that or the man, creature, whatever he is, is a pathological liar," Dick offered. "But I'll wager he had his reasons for lying . . . and convincingly, too."

The calliope was belching out "Shake Rattle & Roll," and the midway was rocking.

Rich had just returned from a visit to the van, checking on his little brother. Gary was asleep, covered with a coat that Balo, or someone, had found. Balo had smiled at him, saying nothing.

"Rich," Martin said, facing the boy. "While this Nabo tells one lie after another, a few things he said were true. One is, we can't get out. Two, this battle is for our survival. Three, it's going to take place on that midway over there." He pointed. "And that is where some of us have to go. I'd feel better if you were back at the van with your brother. What do you say?"

315

The boy didn't want to appear a coward, but back at the van seemed like a darn good place to be. As long as he could sit up front with that pretty Balo and the snake stayed in the back with Gary. The boy swallowed hard, remembering that Balo was *dead!*

"Sounds good to me, Mr. Holland."

"Fine. How about you girls?" But he also knew by the set of their chins they weren't about to leave the group.

They shook their heads.

Martin had to make one more try, for their safety and for his peace of mind. He knew, or at least felt, that once they got on that midway, there would be no turning back for any of them. And Martin did not have even the foggiest notion what any of them might be facing. "Girls, I can't tell you, any of you, what we're going to be up against over there. It may very well end up to be every person for themselves. Probably will turn out that way. I wish you'd reconsider."

They stood firm.

Martin looked at Dick. The man minutely shrugged his shoulders.

"Martin!" the loudspeakers blared. "Oh, Martin! Come to the midway, Martin. Let's have some fun."

Martin looked at the group. "Frenchy, Mark, Amy, Ned, Janet, Don. You're with me. We'll go in from that end." He pointed. "Dick, you take the other group. I have no idea what we're going to find there. I know only that we can't live like this. Time has stopped. So let's join hands and ask Reverend Alridge to say a prayer for us."

"I'm afraid my thoughts are not very Christian at this moment, Martin. Peace and love and all that," the pastor said.

"I don't intend to go on that midway promoting peace and love, Ned," Martin told him and the group. "I intend to go in there with every intention of killing just as many people as it takes to bring this thing to its conclusion."

"How you doin' back there, Ruth?" Doc Reynolds stuck

316

his head out of the window and hollered when Holland finally managed to bring the pickup to a halt. Sort of hard to do with no brakes.

The woman with a meat cleaver stuck in her head waved the meat cleaver in her good hand. "I'll get out of here, Doc. I don't know why Matt did this to me. I don't know why I'm not dead. I don't know what it's going to take for me to find peace, but whatever it is, I know it's here. And I know I've got to help your boy." She lurched off toward the brightly lighted fairgrounds, her stovewood leg clopping on the pavement.

"Impossible," Doc muttered. He looked at Holland. "And for that matter, so are you."

On the midway, the young man who had taken a header off the ferris wheel moved his hand and opened his eyelids, exposing empty sockets where his eyes had burst on impact. He did not try to rise.

The woman with the darts in her body moved behind the concession. Sat up, her back against a support post of the tent-covered concession. She opened dead eyes.

Just outside of town, several hundred dogs and cats, all of them horribly maimed, crushed heads and entrails dragging the ground, had gathered. The leader, a big German shepherd with one side of his head caved in from the deliberate impacting of Karl Steele's pickup truck tire, looked around him. He sensed it was not yet time. But very close. When it was over, they would have had their revenge and then could go to that special place, set aside for animals who had suffered cruelly at the hands of man. And there they could find relief from their pain and find what they had always wanted: someone to love them. For they did not understand why some humans would deliberately hurt them.

For several minutes, both Davidson and Mayfield had sat in the parked patrol car, silent, each with his own private thoughts.

"It isn't our fight, Captain," Davidson finally broke the silence.

"Looks like we've been sharing the same thoughts,

317

Gene. Or orders," he added.

"Orders, Captain? From who?"

"I don't know, Gene. But I can make a guess and so can you. But this isn't our fight; you're right about that."

"Frenchy? . . ."

"That bothers me. But she voluntarily requested to come off of leave, didn't she?"

"Yes, sir. As soon as she did, she was ordered to stay and investigate whatever was happening here in Holland."

The men were parked outside the fairgrounds. They had spotted no one with a gun and no one that even looked like a guard. What they had seen were hundreds of people, the men dressed in out-of-date jackets and the women dressed in bursting-at-the-seams old formal gowns streaming into the fairgrounds.

Captain Mayfield made up his mind. He pointed toward the front gate. "We stay out of there until we hear gunshots or see violence."

They both heard the rattle-bang of the old pickup truck. Without looking around, both knew the leathery, bony old man would be behind the wheel, grinning his death-smile and waving at them as he passed, the old doctor on the seat beside him.

As the truck passed, they noticed the naked lady with the meat cleaver in her head was missing.

"If she was real at all," Mayfield muttered. "If *any* of this is real."

"You didn't stand in the middle of that dark evil place, Captain," Davidson reminded him. "If you had, you'd know it was real."

Mayfield sensed his sergeant's words were true and he was very glad to have missed Davidson's experience. He nodded his head and spoke very softly. "Yes. I know it's real, Gene."

The women embraced and the men shook hands. None of them felt it was a bit overly dramatic. They all sensed that some of the group would not survive, although none

318

of them said it aloud.

"Our new friends are watching us," Frenchy whispered.

Martin turned in the direction of her eyes. JoJo, the Dog Man, and Baboo were standing in the shadows, looking at the group.

"We will assist you in a small way," Baboo said. "The only way that we can. You are all approaching the climax of this . . . game. You are all standing very close to death. Be very careful on the midway, and keep in mind that simply because you see something, that does not mean it is what it appears to be. We can tell you no more than that."

In unison, they stepped back into the night and vanished.

Weapons were checked, nerves were steeled, and eye contact was, for the most part, avoided. The music on the midway had slowed, with Nabo—Martin assumed it was Nabo playing the calliope—doing a slow 1950s hit. The group could just make out the people on the midway slow-dancing.

The group walked toward the midway.

FOURTEEN

The big shepherd turned his mangled head to look at the dogs and cats behind him. A silent animal communique passed down the line. The animals began moving, slowly, because many of them had to drag themselves along using front paws, their crushed hindquarters useless. Wolves and coyotes had joined the group, and as was their way, they helped each other. A huge gray wolf with a missing back paw and a gunshot wound in his side joined the big shepherd. They looked at one another and made peace with body language and head movement. The animals moved toward the fairgrounds, the lights just visible in the distance.

Saint Francis was not pleased with this trek by those he looked after, but the animals would deal with that later.

Those who were so badly mangled that they could scarcely move at all—for many of them, their condition brought on by the uncaring ruthlessness of Karl Steele, his perverted mind and deadly pickup truck—kept the procession to a slow crawl. They could feel. They had to give up part of the immunity granted them in their afterworld to make this quest. And part of that surrendering was the ability to feel—once more—the searing pain that had eventually killed them . . . although for some that final end to life had taken days. That agony brought on by human beings—and not just Karl Steele. There were others like Karl, and on this night of retribution, they would pay.

The animals crawled, limped, staggered and pulled

themselves on. But they did not whimper, did not whine, showed no outward signs of the terrible agony they were experiencing as they inched through the bloody trail left by those who fronted the pack.

Heading for the fairgrounds.

The carnival was in town.

Martin was the first to step out onto the midway. His pistol was in his holster; he had given the big mag to Ned, after the preacher had asked for it, assuring Martin that he could and would use it.

"I'm a preacher," he told Martin. "But I despise the godless." And he let that remark stand on its own.

Warily, cautiously, the group walked the length of the midway. Nothing happened. The dancing, laughing couples did not give them a second glance—or in many cases, a first glance.

The two groups met in the center of the midway and Martin motioned Dick to head his group into the shadows behind the rows of tented concessions.

"Highway patrol car parked just outside the main gate," Dick told them. "It's unmarked but the emblem is on the door."

If Frenchy wondered why the man or men in the unit didn't come in and assist them, she kept it to herself. But meeting her dark eyes, Martin could see the puzzlement lingering there.

"And I think your father is here, Martin," Dick added. "There is an old rusted-out pickup truck sitting on its rims just inside the gate. Two men inside. One of them is Doc Reynolds."

Martin felt a hard surge, a myriad of emotions. But he knew he could not let them show. He knew that he could not show any signs of breaking. And he also knew that the others were watching him closely.

"I'll deal with that when it comes," he finally spoke. "Right now, I'm open to suggestions. I don't know what Nabo wants of us. He told us the midway was the place where we'd bring an end to all this . . ." Martin continued.

"No. No, that's not right. *He* did not say that. I suggested it and he agreed. But we've wandered the midway and nothing happened."

"Maybe he meant the shows, Dad," his son suggested. "Maybe he meant we have to go inside those things." He pointed through the tents to the House of Wax, directly across from them, then moved his hand up and down the midway.

All the group grew a bit uneasy at that thought. "I've never seen anybody go into those places," Dick said. "Or," he added, "anyone coming out of them."

A roaring sound overrode the calliope, with screaming following that. The faint sounds of flesh being crushed and ripped could be heard.

"What was that? . . ." Martin mouthed the words. They were not audible because of the roaring and screaming on the midway.

Martin stepped between the tents and stood rooted to the spot, like so many other sights over the past hours, this was just as mind-boggling.

A rusted, tireless, dirty pickup truck was bucking and lurching and snorting blue smoke, hammering its way up the center of the midway, the rims digging into the sawdust, the nose of the truck slamming into people, knocking them sideways, the bodies mangled and bloody. The fenders on the old truck were flapping like curved wings.

Two men in the truck: Doc Reynolds . . . and Martin's father. Both of them grinning.

Martin stood in the shadows, not exposing himself to the dead eyes of the driver. The others gathered around him, silent, watching the carnage on the midway. As the calliope pumped out music, men jumped onto the hood and into the bed of the truck, clubs and stakes in their hands. They hammered on the top of the cab and on the hood.

Holland, grinning wildly, spun the wheel and sent half a dozen flying off the truck. Some crashed into the crowds, sending more to the sawdust; others flew into poles and onto the wooden counters of the concessions. The sounds of bones breaking could be heard. The old pickup truck

323

roared to the end of the midway, turned around, and stopped, the engine running, the broken lights like deadly eyes, the grill looking like a shark's mouth about to rip and mangle its prey.

The music stopped. The angry crowd, all of them waving clubs of some sort, faced the growling old rusted truck, shouting curses at it and its occupants.

The driver's side door squeaked open and the dead, leather-like shell of a man stepped out. "We're doing this for you, boy!" the old man clacked and whistled the words. "They'll eventually stop us. And when they do, it's all up to you and your group. Go with God, boy. I'll see you years from now."

Martin felt the sting of tears in his eyes. Turning his head, looking at his son, he saw the boy was crying, tears running down his face for a grandfather that he had never known.

Holland stepped back into the truck and slammed the door. When he did, one fender finally gave up and fell off, the sawdust quickly soaking up the blood that dripped from it. Holland gunned the engine and ground the transmission into gear. He floorboarded the pedal and the truck lurched forward. The crowd would not move.

Nabo's voice boomed over the loudspeakers. "Get out of the way, you fools!"

The crowd stood their ground, yelling curses at the men in the truck. They were still yelling and cursing as the truck slammed into them, knocking men and women to both sides and into the air.

"It's so . . . senseless!" Janet said, her eyes taking in all the gore that splattered the sawdust and the concessions. "Why? They're rushing like lemmings to their deaths."

"Senseless?" Ned spoke over the roaring of the pickup truck, the screaming of the people and the almost maddened howling of Nabo. The minister's voice was very calm. "Not at all. It's simply more grist for the devil's mill, that's all. Probably that's all it ever was. Nabo pulled in any unsuspecting carnival people with the promise of revenge."

"Pulled them in!" Her voice was horror-filled. "But

they were all *dead!*"

"We shall never know what voices speak to and from the grave until we hear the dirt shoveled over us," Don said.

"That's awesome!" Jeanne looked at him, all the love in her being shining at him through her eyes.

The cowboy blushed.

The pickup truck came roaring back down the midway, coming with a full head of steam, rolling over people, knocking them bloody and battered to either side. Doc would occasionally reach out of the open window with his heavy cane to bash a head.

But it was Doc's turn to meet his Maker—for the first time. Who knew whether he would come back, like Holland.

Fat Binkie ran up to the truck as it had slowed after impacting with half dozen men and women and shot the old doctor in the head with a pistol.

"I killed the old geezer!" Binkie shouted, dancing around on the midway, his beer belly jumping up and down like a sack full of Jello.

John Stacker, Karl Steele, Robie, Hal and the others applauded and cheered. Binkie took a bow on the bloody midway.

He was still bowing and grinning when Holland backed the truck up and ran him over.

He stopped grinning and started howling as the rims crushed his legs.

Holland, cursing the devil and all who followed him, did a state trooper turnaround in the middle of the midway and began wreaking his vengeance with gruesome results.

Around and around in an ever widening circle he roared, the rear rims kicking up sand and sawdust as they dug down, spinning as they searched for traction. He ended the earthly lives of too many for Martin and the others in his group to count, and tore down concessionaires' tents on both sides of the midway.

Then the old pickup stopped abruptly. It had run out of gas. The mob stormed the truck and jerked the bony old man out of the cab before Martin could react.

The cheering crowd hacked him into dry dusty pieces

with knives and fire axes, beating him into nothing with clubs and iron stakes.

But they failed to notice a leather-like object, with fingers attached, pull slowly away from the screaming mob and slip under the old pickup. The hand, wrist and forearm slipped behind a rim and waited.

Before Martin could react, Dick and Audie had grabbed him, holding him, preventing him from running out onto the midway.

"Nothing you can do, Martin," Dick told him. "Except get yourself killed. It's like Doc said: they bought us some time. And they sure knocked down the odds for us."

Frenchy led him away, back behind a concession. She put her arms around him and he responded, drawing from her woman's strength. They stood for a time, each seeking and taking comfort from the other.

Frenchy pulled away and looked up at him. "Why don't they just come after us and end it, Martin? They could easily overwhelm us."

He shook his head. "Maybe that isn't in the rules, Frenchy. I don't know." The sight of his father, bony and leathery and grinning his death's head grin would not leave his mind. The image was sharp and clear.

"They've pulled old Doc Reynolds out of the truck and are having a good time chopping him to bloody pieces," Dick said, joining them.

"Did any of them see you?" Frenchy asked.

"Looked right at us. Some of them waded through the gore and got close, grinning at us. Didn't make a hostile move. I'm getting a funny feeling that we're really going to win this . . . war—for want of a better word—but we're going to lose it all in the long run. Does that make any sense to either of you?"

Before either could answer, the lights of the midway dimmed and then went dark. The gloom settled around the embattled little group, enveloping them, almost smothering in its too real touch.

The music from the calliope began, a slow melodious tune.

"Now what?" Frenchy muttered, standing very close

to Martin.

"Martin?" Ned called. "You people better see this."

They made their way to the space between the concessions, the passageway illuminated by a strange glow from the midway floor.

Martin almost lost it. All his cold control almost shattered at the sight before him. Looking at the others, he could see that their reservoir of strength was shrinking; the dam of resilience leaking badly.

The dead were dancing.

In the dark.

Dark except for a strange illumination emanating from their bodies. As the macabre dance continued, a greenish glow sprang from the grinning townspeople as they slowly turned in the bloody, gore-covered sawdust. The ladies pirouetted gracefully and the men bowed in a strange dance of the dead.

The scene was so hypnotic, so spellbinding; the music from the calliope so low and soothing that Martin and the others could not take their eyes from the midway bathed in eerie light.

Ned uttered a strange cry; a choking pain-filled exclamation. Martin literally had to tear his eyes from the dancing dead and turn to see why the almost silent scream from the minister.

Eddie was standing behind the minister, his face a tortured and altered head of a beast. Blood leaked from a heavy and fanged jaw.

Ned's neck had been ripped open. The one savage bite had almost decapitated the minister. Eddie was holding the minister upright in his thick hairy arms, the massive muscles having torn his jacket into rags as they had grown. He roared, the jaws opening wide, and took a bite out of the pastor's head, the long teeth penetrating skullbone.

Mark's crossbow twanged. The bolt, coming at full strength from only a few yards away, tore into the lawyer's side and disappeared into the man-beast's body, the ribbed arrow destroying the heart.

Both beings dropped to the ground. Eddie lost his hold on the minister as death reached his clawed hands. The thud of the bodies was lost in the music that filtered through the gloomy light.

"Goddamn you all!" Young Ed screamed his shock and outrage at the dancers in the sawdust.

Before anyone could stop him, he ran onto the midway, the .30-30 rifle in his hands.

His sister, Missy, and Karl Steele were on the boy as he shoved his way through the gory dancers. They brought him down.

With a presence of mind that belied his age and his circumstances, Ed looked back at the group, terror in his eyes and etched on his face, and threw the rifle with all his strength. Susan caught the weapon, eared the hammer back, and shot Missy in the chest, the recoil of the .30-30 jarring her back on her heels.

Missy jerked as the lead struck her, then turned her head and grinned at Susan as her face changed into a snarling demon. She reached down and tore out the boy's throat. Ed jerked in pain and the beginnings of death as his blood gushed out onto the sawdust.

Mark's crossbow twanked, the bolt catching the girl-beast in the temple, the impact knocking her down. The bolt had penetrated all the way through, with about three inches of steel sticking out each side of her head.

Karl screamed. Like the coward he was, he jumped to his feet and ran off into the gloom. Missy struggled to her feet and staggered after him, shoving her snarling way through the seemingly uncaring and unnoticing dancers. The arrowed bolt ripped the flesh of the dancers as she ran staggering and howling after Karl.

The dancers did not notice as their flesh was torn.

The calliope continued its playing.

Young Ed lay still on the sawdust.

The music stopped. The dancers paused in place. The lights popped back on, lighting the body-littered midway. The ferris wheel began turning. The merry-go-round began slowly whirling, the wooden horses grinning and moving up and down on their chromed poles.

"Fun! Fun! Fun!" the loudspeakers called. "Come one, come all. The carnival's in town!"

FIFTEEN

The group, minus two, shifted locations, moving to the space between two other concessions. The dancing had stopped. The midway was fully lighted. The concession operators were once more calling for the marks to play. Many of the townspeople would glance over at Martin and his group, but not one of the blood-splattered and '50s-dressed townspeople made any move toward them. It was as if they could not be seen by the townspeople.

Martin automatically looked at his watch, blinked, and glanced at it again. The second hand was moving, ticking off the seconds. The watch read 9:40. "Check your watches," he told the group.

Time had once more started for all of them. At 9:40.

"What's it mean?" Janet asked, her voice as trembly as the shaking of her hands.

"I think it means we have two hours and twenty minutes to win this war," Martin answered her.

"And if we don't? . . ." his son asked.

"I don't know for sure," the father replied truthfully. "However, if we don't win, this thought comes to mind: We start all over again."

"And we do it over and over and over," Frenchy added.

"Until someone wins?" Amy asked hopefully.

"No." Martin shook his head. "Forever. Dick, pull out one of those tent stakes. Rest of you get one apiece from behind other tents. We're going to attack." Stake in one hand, he reached into his pocket, took out a pocket knife, and slashed the canvas wall of the concession, ripping it open from top to bottom, stepping into the game tent.

The concessionaire turned his head and grinned at Martin. His eyes shone with undisguised evil, but he was not a shape-changer and remained in his human form. He held up a doll. "Spin the wheel and win one, Mayor. You can take it to Hell with you."

"Take this to Hell!" Martin told him, then drove the stake into the man's chest.

The evil in the man's eyes faded as his heart was shattered. He slumped to the sawdust floor and within seconds nothing was left except a mass of charred clothing and baked bones, a tent stake lying amid the mess.

Frenchy looked at the small pile on the sawdust. "The fire. They've returned to what they were back in 1954."

"My, how intelligent we are!" the sarcastic voice came from the midway side of the counter. "We all wondered when some of you would finally put it all together."

Slim Rush, the carnival's front man stood smiling at them. The townspeople had frozen in place on the midway. Standing like human statues amid the body-littered and blood-highlighted midway.

Nicole stepped out onto the midway, a long metal tent stake in her hands. Slim sensed movement behind him and turned just as the long stake drove into his chest and nicked his heart.

He sat down on the sawdust with a thud, fell over on his face, and became a pile of burned rags. Nicole reached down to retrieve the stake and cried out as her fingers wrapped around the metal. The smell of burning flesh touched the nostrils of the group.

Nicole's fingers and palm had been cooked to raw meat.

"We've got to find a first-aid kit!" Jeanne said, staring at the cooked hand.

"No time," Nicole told her, biting her lip as the pain settled in for a long stay. "Can you shoot a pistol, Jeanne?"

"Yes."

"Take mine." Pain filled her voice. "I can't shoot left-handed and I sure can't use my right hand."

"There you are!" a woman's voice boomed from the

dark end of the midway.

"Jesus God!" Dick summed it up for all of them.

Ruth Horton stood naked and hideous in the glare of lights. She came clumping up the midway, a meat cleaver in her head and one in her hand.

"You're dead!" Matt screamed. "Dead! I killed you." His voice was working, but his legs and arms remained locked in position in the sawdust. His eyes were wide with fear.

Nicole hurriedly left the midway to join the others, but not before she noticed that the other concessionaires had not left their tents. They were standing, watching. They seemed to be waiting for something.

"Damn you all!" Nabo's voice came squalling over the loudspeakers. "Fight them. Kill them. You traitors!"

The concessionaires did not move from behind their counters.

Ruth Horton came staggering and lurching up the midway.

"Get away from me!" Matt squalled.

She reached him and swung the meat cleaver, neatly lopping his head off.

The Geek came rushing out of the tented darkness, screaming some unintelligible, hate-filled words. A crazied look filled his eyes and uglied his face. Martin stared at him, concentrating on the Geek alone. The Geek's long, tangled, dirty hair exploded in flames, the fire rolling around his head and spreading downward. Within seconds it covered his entire body. He threw himself to the sawdust as his body exploded, flinging dusty and charred bones in all directions.

Martin closed his eyes, sweat beading his forehead. The fire abruptly ceased.

"You slimy Christian punk!" Nabo's voice ripped from the loudspeakers.

"I think he's referring to me," Martin said.

Ruth Horton had lurched off behind the tents on the other side of the midway.

"What's that sound, Dad?" Mark asked.

Martin listened. "Dogs," he finally said. "Barking. Sounds like hundreds of them; and getting closer."

As the pack of mangled dogs, cats, wolves and coyotes made their way slowly past the highway patrol car, Capt. Mayfield and Sgt. Davidson sat and stared in horror at the sight. The animals mingled around the front gates, seeming to be waiting for something or someone.

Both cops were startled at the sight that appeared at the now-open gate. "What is that thing!" Mayfield blurted, as his eyes touched Ralph Stanley McVee.

The dogs fell silent. They sat on their haunches or lay on the ground, panting from their exertions and their pain.

Before Davidson could reply, the voice of the Dog Man reached them. "Now I can help. Now I am free!" The words were difficult to understand, part yap, part human tongue.

"It looks like a human *dog!*" Davidson finally found his voice.

The Dog Man stepped out of the gate to walk among the animals. He petted them, talked to them, shook his head and made animal sounds of dismay at their injuries, their pain and suffering brought on by uncaring, and, for the most part, worthless human beings.

"You know who did these terrible things to you?" the Dog Man's words reached the state cops.

The animals spoke in body and head movements.

The Dog Man moved to the huge gray wolf's side and looked at his gunshot wound. "Why?" he asked.

The wolf's reply angered the Dog Man.

"Sport."

The animals snarled in rage at the inhumanity humans exhibited toward their kind. This was not sport. This was murder.

"Kill him!" Nabo's voice surged through the loud-speakers. "Kill the traitor!"

Ralph Stanley McVee turned around. Samson was

running up the midway, knocking the statue-like towns-people to one side or the other as he mindlessly rushed toward the front gate.

"Kill him, Samson!" Nabo's voice screamed.

Samson charged through the front gate, his massive arms outstretched, his one thought to crush the life out of the Dog Man.

The shepherd, the wolf, and several more animals had a different thought in their minds.

A big house cat leaped onto Samson's head, its claws ripping and tearing at the big man's eyes. A husky threw herself at the man's midsection and tore out a fist-sized hunk of meat as the wolf and the shepherd mangled the strong man's arms and legs.

Time had once more begun; the world outside could now enter the area that Nabo had sealed off; the powers of the dark forces had been greatly diminished as the howling hairy Prince of Filth pulled his presence away rather than witness a loss. A loss brought about by a tiny handful of humans who refused to bend or break away from their beliefs.

Samson's eyes were ripped out. Ralph Stanley McVee stepped on them.

The animals brought the devil's strong man down and tore his heavy flesh.

Ralph Stanley McVee watched this and grinned a doggy smile. "JoJo!" he yapped, his canine eyes catching sight of the half human. "Find the mayor and his people. Tell them the evil black hearts no longer need be pierced to destroy. Their master has left them. They are alone!"

JoJo, his long arms almost dragging the sawdusted midway, loped off to find Martin.

"Come, friends," Ralph barked. "I will go with you; I belong more to your world than to the world of those who paid money to laugh at me."

The animals poured through the open gates and onto the midway.

"Something has changed," Capt. Mayfield said. "Some . . . pressure has been lifted. You feel it."

"Yeah. But what?"

"I think conditions have returned to normal."

"Normal!"

"In a manner of speaking," Mayfield drily put a disclaimer on his remark.

Davidson lifted a shaking hand and pointed a shaky finger at the ferris wheel. Mayfield's eyes followed the finger.

Missy had caught herself in the framework of the ferris wheel, the bolt that protruded from both sides of her head caught between gondola and metal. She hung there, flapping her arms and screaming in pain.

"Normal?" Davidson cut his eyes.

"I cannot tell you how much I regret saying that, Gene."

The animals had forgotten their pain. Led by Ralph Stanley McVee, they dragged themselves along the midway, searching for the humans who had ended their lives.

Sharp eyes spotted Hal Evans and John Stacker just as the teenage thugs spotted the animals. The young hoodlums tried to run. They were brought down, screaming and begging, by a furry pack with slashing fangs.

With blood dripping from snarling snouts, the animals looked around for the leader of the punk pack. But Karl Steele had witnessed the carnage of his friends and had raced behind the concession-lined midway. In his fear, he ran directly into Martin and his group.

Mark handed his crossbow to Audie as the group circled the two young men.

"I have wanted to do this for a long time," Mark said, then stepped in close and busted Karl in the mouth with a hard right fist.

Karl went down, but he didn't stay down. He was back on his boots in a heartbeat, wading in, swinging both fists. Mark stepped back, blocking the punches with his arms. He found an opening and drove a hard fist to Karl's belly, doubling him over. Mark brought a fist down on Karl's lower back, bringing a scream of pain from the kidney punch.

Karl backed off, trying to regain his wind. His eyes were wild with hate and confusion. "It wasn't nothing that any of us could help doin'!" he yelled. "Them people come in an' made us do it."

"He's a shape-changer," Martin quietly reminded his son.

Karl screamed at the surrounding circle as his face began its transformation into a mask of thousands of years of evil.

"Let us through," the quiet slurry voice came from the darkness behind the circle.

Ralph Stanley McVee and his friends.

The small circle opened. Karl's face was once more in human form.

"The power is waning," Ralph told the gathering. "But there is still much danger."

Karl's eyes found the mangled shepherd. "You're dead!" he screamed. "I kilt you last year. I 'member you by that off-colored leg. I run over you and won ten dollars from my dad. He said I couldn't hit you on the highway."

The shepherd jumped, the fangs working at Karl's face. Karl screamed in pain and managed to break loose, running from the group, into the surrounding darkness. Martin noticed the young man had begun running on all fours.

"Let him go!" the Dog Man yapped. "I am feeling that his punishment is yet to come." He grinned his canine smile. "And I am feeling that it will not be to his liking."

Before Martin or any of the others could ask what that punishment might be, Ralph and his friends were gone, vanishing into the night that surrounded the lighted midway. Within seconds, screams were heard as the animals took their revenge against those who had deliberately hurt them in former lives.

"You'll still lose!" Nabo's fury-filled voice raged from the loudspeakers. "I shall destroy this miserable place and leave you with nothing! Nothing!" The sound of the amplifier being turned off was a loud click in the night.

"My watch is still running," Frenchy said.

The others checked their watches. Time had indeed returned to them.

"Now what, Dad?" Mark asked.

"We don't run anymore. We take the fight to them. And I have a feeling that I'm going to have to face Nabo alone."

The physically exhausted little group moved toward the lighted midway.

SIXTEEN

Several canvasmen and roughnecks came at them when the group had walked to the center of the midway. Had the circumstances been just a bit different—and also the God they worshipped—the creatures might have been pitiful things, for some were caught between human and demon transformation, unable to fully attain either.

The music-filled air and the dancing midway erupted in gunfire. The canvasmen and roughnecks were stopped in mid-charge, dropping to the already blood-soaked and body-littered sawdust.

The dancers did not even look up from their 1950s-style gyrations. But Martin had noticed that the number of dancers had lessened, and hoped that those left were not yet fully under the rule of the Master of the Netherworld, but just caught up in something they didn't understand—and could be saved.

He didn't have long to think about that.

The front of the Crazy House went wild in an explosion of flickering lights and loud music.

"I think that's our cue, Martin?" Frenchy shouted over the din.

Martin cut his eyes. *"Our cue?"*

"We're together, baby," she told him. "Get used to the idea."

And there, standing in the midst of danger and the stink of bodies and blood, Martin knew he had found what most men only dream of.

He winked at her.

She returned the wink, screwing up one whole side of her face. "Let's do it, Martin!"

Alicia appeared on the bally deck, her face a mixture of beauty and beast. She screamed at him. "Oh, yes, Martin! Come to baby, Martin!" Her voice changed to an inhuman howling, her mouth open wide, exposing long fangs.

Martin lifted his Colt and sighted her in. Images flashed behind his eyes. Their honeymoon. Their lovemaking. Their years together. The birth of their children.

Alicia's howling intensified. Green slime dripped from her mouth.

The memories were gone.

Martin shot her between the breasts. Pulled the trigger again, the muzzle lifting from the blast, the slug taking her in the throat. He fired again, just as she was falling backward.

Alicia dropped to the wooden bally floor and lay still, forever trapped between human and demon form. If she ever did any more of Shakespeare's lines it would be to a french fried audience. At least that was Martin's silent prayer.

Frenchy's .357 barked and a young man went down, a homemade spear in his hand. The face was human; the hands were clawed and hairy.

"You fiend!" a man's voice screamed from the ground corner of the Crazy House. "You hideous fiend!"

Mike Hanson. His face, as Alicia's, was caught between worlds. Mark's crossbow thunked. The bolt slammed through Mike's neck, pinning him to the wooden bally stage. His legs kicked and jerked as one hand tried in vain to remove the bolt.

Mike drifted on into the Netherworld, dutifully mincing after his sweetie.

Martin and Frenchy looked up the midway. Lyle Steele was running just as hard as he could, a pack of snarling animals close on his boot heels.

Martin stuck out a foot and tripped the man. He rolled and came to a sliding halt by the merry-go-ground. He scrambled onto the ride and grabbed onto a wooden horse.

Martin and Frenchy stared as the wooden horse turned its head and smiled at the animals that circled the ride.

The merry-go-round began to revolve. The wooden horse threw back its head and whinnied happily. Faster and faster the ride revolved. Lyle had managed to climb into the saddle of the wooden horse, his boots almost dragging the floor. He was screaming his fear as the horse went up and down on the pole, around and around, faster and faster.

"Ride 'em, cowboy!" Dick yelled from the edge of the midway.

Lyle howled his fear.

The man was almost a blur as the merry-go-round revolved at an impossible rate of speed.

The animals watched with undisguised glee in their eyes.

Lyle lost his grip on the wooden horse's neck and was propelled through the gaily lighted night air at what seemed mach-one speed.

He crashed into a light pole, arms and legs spread wide in an obscene embrace of body against pole.

The animals moved on, seeking others who had harmed them.

"Loose the stock!" Nabo's voice screamed from the loudspeakers. "Turn the tigers on them."

Roughnecks ran to the cages and threw open the barred gates.

But the animals would not leave their cages. They were savoring these moments.

An ape reached out and tore a carnie's head from its shoulders.

Nabo screamed his outrage at this betrayal.

Tiny the Giant lumbered onto the midway, heading for Martin and Frenchy. A howl turned him around.

JoJo stood in the midway. "You will not harm them," he spoke calmly. His ape-like face almost serene.

Frenchy lifted her pistol. Martin pushed the muzzle down. "No. JoJo wants him."

With a howl of pure hate, the giant lurched toward the

Ape Man. JoJo gracefully sidestepped the charge and tripped the giant, sending him sprawling facedown in the bloody sawdust. He leaped onto his back and began beating the man with his big fists. He looked up only once to call to Martin. "Go! The Crazy House. Go. But be careful!" He then resumed beating the giant into death. Again.

Martin and Frenchy stepped up to the wooden walkway leading into the big tent. They walked up the steps, pushing aside the canvas flap, and stepped into the madness.

King suddenly lifted his head, a hissing sound coming from his mouth. Gary and Rich were sleeping soundly.

"I hear her, pretty," Balo's words soothed the python. "Stay with the child." She slipped through the closed door of the van and stepped out into the night to face the woman with a face of a monster. "They shall not be harmed, Colleen."

Dr. Rhodes' wife opened her mouth to howl. Balo stepped into the woman, enveloping her in a sparkling mist.

Total evil was enveloped in good. King slithered up and watched as his friend turned the enraged demon around and sent her back to the pits, silently howling as sparkling bits of her being flew out of the envelopment and exploded without sound in the darkness.

The snake watched for a time and then once more coiled up on the seat. King would have handled it differently; would have made it last longer and with much pain. But . . . to each their own, he supposed.

He listened to the children's untroubled breathing and found comfort in the innocence of the boys.

"You want me to drive through those gates and put us inside the fairgrounds, Gene?" Mayfield asked.

"No, sir. I sure do not."

Neither one of them heard the man and woman walk up to the side of the car; the same man and woman they had encountered when first entering the town. When the man's voice came out of the night, Gene Davidson almost fainted.

"We're going home now," the man said. "The prom is almost over."

"Where did you come from?" Davidson hollered, turning his head.

Both cops looked at the odd couple who were splattered with blood.

"Yes," the woman added. "The dance floor is filled with rowdies. Those pooty types always come along to mess up everything. Good night, boys."

They walked off into the night. The cops sat and watched as more couples began walking out of the fairgrounds, passing the patrol car, holding hands and chatting.

"I sure am glad you're here, Captain," Gene informed the man.

"Oh? Why is that?"

"'Cause you get to write the report."

Whatever Martin and Frenchy expected as they entered the Crazy House . . . the sight that greeted them certainly wasn't it.

The placed was filled with cobwebs. Banners and streamers hung in tattered rags from the ceiling and the walls. A clown suit hung from a hook. The place looked as though it had not been used in years.

About thirty-five years, the thought came to Martin.

Both turned around as footsteps echoed hollow on the old creaking wooden floor. They expected to see the rest of their group.

They got Nabo.

The man stood smiling at them.

"It's been interesting, Mr. Mayor."

"That's one way of putting it," Martin replied. He was

341

so tired he knew he could not last much longer. He had to get this done. He wondered where Linda was?

Mayfield and Davidson watched as the teenager ran out of the fairgrounds and up to the patrol car. "Please!" she panted the word. "You've got to help me. Everybody's gone nuts in there!" She pointed to the lighted midway. "Dead people all over the place."

The cops got out of the car, to stand beside the badly frightened girl. "Take it easy, Miss," Mayfield told her. "You're all right, now." He opened the back door and motioned for the girl to get in. "Tell us what happened."

She leaned back against the seat and closed her eyes. Both men could see she was exhausted and badly frightened. "You're not going to believe me."

"Miss," Davidson said, "after tonight, I'll believe anything? What's your name?"

"Do it, Mr. Mayor," Nabo urged.

"Do . . . what?"

"End it. You've disgraced me. Humiliated me." He looked at the confused expression on Martin's face and grimaced. "You've *won!*"

The wooden floor shook as the rest of Martin's group entered the Crazy House. "The place just calmed down, Martin," Dick announced. "Carnival people just standing around, looking scared and confused."

"I figure maybe six or seven hundred people walked out of the fairgrounds," Audie said. "Must be several hundred dead."

A leather-like hand began slowly making its way up the steps of the Crazy House, the fingers gripping the step above and pulling up, carefully. It reached the bally deck and scurried across, slipping into the gloom of the big tent.

Martin counted heads. One more was missing. "Where's Don?"

"He spotted Joyce running away," Jeanne said. Her voice sounded very tired. "He went after her."

"To kill her," Susan added.

"Silly boy!" Nabo shook his head. "By now, she's at her house, sleeping in her bed. She . . . well . . . if he kills her, the charge will be murder."

"You lied before," Martin reminded him. "Every time you've opened your mouth, as a matter of fact. Why should we believe you now?"

"Well . . . that's a good point. But I have no reason to lie now. I am defeated. My troops are finished. Oh, they'll regroup . . . maybe. But without me."

"And they'll . . . be back?" Frenchy asked.

"They'll return somewhere. Oh. Here?" He smiled. "Perhaps. It's something to think about, isn't it?"

Chief Kelson waited in the darkness by the canvas wall, a pistol in his hand. He had his orders, and he was, by all that was unholy, going to carry them out. He was going to kill Martin Holland. That was his single thought.

Something tapped on the toe of his boot. He looked down. Nothing. Must have imagined it. He waited for the signal from Nabo. Something moved behind him. He turned his head. Canvas was moving. Big rat, he figured. Something tapped him on the shoulder. Really annoyed him. He turned fully around in time to feel old bony fingers clamp onto his throat. He dropped the pistol and lifted both hands, grabbing the object that was cutting off his air. He tried to pull it free, staggering backward, fighting for air.

"Well, now!" Nabo said, his voice filled with disgust. "Of all the places I could have gone, I had to come back here. To a town filled with incompetent jerks." He walked over to Kelson and put his shoe on the man's backside. He gave him a shove and sent the chief tearing out the rotten old canvas to the ground below. Kelson drummed his heels against the ground as death took him. The hand remained clamped around his crushed throat.

Nabo walked back to face the group. He stared at Martin. "Do it, Mr. Mayor. Put your burning eyes on me and end this night."

Martin stood, returning the stare. Then he slowly began to smile.

"What are you smiling about!" Nabo shouted. "There is nothing amusing about this! I demand that you kill me. That is my right. That is my wish. I command you to kill me!"

"No," Martin told him.

"*No?* You can't do this to me!"

"Why not, Nabo?"

"It's . . . it's . . . not a gentlemanly act. There are rules you must follow. You can't do this to me! I will not tolerate this . . . this indignity!"

Martin walked to the man and slapped him, the heavy blow knocking the man down onto the dusty floor. Nabo lay on the floor and cursed. But he made no attempt to rise. A thin trickle of blood leaked from the corner of Nabo's mouth.

"Martin? . . ." Frenchy whispered.

Martin held up a hand, silencing her. "Audie, you and Nicole go head off Don. Stop him. Move."

The deputy and the city cop left the tent. Martin squatted down beside Nabo. He pinched the man hard on the arm.

"Owww!" Nabo shrieked.

Martin stood up just as Mayfield and Davidson stepped into the room, automatic weapons at the ready.

"Frenchy," Martin said. "I want you to arrest this . . . person." He looked at Nabo, cowering on the dirty floor. Nabo cursed him and spit at him. "There must be a hundred different charges you can bring on him. Everything from inciting a riot to operating a carnival without a license."

"Curse your soul, Holland!" Nabo screamed. "You can't do this to me."

"I've done it, Nabo."

Nabo squalled and kicked on the floor, the dust rising from his childish temper tantrum.

Frenchy looked at Martin. "He's mortal," Martin

explained. "That's his punishment for failing here. All those who survived are now mortal. Doomed to spend the rest of their lives here on earth as mortal beings. He gave it away by having Kelson hiding in here, waiting to kill me—because Nabo knew he couldn't do it—and by insisting upon me killing him. He'd rather die than have to spend eternity as a mortal. He probably can't kill himself. His . . . master would not permit it."

"It'll probably never come to trial, Martin," Frenchy warned him.

"Probably not. But Nabo will be confined to a mental institution for the rest of his life. Forever locked down in a place for the hopelessly criminally insane. A far worse fate than death."

Nabo lay on the floor and cussed.

The sounds of what appeared to be a hundred sirens drifted to them.

"I called for backup," Mayfield explained. "And for the attorney general to be helicoptered in." He jerked his thumb toward the midway. "I have never seen so many dead people in all my life."

"How disgusting!" Nabo said. "How humiliating!"

"Halp!" a woman's voice squalled through the now-silent midway. "Halp me!"

"Dolly Darling," Nabo explained. "She can't get out of her chair."

"Doomed to be a freak forever," Jeanne said. "Serves her right."

"I have never been so humiliated in all my lives," Nabo ranted.

"Cuff him, Gene," Mayfield ordered.

"And be sure you read him his rights," Frenchy added.

"Halp!" Dolly squalled. "Halp!"

SEVENTEEN

Frenchy was with the state police. Audie and Nicole with them. The kids were asleep. Holland, Nebraska was literally crawling with officialdom.

Martin sat on his front porch. He could not recall ever being so tired.

His daughter sat in the porch swing, glaring at him. "You're stuck with me and I'm stuck with you," she said sourly.

"That's right, honey."

"I hate you!" She bluntly told her father. "And you just wait. I'll find a way to once more become what I was before."

"No doubt you will try. And you might make it. But until that time, you are going to be a perfect lady. The pride and joy of the Holland family."

"We'll see about that."

Audie stood over the still breathing body of Binkie. He lifted his walkie-talkie and called for an EMT.

"I'm scared," Binkie whispered.

"You ought to be." He looked at the boy's crushed legs. Someone had put pressure bandages on the wounds, easing the bleeding to only a thin ooze.

"Nicole walked up to Audie. "Highway Patrol found Joe Carrol beaten to death in his bedroom. Billie Watson was found wandering around in the grasslands. Naked. Out of her head."

347

"Any sign of Balo, JoJo or the Dog Man?"

"Nothing. One carnie said the Dog Man just vanished into thin air with the animals. Audie? You got to see this, man. Come on."

She led him to the wax museum. "Brace yourself," she warned him, pushing back the canvas.

Audie hissed in shock. Unlike the Crazy House, the inside of the wax museum was clean and new-looking. But it was the wax creatures that trapped his attention.

The dead had been transformed, to forever stand—he hoped—as exhibits. Alicia was there. Mike Hanson. Lyle Steele. Matt Horton. Missy. Kelson. Gary Tressalt. Eddie. They were immovable statues. Except for their eyes, which followed the city cop and the deputy as they walked around the dimly lit room. Audie's flesh seemed to crawl, as if maggots were sliming about on his skin.

Audie swallowed hard and walked back outside, to stand in the warm welcome light of God's day. "What do we tell the investigators, Nicole?"

"Frenchy's taking care of that. She said the attorney general is going to call it a riot and nothing more.

"I figured a cover-up."

"What else could they do?"

"They're . . . we're . . . somebody's going to have to dispose of those . . . wax things."

"If they can," Nicole said grimly.

"You can't do this to me!" Linda squalled at her father.

"Bend over the end of the bed, kid," he told her, a leather belt in his hand.

She cut her evil eyes, her lips grinning at him.

Martin backhanded her, jerked her up, and bent her over the end of the bed. He began applying the leather to her denim-clad bottom.

"Aren't you going to tell me that this hurts you more than it does me?" she wailed.

"No indeed, girl. I'm taking a great deal of satisfaction from this. I'm going to blister your butt until you can heat

your own bathwater just by sitting in it. And then we're
going to church, baby."

"Church!" she shrieked. "No way!"

"Church," Martin said grimly. "To pray for your lost
soul. And to pray for me—since I'm obviously going to
have to put up with you for only God knows how long."

Karl Steele lay whimpering, gritting his fanged snout
against the pain in his foot. Since animals do not have the
ability to cry as humans, Karl could only whine and
whimper.

His rear paw was caught in a small animal trap.

His metamorphosis was complete. He no longer in any
way resembled a human. He was a dog.

Karl whimpered against the pain. And then he began
doing what he—when he was in human form—had caused
other animals to do, many times. It was the only thing he
could do to regain his freedom.

He began chewing off the trapped leg.

EIGHTEEN

Christmas. Holland, Nebraska.

The sightseers and morbidly curious had stopped coming to rubberneck at the town and the remaining inhabitants.

After the riots.

Martin and Frenchy had been married for a week. They sat in the den before a crackling fire. Mark was in his room, studying. Linda was in her room, doing only God knew what.

And Satan.

Frenchy had resigned her state police commission a day before they were married.

The town was looking around for a couple of new doctors.

Janet and the kids had moved away.

The police had tried to destroy the wax statues. They would not burn. Nothing could burn them. They tried blowing them up. A big bang and lots of smoke was all that was accomplished by that. The statues were finally stored in a concrete block building with no windows and a steel door. Just outside of town. The carnival had been dismantled and stored. Just outside of town.

Dick Mason had purchased the old Bar-S ranch. Renamed it the Flying-M.

Jeanne and Don were planning to be married in the spring.

Nicole and Audie were married shortly after the incident. The incident at Holland was how the official

351

report read.

Nabo was confined at a state mental institution for the criminally insane.

Dolly Darling and a few more had joined other carnivals. They would be touring the nation come spring.

Frenchy stirred beside Martin as a strange but now familiar chanting came from Linda's room.

And they knew that in other homes around the town, other kids would be picking up the same chanting, and other parents would be wondering what to do.

"I know what I should do," Martin said, putting his arm around Frenchy's shoulders. "But I can't just walk up to her and kill her. I just can't do it, Frenchy."

"I know."

"While you were wrapping up the reports on the . . . incident, I tried to have her committed. She was calm and quite lucid. The psychiatrists said she was as sane as anyone else. I had no choice; I had to bring her back home with me."

The chanting picked up in tone and volume.

Martin stood up and tossed another log on the fire.

And in the concrete block house, Alicia opened her eyes and smiled as the sounds of her daughter's chanting finally reached her.